Gilliss
Books

TOPEKA,
ma 'shuge

A NOVEL

RAYMOND HUTSON

ISBN: 0615809634
ISBN 13: 9780615809632
Library of Congress Control Number: 2013939818
Gilliss Books
Spokane, Washington

This book is a work of fiction. All circumstances and characters appearing in this work are fictitious. Any resemblance to real persons, living or dead, is purely coincidental.

1

Sam Etulain gazed across the highway and down at the lethargic water of the Columbia beneath the glare of a milk glass sky. No vessels were in sight, not even a wind surfer. He had slept poorly and lain on the bed awake through the cooler morning hours, but now a merciless radiance rose from the asphalt. He crossed the sticky pavement and snapped open the door of his mailbox, grasshoppers darting out of the tall stands of kale that grew in the culvert. He pulled out the newspaper and a few envelopes, then turned and walked the sixty-two strides down the crushed gravel lane to his house, subvocalizing as he went. One day it had been sixty-one, another day, sixty-four. Pacing off the distance made him feel like he controlled one small axis of rotation in his life.

The front door of their bungalow, a three-bedroom cottage that had reminded them of England when they first toured it with the realtor, swelled with the summer humidity and stuck slightly, and he cursed softly as he forced it open. It had opened just fine during the winter, he thought. Since then, the whole world had turned to shit.

He opened *The Oregonian* for July 8, 1989, reading the classifieds first, praying for some cryptic personal message. Teresa sat catatonically in the living room, her vision fixed on some indefinable focal plane beyond the glass, suspended in the sunlit air of a July afternoon. He watched until her chest rose. Satisfied she was breathing, he turned to the entertainment section.

The weekends were the most difficult. During the week, her position at the school gave her a framework within which to function for seven hours. On Saturday mornings she absorbed herself in housework, initially reshelving all of his books to a point of annoyance. He didn't object to this because it kept her occupied for forty-five minutes. She would dust the shelves in front of the books, passing the wand of the vacuum over the tops of them. She would dust the piano that no one played. She would turn off the vacuum and open the door of Erika's room as if she had heard something. She would vacuum the rugs of the living room and the carpet of their bedroom. The wheels of the Electrolux would rattle over the grate of the floor furnace in the hallway in front of the bathroom. She would go into Erika's room and vacuum the hardwood floor.

All of the laundry was washed, every type of garment in a separate load. She would take clothes from Erika's room, clothes that had been washed the previous Saturday, clothes that had not been worn. After this, every garment returned to a hanger, hung in a certain orientation, as if once again for sale in a department store, and she would begin on the kitchen. Sam would rise and stand beside her at the sink without speaking. Each week a glass or saucer was broken, without anger or malice, just an inattentive grip on wet dinnerware, plain things they had bought for everyday use. She had cut herself badly last month, and standing beside her made him feel like he could prevent this from recurring.

Then she would vacuum again. She would stop midway and look into Erika's room. The vacuum would start once more. This ceremony would consume most of Saturday. By late in the afternoon she would begin the retreat into herself. If another faculty member stopped by she would acknowledge them, then busy herself with correcting disorder. She would apologize; the house was not clean enough for guests.

By Sunday she would be spent, empty. Sam thought the medications made her empty. Half of a biscuit. One cup of tea. Then that chair, that window, that silence.

He looked at the movie listings, *Halloween IV, La Bamba, Old Gringo, Sticky Fingers*. A comedy? No. A human interest story with a happy ending? How could you tell what was going to be a happy ending? It depended on your own circumstances. One could no more guess the effect of a film on one's disposition than guess the content of tomorrow's front page.

The phone in the kitchen rang. He smoothed the paper and stood, glancing again at Teresa, then went into the kitchen.

"Yes…that is correct."

"Eh-*two-lane*, Etulain. Yes." There was a long pause.

"Since March twenty-sixth…"

"She would have…she'll be sixteen on July twenty-eighth." He stared at the floor and a shadow fell across his feet. Teresa stood in the doorway, watching his lips move, eyes wide, bloodshot.

"You already know these things, I believe…"

"I understand. If it will help."

"We can be there in two hours or less."

"Thank you." He hung up the phone. "That was the coroner's office, in Portland. They want us to come see, to look at a girl they found. In the river."

She crushed her face into his chest.

"No, no, no. I don't think it's like that." He pulled her face up to his with his palms. "I think maybe they just want us to say that it's *not* her. They need to know these things, when they try to solve other cases. We can help. It's our duty."

They turned left onto the on-ramp and into the westbound traffic. Life swallowed people, thought Sam. The earth swallowed them. History could rip people from the ground where they flourished and carry them elsewhere to wither. What happened in a lifetime to one individual only reflected the tide of history at that point, like grains of silver in an enormous photograph. History was like that; one layer consumed another, absorbed its parts. One afternoon, a bomb had come through the roof of the school where his parents taught, killing his father. Dropped by a Stuka. Surely the Stuka had a pilot, just another grain in the photograph. History had moved his mother to England, where she had died of tuberculosis. Now some force had sucked his daughter from their home in The Dalles and deposited her, possibly, on a table at the Portland coroner's office.

He looked over at Teresa. She was silent but she was crying. Perhaps she would be swallowed as well. By the end of the school year her sick leave would be exhausted. She was growing thinner, never finished her meals, and could not concentrate on the simplest things. Yesterday morning she had nearly backed into the path of a passing car as he watched from the dining room. It was only a matter of time before something like this ate apart the basic fabric of one's instinct to survive. As they moved along the highway along the curves of the Columbia, in and out of the shadows of the hillsides, the sunlight highlighted the shallows of her temples, the folds beneath her eyes, bleaching the color from her face until it was indistinguishable from the blanch of the pavement.

They arrived at the address the voice on the phone had provided. A large white van, like an ambulance without lights, sat behind the building. Next to it an unoccupied, unmarked patrol car, the voice of a dispatcher sporadic and indecipherable inside. Two parking spots remained, both marked "Police." Sam took one of them.

Teresa looked at him, alarmed. "We won't be here long," he said. He rapped on the windowless steel door and took the knob, and it struck him then how a situation they had tried to dismiss with euphemisms and optimistic platitudes when they spoke to others had crossed into the irrefutably bizarre. How many parents had come here before, looking for their children?

A slight black man with wire glasses answered. He introduced himself as Larry. "I assist the pathologists when there's an autopsy to be done."

Larry introduced them to Detective Betancourt, who rose from a desk in a small office, shook their hands, and asked them to sit. He was beyond fifty, round-shouldered, his black hair streaked at the temples with white, the skin sagging beneath his eyes and jaw like a plastic mask that had been left in the sun. The detective went over some basic formalities, then explained the circumstances. The subject had been found by a father and son while fishing along the riverbank, at about Milepost 75.

"Where is that?" asked Teresa.

"Near Myer State Park. Just west of The Dalles."

Sam crossed his arms and tilted his head back. "My daughter's been gone for almost four months, I would think she might have traveled farther than ten miles."

The detective went on. "The subject's body has been in the water for about six weeks. There's been some damage. Nature does things."

Teresa looked at Sam, and he placed his hand on top of hers. She pinched his fingers between her own. "How did she…?"

"Her neck was broken, but that might have happened from a fall, or the turbulence of the river. If you two will step this way."

Teresa started to rise, but still grasped the arms of the chair and clumsily started to pick it up. Sam pressed gently on her shoulder and she sat down again. "I think I can decide if my wife needs to see this."

The room was tiled and stainless. Sam could see the detective's breath. The temperature had been lowered to retard decay, but decay triumphed. Purines and amines filled his nostrils and surrounded his skin. He could taste decay in the air. A rimmed steel table occupied the center of the room beneath the enormous dome of a surgical lamp, upon it an irregular form about five feet long, covered with olive green plastic. Beneath the table hung a stainless bucket.

"Do you feel alright?"

Sam nodded.

"If you want to sit down, just let us know. I want you to study what you see and think carefully. Do you feel like you're ready to look?"

Sam nodded again. The detective folded back the top edge of the plastic to the shoulders of the figure on the table. The sting of decay found its way to the back of Sam's throat.

He looked first at the eyes, searching the vacant hollows for the familiar, where only a curdled gray remained. Some of the hair, straw black and green, had been teased apart and spread unnaturally over a folded white cloth to the left of the face. The skin, where it remained over the right side of the nose, was swollen and deep purple like a too-ripe plum, fine bubbles of gas appearing at the edges, their movement drawing his attention, something that continued to digest the girl in spite of the refrigeration. The jaw hung agape, most of the lips torn away. Sam stared at the teeth. He slowly shook his head. The doctor and the detective both looked at him. He cleared his throat.

"This girl has fillings. Erika does not, unless she's gotten them in the last four months."

Someone sighed. A drop fell into the bucket.

The detective put his hand on Sam's shoulder and turned to the door. "We're so sorry. We didn't have any dental records in the file."

"You didn't have any because there were none to submit. I don't think she's had her teeth X-rayed since she was seven or eight." Sam shrugged. "Absolutely compulsive child, about brushing her teeth, anyway." He stopped before the open door. "I understand why you felt like you needed us here today." He paused, wiping the edge of his eye with a fingertip, then stared at the table searching for something more to say, but it had escaped him.

They were eastbound, a steady flow of traffic in the other lanes driving into the sun, glare on the windshields concealing the people inside. She was still alive, he was sure. She could be in any of those cars. Exit thirteen. He sorted several strands of logic, calculating, needing to begin at an arbitrary boundary. Exit seventeen. They had just seen the body of the girl who would die, no, who would be found dead, along this stretch of highway. There was a randomness about these things; that was a given, and there was likely to be just one body. This year? Yes. Along this first hundred miles—that would be a reasonable boundary. They had just seen that one girl, and she was not Erika. These embryonic strands were brilliant and true and remained suspended before him. He relaxed his grip on the wheel and sighed. He could not share these theories yet with Teresa; the weight of her sorrow would crush them.

Theresa remained silent and watched the shoulder of bone-white concrete race past and thought of all the little animals that had been hit and died there, and how, in a few days, not a trace remained.

*

Erika awoke in double time, sixteenth notes of image and memory, a dreamy snarl of what had certainly happened yesterday and what might be, mosaic fragments of some elusive truth vibrating away from each other with the pounding of her heart. She wondered if she had been asleep at all. A singular burst, like an eardrum ruptured, had punctuated a nightmare, and now she wondered if a door had been slammed, a passing truck on the interstate had sounded, or if he had just snored or sputtered. Perhaps someone had shaken their doorknob. Motionless, willing to suspend the rhythm of her own pulse, she waited for a second sound. The scene of the crowd, serpentine and faceless, carrying the body, came back to her. She touched the man beside her on the hip and felt his torso rise, breathing with the innocence of a metronome. Everyone is innocent, she thought, when they're asleep. "Tomorrow we will go to Colorado," he'd said, before he had drifted off.

"But why Topeka?" she'd whispered, but he was asleep by then.

The medication had been wearing off earlier and earlier for weeks, retreating sometime before the sun came up. Maybe it made a sound inside her head when it did, a thousand invisible soldiers gathering their metal and marching away, leaving a haze across her vision. She ran her fingertips lightly over his blanketed shoulder and rose so she could see over him, the bedside clock rhythmically blinking 12:00 a.m. without a sound. At least it will not go off at five or six, as they sometimes do, she thought, set by the previous occupants of the room. He never asked the desk clerk to call them in the morning, like her father always did. At first she thought this was some indulgence of freedom, to sleep as late as they wished.

"The less they know of us the better," he had said, and now she understood. A desk clerk who knew what time you were going to get up was a threat. To live like that must be exhausting; any detail, however small, could be used to hurt you. He paid cash at every restaurant and every gas station, and when he could, he parked the car so the license plates were not seen. He glanced at the security cameras in the 7-11 and then admonished her not to look. If someone began to speak to her, he was at once between them, saying, "So there you are!" or, "Hurry, we are already late," and once, "Your mother is looking everywhere for you," after which she had cried for an hour as they blazed down the interstate while the wind obliterated her sobs and dried her tears. At the end of the day, she had seen him in the parking lot, burning a fistful of receipts; he must have lived at some point where that was the predominant truth, and those days now stained his present, and also hers by association. She sensed this, but she could not articulate her unease. She caressed his shoulder with greater compassion. She would show him, eventually, that her life, her world, was not like that and that his could be the same as hers. When his fear was gone, he would love her better. It was the lie that lessened their love now. It was the lie that had fractured her sleep.

She had taken a seat at an old black upright in the lobby while he had registered, the yellowed ivory keys comfortably weighted beneath her fingertips, and she'd started slowly into a Gershwin exercise, then sixteen or twenty bars of "Tiny Dancer," thinking of her mother's album, the blue cover worn to the cardboard in places. It was a favorite, her mother had said, the day she'd handed it to her. All the time Majij had watched her, not knowing the best way to respond, while the balding clerk leaned over the counter and said, "It's okay. Let her play," and smiled. She had moved to *Isle of the Dead,* when he added, "Your girl has some fingers, doesn't she?" And the way he had said "girl," his brief leer, made them both realize later as they lay close in the only bed in the room, that the clerk understood something wasn't right, an incongruity he was willing to overlook for the cash he had just collected but which he still felt he should highlight, just to assert his vision. Nothing slipped past him in *his* motel. The compliment had stripped away her costume, leaving her gritty and naked before the balding little god of the world they had chosen to make their own for the night. But only for a while, until they touched, and the heat came inside of her, and then nothing after was more important.

She took a deep breath and held it for five seconds, then slowly exhaled. He had shown her this once, in their first month together, telling her that fear could be seen, wild dogs knew this. Even before you turned away to run, they smelled it, before they tore out your throat. People would know about her sin and punishment would follow.

They occupied a room at the end of the motel on the second level, and in a rare oversight, he had left the curtains open. She slipped out of bed, buoyant, ethereal, and was by the window. In the vast Wyoming sky beyond, the moon was rising, nearly full, an orange thumbprint above the hilltops. Her father had shown her once how the moon could be covered with a finger or two on the horizon and how it seemed smaller, but wasn't, high overhead. "See how we fool ourselves," he had said.

She had bathed well and shampooed, but found him asleep when she came out of the bathroom, and decided he didn't want her that night. He had seemed distracted since they had watched the funeral. Later, when he was half awakened by her accidental touch, or sensed her dampness, he had rolled over and taken her with a lazy rhythm and a few words of French she did not understand, murmurs in the darkness. That he could be so automatic seemed dear to her. He must dream of me, she told herself. But there was apathy in his interest that she couldn't fully deny, and so it was a disappointment knowing her intuition had been wrong, and, in a way, a relief that her own lassitude would go unnoticed. Once, the very thought of such closeness could precipitate agonizing excitement and anticipation. Now it could be exhausted.

She imagined her parents talking to her and this man she had chosen, like they would talk to any other faculty, and her father would look at the moon and say something that would reveal that they all spoke the same language and knew each other as adults. But she couldn't picture her mother having anything to say to him, knowing what they had just done and had been doing for three months, and with this came a sense of loss.

She looked back at the dark mass of him on the bed and thought about waking him up, pulling him to the window, sharing the moon with him. Do what they had done earlier, all over again, when they could see each other's faces. But a week ago, she had studied that same moon with the binoculars from his glove compartment at a rest area one evening, then handed them to him. "You look," she'd said. But he didn't look; instead, he just put the lens caps back on the binoculars and put them away without speaking. There was a place in him she could not reach, a place in herself he refused to go. Standing in the window, she suddenly felt an abysmal sense of loneliness.

Flickering blue-and-red lights crested a pass on the horizon and followed the highway, moving quickly. She stooped and turned off the fan beneath the window, but the lights made no sound and soon passed from view as they arced around the edge of town.

2

Pregnant late in life, Teresa and Sam are congratulated by other faculty with joy and reservation. Some speak of Down's syndrome, or babies born without feet, or flippers for arms, but the couple is stoic. Determined but nonchalant, so *British*; perhaps *over there,* they just don't concern themselves with those kinds of risks. Teresa is seated across the desk from her obstetrician each month, steadfastly refusing the amniocentesis. Teresa feels guilty as Erika is laid in her crib in those first few weeks. The labor was complicated and there will be no siblings. When the child cries she holds it close to her but offers no lullaby, and worries that nature has made a beautiful, delicate mistake. The sound of Teresa's voice might call attention to the injustice, and her daughter will be given to another.

Their house sits high on a country lane in Oregon overlooking the Columbia River. Every living thing on their acre becomes Erika's playmate. Talking incessantly to the invisible, she plays for hours alone, building homes of Popsicle sticks in her sandbox and attempting to populate them with unwilling grasshoppers and beetles. Teresa listens through the screen windows of the kitchen, intoxicated with the magic of this fragile life she has brought forth. She points out to Sam how Erika lacks social maturity and needs just a little more time to grow out of her toddler world. There is no need to hurry; the child is still unsteady on her feet. Just look at her! This will be their only chance. Sam finally agrees to keep her back just one year from starting school.

"She's a smart little girl," Carl Waterbury, the family practitioner, tells Sam and Teresa after Erika's eventual preschool exam. "You know what she told me? Not to *condescend* her. Con-de-scend." He leans back in his squeaky chair, his bulging belly concealing the aneurysm that will kill him six years later, and runs his fingers through his graying, rusty bristle before locking them behind his head. "Where did she learn a word like that?" He raises his eyebrows at Sam. "She'll be an agent of heaven or hell, but there won't be anything ordinary about that child."

For her sixth Easter, Sam and Teresa give her a kitten, white with a black patch over its eye. Erika names her Natasha, after a character on the *Rocky and Bullwinkle Show*.

Eight weeks later, on the last afternoon of first grade, Natasha is sleepy, just home from the veterinarian, lying in her basket on the kitchen floor. Her tummy shaved—a stitch, a crust of blood. Erika picks her up and stands behind her father, tugs at his pant leg, and points at the cat's wound.

"So she won't fall in love and run away from us," her father explains, jovial, and turns away to talk to her mother again. When he looks again, she still stands there, the cat cradled in her arms. "We're responsible for what we're given to take care of," he says, squatting in front of her. "Without the operation, something unexpected could happen to her."

"So what could happen to her?" she asks, looking into the face of the flaccid cat.

"Well, she might have kittens before she is ready."

"Will she be able to have kittens later?"

"Yes."

She draws the cat closer, pressing her own cheek against its folded ear. She reads to the cat, dresses it in doll clothes, and tries to compel it to sit patiently on a dining room chair while she pours dry cat food in a bowl. For a while, she is bored with the taciturn animal. A few weeks later, she stands behind her mother in the laundry room, Natasha weaving lazy eights between her ankles.

"Can I have a little brother?" she asks.

"Mummy had an operation," Teresa says. "I can't give you one."

"An operation?"

"Yes. An operation like Natasha's. No more babies, ever."

Five years later, Erika becomes fascinated with Russia after watching *Doctor Zhivago* on television. She dwells for months on the unconditional loyalty of true love, the necessary tragedy for perfect romance, and finding a Russian-English dictionary in her father's den, practices writing love letters in the strange characters. Eventually she writes Natasha's name in Cyrillic on the cat's bowl and wonders if Natasha mourns in the night for kittens she will never know.

*

Teresa Etulain was quiet, diplomatically polite, her impressionable years passed in a girls school in postwar England, learning perseverance without complaint. Eventually she earned a degree in English literature from Cambridge and a teaching certificate as well, but the disinterest of her American students in literature of any kind, their "learned laziness from the telly," she said, drove her from the classroom after a few years to the shelter of the business office of Wilson Junior High. On her desk sat the school mascot, a salamander wearing a numbered jersey, a gift from the office staff. It puzzled Teresa, because the junior high didn't actually field a team in any sport.

At home Teresa worked around Sam's eccentricities, piles of ungraded essays on an old mahogany dining room table, his abandoned, half-empty teacups scattered throughout the house, and everywhere books, mostly history, filling shelves in the living room and down the hallway, covering one wall of the master bedroom and three walls of the guest room where he kept his desk. Stacks of books with old leather bindings or fabric covered, dog-eared paperbacks piled by the arms of his overstuffed chair, and always half a dozen or so on the windowsill of the bathroom. The entire house, save the kitchen, exuded the faint musty aroma of leather, old paper, and glue.

Rehearsing his lectures, Sam frequently mumbled a stream of consciousness on almost any subject to any audience, including his young daughter, addressing her with the same rich fabric of language, as she sat playing on the floor beneath the dining room table while he corrected papers, as if she were another of his college sophomores. He stopped periodically, defining a word for her when she was paying attention. "Say 'ca-pit-u-late.'"

She looked up at him, two huge opals full of wonder, delighted that he knew she was still there. "Cawwtipew-ate."

"Excellent, darling. Excellent. Can you say, 'never capitulate?'"

"Eff-er cawtipewate."

Then he was off again, down another vein of history, the details linking the story of humanity like so many roots of crabgrass.

Near the entrance to their hallway he placed a small frame with postage stamps of the counties he had lived in: Spain, Andorra, France, and England, small cameos of dead royalty on tiny squares of magenta, rose, or aquamarine. Erika was taught to identify the faces and the countries they ruled; Sam would place a finger on each and she would recite their names. As she grew older, the frame seemed to climb the wall, always at her eye level.

*

Trish appeared the summer after second grade, outside the fence of Erika's backyard, throwing pebbles of crushed basalt into the sandbox until Erika turned around.

"Why are you throwing rocks at me?"

"They're not rocks. They're five-eighths crush. My ex-dad makes them at Fred's gravel pit. What's your name?"

"Erika."

"I'm Trish. My real name is Patricia."

Erika put down her pink plastic shovel as if she had never intended to pick it up, and brushed off her hands. "Why don't people just call you Patty?"

"Cause Patty sounds stupid. I like 'Trish.' It sounds slippery. You ever been to Fred's Gravel Pit?"

"I don't think so."

"My dad says teenagers swim butt-naked down there. Boys and girls at the same time."

"So how is *butt*-naked different than just being naked?"

"I think it's when you're naked and you just don't care. What's your cat's name?"

Natasha sat on the porch step, licking a paw. "Natasha."

"That's a dumb name."

"It is not. It's Russian. You have a cat?"

"His name is Tiger. He's bigger than your cat, and he's got balls."

Erika could reach Trish's house by walking through the backyard of the people across the street and crawling through a hole in the wire fence covered with a tangle of blackberries. She carried Natasha with her one morning, the girls standing in the damp, cool, closed garage while the two animals circled on the oil stained concrete, backs arched, hissing at each other.

"I guess they don't want to play," said Erika.

"Cats don't play," Trish said. "They just sleep and hunt and do it with other cats."

Trish knew stuff. How to cook canned ravioli in the microwave. How to refill a cigarette lighter. Erika would listen, jaw agape, as Trish telephoned numbers she chose from the air, asking whoever answered if they knew Seymour Butts, crashing the handset and giggling at her impunity. She used the toilet without closing the door. Her mother was seldom home, and crawling through the fence was like falling down the rabbit hole into a small world of disorder, where rules and consequences were jumbled like fragments of an old puzzle that no one cared to reassemble anymore.

*

Columns, numbers, and percentages of net balanced Teresa's day, a cool refuge from the chatter of the schoolgirls who, wandering in between classes, stood in her office doorway and asked her things they would not ask their own mothers. Her British accent mistaken for wisdom, her straight copper hair and bangs so hip, her imperturbability made her appear a counselor by nature. Her own daughter was different from those common girls, she had to remind herself, and could never be so base, Erika simply didn't have those sorts of thoughts; they had raised her better than *that*, with a sense of propriety that was sadly out of fashion.

Erika grew resentful; by the time her mother returned home, she had used up all of her *mom-ness*. Teresa would set her purse on the table, hang up her keys, and ask flatly without looking at her, "Can you please empty the trash? Act like you live here."

When Sam and Teresa recruited a piano teacher, determined to keep Erika unadulterated, they made careful inquiries, settling on Mildred Turner, a recent émigré and classical pianist from British Columbia. Teresa listened as her nine-year-old daughter practiced scales, Chopin, and later Mendelssohn on the old blond spinet.

For her twelfth birthday, her mother gave her *Pride and Prejudice* and a collection of Henry James short stories. Bored, Erika borrowed *Lady Chatterley's Lover* from her mother's bookcase, keeping it hidden under the lid of the piano. Playing until she was distracted, one intruding fantasy followed another until she heard the screen door slam and her parents' car start. She would retrieve the book, snatching it with a rumble from the dark sliver of space left of the soundboard. She pictured the man's hands and his lips and parts of him she couldn't imagine. He behaved very differently from the way her parents held each other, smothering and unspeakable. A chill rose up the back of her neck that made her close the cover, then peek again, like watching a frog swallow a large moth.

After her homework she would stay in her room, beneath the blankets with Hemingway, Fitzgerald, and Graham Greene, finding souls in the books that, like herself, had no brothers or sisters, men who lived tragic lives, never forsaking their beliefs against the popular wisdom. Erika read of wars and men and nations and the reasons things came to pass. At an age when most girls were infatuated with horses, a passion for clarity and truth grew in her, a fascination for knowing what was and what was not—the vision of hindsight, the vision of all historians, her father's truth. A smoke ring relief of *Epictetus*, fragments in her father's voice, followed her silently on the playing field. Students who ridiculed her idealism were never forgiven. Her unerring confidence and irrevocable resolve, her polarized vision of white and black, went unrecognized, other students as oblivious to her sense of identity as they were of subatomic particles. They only decided that she was easily pissed off, and rifts began to form. Eventually a seventh-grade teacher at Wilson Junior High School described her as "arrogant and oppositional."

The summer after sixth grade, a trio of friends remained who respected her wisdom, pedals and handlebars moving as one across town to the swimming pool: Steven Ortega for his mechanical savvy, Aaron Parsons, self-deprecating and funny, and Melinda Mathews, because Aaron said she was prime and he was going to marry her and preferred her tucked onto the banana seat behind him, her face against his bare shoulder. By the summer after sixth grade, Erika watched Steven with an understanding she could not explain to Melinda, who regarded her like a big sister, and with thoughts about Steven that felt too noble to share with Trish.

*

It was later that same summer, early one afternoon, that Erika and Trish played Monopoly in the attic where Trish slept— Trish's version, with stacks of pennies and nickels about the perimeter, for all the paper money had been lost along with half of the deeds. Two small plastic army men served as proxies on the board, Erika's was missing an arm. Trish kissed hers before each throw of the dice, eventually leaning back on her elbows, a leg to either side. "Older guys know how to kiss." She regarded the tiny figure in her fingers with veneration.

"How do you know?" Erika thought of her parents kissing each morning. "Everybody knows how to kiss, anyway."

"No they don't." Trish tossed her head defiantly and sat up, Indian style. "Some guys don't know jack crap." She leaned forward and narrowed her eyes. "You ever been kissed by a guy?"

"My dad." And as quickly, Erika wanted to mention Steven, but could not. She had turned away so he only kissed the side of her head, a cowardly move that would only invite ridicule and maybe end the game. She hoped Trish wouldn't ask.

"He doesn't count. Dads don't count, ever." Trish kissed her soldier, rolled the dice and tapped him along the board eight spaces. "You should practice with me."

Erika wrinkled her nose and leaned away from her.

"Come on. You're thirteen years old now." Trish scooted forward. "Just pretend I'm a guy, Jon Bon Jovi or something."

"Too weird."

"It's not weird if you're pretending you're with a guy. I just don't want you to screw up when your chance comes."

Erika tensed, puckered tightly, and closed her eyes. Trish's lips were wet and smelled of the cigarette they'd shared, Trish drawing the smoke deeply as if it might fill her entire being, Erika holding it only in her mouth until it started to go down her throat, expelling it with a little cough. Now it occurred to her that Trish might fill her up with smoke, inflating her like an air mattress.

"Open your mouth a little bit."

Erika opened her eyes.

Trish was over her on all fours. "Really, you kiss like a chicken. That's what my uncle Phil would say."

The tobacco fragrance, honey-thick, mixed with *Claiborne* and the heat of her friend's body. Erika parted her lips, her eyes still open. Trish closed hers and kissed her again. No smoke came, and Erika relaxed, allowing herself to be filled with the foreign, intimate warmth of her friend's lips, the tip of her tongue until her balance quavered.

Erika pulled away and shook her hair, confused, flushed. She looked under her arm, back to the game. "You owe me ten cents."

"You're going to *charge me?*"

"You're on my boardwalk."

Trish sat back on her own side of the board. "You think too much."

Erika stood up. "I have to pee," she said and retreated down the narrow staircase that ended in the kitchen. The air was colder as she approached the first floor, a draft that smelled of old cedar and dust from a boot-sized hole in the Sheetrock near the bottom tread. As she crossed the hallway to the bathroom, a hinge squeaked. The door to the first-floor bedroom opened and a pasty looking man with red hair, wearing only a pair of stained boxer shorts, stood watching her.

Erika glanced up the stairwell behind her, darted across the hall, slammed the door and pressed the lock button. The knob rattled twice, then was still. Erika finished, washed her hands with a dirty bar of soap, and opened the door. The man, about forty, stood there, feet spread as broadly as the width of a second door, hands thrust into the waistband of his rumpled boxers, a rigid stem protruding under the fabric. "Trish, sweetie," he said.

She recoiled, and he smirked as he stepped into her path to the left, then to the right. She squeezed past finally, feeling the pressure along her waist of whatever sprouted rigid within his shorts. She threw herself against the kitchen door and tugged, but could not gather her senses to turn the dead bolt.

"What's with the damn noise?" Trish looked up. Erika reappeared, breathless, at the top of the stairs. "You'll wake up mom."

"A man, downstairs," she gasped.

Trish gave her a knowing nod.

"He stuck his…" But she stumbled on the word and stopped, glancing at the top of the stairwell. "Isn't there any way to close the door?" She realized as she spoke that there wasn't a door. She looked out the window behind her and wondered if she could jump, like Natasha, into the top branches of the tree and climb down, but the limbs were barely thicker than pencils.

Trish bounded to a closet and dragged out an aluminum softball bat, one side indented as if it had been used to drive nails. "I'll smack him good if he comes up." Trish swung the bat through the air in what felt like an established protocol, with a grace that Erika had only seen on TV.

Trish crouched down behind the stairwell with the bat across her knees as Erika barricaded herself behind the bed with her back to the wall. Trish whispered, "Now you've got his cooties."

They both listened. A door opened and closed. A toilet flushed. A glass was put into a sink. The floor creaked with footfalls that once approached the stairwell but then went away. A murmur of voices followed, then a latch and a screen door slam. Trish moved her weapon to one hand, tiptoed over to the small window at the end of the peaked ceiling, and looked down. "He's leaving," she said. A motor started, idled for a moment, and retreated. Erika climbed over the bed and stood by her. A yellow Ford was driving away, already a few houses down the street.

Erika slowed as she crossed her own yard that evening, as if her parents might know, her experience visible as soon as she opened the front door. It hadn't been right, but the man had thought she was Trish, and maybe men, when they came to Trish's house, did that. Maybe it was what made Trish so strong. Nonetheless, she felt torn open and could still feel the tip of his thing (his *finger*, it must have been his finger!) in her tummy, an awful, secret feeling, as if an alien she could not dislodge had slipped into her chest. Could something so small that you couldn't see crawl down your skin and get inside? Make you pregnant with an ugly, red-haired baby, a miniature of the man? She wanted to wash it away, but it was still there, concealed inside of her, hanging on with claws, between each sip of milk that night at the table between them, where it was warm, near the books, and could burst forth at any moment. Her parents acted so normal because they knew, they just had to know, and maybe there just wasn't anything they could do about it. Maybe it was supposed to happen, like some kind of ceremony they'd expected all along. After they ate, she went into the bathroom and pulled up her T-shirt and looked, but there wasn't even a red mark or a scratch, nothing but her memory of his hand, of his finger.

A month passed. One evening, when wind filled the gorge and rain followed minutes later with darkness, Erika sat in the chair by the living room window with her geography text. She sensed motion on the street, peripheral, perhaps something blown. In a flash of lightning, she could see the Ford parked along the far shoulder, white or yellow, she couldn't tell, and she stared at the driver's window. In another flash, she saw that it was closed, that it might be parked, that whoever had driven it there might already have gotten out. She set her book on the floor and sockfooted to her parents' bedroom.

"Dad?"

"Your father's in the bathroom. What is it?"

She stood silent. There was no way she could tell part, without all, of such a terrible, terrible mistake. In waiting, she had caused this, drawn it to her, invited it, even. Complicity, that was the word. "Nothing," she said and went back to the living room and leaned against the front door as if it were already being forced, twisting the deadbolt tightly, then stooped near the window and stared into the dark until a neighbor's car came down the street. The Ford was gone.

Her period came in October of that year, before geometry, an unexpected stickiness that arrived so insidiously that she was unaware until a splotch of deep burgundy appeared on her jeans as she turned before the bathroom mirror during the last hour of the day, other girls making a wide berth around her.

Teresa explained everything she knew that evening in the sterile, functional manner in which she herself had been told, then approached the subject again in the weeks after, apologetically.

"If we had a son, it would be my job," Sam whispered to Teresa one night. "Besides, boys just know these things." Later he put a large bookmark in the Britannica at "Reproduction" and left the volume on Erika's desk, going off to bed, satisfied with his insight.

In seventh grade, Erika walked beside Trish in the hallways, Trish proud of her brainy but not especially pretty mascot, Erika loaning her a respectability her mother had told her she'd never have—tough, gorgeous Trish, who knew older boys and wore heady perfume. Other girls envied her for her wit, her tight clothes, the small purple dragonfly tattooed near her cleavage, and the cars with dark windows that took her away at lunch time. Trish would find Erika before class in the afternoon, moments before the bell rang, humble, desperate for rescue before an exam. Erika could see her from her own desk across the hall, Trish crouching over an exam on the Roman Empire, and imagined her killing Goths with the aluminum bat.

It was a November evening when Erika first comprehended the finite span of a lifetime. When the ethereal awareness of her own reproductive potential drifted into view, it arrived with a sense of desolation and an insatiable want, the feeling that there was no one who would ever understand the emptiness she felt inside. She dreamt of a man one night, a dark man with an exotic voice, smooth skin, and dark hair, who touched her, held her, drew her all around him, and protected her. She did not know him, but she awakened with the warmest familiarity, feeling that she did and that *she* had protected *him*, and she searched the mattress beside her before she was fully awake. She did not tell her mother. No one could fill the want. Each night in the months that followed, she longed to repeat the dream and the fullness in her pelvis that came with it.

Late one evening, she came out of her room as her father sat in the dark, watching television. On the screen, veiled women moved through a dusty market.

"Why are all of the women covered up like that?" she asked.

Sam studied her for a moment. Another faculty member had mentioned, just the week before with a gentle euphemism, that his daughter could look simultaneously quizzical and critical in the same moment. "Like a James Thurber drawing," he had said. *Odd,* he had probably wanted to say. She had that expression now. "I suppose it's the way they honor them. Keep them away from the sticky fingers of other men."

She flinched and hoped he hadn't noticed. "All you can see is their eyes."

"I suspect they might be hiding a few old ugly ones too."

She pushed his feet to either side and sat down on the wide ottoman in front of him. The women's figures glided across the screen between market tables, along sidewalks or stood in small clusters at an airport without mouths that could be seen, like breastless chess pieces. "I wonder if they have fewer rapes that way." She imagined the form of them, their legs, hips, sliding silent inside the tents of clothing.

"You're too young to be worrying about that sort of thing."

She turned around and looked at him with a hint of indignation.

"Aren't you?" he asked.

"I guess. Neat idea. Protect your women. What country is that?"

"Yemen. Southern Yemen. The whole Islamic world subscribes to that idea, more or less." He turned his gaze back to the flickering screen.

"Cool. Good night, Dad."

*

Now, no students come by. The stereo is silent, the quartz clock ticks. The occasional low horn of a tugboat is heard from the river. The silence has assumed an authority of its own, and they humble themselves before it; when they speak, it is in half whispers, and doors are closed softly and shoes are left on the top step outside. The zone of silence has grown around the little house. Old friends feel embarrassed to step within, ashamed and awkward to remain outside its boundaries, and so the phone seldom rings. They don't know what to say to a couple who have lost their only child, their legacy. Is this nature's way of abortion? Was there something wrong with their parenting that blighted their daughter's future? "It is better we don't bother them," people say or, "They need some time for closure." And then they change the subject to cholesterol or Gorbachev or gas mileage or the ozone layer.

The frame of stamps, broken into pieces, has been tucked in a manila envelope and placed out of sight in a cabinet beneath the living room bookcases.

Sam sits up late in the dark, long after the TV is turned off, in the summer, listening to the sounds of the crickets through the screens, retracing the steps that led him to bring Teresa to this peculiar corner of the earth. The reunion with his bohemian brother short-lived, he only hears from him now when he needs money. Teresa's father had died shortly after Erika's birth and her mother a few years later. His stepfather he can remember clearly only as a young man in an English uniform at the wheel of an open car, the man who extricated them from the chaos in Marseilles like a magician while his mother smiled over the seat at him.

In earlier years, Sam would rise eventually and shuffle down the hallway, stopping by his daughter's door to hear her breathe. Sometimes he would stand by her bed for a moment, watching her, and wonder what the world was going to bring her, this odd girl who was his daughter, then he would take whatever book she had fallen asleep reading and place it on the nightstand.

Now he stands by her empty bed late at night, remembering the old doctor's words, imagining that Erika is still there, wishing he had not reshelved all of her books. Thinking that if he had left the room alone, especially in the beginning, she might be there one morning, perhaps crawl in through the window after they had gone to sleep. He has even left one window unlatched.

"I won't ask her a thing," he says.

3

By fifteen Erika has grown taller than most of her classmates, and her small seniority in age is forgotten by most. Her knees, so prominent in childhood, now appear proportional as calves, thighs, and hips blossom. Her waist remains small and her shoulders thin. Her neck is slender, *elegant like that of a princess*, her father thinks but never says. In Erika's eyes, it only contributes to a graceless height, and for a while, she adopts a diffident slouch, unconvinced by her mother's reassurance. Each morning in the bathroom, she surveys her face with exasperation; her nose grows longer each night. If the dark-skinned man of her dream returned, would he want her now?

Her hair, like corn silk in childhood, has acquired the hue of moldy hay. She has no acne, but her skin remains pale, "fish-belly white" says her father, all he can say comfortably, believing privately that her skin resembles porcelain, but one does not tell a fifteen-year-old such a poetic thing, lest it lead to a lot of self-admiration. Teresa thinks her daughter has a ghostlike appearance and tries to feed her more liver. When the door to her room is open, only a path can be seen to the bed and closet, all the rest of the oak floor obscured by abandoned magazines, sheet music, and dirty clothes.

Classmates grow aloof. Trish talks more and more about parties the high school kids have and boys she meets in the dormitories at the junior college. The world is not indifferent but a paragon of harmony, circles of favors between popular suntanned girls and a web of extended families from which Erika is excluded. And nobody, nobody has a dad as weird as hers.

She dances reluctantly with her father in the living room, her mother leaning in the kitchen doorway, smiling, as she learns to swing, foxtrot, and waltz. These few minutes, her palms against his, and the one-on-ones in the driveway shooting baskets, increasingly become the only moments of truce. In her room alone, she gyrates, twirls and splits, every motion she has seen on MTV, while the rest of her existence diminishes.

When she tries to get her father to play their language game one evening, each one of them required to finish the other's sentence in Spanish, German, or French (Erika is permitted to hold language guides), he suggests that she master English first. Long pauses emerge at the dinner table, Teresa glancing from one to the other, searching for a crevice to anchor some connection between them—the right word, the beginnings for a bridge.

They are so clueless. The television news drones for a few minutes before her father *pontificates*—the right word, she thinks. Pon-tif-i-cate. Like living with the damn pope. She goes out the back door and stands in the yard at the edge of the deep grass by the rusty swing set until the mosquitoes land on her white legs.

Party invitations come in the mail or by word of mouth, and she hears, "But we don't know that boy" or "I'll have to ask your father" or "You've got some catching up to do in math, don't you?" Erika stops asking. The invitations stop coming. Fantasies materialize at night in bed, the nearness of a man, her dark man, not a boy, and she explores every inch of him.

For a few weeks at the beginning of the year, she joins any cluster of girls where there is excitement in the conversation, the foretoken of an event. Trying to approach casually, her height betrays any effort at complete invisibility. One or another girl says, "Hi," not her name, just "Hi," and returns to the cluster.

Eventually it comes, a yellow strip of legal paper folded lengthwise and shoved through the air slot of her locker by an anonymous hand, falling at Erika's feet when she opens the door. Her heart skips—a note from a boy, or another invitation. But in round script she feels certain is a girl's is written, "*Do you FUCK like Trish?*" She glances around, thinking the perpetrator might be watching for a response, but she is not even that important; the hallway is nearly empty.

She wants only to be *there*, to listen, to watch, where there is music and the voices of the cruel, pretty girls and the confident boys they possess. To be part of the talk the next week. To be included, if only for a little while, before someone turns down the living room lights. At night she imagines what she has heard in half sentences, tucked in the privacy of whispers between open locker doors, boys and girl getting close. It is closeness she wants.

*

It was a quarter to eight. Erika sat on one side of the living room and Melinda opposite, between them nine chairs borrowed from other corners of the house. Aaron, drowning in their embarrassment, had disappeared down the hallway, pretending to ask a question about Charlemagne of Sam, who, anticipating a houseful of teenagers, had sequestered himself in his study. Great White had played through on the turntable, and now the room was quiet except for the repeated scratch of the needle against the record's label.

"What time did you put on the invitations?" Teresa asked again.

Erika sat mutely staring up the street.

"Six-thirty till ten," Melinda answered.

"Well, maybe there was a game or something tonight."

"There wasn't any game," Erika said without moving her gaze.

"Perhaps one of the other girls had a party." Teresa looked at the square metal tray of cold pizza rolls. Aaron had eaten nine of them before Melinda hissed at him and drew her finger across her throat. Teresa picked up a bowl of Doritos. "Or perhaps they needed to study." She took the Doritos to the kitchen, then crossed the dining room on her way to bed.

"All of them? That's not a lot of comfort, mom."

"Maybe they forgot. I could call..." But she was already down the hall, passing Aaron, who reappeared, wearing a face of neutrality.

"No!"

"Hey." Melinda stood. "We could just have a party ourselves. It's their loss."

"Yeah." Erika stood and turned off the record player. "Let's clean all this crap up." She carried the tray of pizza rolls as far as the kitchen door and, unbridled, hurled it the length of the room.

Her mother's door opened. "Dear God, what's going on out there?"

Melinda seized Erika's arm. "Nothing. We just dropped a pan."

The door closed.

"You okay?"

"Yeah. You two just go. I'll talk to you tomorrow."

Erika went into the bathroom. On her back were seven moles; she studied them in the mirror that night for a while after Aaron and Melinda had gone, imagining they were a divine mark, trying to match them to a constellation but finding nothing in the sky charts of either hemisphere that matched. "A curse," she said to herself. Her parents' bedroom door was shut. She went back into the living room dressed only in her underwear, knowing that no one would come by so late but with a small wish that one of the boys might and would catch a glimpse of her through the window and feel some sense of loss that he had ignored her invitation. She unplugged the portable stereo and carried it back to her room.

*

Trish was now at the high school and moved among an important circle of friends. On Christmas afternoon, she came to their house with Ronnie, arriving in his 1977 Dodge Diplomat with throaty mufflers and creaking doors. Trish hopped out of the passenger side, the front seat, with an authority that awed Erika. They loitered in the living room, the winter air laced heavily with cigarettes falling off their clothes. Sam looked up from his seat at the table.

"You kids smoke?"

"Oh, no, sir…but my brother does." Ronnie crushed the pack a little deeper into his pocket.

"Yeah, we had to drop him at work, and he smokes, and he won't let us roll the windows down," added Trish.

Bullshit, thought Sam and turned over a paper.

Trish picked up a piece of fudge and bit off half of it and put it back on the tray.

"Hey, kiddo. Wanna go to the movies? *Tequila Sunrise* is at the Coronet."

Erika glanced in the direction of her father and rolled her eyes. "I don't know." She looked out the window at Ronnie's car, a retired black-and-white with a spotlight on the driver's door. "Neat car. Does the spotlight work?"

"It's disconnected," Ronnie said. "But I could hook it up any old time I wanted."

The afternoon sun was melting the dirty snow packed behind each wheel. In spite of the oxidized paint and the rust stains that ran from the remaining brightwork around the doors, the car glistened. It was an icon of freedom, and Erika ached to climb into the front seat, or even the back, and go with them. She studied Ronnie's beefy hands, his teeth as he smiled, and the outline of him in his tight Levis, and imagined Trish letting her sit in the front seat. In the middle. She reimagined it again without Trish at all.

Teresa sat in the kitchen and leafed through the entertainment section of the *Oregonian.* "Sweetheart, that movie's rated 'R.'"

Trish picked up a second cube of fudge with her other hand while she licked her fingertips clean of the first.

Sam opened a paperback copy of *Before the Deluge.* The boy's name had come up in academic circles after he'd applied to the college auto body program. From the fragments he could recall, the boy's locker warranted a search for some stolen tools, and Sam thought of his own brother. "I believe your mother could use your assistance this afternoon," he said without looking up.

Teresa stood up and went to the kitchen. "I'm sure I'll think of something," she said under her breath.

Sam wandered into the living room and searched for a book on the Wundervogal in a pile by his favorite arm chair, unobtrusively inspecting the boy sitting in it. The boy had a tattoo on his left forearm, but Sam couldn't read what it said. Trish and Erika vanished into the bathroom.

"So what level are you, lad?"

"Huh, level?"

"I mean to say, what grade are you in? You are in high school, I presume."

"Oh, yeah, tenth grade, sir." The boy shifted in the chair and sat up slightly.

"You like to work on cars?"

"Yeah."

"Looks like you picked a dandy one, then." He looked older than sixteen. Probably held over a year or two.

Trish locked the bathroom door, pulled down her jeans and sat on the toilet. Erika pulled an eyebrow pencil from the drawer next to the sink and began slowly to drag it, for the first time, over each eye.

"Wait a second, don't use that." Trish stood up, zipping her jeans. "It's brown. You've got too much eyebrow, anyway. Have a blue one? Your eyes are blue, and you can use it for eyeliner."

Erika fingered through the drawer, all of the little tubes and brushes her mother's. "Don't see one."

"Okay, forget that. Let's do something for your eyebrows." Trish opened her purse and dumped it by the sink, fragments of paper, ashes, hair, and lint falling; an inverted mushroom cloud poured onto the vanity. She brushed it onto the floor. She picked up a pair of tweezers and sat facing Erika.

"Look at me. They're growing together in the middle. Like the cookie monster."

Trish's fingers were smoky and resinous. Erika held her chin up but scrutinized the mess on the counter: A pack of Marlboros and a yellow plastic butane lighter slipped into its cellophane cover, three tubes of lipstick, a dozen pennies, some Tic Tacs, a package of Zig-Zag papers, and a circular pink plastic compact with a foil pack visible on one side.

"You on the pill?"

"…umhum."

"Ouch!"

"Sorry. A couple more to go. Doctor Stevens said it would help my acne." Trish squinted and leaned closer.

"So, are you and Ronnie…"

"Yes." Trish glowed.

"So where do you go? Where *can* you go?"

"Well, until it got cold and they closed it, we'd go down to Myer Park."

"Aren't you worried about weird people? Guys with hooks?"

"Ronnie keeps a gun under the seat."

"You're lying."

"No shit. I kid you not. He showed me how to shoot it too."

Trish produced a blue eye shadow brush from her own purse. "Close your eyes. And there was a time in his mom's garage while she was home." A silver blue ribbon of color grew across Erika's ivory eyelid. "And then sometimes, just after school, we have about an hour before my mom gets home from work."

"You're gonna get caught."

Trish smirked. "We did, kinda."

Erika flushed and let out a little squeak. "What happened?"

"Nothing. It was just the park ranger at Myer. He banged on the window with his flashlight and yelled." She started to giggle. "Now he knows Ronnie's car and follows us around in his little green truck if…" Both girls started to snicker uncontrollably. More blue was applied, its iridescent sheen as fine as the dust of a butterfly's wings.

"I think Mom sort of knows, anyway. I mean, she kinda' made sure I was on the pill." Trish leaned closer. Shorter, softer strokes. Trish squinted, searched her work critically, and stepped back.

"Doesn't it hurt?" Erika asked, thinking it might be a stupid question, but the opportunity to ask might be gone if she did not. And *smell*. It must smell, she thought.

"I don't know." Trish shrugged. "Maybe a little bit. The first time. There. Look."

Erika stood before the mirror, fascinated, uncertain. She blinked and felt the slightest stiffness in her eyelids, like a thin layer of glue had dried there.

"I bet Ronnie will like it." Trish beamed.

"My parents will just make me wash it off."

"I bet they won't if they're making you stay home."

"What's the point, if I stay home?"

The two girls blew into the living room. Trish flopped into the chair opposite Ronnie's, and Erika stood, bashful, behind her. Trish rolled her head back and grasped Erika's hands, swinging them from side to side.

"What do you think, Ron, my man?"

Ron looked up at Erika. "Yeah, wow. Hey, she's really, like, Erika, that's really pretty."

"C'mon, dude." Trish bounced up on her feet and grabbed his hand. "We're gonna miss the show."

They fumbled with the screen door and said good-bye to Erika's parents. Trish turned to Erika and smiled a smug smile, a smile of confidence. Freedom seemed to rise and follow her to the porch. Ron looked back and smiled, a smile reserved for little sisters.

The Dodge started with a black puff, rolled back into the street, stalled, then puffed again, and the two drove off. Erika sat down and contemplated sulking.

"Let me see your face, honey." Erika swiveled the chair around.

"Really, I think that's a bit much. What do you say, Sam?"

Sam looked up from his book at the dining room table. Her neck, her jaw, so much the form of his own mother in her young years. "I think she's looking more and more like a young woman every day."

It sounded patronizing. Erika stood up and walked down the hallway to her room, closing the door behind her. She had stacked her opened Christmas presents on the bed late that morning, and flopped down beside them. The pile of boxes slid toward her thigh and she sorted through them again. A pair of white flannel pajamas with little powder blue sailboats printed all over them. The *Girl meets Boy* album she had wanted. A French-English dictionary of her own, and a plastic case of makeup with a dozen shades of eye shadow, lifeless pastels laid out in a tray like a child's watercolors, far too large to fit in a purse. *Meant to stay home, like me.* She couldn't imagine herself wearing them now; she would look like a clown.

She opened the album and placed it on the spinning turntable on top of her dresser. The music unfolded in a cascade of crystal notes and she turned up the volume, then spun, her hair feathering across her eyes and lips, and her spirits rose and pirouetted about the room. It grew dark outside and she switched on both bedside lamps and turned up the thermostat, basking in the heat and the light and the music. A star could fall into my life, she thought. She took off her clothes and slipped into the pajama top and admired her long, bare legs. She turned again, stepping away to the rhythm, fingers light in the air, swaying and sliding in circle upon circle, imagining her shadow and another, gliding magnetically, each turn, each breath, every spin faster. The song ended.

Her father rapped on the door. "Turn it down a tad, will you?"

She stopped and stood before the mirror on the back of the door and looked at the awkward girl wearing a child's pajama top and eye makeup. The album rolled into the next song. She'd considered showing the pajamas to Trish, but imagining Ronnie following them down the hall, thought better of it. She was surprised her parents hadn't gotten her the kind with feet sewed into the bottom. She lifted the pajama bottoms from the box, held them at length, then pulled them on. Her father rapped again. She pushed "Reject," the tone arm rose and the room fell quiet.

On the desk in its opened cardboard box sat a twelve-inch globe that Aunt Helen had given her. She lifted it out and cleared a space on the desktop, staring at the multitude of colored nations separated by great expanses of black, the oceans of the world filled with ink. Helen's gifts always arrived unsolicited, a day or two early, things they might have never thought of purchasing themselves, but somehow indispensable later. Helen Bierwirth, married to Uncle James long ago for just eight months, lived a mile closer to town in a two-bedroom bungalow. Each room meticulous, her home displayed but one old black-and-white photograph in an oriental frame. "That's me," Aunt Helen would say with the detachment of a curator of a museum and would point at the toddler, "and that's my father in his uniform, and that's General Stillwell."

What artwork she owned—a few swords, tarnished masks of bronze and leather, a small collection of blue-and-white porcelain—recalled her growing up in China, the daughter of a marine assigned to the US embassy. One did not visit her home without invitation, and her telephone conversations were brief, even curt. One felt more welcome at her office at the hospital.

Erika slowly rotated the globe and stopped at New York, feeling the surface of the tiny bull's-eye labeled, "New York City," as if she might feel the texture of the skyline. In the kitchen, the telephone rang. A moment later, her mother tapped at the door.

"Erika, its Melinda. Keep it short. Dinner's almost ready." A friend. My only friend, she thought. She shuffled down the hardwood floor of the hallway, across the dining room carpet and into the kitchen, stepping on a crumb of cat food as she took the receiver.

Melinda spoke in short, excited fragments interrupted by snorts and sniffles. In summary, her mother was taking Aaron and herself the next morning to go skiing at Mt. Hood, and could she come along? Teresa nodded. Sam mumbled something about paying her lift ticket but added that she should pack a lunch, the food at the lodge being so expensive. He had pulled the console television away from the wall and sat on the floor behind it, glasses resting on his nose, attaching a VCR he had purchased for the family. Every girl in her class owned one, it seemed, but it was their first. Erika hung up the phone.

"Well, you're all ready for bed. Are you feeling sick?" asked Teresa.

Erika watched her father. "I just wanted to try them on. We have any tapes for that thing?"

"That's the real surprise," he said, pushing the console back to the wall.

Erika ate little of her supper, alternately looking out the window and staring at her plate. Trish and Ronnie would be getting out of the movie by now. She picked at her plum pudding.

They watched *It's A Wonderful Life* that night, Erika curled up at one end of the sofa. Teresa cried at the end. Sam thought of his own childhood and realized again how much better things had been in America. Erika wondered if she had a guardian angel of her own, if he was an old man, and if he watched when she showered or got undressed.

She lay in bed, turned off the lamp, and thought of Jimmy Stewart again, how Donna Reed glowed at him.

Trish and Ronnie—and a flush came over her. It was magic to have someone want you so much like that and to want him, skin against skin. It wasn't really dirty, she thought; you just kissed and kissed, in different places, and she stroked her hips. She twisted herself around her blanket until it crossed between her legs like a barber's pole, and crumpled her face jealously into the pillow. Trish dared to do *that*, with Ronnie; it was a heady notion. Her heart beat quickly and her breaths grew shallow, trying to imagine Ronnie, the mass of him, all of him, and Erika shuddered as she approached the darkness at the edge of her unspoken dreams.

Abruptly she felt small and ineffectual, her parents somehow to blame. She got out of bed and pushed aside the lace curtains. It had begun to snow again, enormous flakes settling over the neighbor's backyard, the picnic table's sharp edges softened by the contour of the snow, shadow and relief illuminated by the bulb on the Grants' back porch. She stood there for several minutes as the falling swirls of white settled something in her chest.

Her feet got cold. Skiing had been frustrating the year before, with snow under her collar, beneath her jacket, melting in the small cleavage of her chest where she could not reach it. She left the curtains parted and climbed back into bed, rubbing her feet together. A star might fall, she hummed to herself, and fell asleep.

*

The following morning Melinda arrived, her mother driving their Subaru station wagon, Aaron and Melinda's skis on the roof. Erika put the last bite of a waffle in her mouth and got up to let Melinda in. Melinda chattered and sniffled as she followed Erika to the bathroom, where Erika repeated the mascara ceremony of the afternoon before while Melinda watched with the solemnity of a witness to brain surgery. "Awesome," she said finally. "Like Madonna or somebody."

Erika stuffed her lunch, her gloves, and a pair of Snickers bars into her backpack and kissed her mother on the cheek. Teresa held her at arm's length for a moment and studied her face and the makeup.

"Isn't that going to run if it gets wet?"

"Nope. It says 'waterproof.' You got it for me." And Erika turned away. "Come on," she said to Melinda, and the door slammed behind them.

Melinda slid in next to Aaron in the back, who immediately tried to tickle her. Erika hopped into the front. Mrs. Mathews said something about seat belts, Aaron interjected something about fresh snow, and Erika said "That's great," wondering herself how it would be different from old snow. Maybe fresh snow would be softer when she fell down.

Erika talked to Mrs. Mathews about why the river couldn't freeze, how roll-on deodorants were better than aerosols, and what she thought of Mahfouz winning the Nobel for literature, all the while watching her foot movement as she shifted the gear lever. She studied the instrument panel and leaned forward to peek into the rearview mirror. She watched the road disappear before them, a quiet little thrill sitting in the front, even without a boyfriend. It was overcast as they drove through town, and along the river, a dense fog enveloped the interstate. Mrs. Mathew's conversation subsided as she concentrated on the taillights ahead of them. The fog thinned as they rose through Hood River. Climbing the highway into the mountains, one curve followed another, the sunlight fell suddenly down through the trees from the blue sky and the bright white hillsides above them.

"Melinda's going to be a candy striper next month." Mrs. Mathews finally spoke without looking over. "Do you think that's something you'd like to do?"

"Melinda told me last week." Erika paused. "It would take up piano time. I only get to play stuff I like before dad gets home."

"Well, if you decide, just let your mother know. I'd be glad to pick you up when I pick up Melinda."

At the lodge, the three of them bought lift tickets, then Erika went off to the rental shop with her pack on her shoulder. She clomped over a few minutes later, skis and poles crossed against her chest. Her lesson would be over by ten thirty, she told Melinda. Could they be by the easiest lift about that time?

Four others joined her for the lesson: three high school boys from Portland and a fat woman with red hair, who talked at whoever stood beside her and kept falling down and laughing. The three boys antagonized each other, too preoccupied to notice her. Erika found that her toes got cold if she stood still too long. She wondered where Trish and Ronnie went after they left yesterday. She pictured them just holding each other, warm under piles of blankets in Trish's little white twin bed.

What would she be expected to do as a candy striper? It was, it dawned on her in that moment, *a way out of the house.* An entire universe of independence unfolded before her in the minutes that followed, her class moving fifty yards down the hill before she noticed. She imagined tables crowded with friends, her new friends. Connie and Becky and of course, Jarrod, the guy from California, and whoever Becky had that week. And there would be other boys, boys who hadn't noticed her before, but now they would with her new makeup. They'd realize how smart *and* beautiful she was, and they'd ask her to go cruise for a while and would drive her home. She would have to talk to Aunt Helen after school on Monday. She managed a turn and then another. With Herculean effort, she snowplowed to a stop. She studied the lift chair above them. Just watching it rise into the sky made the surface below her seem to slip, and Erika wondered when the instructor would take them over there, but she never did. The lesson ended, and Erika was alone. She floated in a black-and-white montage of adult freedoms. It would be just another year, and she'd have her own car; she might become a nurse, recognize the obvious in the emergency room during some panic and save a life, and wouldn't she be so important at school then. She drifted down the hillside toward the corral of rope, intending to stop near the end of the line, but miscalculated her speed and joined the line instead, colliding with two small girls, nearly knocking them down. More skiers arrived and she was swept along by the crowd, when she spotted Aaron and Melinda a dozen yards behind. They shouted to each other.

Erika shared a chair with a man she thought to be about twenty-five, slender, clean-shaven, with a few curls of dark hair dangling beneath his ski cap and his eyes bluer, so much prettier, than her own. Her nose was running and she turned her head away, trying to wipe it inconspicuously. As the chair climbed, he dug in his pockets and produced a roll of Mentos. He put one in his mouth, then offered her one and asked how long she'd been skiing.

"Oh, this is my second year." She watched the treetops pass from side to side as the chair swayed gently. She looked down between her skis at the myriad skiers passing beneath them at incredible speeds in the opposite direction. She placed an arm behind the chair, behind him, careful not to touch his jacket. She grasped the edge of the seat more rigidly with her other hand, as if whatever friction held her there could be broken by a sneeze. "This is actually my first time on the chair," she said, looking at her knees.

He smiled. "Well, I don't think I've ever heard of anyone slipping out."

"I guess what bothers me more is knowing how high I'm gonna be when I get up there. Knowing I'm going to have to get all the way to the bottom without falling."

"There's no rule against falling," he said. He looked off into the treetops. He spoke again, looking at her. "The secret is to just use the few muscles you need to control your balance. Don't try to control gravity or the mountain. It's all about relaxing and just shifting your weight."

She heard half of this. He pulled an amber pair of goggles down over the beautiful eyes. The wind started to push the chair.

"Better get ready to get off," he said, as they leveled and approached the operator's booth.

She stiffened and the wind grew colder.

"Now get the tips of your skis up, keep them side by side. When the chair passes that little green sign, just stand up and push the chair away from your butt with your hand." The cable clattered and there was the sound of loud machinery. He raised his voice. "We'll both need to go to the left. I'll get out of your way..."

The ramp suddenly looked terribly steep and she began to brace herself and panicked, gliding for a few yards before her skis crossed. She gyrated for

a second, fell forward, and slid another forty feet on the glazed surface, horrified that she might slide down the entire mountain. She slowed and stopped.

She heard the scrape of skis as he reappeared, gliding slowly backward
before stopping in front of her.

"You okay?"

"I think so. I feel so stupid."

"You just fell down. It'll happen less and less."

God, he's cute. He was talking to her again.

"Put both of your skis side by side, downhill, toward me." He took a pole
from his hand and stooped, taking her by the arm.

She stood up. Slightly uphill, she was at eye level with him. His goggles
were up again. She liked the touch of his hand on her arm, but already he
was letting go. *In the movies, I'd kiss him now.* She teetered and thought she
was going to fall on him and knock him down. The feeling lingered and she
blushed.

"See, you're fine. I bet you won't fall again all day." He pulled his goggles
down and was gone, vanishing over the white.

Airy confidence filled her, her skis buoyant. She slid forward across a
shallow slope and felt her weight shift to the downhill ski, a cautious turn, she
stooped forward slightly and traversed slowly in the opposite direction. She
stood more erect and looked across the valley below, the sun brilliant from
every tiny crystal, and wondered where he had gone. "Older guys know stuff,"
Trish had told her once. "They won't mess with your mind." She looked for
him in the lines at the chair, and as she rode the lift, she watched each hat
below, careful of her form the rest of the afternoon, just in case he might be
behind her. She stopped periodically, high at the edge of a falling meadow of
snow, and took in every tree against the blue sky, breathed the cold oxygen,
and felt certain that he would ski up to her side at any moment and this world
would belong to them. She wondered if he was in college, or sold expensive
bicycles, or traveled the world doing something secret for the government.
She fell just once more.

She wanted to pour all of it out before Melinda when they sat down to
lunch, but Aaron was there, arranging his French fries on the table to look
like little animals, so she decided against it. What if he appeared again and
Melinda thought he looked too old?

By three thirty, Erika was exhausted, and her blue jeans wet up to the
knees. Her buttocks and shoulders ached as well as the muscles across her
chest. It was a good hurt, she thought, as she checked in her equipment. She

had mastered Cannonball Run, riding it to the base three times without falling. It was identified by a green circle, but she felt the same triumph of those who had climbed Everest. She handed her plastic tag to the closet clerk, then sat down and pulled on her own soft, dry snow boots.

Mrs. Mathews waved to them from the parking lot. She had gone into Portland for the after-Christmas sales and the back of the station wagon was a nest of sacks and boxes. Melinda put her ruddy nose in one as she got into the back seat. "You just stay out of those, young lady," her mother said.

Aaron's cap was covered with ice, his face red and exhausted, and he fell asleep as they pulled out of the parking lot. It had become overcast again, and a freezing rain had started to fall. The defroster roared against the windshield and the wipers swept back and forth through the brown slush that rose from the wheels of the cars in front of them, brake lights glaring in quick succession at each curve as they crept in foggy procession down the mountain.

Erika reclined her seat and closed her eyes, thinking all the while about the stranger with the blue eyes. *Older guys know how to kiss,* she remembered, and constructed various fantasies of how they might meet again. In one, she was an Olympic skier and he was a magazine reporter. In another, she met him on the set of a commercial where she was endorsing some winter sports equipment, having become a famous skier herself. In her favorite, she was a nurse, and he had been injured, in an avalanche perhaps, and she helped him take his first steps again. She would definitely go talk to Aunt Helen on Monday. Melinda chattered incessantly with her mother, her voice fading in and out of the daydream.

*

Robert Myron Quigley sat at his desk and reorganized the stack of computer generated ledgers in front of him, comparing one column with another in a second set, trying to unearth a pattern to explain the irregularity that had triggered an audit at First National Bank of Kansas. One stack sat accordioned in his lap, its folds of pale green-and-white stripes traveling up over the desk calendar and disappearing over the front of his desk. He didn't like bank investigations, they felt like they should be well within the realm of the Treasury Department. He had procrastinated, and the sun sat low in the winter sky over the St. Louis skyline, a few buildings outlined in red-and-green or white lights, a streak of gold refracting off the nickel-plated frame of his wife and daughter. He reached out and turned the frame a few degrees with the theory that it would fade more slowly, a motion he had repeated every afternoon for the past twelve years that his office had been on the ninth floor, facing west. He pushed the frame sideways a few inches, concerned that the paper might knock it off.

On the wall near the door hung a portrait of George Herbert Bush, with William Sessions on his left and William Webster on his right. The ready-matted photograph had arrived two years earlier, an official fixture for every special agent with his own office, and a larger one hung in the lobby. Almost immediately after the photographs' arrival, someone had fashioned an alien head from a green Post-it Note and plastered it over Webster's face, with a caption denying the existence of Area 51. Sessions was rumored to be making a tour of the Midwest after the first of the year, and it seemed to Quigley that everyone had had their laugh and it was time to scrape it off.

He picked up the top sheet of a second stack. The column of initials down the left margin had been partially obliterated by a magic marker. At five that morning, he and two field agents had left for First National, driving through the dark to a small branch in a strip mall in the east district of Topeka, and they'd started the day with a stack of ledgers in what they were assured was an unused storage room. Thirty minutes later, they found themselves sharing it with two argumentative would-be home buyers and their loan officer, who, glancing at the agents, said, "Never mind us," before unreeling a long recitation of legalese to the couple, a situation that escalated to raised voices, clenched fists, and fold-ers slapped like whips on the tabletop, the other end of which served Quigley. When he and his two assistants hurriedly stuffed the ledgers into a bank box and started to leave, a skinny dishwater teller had stopped them.

"You can't take these out of the bank like this," she said. "It would be a violation of confidentiality."

The three of them had watched, stunned, while she ran the marker the length of every page with mechanical efficiency. Earl Hurley, the president of the branch, was already out of the building. Earl was too stout to wear his side-vented suit gracefully, and the back of it had stuck out over his buttocks like a little shelf as they followed him into his office at their arrival. Earl was in a perfect position to execute illegal transfers, but his patronizing smile and his clumsy two-handed handshake made him seem too stupid to pull off what was, at this point, a very clever embezzlement. Or maybe it was just an act. Earl had called just after lunch, however, and promised to send unblemished copies by courier that afternoon. Now he compared the two, watching for any change that might have been made. It was his nature.

"You staying late?" Cory Johnson leaned in the already open door.

"Might. Sometimes if you stare at something long enough, the answer jumps at you." Quigley leaned back. "You like working with Allen?"

"He's fine. Talks about cars a lot though."

"He was eight years with the state patrol." Quigley thumbed the pile on his desk. "I might have a surveillance coming up for the two of you."

"Thanks. See you in the morning."

After Johnson left, Quigley leaned over the first sheet and started to tabulate the three-letter columns, still faintly legible beneath the long black smear. Earl had introduced him to each employee, going office to office. Clyburn, "David Clyburn" it had said on his desk, hadn't looked him in the eye, there was something in the way he shifted paper on his desk and in his terse manner when he answered the phone while they spoke. "What do you do here?" Quigley had asked.

"I, ahh," and Clyburn looked at the desktop as if it might whisper the answer. "I do, I handle," and he nearly grimaced, "small business loans, commercial real estate. That sort of thing."

"That sort of thing," Quigley repeated. "Nice to meet you."

"H. Malouf" had occupied the smaller desk in the next office, his whole demeanor timid, courteous in the manner of someone who will do anything to avoid contention. He had been sitting with his back to the door when they had knocked on the doorframe, crouched, leaning forward, tapping away at his keyboard so lightly from arm's length, as if it were a sleeping animal he feared.

"Are you from India?" Quigley had asked him after they were introduced, the little man having initiated a handshake.

"Oh no, sir. Lebanon. But I lived for a while in Turkey before I came here."

"Beirut," Quigley said, "where all that fighting is. Do you worry about your family?"

"The Lebanese do not fight. Everyone else brings their fight to Lebanon. My family is dead, sir."

"I'm sorry." Quigley's small talk had opened a scar. The little man would spend the rest of his life with the notion that auditors, for Earl had not introduced them as the FBI or anyone of governmental rank, were bigots. "People fear us more than dentists," Quigley's director had told him once, just after he'd been accepted to the Bureau. Attitudes couldn't *always* have been like that, everyone looking over their shoulders. Arresting gangsters, bank robbers, finding kidnapped children—the public used to eat it up. Quigley touched the cap of his pen to his daughter's image. No one kidnapped children anymore, they just left on their own.

He traced his finger down the inked column, reading silently, 'EPH, EPH, DLC, EPH, SAS, HHM, DLC, SAS, EPH.' He scanned down the next six sheets,. most of the transactions initiated by Clyburn or Hurley. He picked up the phone and pressed one button. "Jeanette. Run a search on a David Clyburn. Anything at all."

Sally Swartz. He wondered what her middle name was. Anne, maybe. She had been with a customer when they arrived at her desk, but she had bounded around it and taken both of his hands and greeted him, her perfume heavy, her makeup applied with a trowel, he thought. She had so reminded him of his own schizophrenic aunt that he couldn't remember what she had said at all, only that it was insubstantial.

After a few minutes, the phone beeped. He went back to his desk and pressed the speaker button.

"Nothing federal. The locals are looking for David R. Clyburn for a whole bunch of parking tickets. And there's a D. Larry Clyburn wanted for domestic abuse and child support."

"How old are they?"

"Looks like the first one is seventy-one. Larry is thirty-eight."

"See if you can get an address history on the young one."

"Yes, sir. Will there be anything else?"

"Make a note for yourself. Contact INS, see if everything is credible on an 'H. Malouf.' Take his social from the First National face sheet."

"Los Angeles is still open. They could check now."

Quigley looked at his watch. A quarter to six. It was fully dark outside. "No, that's okay." He turned on his desk lamp. "Go home. You can do that tomorrow."

4

Majij Aziz rolled down the window and slipped the parking card into the slot. The barrier raised and he pulled into the doctor's parking lot of The Dalles Community Hospital, turned smartly into the second space, and shut off the engine of the black Saab. On the passenger seat lay a clipboard grasping a bundle of curled pages, three patient names scribbled on the top sheet in black fountain pen. Dolores Peterson, *pancreatic cancer, jejunostomy feeding. Pain control.* Juan Ramirez, *diabetic. Cellulitis left leg.* Raul Aguilar, *pneumonia. Alcohol withdrawal.* He picked up the list and an imitation Mont Blanc from the console.

Had he remained in Tehran three years ago, he would have a position at a hospital by now, highly regarded, but he would have no car, or maybe just a *Pakon,* he mused. He looked around the black vinyl interior. The car was used, but not badly, he had paid three thousand dollars and it was European. Leather seats. A flat engine like a Porsche. His first car, an oxidized Escort with shredded upholstery that clung to his jacket, had been an embarrassment, and he'd always made an effort to park it in the visitor's section and walk away quickly. In this car he belonged.

Two figures approached his peripheral vision. A fresh fall of snow remained from the night before, but the sun warmed the pavement in the afternoon and steam rose from the sidewalk between their legs. American girls. One girl, shorter and thicker than her companion, wore a quilted waist-length down coat that by way of multiple creases and billows obliterated any semblance of female form that might have been present. A pleated red-and-white striped skirt was visible above the white hose and black winter boots. She seemed to be doing most of the talking, waving a stubby, quilted arm occasionally for emphasis. Her voice was audible only for a moment as the girls passed finally along the sidewalk in front of his car. They hadn't noticed him and he studied them impassively.

The taller girl wore a knee-length wool navy jacket, a belt drawn tight about the waist. She carried a backpack over her left shoulder and stopped to inspect its contents, as if she'd forgotten something, just as they stood before his bumper. Her cheeks blushed with the cold, but her neck was pale in profile against the navy of her lapel. She spoke to the other girl, then walked on, the contour of the coat reflecting the motion of her hips, fluid, neither exaggerated nor juvenile. She grew smaller and then disappeared into the building. American girls. They wasted a long time being teenagers, learning things they didn't need to know, wasting a great deal of money and demanding trivial amusements. At home, these girls might be married, doing something useful. One of them might even be offered as a wife to some fine young doctor, her attributes assessed, a match arranged by wise parents with an eye for value. But here, you could pick the woman you wanted; you could see her, touch her, and try her out. You decided on your own, just like he had picked this car.

He looked again at the list, his initiative to get out of the car dampened by an ever-renewed bitterness. He loved the patients because they treated him as their doctor. They relied upon him and seldom challenged his word, and this made him feel worthwhile, that someone thought what he had to say was valuable. But he was also aware that they had nowhere else to go. They had chosen him from a short list. They could not afford to travel to the University Hospital in Portland, and few physicians accepted Medicaid in this town. Pathetically, they had accumulated no wealth. After a long office day full of them, half of them edentulous, each another variation of the same litany of neediness, he felt only contempt. Dissatisfied and self-absorbed, they clung to their alcohol and gluttony with fists of righteousness.

The meat, of course, was good here in America, soft, pink, ground and buttery, pressed dripping with mayonnaise into bread too small to contain it. Eat quickly, or it would escape, falling onto your clothing or the seat of your car. It was unjust; somewhere at home, good Muslims who might otherwise be healthy were dying of a lack of food or clean water. Even the pork, forbidden pork, was as sweet as lamb—baked pork roast, fried pork chops, bacon; only the ham had been too salty. Sausages, for a while he could not eat enough of them, but he quit pork after realizing that Americans were fat, all of them as fat as Reinholdt, the man who had taught him chemistry, and as arrogant. Pork had made them as pigs, his brother liked to remind him. How much greater this wonderful land might be if it belonged to people of the faith. It was a tenet Majij accepted in silence, with a certain ambivalence; at the end of the day, he was generally happy here, if not lonely.

Majij sighed and touched each name on the list. Ten dollars for each office call, ten dollars for each hospital visit, twenty dollars for admitting a patient to the hospital. Majij had left residency before finishing and was consequently unable, in most states, to be licensed as a physician. He had to remind himself almost daily that he was as well-off functioning as a physician assistant under the proctorship of Ahmed Rashid, MD. He had no liability, no cost of overhead, Rashid had pointed out at the first interview. Rashid would remind him again whenever he detected a passing breeze of unrest. The patients were all, in the eyes of Medicaid under the practice of Dr. Rashid. Rashid would take down a book and open it on the desk, and Rashid would speak, pointing to one paragraph or another, paternal and condescending. Majij would listen. But Rashid was from *Iraq*. Iraqi soldiers were killing young Iranian men, a fact Rashid never acknowledged. On the credenza behind his desk, there was always a pile of *The Arab Voice*, but he would never answer a question posed in Arabic. Was it because Rashid felt he was not obligated to, because he owned all the little clinics? Ownership changed people. He would sit with his desk between them, leaning forward in his red leather chair, shaking his finger or gesturing with his hands. He might slap the desktop as he finished what he had to say, like a judge with a gavel. Rashid had spoken of raising office fees, and that would allow Majij thirteen dollars per visit. Majij had not decided whether this was greed on Rashid's part or an effort to manipulate. Majij felt manipulated. He pulled the paper off the clipboard and folded it into thirds, then tucked it inside his coat pocket. He picked up the stethoscope from the passenger floor, opened the car door, and pulled the black corduroy collar up around his white turtleneck. He danced between the puddles of the potholed asphalt, stomping his feet as he reached the doorway. A few drops of melting snow fell into his hair and he shook them away.

Across the lobby sat the information desk, which, in the eighteen months he'd passed there, had never been attended. The first door in the hallway just beyond it opened to the doctors' lounge, and Majij entered. To the left was a stainless steel coffee maker with several carafes on an old credenza. A leather couch, its central cushion caved away, occupied the far wall beneath the curtained windows, which looked onto a small courtyard with several bare trees. In the corner was a modest television, a CNN anchor droning on about a plane that had exploded the week before over Scotland. Majij picked up the remote from the credenza and muted it. The remaining wall was covered with well-worn textbooks no one looked at, most of them past editions donated by senior physicians at retirement. Majij had taken several of them back to his apartment, where they lent an air of legitimacy to his own bookshelf but remained just as useless. He felt the carafes. One was still warm, he smelled it and then poured himself a Styrofoam cupful. He added three packets of sugar and swirled the cup a few times. He stepped back into the hall and walked toward the light of the nurses' station.

Aguilar had spoken Spanish to him yesterday and the day before. Majij found that annoying. How could a man, even an alcoholic fool, mistake him for a fellow countryman? Maybe Aguilar *only* spoke Spanish.

One nurse, a slender, blond-haired woman about forty, sat at the desk, writing. She barely glanced up.

"Good afternoon, Doctor Ah-ziz," she said in a singsong fashion, stretching the last syllable of his name like putty. The second nurse, with short red curls, filled most of a small drug closet. She stood with her back to him, broad buttocks taxing the seams of her uniform. She was reaching up, tampering with an IV bag on a pole, arms like two great hams, all the while making little puffing sounds. She glanced over her shoulder but did not acknowledge him. He sat down at the desk in the remaining chair and with deliberate embellishment, moved the fat nurse's coffee cup aside. He pulled Aguilar's chart from the rack.

A door opened somewhere up the hall and a murmur of young voices could be heard, intertwined with the intermittent protest of an unlubricated caster on something rolling, slowly growing closer. It was neutral conversation, the conversation of friends, heedless of the tension that hung like ozone around the three adults. A cart stopped just before the nurses' station, pushed there by the two girls. They no longer wore their coats, and the taller one stood with her back to him, the fine red-and-white stripes of her dress converging at a petite waist before flowing like a waterfall over her hips, her arms pristine as porcelain in the fluorescent light. He straightened up in the chair and tried to see her legs, then rubbed his eyes and stared again at the page in his fingertips. The two voices fluttered benignly, their two forms moving softly around the tasks before them.

"Excuse me," she said, and in a curtsey had leaned over his shoulder and removed a ballpoint from a basket beneath the edge of the counter before him. Her hair brushed his cheek, and he looked into her eyes for a fraction of a second, then she was gone. He turned back to the chart before him but had lost his train of thought. He flipped to the laboratory section and realized after a few seconds that he had read the reports already. He returned to the progress notes and uncapped his pen, adjusting his chair. He looked timidly over the top of the chart and watched the two girls as they placed amber plastic glasses of juice on a stainless steel cart, trying to absorb chatter he could only hear fragments of. She had been so close! The tall girl glanced at him, he stared, and she glanced again, but looked at him for longer as though she recognized something. Her voice was low and velvety, and she spoke as she watched him, and for a moment it seemed she was speaking only to him. But the second girl responded in the nasal voice of a child. He looked down again at the chart and imagined her face near his again, but this time he held the image before him: almond-shaped blue eyes, lips like carnation petals, her white teeth barely visible. He'd felt a wisp of her breath or perhaps just the current of air as her hair tossed away. Now he imagined it again on his cheek, across his lips, and wondered what it might be like to kiss her.

"Doctor Aziz, Mrs. Peterson just vomited again. We have nothing ordered for her."

He turned and looked up into the stout face of the red-haired nurse. Like a Kurd, he thought. The big woman thrust a chart beneath his nose as if she might poke him with it. He glanced over the list of medications and scribbled. Looking into her eyes, he enunciated, in the deliberate tone he would use to address the simpleminded. "There. Phen-ner-gan, twelve point five, eye-vee, every four hours as needed." He turned in his chair again, but the two girls had escorted their cart to the end of the hall. He had no patients down there.

When Majij arrived at his room, Aguilar was tugging at his wrist restraints, snapping his head alternately from one side to the other, trying to look above him, determination alternating with terror. He could not quite see what tied his hands because of his pillow, but was evidently cursing them in Spanish. He had kicked away his sheets and was naked from the waist down and a clear vinyl catheter led from his penis and over the side rail. He looked down and snarled at it but could not reach it. He focused only briefly on Majij and stopped struggling long enough to say something in Spanish that ended with "…amigo," followed by a laugh, then he was at it again, rattling the side rails as he jerked at the restraints more violently. Majij watched dispassionately, then, thinking of the two girls, pulled the sheet back up to its place.

Aguilar might injure himself; this would reflect on Majij. The nurses plainly had not been giving the Librium as he had ordered and now the man was in delirium. This happened sometimes, a passive-aggressive gesture by the nurses. Some nurses, he reminded himself. The Librium had been ordered "as needed," and the nurses, believing that their own judgment was now a factor, decided among themselves not to give the medication at all. If he ordered the drug given according to a schedule, the only alternative, they might dose the patient right into a coma. So they would torture this man, the harpies, and make him an instrument to express how little they respected Majij's orders or his medical judgment. They'd known when he'd arrived what was going on here and had said nothing.

He stuck his head out of the door and called the blonde nurse by name.

"Draw up fifty milligrams of Librium. Now. Bring it to this room." The nurse arrived, and Majij explained flatly how the treatment had failed and why the drug should be given in a timely manner. She looked at him, non-plussed, then moved about the bed, administering the drug and retying the wrist restraints lower on the frame to Majij's satisfaction.

"He'll be able to pull out the catheter now," she grumbled.

"This is true, but perhaps he will not if he gets his medication on time and he stays sleepy. Remove the catheter."

She clenched her jaw. "He'll piss on the sheets."

"It is not my concern. Remove it anyway."

She flushed and did not look at him until she was finished. "Will that be everything?"

He nodded, never taking his gaze away from his patient. Then he turned, washed his hands, walked to the nurses' station, and picked up Ramirez's chart. The stainless steel cart was even further down the hall, and the two girls were nowhere to be seen. As he leaned over the desk he imagined that he could smell her.

Mr. Ramirez was sitting on the edge of his bed, rummaging through his nightstand. An overweight man with graying hair and a stubble of beard, he looked more like a Chicago cabby to Majij than a farm worker. Beneath his hospital gown, he wore a pair of dirty white socks and athletic shoes stained with clay. His right leg was still larger than his left. Resembling the brilliance and tension of a ripe tomato at admission, it now looked more like a yam. *"Cuando puedo hir para la casa?"* he asked.

"Speak English, please."

"So when do I go home? This place is going to charge me a lot."

"Now, if you like. Can you get a ride?"

Mr. Ramirez tore open a small package of sunflower seeds he'd found in the drawer and stuffed several in his mouth. He nodded his head and spit some shells into the trash can by his feet.

Majij turned to walk away.

"Hey doc, how about after dinner?"

"Certainly."

He sat at the nurses' station, scribbling his note, leaving a prescription in the pages of the chart. His coffee was cold. He swirled the slurry of sugar at the bottom and swallowed. The cart had moved again. He picked up Mrs. Peterson's chart and walked down the hall. Too much drink when she was younger, he thought, might have caused her tumor. She was divorced, perhaps because she drank. She'd smoked—unbecoming, but not forbidden. During her last admission, when she could still eat, he'd find her outside the front door in her wheelchair, wrapped in a hospital blanket and robe, her gray cheeks drawn and eyes lost deep in her skull, a death's head sucking on the cigarettes. He was embarrassed when she greeted him, announcing without sarcasm that he was her doctor. When she had been in pain, she'd told him, but she'd maintained a certain dignity, some strength that reminded him of his own mother. Now her cancer obstructed her bowel completely, and she would vomit all of the mucous and bile her body could make unless they vacuumed it from her stomach continuously. Below the point of obstruction her surgeon had placed a tube into which they pumped thirteen hundred kilocalories over twelve hours each day. Much of this time she would sleep, but continued to hurt when she wakened, and she now absorbed two hundred milligrams of morphine daily. Ninety-seven pounds this morning. She was dying, at forty-six, and there was nothing he could do about it. All of these issues continued to fuel an ambiguity within him. She had accepted her illness and accepted him, unconditionally. He did not know how he should judge her. She seemed to genuinely like him, and this made it all the more difficult. He always prayed he would find she had died in the night when he arrived for his rounds in the afternoon.

Her curtain was partially drawn and he peeked around. In the wake of the Phenergan she was asleep, her mouth open, her lips the palest gray pink, the remaining flesh of her face yellow and fragile as the skin of an onion. A trivial effort had been made to wipe the vomit from her pillowcase (instead of changing it), and he could still smell it. It made no sense to wake her. There was the tap of light footsteps on the tile behind him, and he turned. The tall candy striper stood there with a plastic glass.

"Oh, I'm sorry. I'll come back." She started to turn away.

"No, don't. I mean, don't ever offer this woman *anything*. Do you understand?" He had been angry before she arrived, and it emerged unintended, indiscriminate in its target.

The girl backed to the door, spilling some of the juice on her uniform. "I think so...yes, sir." She vanished.

He listened to the cachectic woman's lungs, letting the weight of the stethoscope rest against her uneven ribs. He brushed her thin hair from the edge of her mouth and then wrote a quick note in the chart at the bedside before returning to the nurses' station. The cart had disappeared.

He walked up the hall, toying with the car keys in his jacket pocket. As he passed the cafeteria, he saw the two girls, one rubbing her blouse with a towel. His pace slowed as he crossed the lobby. He pivoted, stopped. Don't be silly, he thought, she's only a teenager. He walked back to the cafeteria and went in. The two girls were sitting alone, talking, and he stood before them.

"I want to say that I did not mean to be so harsh, back there..."

The shorter girl looked puzzled.

"In Mrs. Peterson's room. I only meant to say that whatever she might ask you to get for her to drink, it will only make her vomit more. It would be very bad for her." He now felt more awkward than when he'd entered the room. The two girls continued to look at him, bewildered. *Oh.* It occurred to him. "Forgive me. I'm doctor Aziz," he said, and he held forth his hand.

The taller girl stood. "Erika, Erika Etulain." And she took his hand in hers.

"Etulain. You are French?"

"My dad was from Andorra."

"He is dead?"

"Dead? Oh no, I mean he was *from* Andorra. He's from here now." She laughed and smiled at him. Her laughter brought color to her white skin, and he found himself once again absorbed with her lips. Afraid he was staring, he turned to the other girl.

"Melinda Mathews." She grabbed his hand and shook it, giggling nervously. Erika sat down and crossed her legs. She wore white hose, and her calves were larger, fuller than he expected for a girl her age.

This was much better. Confidence returned. "Well, if there is ever any question you want to talk about, or anything about my patients that you do not understand, please, be free to talk to me." The girls seemed charmed by this, and he retreated slowly, his eyes on Erika. He stumbled into a chair but caught himself. "Goodnight," he said.

"Goodnight," the girls returned. Melinda waved at him as if he were departing on a train.

*

Majij pulled out of the parking lot and down the hill. A few minutes later, he had parked in the snow-crusted gravel behind his apartment building and stared up at his own darkened window. His foot touched something spongy in the shadows at the bottom of the stairs and he bent down and picked up a frozen newspaper wrapped in a plastic bag. Mrs. Greyson's paper. He looked over at her apartment, where her window was still illuminated, and made his way up the icy boardwalk to her door. She answered after the third knock.

"Thank you, you dear boy," she said.

The heat poured out around her like an inferno. Her glasses, two huge parabolic lenses, made her look like a squirrel in a cartoon. Majij smiled. "You're welcome."

As he walked away he looked over at his own apartment window again. He turned off the heat before leaving on his longer days and it would be cold. He trotted down the steps and got back into the Saab instead. Twenty-two patients had shown up that day at the clinic. That would be two hundred and twenty dollars, a thousand to save each week, four thousand, no, thirty-six hundred after rent was paid. He had worked through this exercise before. A location in Tehran would be best, the central district perhaps, so a few of the poor from the southern neighborhoods could be worked in.

He relived his conversation with Erika and felt sure he'd repaired whatever damage might have been done when he'd spoken so harshly. He thought about holding her now, putting his mouth to hers, his hands on those hips, those calves, the white hose, and something stirred in him. Americans, so proud, so protective of their daughters; they would think it obscene. He guessed her age to be sixteen. In Iran, she could easily be a bride by now. It was a desire he did not feel he deserved yet, and the whole fantasy began to make him uncomfortable.

He drove up a ramp onto I-84. The roads were wet, and there was no ice forecast; he could be in Portland by eight. On Burnside he'd found a bookstore, unlike any Iranian store he'd seen before the revolution. They also sold movies, and he could go there without pretension. In Chicago he had gone to Barnes and Noble when he could not sleep. Their selection was limited, each copy wrapped in brown paper; one could not examine it beforehand, so there was no reason to linger. Nonetheless, he kept ready certain phrases of indignation, a posture of reluctance to be displayed should he be noticed by another passing Muslim. He practiced this superficial outrage to himself as he drove, as a duty, a self-admonition should his fidelity to his religion be challenged.

Fine rain peppered his windshield as he drove into Portland. He passed Powell's on the right. They would be open late. He'd stop and pick up a copy of *The Arab Voice* on the way back. A torrent of headlights came down Burnside in the opposite lanes as he approached his turn. A break in the traffic opened and he crossed, an unknown part of his car scraping the curb as he pulled in and parked. The windows of the shop were painted black, and only a generic blue-and-red neon sign above the door gave any indication that it was occupied. He bounded through the rain and pushed open the door. A young, unshaven clerk reading a textbook glanced up at him blankly for a moment, then returned to his study. No one else in this store would make eye contact. A white-haired man of about fifty with steel glasses and a silk ascot was looking at a magazine with two pubescent boys wearing cutoffs on the cover. In the back of the store where the videos were shelved, two young men stood holding hands.

He could linger here, and no one would object. The top copy of most of the magazines was dog-eared; people expected it. The more one looked, the more one wanted, and bought. Everywhere in America it was this way. He hesitated and swayed from one foot to the other, oblivious for a moment to the rows of glossy covers. Something objected beneath the sole of his shoe, and he stared down at a cigar butt, crushed and smeared across the tile floor like an enormous beetle. He thought of Mrs. Peterson and how the rancid air of the shop might settle into his skin and infect her at the next visit. He thought of the exquisite girl who had spoken to him two hours ago and of what she might think if she saw him here. Suddenly he felt brutish, uncouth, every flicker of flesh on the rack in his stomach now, rotten with larva, ready to come up. He took a copy of *Oui* and handed the clerk a ten-dollar bill, shoved his change in his trousers without counting, and ran to his car.

At Powell's, the lights were bright, there was scattered conversation and the steady rumble of footsteps up and down stairs, with coffee brewing somewhere. Single women were here, sometimes handsome women, but most, it seemed to Majij, intent on appearing as bizarre as possible. They moved among the shelves sideways like crabs, looking up or down or directly forward. He knew better than to try to talk to any. Still, he would move behind them sometimes, pretending to look at a higher shelf, and inhale their scent.

In Chicago, he had dated some American girls: two nursing students, a nurse, and a shelving clerk at the medical school library. Two he had gone to bed with. The librarian had pursued him, calling him initially to request that he return a book. She had wanted to do painful things to him in his bedroom and he'd decided she was crazy. Two of them said they'd been offended by his magazine collection and never returned his calls. One girl talked incessantly of her plans as a doctor's wife. Then came the accusation, an incident, misconduct they said, and exaggerated rumors spread through the hospital.

Along each side of Burnside, the lights of taverns glared through the wet windshield. Couples walked arm in arm, weaving along the sidewalks. Young women with long waves of honey hair, leaning on the shoulders of their young men. Beautiful girls with tall handsome men. What could one do to keep such a girl? Why would she be interested in a small man from another country with so little to say that she would think was romantic? Ugly girls with toad-like men, an equal package. What sort of girl would pick him? She would be short, he decided. He glanced in the rearview mirror. She would have a moustache, he mused. Maybe people loved when they found someone who met all of their needs. It made sense. He wondered what girl could have all of her needs met by himself. No one, he thought, would be worth having if they would have him. He slowed to a stop at a crosswalk. Erika was her name. Erika.

Rashid had a wife. Jolly and plump and talkative, she'd birthed Rashid's four children, whose glowing little faces, three girls and a boy, occupied a rectangular photograph on his desk. How could four children be happy at the same moment when the camera shutter clicked? Majij hadn't seen them firsthand, and Rashid didn't speak of them, they were like an old purchase that one had grown bored of. He did speak of Jolie sometimes, of her cooking, her obedience, and the comfort of her breasts.

Majij thought of his own needs again and how short a list it was: someone to lie with at night, someone to listen to him, follow him where he went in the world, and carry a son for him. There was a decency about that business of possessing one woman alone, devoting oneself. He tried the idea on again, as he had sometimes at night, and felt himself nobler. And he thought once again of Erika. Someone flashed their brights. The light was green and he moved forward as it turned amber.

It was difficult to be a good Muslim here. To feel as if he belonged, to be among the crowds of laughing friends in the smoke and the music, he would have to go into one of those taverns and become drunk and say clever things, like on television. Even then, girls would walk away while he talked to them. He would leave alone. But, *God would mock them and keep them long in sin, blundering blindly along.* It was a feeble retort he cast over his shoulder, unjust and full with his own bitterness, as he crossed First Street and drove up onto the bridge.

His brother, Hakim, had quoted once from the Koran that happiness of the flesh was God's way of leading the nonbelievers to greater sin, so they would endure a greater hell. Majij grappled with this notion at least once a week, that all of the people he saw would either be cast into hell or converted to Islam, and it collided with his sensibility that God, who perhaps in error had made him a physician, would deliberately scheme the failure of so many souls.

He told himself that he wanted to be a good Muslim. But by the time girls in this country were allowed to leave their parents' houses, they were ruined. They had opinions to offer on everything, they were never quiet, and they never listened. It was no wonder Christian men would marry only one.

By the time he reached the on-ramp of 84 East, he was bitter, feeling cheated, a man in the market with the wrong currency. He accelerated hard, and the car slid a half lane onto the shoulder. He knew he was driving on ice.

*

The Sikhs, it was said, were Aryan. Or did this mean their language was Aryan? Erika had started an essay on the geography of India, but had sidetracked herself with a detail she was unsure Mrs. Emerson would even give a shit about. She stood from her desk, straightened her nightgown, and opened the bedroom door, but the living room was dark. A band of light was visible at the bottom of her parents' door, and she could hear them stepping about. She would ask her father in the morning.

She sat down again and turned the globe, stopping with her finger on Egypt. "Doctor Aziz," she said, "what a grouchy prick you are." How could someone so young and so close to her own age have so much attitude? The idea stung a little bit, even as it crossed her mind. Jeee-sus, he was so good-looking, she wasn't sure she could stay mad at a face like that very long. He couldn't be more than nineteen. Alright, college and then med school, three years, she thought, like lawyers. She settled on twenty-four. When I'm eighteen, she calculated, he'll be twenty-seven, and a little chill went up her neck. She pulled her feet up into her chair and rested her chin on her knees. She opened the algebra text as if it were a box of snakes and stared at the first equation for several minutes. Then found herself asking the young doctor how he would approach it, and moved her chair over an inch, his face next to hers as it had been at the nurses' station, as if he were there. His fingers flashed over the keys of the calculator. No, he just mumbled something, some math terms, he was so smart he could do this in his head. She sketched a small heart in the margin of the sheet, then erased it. Let N equal one, she purred to herself, trying to remember his cologne, and a few minutes later, an answer appeared at the end of her pencil. She flipped to the appendix at the back of the book and it was correct.

Black corduroy, that was what his jacket was. She slid open her closet and flipped through the hangers, to be like, to feel, oh, to feel like him! Her only corduroy were brown, but black velveteen, yes, those black velveteen slacks! Trish had said, "They make your ass look good." She could be so gross. But Erika pulled them off the hanger and wriggled into them, hiking them up to her waist, and turned to look in the mirror. Trish was right. I'll say the uniform got dirty, my mom didn't wash it.

*

Different nurses were on duty through the weekend, and Majij walked the hallways invisible to them. Many of the rooms were dark and empty. A new coat of wax had been applied sometime in the night and buffed to marble brilliance. The candy striper's cart was absent. All of the clutter of the week that migrated into the hallway, IV poles, spare chairs for visitors, extra bedside tables, had vanished. Majij breathed in the quiet and relished the sound of his soles on the tiles. Mrs. Peterson spoke only two words to him on Saturday and by Sunday had slipped into a light coma. A zealous night shift had medicated Aguilar so sufficiently that he snored through his exam on both mornings. There was no coffee in the doctors' lounge, and someone had allowed the last carafe to burn, its contents the viscosity of asphalt. Majij walked down to the dining room where an industrial-sized urn always delivered a tannic brew. He looked at the table where the two girls had sat. He should have said more. Something academic.

On Monday, he saw twenty-five patients in the clinic, almost all with some sort of respiratory illness. He bolted from one room to another automatically, prescribing the same regimen for them all, a cheap antibiotic, a generous quantity of codeine cough syrup. It recurred to him every few minutes throughout the afternoon, sometimes as a patient confided in him—he would see Erika, possibly in just a few hours—and a pleasant weakness came to his legs.

Two workmen were installing a powered door at the parking lot entrance and having some difficulty with it when he arrived at the doctor's parking, and they suggested he walk to the back and enter through the emergency room. Beyond the Emergency Department, the hall took him past the obstetrics ward and the wired glass window where visitors could view the newborns. He was startled to find Erika standing there alone, her arms raised, fingertips against the glass, leaning forward just enough that her nose touched the window as well. Her hair was pulled back into a twist, and he was struck again by the delicacy of her neck. She was smiling. He slowed and stood quietly behind her. She had meticulously painted her childlike nails carmine, and wore a pink oxford blouse. Radiance fell all about her. Beyond the glass were two bassinets taped together, tilted to face the window. In each lay a wrinkled, rolled powder-blue blanket, a small ruddy face at the top. Beneath them, hand-printed placards said, "Burnett baby one" and "Burnett baby two." He could smell her again, and breathed slowly, not to betray himself. Her scent was floral and warm, stale and sweet at the same time.

"So they have brought us twins today," he said, almost in her ear.

She squealed and spun around, striking him on the arm as she did.

"Oh, I'm sorry! I didn't know you were behind me." She touched him again, smoothing the wrinkles of his sleeve, her joy so luminous he had to look away. She rubbed the print of her nose from the glass with her elbow.

"So how was your weekend?" he asked and began to walk.

"Well," she began, "one of my best friends ran away."

"Melissa, the young lady I met last week?"

"Melinda. No, Melinda would never run away. Her mom's cool, and she's got Aaron. She's just sick today. It was a girl ahead of me, Trish. She's in high school. Neither her or her boyfriend came back."

"From where?"

"Came back to school after Christmas. Everybody says now they've got an apartment in Portland."

"So how does this boyfriend…" He put his hands together behind his back.

"Ronnie."

"Yes. So how does this Ron-nee pay for this girl? It takes money to buy an apartment."

"He works on cars, I bet. He's good at that."

"Is this common, for girls in your school to run away?"

"Trish is the first, I think. That I've known."

He slowed and looked her up and down. "Your pants. They are quite lovely." And he touched them timidly, quickly, with a motion of his hand.

She halted, pigeon-toed, unbalanced, "I, my mom," she stammered, but her thoughts fell all apart.

The conversation lulled. "I am going to the cafeteria. Will you join me?" he asked.

"Sure."

Erika sat down and Majij drew a cup of coffee from the urn.

"So what do you want to learn today, about medicine?"

She put her hands together and pressed them between her knees, taking a deep breath. "I was wondering, are twins really exactly alike in every way, even in the way they think? We saw a film in school about two girls who got adopted, by different families I mean, and they were twins, and when they finally got together when they'd grown up, they'd both married lawyers, and they both worked as receptionists."

He rolled his eyes and looked at her paternally. "Well, there are a lot of lawyers in the world, some people say too many. A lot of them get married. Of course, everyone must have a receptionist." Through the windows, darkness gathered over the city below.

She started to speak, then shut her mouth in a small pout instead. It was not the response she had hoped for; he had missed the irony, the amazement she'd contemplated all afternoon and hoped to share. She started again, "But don't you think…"

He turned toward her but looked at his coffee. "There are always differences. Differences one cannot see. One is always stronger, or wiser, or more resolute, the other weaker. I suppose, if there is to be birth trauma, say, not enough oxygen, it is usually the second baby that is at a disadvantage." He looked up. "Some believe that the first to be born will follow the right path, will have greater virtue. How do you say? Will be more *moral.*" He stroked his moustache.

She watched his fingertips, thinking he looked like Omar Sharif. "Even if they both grow up with the same parents?"

He smiled and looked at her. "Oh, it is just something that old women say. Forget that I have said this thing." He rotated his cup on its saucer. "With the same parents," he repeated, softly, to himself.

Erika looked at the clock and leaned forward. "I'd better get started. There's only eight patients today, but I'm by myself." She pushed her chair back and stood up.

He watched her as she walked to the door, feeling drawn to follow.

She stopped at the doorway. "Dr. Aziz..."

"Majij. Please call me Majij. Or Maj, if you like."

She put her hand to her chin and giggled. "Maj. okay, Maj. What I was thinking, what I wanted to ask you, if we're just sucking everything out of Mrs. Peterson's stomach anyway, couldn't we just give her something to taste, to wet her mouth? She'd at least feel like she was drinking something."

Majij smiled. "You want to break the rules so that you can be compassionate. I think that is...beautiful." He went on, "It will be safe, I suppose, to give her one cup of ice chips. But only one. Understand?"

Elated, she nodded vigorously and disappeared.

*

An untouched cup of melting ice sat on the bedside table. Dolores Peterson lay with her mouth agape and her tongue dry and cobbled like baked earth. She was deeper in coma, her eyes still partway open. He closed them with his fingertips. A small voice within him had looked forward to speaking with her today, a finite measure of self-worth, and he was aware for the first time of its absence. He was going to miss her, this old derelict American woman. Perhaps she might have still been awake had he come directly to her room. He wanted to tell her about Erika.

"Do you think she's dying now?" Erika had entered quietly and stood behind him.

It had been a private moment, and he stared at her.

"She was like this when I came in," she apologized. "She never touched the ice. I'm sure. I didn't know what to do, so I just set it there."

A blond-haired man with a moustache, a laboratory technologist about forty, walked in behind them carrying a small plastic tray full of syringes. He nodded toward the bed. "You order a blood gas?" He asked Majij.

"Yes."

The blond man wrinkled his face in futility. "She's a tough stick," he said, and knelt by the dying woman's arm. Erika and Majij watched while the tech scrubbed her wrist and then probed her flesh miserably. He began to sweat. Erika moved behind him and stretched onto her toes, trying to watch. Majij watched Erika, her curiosity, her restraint registered in the fists she made with her beautiful little hands behind her back.

Majij leaned over the bed. "It is fine. You are just not lucky today," he told the tech. "Just leave me a syringe. I will draw this."

"Thanks." The tech retreated, looking embarrassed.

Majij watched him go and then pulled the curtain. "Come here," he said. "First, you hyperextend the wrist, like so." And he bent Mrs. Peterson's other wrist back gently. "Now, feel." He took Erika's hand and set her index finger on the fluttering artery beneath the pale skin. "With the bevel up, keep it at forty-five degrees," and he put the syringe into her fingers like a fountain pen.

"No! I shouldn't…"

"Of course you can. You want to. I can see that."

"Yes, but…"

He took her hand and guided it and let go. "It is there for the taking. You will be helping her as well." She pressed down in a single gesture, and the syringe filled briskly, cherry red.

"My God. It's so bright."

"It is from an artery." He pressed a gauze gently at the site. "Now just pull it out and push the tip into that little rubber stopper."

Erika did as she was told and wrapped tape around the wound, very firmly, as Majij instructed her. She stepped back when she finished. "She's still going to die, isn't she?"

"We all are, someday." He stepped back and placed his hand on her shoulder. "That is okay. It is not for you to worry." Her shoulder was warm, substantive through the cotton of her blouse. "You did that well," he added. His fingertips rested gently in the concavity above her collar bone. He stroked the back of her neck with his thumb. She did not lean into the pressure of his palm. She did not move away. He felt driven to put his hand on her waist, but pulled it away instead. "There is nothing either of us can do for her now. *In sha Allah.*" He pivoted and walked out, not aware until he left the syringe on the laboratory counter how moist his hands had become.

Aguilar was complacent, essentially absent, looking over at the sky, humming to himself, his bed linens clean and orderly. Either he was less agitated, or his bed had just been remade. He was still in restraints but did not tug at them, as if arms flung wide and legs spread like an infant were a natural position for any forty-four-year-old man. Aguilar did not acknowledge Majij's presence or his touch as he examined him. The man's pulse was rapid, but at least he was coming out of the delirium.

*

Majij had just gone to bed when the phone rang. Mrs. Peterson had expired, and could they release the body to the mortuary? The call was a formality, its only practical value to alert him that there would be one less face to talk to and one less family to contend with in the morning. He flopped back on the pillow and stared at the ceiling in the dark, illuminated at intervals by the headlights of cars passing on the freeway. It was a peculiar, cruel game Rashid played with him each time a patient died. Rashid would be very critical, find some error he felt was obvious, some artificial juncture in the patient's management where the wrong decision precipitated death, and strut around his office with his hands behind him, frowning, his face collapsing in upon itself like a rotting squash. First sorrow, then amazement, then careful sarcasm. He would ask Majij a question and answer it himself. Finally he would stand behind his chair and curse in Arabic. The less directly Rashid had been involved in the case, the more merciless he would be. Mrs. Peterson had seen Rashid once about six months ago and told Majij afterward that she didn't like him. Majij grew hot with frustration and pushed away the blanket. As if he was expected to cure pancreatic cancer. He ruminated on this and began to rehearse the confrontation silently in the dark, certain to come within the week. Both men were educated, and both knew, at some level, that it was bullying, a pointless humiliation to which Majij had become accustomed, which he felt always that he would eventually deserve, and which perhaps he even longed for.

He knew now that he would not sleep, and sat up, then stood at the window and pulled the curtain aside. A tavern sign flickered in red neon at the end of the block. "Not people of the book," his brother would say. He looked at the highway. So Erika's friend had run away with a young man. Fatima had run away. She had lived in the apartment above his in Tehran when her parents were burned to death in a theater arson. He was in college at the time, spending the mornings home in study. Fatima would come down to complain, to talk, to borrow something, always when the other people in the building had left for the day. In spite of the morals police, she would come. Finally one afternoon she gave herself to him, and again each afternoon for a week. Then her aunts arrived from Abhar. Two proper aunts moved in, very pleased with the electric light at any time, and the hot water. Fatima vanished. He supposed she had been about twelve at the time. He'd realized only later how frightened she probably was. For half a year, he'd looked for her in every street. In every crowded alley, he scanned for her dirty pale blue muslin *chador*. Her gait he had not studied enough to discern the signature of her body, for he had remembered her most vividly on her back, naked.

The awareness that she had left while he was indebted to her reawakened. He paced the room twice, then went into the kitchen. Buried in his memory, she was still alive. Whore, Hakim had said, but in ignoring her true needs, Majij had committed the irrevocable. Self-denial, that might have been the path to change her course, but he had violated her instead. He opened a drawer and picked up a fork and hefted it, before exchanging it for a knife. The serrated edge vibrated its length along his thumbnail, and he put that down as well. *Tanbih kardon,* atonement. He pressed his fingers to his temples until his jaw ached, then went into the bathroom, and turned on the light and imagined Fatima behind him in the reflection in the mirror. He hesitated. Life must move forward, he thought, then opened the medicine cabinet and dragged his fingers the length of the top shelf. A handful of small plastic cartridges fell into the sink. He picked one up and read, "23 ga, 1 inch." He set it on the vanity and picked up another, which read, "18 ga, 1½ inch." He knew now there was a reason these came home in his pockets, why he had saved them, there was a reason for everything that had happened, and right now it seemed all to flow from this inequity. He wondered where she was now. Clearly Allah had sent her so that he could care for her, and he had degraded her instead. He twisted the cartridge and pulled out the stainless needle and held it in silhouette to the light. He wondered if he should strike it on the tile to create a barb, but no, that would cause infection, and he slammed the point down straight into the back of his left hand. The shock seized his arm up to the base of his neck in one convulsive agonal wave and he gasped and fell onto the toilet seat as his eyes welled and a trail of blood trickled toward his elbow. Would Erika run away with him? He turned his hand over and stared at the point of the needle in his palm.

*

On Tuesday morning, only nine patients appeared at the office and four more in the afternoon. An air of lassitude fell over the staff. The receptionist, an older woman, busied herself with needlepoint. Barbara, his nurse, a slender woman in her forties, a victim of too much sun, sat in the break room, smoking a cigarette and working crossword puzzles.

He was obligated to remain until four for walk-ins. At four the waiting room was empty and the street turning gray as the sun began to disappear. He put on his coat. Perhaps Erika and her friend, perhaps just Erika, would be walking past the parking lot at the hospital and he would be able to walk into the building with her.

The hospital sat high on the hillside where the sun was still shining. He waited a few minutes, enjoying the warmth and rearranging the papers on his front seat. He had time, there was only Aguilar to visit today. What if she came over to talk to him or looked into his car? He cleaned candy wrappers and gas receipts from the floor and stuffed them into a Styrofoam cup. He gathered all the loose change and put it into the ashtray. Still no sign of her, perhaps she was inside already.

As he walked in he tossed the cup into the litter barrel by the door. He started to cross the lobby when he glanced at the wall to his right and sensed a small void in the display where the physician staff photographs had been mounted on a long walnut plaque. One was missing. As he grew closer, he realized it was his own picture that had been taken down, leaving a little rectangle of darker walnut next to "Eric Aronson, MD." Who would do such a thing? That blonde nursing supervisor, who had asked him if he was taught anything about females "back in Arabia." Katrina was her name. No. It was Bob Borden, administrator puppet, the ugly sweetness of his greeting when they passed. I should have washed my hand after shaking his, he thought. Such a cowardly gesture of disrespect. You could not prove yourself to such blindly bigoted people; it was always like that in America, insidious stupidity. And they called it freedom. He swiveled, his pace quickening with resolve as he approached the ward.

The nurses' station was oddly vacant, and there was a din of conversation from down the hall, from Aguilar's room. Two nurses emerged and walked past him, followed by a respiratory therapist, disheveled and weary, pulling off his gloves. Miller, an ER physician from Tennessee, stood in the room alone, scratching some final notations on a chart. He glanced up at Majij.

"This guy yours?"

Majij looked at Aguilar, who looked lifelessly at the ceiling. His eyes had a gray film over them, and an endotracheal tube projected awkwardly between his rotten teeth. He was naked, vomit on the mattress pooled in little eddies on either side of his torso. He was still in restraints, empty plastic and torn cardboard packages scattered around his bed like fallen leaves.

Majij shook his head, incredulous. "What happened?"

"Dunno. They called a code about," Miller looked down at the chart in his hands— "four oh five. He was flat-lined when we started. Never got a rhythm in twenty minutes. Finally, I just called it." Miller leaned forward and lowered his voice. "I think he probably puked and aspirated a long time before anybody found him. He was damn cold when I got here."

"Oh Jeesuss…" A girl's whisper. Miller and Majij both looked at the door, where Erika stood like a sculpture, a glass in one hand, a pitcher in the other.

"Excuse me, please." Majij walked away, taking the pitcher and leading her out the door. They walked side by side, slowly, down the hall.

"I'm sorry," she stammered, not looking at him. "I shouldn't have interrupted. It's just that, I've never seen, well, I didn't know that's what they did when…"

He put his arm around her shoulder and led her into the cafeteria and sat her down. "No. You are fine. That is a shocking scene for anyone to see. I was surprised also."

Her eyes filled with tears. "That look, on his face."

"Please. These things happen. It is no one's fault." He lied. Aguilar had been neglected and by all rights should have lived to drink again. "Can I buy you a Coca-Cola or anything?"

"No, that's okay. I'll be fine."

Majij poured her a glass of ice water and set it on the table. She took a sip and swallowed.

"So do you have to do that, a lot, when you're a doctor?"

"No, not so often." Majij shrugged. "Sometimes people say, 'Do not do this thing to me,' and we follow their wishes. Mrs. Peterson did not want us to do this."

"I noticed she was gone. I guessed she didn't get better."

Majij shook his head. "I don't think Mr. Aguilar ever said anything sensible at all, and if a person doesn't tell us what they would like, then all of *that* happens." He gestured toward the hall, toward Aguilar's room. "Are you sure you're okay?"

"Yeah, I'm sure." She set the glass on the table and straightened her posture and began to smile, then looked dismayed. "What happened to your hand?"

He lightly picked the Band-Aid on the back of his fist. "I cut it, in the bathroom."

She reached out to touch it. "Are you okay?"

"Thank you, yes."

She stood up with a pretense of composure. "Well, I should go back and put away the cart. He was my last room. I need to head home."

Darkness had fallen outside the windows behind her. Majij watched her leave and then returned to Aguilar's room. He felt certain the man had died of neglect. He had been as useless as a street beggar, but a small rage began to percolate nonetheless. In ignoring Majij's patient, they were, by proxy, ignoring him—because he was a foreigner, because he did not speak like them. A few weeks after he'd arrived, he'd overheard a nurse impersonating him, other nurses laughing.

Aguilar's body still lay there in partial darkness, the light over the adjacent bed left on. Someone had swept the floor, but little else had been moved. He was still uncovered. No one was going to come for him, there was no family listed. The drawer of his bedside table was open, and Majij stared down at his personal effects: a few coins, a wad of dirty receipts, and the man's wallet, which was flipped open. The green card stated that he'd been born in Belize. His driver's license grinned at Majij from one side, and he slipped it out to look more closely, turning toward the light. It was issued by Washington State. Imagining Aguilar at the wheel of a car was frightening. They were both about the same weight and height. He looked down at the dead man again, absent-mindedly turning the card over and over in his fingers. Then, without any specific plan, he put the card in his pocket.

5

Majij exited the doctors' lounge just in time to see Erika go out the front door. Instinctively, he wanted to call to her, but decided it would attract unwanted attention. Instead he turned and walked to the right, past the nurses' station, past Aguilar's room, and through the emergency room at the back of the building. A hearse had backed into one of the ambulance spaces, and a solitary man was unloading a narrow folding stretcher. Majij hurried past into the dark of the parking lot. When he reached the Saab, he turned the heater on high. Erika was well away from the hospital; she'd traveled far on those long legs, almost to the corner. He pulled over slightly ahead of her, reached across the seat, and rolled down the window.

Erika slowed and stooped to look in. He had sublimated himself, hanging onto the wheel with his other hand.

"Do you have far to go? I can give you a ride."

She hesitated and leaned closer. "Oh, I think I'll be okay, really. It's not far."

"I would be very happy to take you where you need to go. You're going to get very cold." Traffic slowed behind him, a horn sounded, and a car accelerated around through the slush and turned the corner.

She pulled her coat sleeve back from her watch.

"It's a quarter to six," he said.

"Okay. If you're sure it's no trouble." She climbed in and rolled up the window. "It took me longer to clean up tonight without Melinda."

She'd only been outside for three minutes, but in the blow of the heater and the embrace of the seat, she felt as if she belonged.

He let out the clutch, turned down the hill, and shifted again.

Unsure of what to say, she watched the snow drifts at the curbside and wondered about his hand on her shoulder, how odd, how good it felt. She thought again of the dead man and of the smell of vomit that seemed to linger. She wondered if she had stepped in anything, and if Majij could smell it too. They crossed the first intersection at three blocks, and he glanced over at her for directions. She looked at him and smiled and then nervously gestured over the back seat.

"I'm sorry, we should have turned back there, to the right." She sighed. "I wasn't paying attention, I guess, 'cause I don't drive."

"That is quite all right." He turned into a parking lot and made a loop. "You are just used to being chauffeured. Left up there?" He pointed to a Texaco station at the corner they'd just passed.

"Yeah." She nodded her head, and they made the turn. He wore no gloves, and it struck her how delicate his hands appeared. My *chauffeur*, she thought.

"You are in high school?"

"Next year." She faltered on the second syllable, and as quickly as she'd spoken, she wished she could take back those words, snatch them from the air in the car. "High school doesn't start till tenth grade here."

"You ask intelligent questions." He drew a spiral in the air with his finger. "I like that. What I mean to say is that I have been very impressed by you, that you care about my patients."

She melted into the seat.

"You should not be ashamed to be young, it is only a way of counting years. Some women have ruled nations at sixteen."

Erika thought of Joan of Arc, burned alive. Streetlight to streetlight, blocks rolled past. In the light of the instrument panel, there was something so much more personable about him, a joy, incongruous with the flutter in her chest. She floundered for something to say.

"What were those words you said, last week, when we left Mrs. Peterson?"

"When?"

"It sounded like Latin."

"Oh. I think, '*in sha Allah.*' It means 'Go with God' or more accurately, 'As Allah wishes.' It is Arabic."

"Is that what you speak?"

He frowned. "No. Arabs speak Arabic. I speak Farsi, which is different. In Persia, that is Iran, we speak Farsi. It is a much higher language. Much older." He cocked his head matter-of-factly. "I speak both. It is the same alphabet, but a different language. Like English in America, compared to Spanish in Mexico. Some of the same words."

"I can speak some Spanish. Steven taught me."

"Steven. This is your boyfriend?"

"Kind of, since we were kids. He hasn't called much this year." She paused and assembled her sentence carefully, anxious to demonstrate her linguistic latitude. *"Gracias, por tomar me casa."*

He glanced at her somberly. "You sound like Aguilar."

"The guy who just died? Thanks a lot."

"No. *Croyez vous qu'il dise la verite? J'aime ie son de ta vox.*"

"French? That sounded pretty."

"I'm impressed. You understand French also?"

Erika thought of her awkward French—her misunderstanding of tense—a miscellany of nouns—stupid little verbs. Obviously fluent, he had spoken so quickly, without constraint, that the translation had raced past her. Only a beautiful inflection remained in its wake.

"Not really. My dad does pretty well, I think. He whispers French to my mom, and it makes her swoon."

"Swoon. What is swoo-on?"

"It means 'faint.' She doesn't really faint, just pretends to, and then she hangs on his neck and they look goo-goo at each other."

"Goo-goo? This is more English? You've made this up."

"Goo-goo," she repeated with authority.

"So what do you mean when you say 'goo-goo?'"

"It's slang. It's not in the dictionary." She could feel herself blush. "It's like when a boy likes a girl, and he's afraid to tell her, or he can't because they're in class, so he looks goo-goo at her." She turned in her seat, leaning closer to him, and studied his profile, the reflection of the instrument lights on his face, his moist lower lip.

He glanced over. "And the girls, they do not look goo-goo at the boys sometimes?"

"Oh, I guess we do, if they're really special."

He straightened his shoulders and pushed his lip out slightly. "Well, in Iran, we were taught not to let such thoughts into our heads. At least during class. You should be paying attention then." He continued, "Because one thing may lead to another, and..."

"Are you Muslim?"

"Yes. I try to be a good Muslim."

"Neat. I'd like to learn more about that." She wiped her nose and bounced once in the seat. "I read *The Seven Pillars of Wisdom* last summer."

"Is that about Islam?"

"Not really. More Arabia. T. E. Lawrence wrote it. He was English."

"Ah yes, the English spy who tried to organize the Arabs for the purpose of the British." His tone grew parental. "So why does a young American girl chose to read such an old book?"

"I sort of found it at the library, by accident, after I watched the movie with my dad. It was an awesome movie."

"I saw that too." And as he said this, a small fountain of possibility sparkled. "Those were Arabs, you understand. There weren't any Iranians. Comparing Iran to Arabia would be like comparing Manhattan to," and he waved his finger in the air again, "...Bolivia."

She wanted to touch him on the shoulder or the side of his face. "I watched a special on National Geographic one time," she said. "You guys treat your women with so much respect."

The pavement grew more irregular and the streetlamps farther apart, each house now on an acre or more; tangled farm-wire fences and rural mailboxes had appeared. The road climbed and banked to the left. His hand rested on the shift knob. Her left knee, round and smooth in the white nylons, in the soft green glow of the instrument lights, rested against his knuckles. He stroked it timidly with his fingertips.

"Stop! Here. That was my street." She turned and looked out the rear window. He pulled onto the shoulder. She slipped a strap of the backpack over her left arm.

"I can take you back to your front door, if you like."

"No, this is fine. It was really nice of you to come out this far." She felt for the door latch, opened it and stepped out, and then turned. "You might be Muslim," she smiled, "but sometimes you look goo-goo." She closed the door, still smiling, her eyes never leaving his, then turned and marched through the snow.

He watched her as she reached the corner, where she turned down the dark street without looking back, and wondered if he was really so transparent. He had told her out of habit that he tried to be a good Muslim. She probably could not tell a good Muslim from a cannibal. The cold air had replaced all of the life she had brought into the car. He placed his hand on the seat where she had been, to absorb the last of her warmth. He wondered if she had really understood what he had spoken in French, and if she would tell her parents, and the idea brought the smallest wave of fear to his stomach. It was suddenly too quiet, and he turned on the radio.

"...and she wants you, and you want her..." The voice on the radio sang.

He looked over his shoulder and made a U-turn and headed back to town.

*

Erika dropped her pack in the armchair and shut the front door. The knocker rattled. The exhaust fan hummed in the kitchen, and the house smelled like warm food. Teresa looked out of the kitchen and smiled.

"I didn't hear a car come in, sweetheart."

"You didn't. She walked down from the highway." Her father spoke from the corner of the dining room where he sat looking out the window. The light over the table was off and she hadn't seen him sitting there. He didn't look at her. Teresa dried her hands.

"Didn't Mrs. Mathews bring you home today? Did you have to walk?"

"Melinda was sick, I guess. She wasn't at school." Erika stooped and picked up Natasha, holding her nose to nose. A *doctor,* she thought. No, they will ask. A nurse? That would be lying. "Somebody who works there gave me a ride." She made a silent note to carefully delete gender if this continued.

"Next time you might not be so lucky. Please call, one of us can come get you." Teresa returned to the kitchen but called back, "Dinner will be ready in a few minutes. Will you take off your coat and set the table, please?" The rumble of something boiling died away as it was rescued from the stove.

Erika hung her coat in the narrow closet and turned on the light over the dining room table. She went into her room and raked her fingers through her hair, glowing at herself in the mirror, a rigor rose up her back.

"Erika, come back in here. Have a seat."

She pulled the farthest chair out and sat on the edge of it, leaning her arms on the edge. She looked at her father, but he had turned to the window again.

"I saw a dead man this afternoon, Dad."

He looked over at her, his trance interrupted. "I suppose that does happen in the hospital sometimes. It was at the hospital, I hope."

"Well, it certainly wasn't at school. He was a patient..."

Teresa emerged from the kitchen, having resolved to set the table herself. "What are you two talking about? Someone died at school?"

Erika drew her face long and puckered, trying to choke a smile.

"No, dear. Erika was just saying she saw a dead man, a patient, at the hospital."

"What could she possibly learn from that?"

Sam raised his voice to follow her as she returned to the sink to rinse something. "Teresa, it's part of the business of a hospital. In any case, it's time she learns about this sort of thing." He lowered his voice. "She seems to be learning about so many things these days." He picked up his dinner knife and looked at his reflection in the blade.

"I can't hear you. Do you think I should call Helen about this?"

He looked at Erika. "Did you get to know this patient very well?"

"Not really. I took him water a couple of times. He was always tied to his bed." And as she spoke, she realized how bizarre this might sound to someone who didn't work in a place like that. "He looked crazy. He didn't speak any English. He was Mexican."

"You could have practiced your Spanish."

"What he said never made any sense." She scooted her chair in. "He called me 'pequeno *pooh-tah.*' Do you know what that means? I couldn't find it in the dictionary."

Teresa leaned over the table and placed a bowl of mashed potatoes and cheese on a trivet. "Fine dinner talk," she muttered.

"Did you ever see a dead man when you were growing up? Any Germans?"

Sam leaned back and knitted his hands behind his head. "No, there wasn't much shooting in Marseilles, that I can remember. I was only six, of course." He looked at Erika, and he thought of his mother, he thought of James. "I saw a man who had been hanged. A Frenchman. Someone the partisans wanted to make an example of."

"What had he done?"

"I have no idea. Somebody thought he was guilty. I remember asking my mother the same thing." He looked off into the night after he said this, setting his fists on the table.

Teresa returned with a small plate of sliced beef and a bowl of boiled cabbage. Sam sat at the table, alone in his thoughts, some barrier materialized in the time she had stepped away. She sat down, the scrape of her chair legs fracturing the silence. "Is Melinda going to be okay? When will she be back?"

Erika, adrift, shrugged. "I dunno. She's probably just got a cold." *God, he speaks French!* "It's not like malaria or something."

"Such a cheeky little girl. Hard to imagine her sick."

"Mom, her nose has been plugged her whole life, I can't remember when it wasn't." *Jeesuss, I wish I knew what he said to me...something about my voice.*

"Have you seen Steven lately? You know, I told you he called a few weeks ago."

He touched me! Twice! Maybe in the car, it was accidental. "No! I haven't seen him. He only calls now when he wants to borrow something, anyway."

Sam looked up from his plate. "You two have a falling out?"

"No, we didn't have *anything*. I think his mom just wants him to call girls that are Mexican, or Catholic or something."

Every answer was a damp blanket that might cool the heat inside of her, the glow so brilliant that she worried it might cause smoke they would see. *She'd ridden in his car! He talked to her, looked her in her eyes, right down to her heart. Like the first time she'd ever seen him.* This was what she wanted to talk about, but could not. It was an invisible glass she drank from, and she wanted to stay intoxicated as long as possible.

"Erika, eat before it gets cold."

Erika looked around the table, at the remaining chair, at their half-cleared plates, and at her own, untouched.

Sam responded in little grunts, a shrug, or an occasional "Humph…" He would glance up periodically and find Teresa looking at him, then break his gaze with her to take another bite, his fork downturned in his left hand, his knife in his right, spearing his beef with more force than necessary, cutting it with rapid, small strokes that made the plate squeak, all of the time glaring at it as if it were still alive.

Sam finished his plate and left the table first, carrying his dishes into the kitchen. He had culled several boxes of books from the shelves throughout the house earlier and now busied himself carrying them from the porch out to the garage, cursing softly each time he fumbled with the latch with his hands full, a small wave of cold air puffing through the kitchen and into the dining room as the door slammed behind him.

*

Sam had dropped the cap of the toothpaste that morning. He stood for a moment scanning the floor, the pattern of the throw rug, and with dread, the damp, dusty area behind the toilet, but it was nowhere to be seen. He descended finally to his hands and knees and peered into the narrow shadow defined by the protrusion of the vanity beneath the sink. There the cap lay, and a few inches from it, a small, flattened, tubular fragment of paper. Sam picked it up and inspected it in the light above the mirror. It was brown at one end—no, burnt. He picked it apart with his nails, and a few green flakes escaped into the sink. He smelled it. *Kif. Majourn.* He had not smelled this since his boyhood in Marseilles, when his brother would bring it home late at night after adventures with the Algerians.

He ruminated on his discovery throughout the day. He walked over to the campus library and reviewed every reference he could find. He pulled out his eyebrows. The more tasks he found to occupy himself, the more it returned to haunt him. Evolving from a tiny fragment of paper, it became irrefutable evidence of delinquency unimaginable in his household and tried to picture who might be selling it at the middle school. He had heard that much of it came up Highway 97 from California, brought by migrant workers and grown in Mexico. But how would she pay? He had no idea how much it would cost, but imagined it would drain her allowance and any money she might have saved from yard work or babysitting the previous summer.

His first vision, that she smoked alone in the bathroom, grew less credible. Sam wanted to know who she had smoked it *with*. It could ignite the libido, his brother had impregnated a French girl several years his senior. What predator had singled her out, cut her away from their family? He imagined a dull-witted boy with an enormous erection in his blue jeans, his arms around her, a compelling monologue of promises and lies. He pondered this until his stomach hurt. He lay awake for a long time that night, thinking about this, staring at the dim relief of the roses etched in the light fixture that hung in the darkness above his bed.

By 2:00 a.m. he was confronting the entire lascivious culture, provocatively dressed teenagers on magazine covers, bulging trousers and exposed midriffs on every television channel, and little girls in makeup. Parents who had given up put their daughters on birth control pills, and something of their youth became an innocent casualty, like spraying an herbicide indiscriminately instead of carefully weeding the garden. He sat up on the edge of the bed and stared into the web of shadows of the winter branches across the windowpane.

"Sam?" Teresa whispered.

He didn't answer. He felt like a captain who has found his vessel far off course in the middle of the night. A radical correction was in order.

*

In flannel, she drew her legs up, then tugged at the cuffs of the pajamas with her toes to pull them down. Obviously he liked her. She buried her jaw deep into the pillow, floating, giddy, fascinated, and imagined that he was married and pictured him in a hallway, removing his coat. Are there children? No. Children drained too much from the fantasy too quickly. Maybe later they would have their own children. Someone was at the table with him, a woman with a scarf, but she could not give the woman a face. She made the woman go away; it was only his sister, she decided, who must go back to Iran.

He didn't wear a ring. Maybe Muslims didn't. Who could be married in medical school? She understood it to be very hard. If he was married, then it seemed all the more impressive that he noticed her, that he liked her. Maybe his wife was mean to him. Erika relived his touch, guiding her hand to the old woman's pulse, they were at the bedside again, and his arm was around her.

He is here, right now, he lights some of her incense, he speaks French to her. She is in his car again. She stretches over and kisses him. Or he kisses her, his arm around her shoulder. She places her nails in his hair. It is soft, black, satin. They have parked. He cups her face in his hands. *Je vous aime,* he says. This phrase she has memorized. He says it again with different emphasis. She speaks in response, and her heart leaps—not out loud! Mom and Dad might hear.

She snapped on the nightstand light. Omar smiled at her from his shrine beneath the window. Peter O'Toole was next to him, but she had covered the English blue eyes and the sun-bleached hair with the corner of another picture, so only his sandaled feet were visible. She dangled off of the mattress and snatched a piece of notebook paper from the floor. *"Je t'aime,"* she wrote. It was too careful in her gentle backhand, she decided, so she wrote it again, this time printing a tall, thin, narrow script. How would he write this in his own alphabet? Probably the same alphabet used on a can of fish her mother had in the kitchen from Morocco. She pondered tiptoeing out there to bring it back. Just to touch the beautiful lettering. How far was Morocco from Iran? Each question she asked herself begged another.

She crept over to her desk and rotated the globe. A board creaked in the hallway and the bathroom door closed. She slipped back into bed and turned off the light. She wanted the covers to be heavier, to press down on her, hold her in bed with their weight. She passed her hands over her breasts, her fingertips along each rib, past the softness around her navel to the angles of her hips, pressing more firmly, a new hunger there, inarticulate and mercurial, a delicious nervousness next to her heart.

She tried to remember exactly what he had said, but the gift had slipped through her fingers. Her father had said French would be important and now, here was a painful lesson. If only she could have answered him. She shouldn't have spoken Spanish; now Majij would think she was stupid. She relived the entire afternoon, wanting all of its joy again, and then Aguilar returned, tied down to his bed. She had heard of crazy people being tied down. The smell in his room—maybe that was *the smell of death* people talked about.

The elation was gone. She thought about Aguilar awhile longer, trying to imagine him as a little boy in Mexico, but couldn't keep the picture clear. She chewed on a strand of her hair. Maybe there would be new babies at the hospital this week. She had just started a paper on India for World Studies, but maybe she could change and do one on Iran; she would have a reason to talk to him more. This plan satisfied her and slowly her eyes closed.

*

Majij sat in the dark in his underwear, seated in a folding chair he had placed by the window, holding the curtains back with the tip of his toe. He watched the headlights on the interstate, indulging various fantasies of the girl who, ever so peripherally, was part of his life now. He imagined picking her up again, what he would say. Would she want him to pick her up? Of course. Maybe he would find her on her way to school, and she would take the day away from classes. American students skipped school all the time. He would encounter her alone downtown some Saturday morning, and she would come here with him. Her parents would be called away, to a funeral in Andorra, and she would stay with him when the electricity failed in her end of town. He erected each scenario with the patience of a cat watching a bird on the other side of a windowpane. He sifted through every sentence she had spoken, searching for reciprocal interest—the last words she'd spoken before closing the door of his car, that look, that smile.

The phone on the nightstand rang and he broke free of the daydream. He crossed the room but stood looking at it, letting it ring a second, then a third time. She could have taken my number from the call list at the hospital, he thought, and hoped, with a small sense of futility, that it would be her.

He picked up the handset. "Hello?"

"How is my brother, the great healer, this evening?"

"I am okay."

"Are you by yourself, or do you have a *date?*"

"I am alone. I had already turned out the light." Majij sat down. His brother was playing with him, his voice taunting, the sarcasm older brothers feel entitled to use.

"Alone in the dark so early. And with no wife. You are still buying the obscene books?"

"And do you have a wife, Hakim?"

"Don't be insolent," the voice crackled. "No one I am introduced to has our mother's qualities. You do remember our mother, don't you?"

Majij paused. He could hear the intermittent patter of fingertips on a keyboard. "You're typing. Who do you write to so late at night?"

"I asked you, you do remember our mother, don't you?"

Majij huffed. "Of course I do."

"I am not writing a letter. I am working, and I am so-o-o-o sorry I bothered you. It is still, just after midnight here." There was an echo to Hakim's voice; perhaps he was on a speakerphone. "Do you still trouble yourself with the slovenly? Think with *ka akday at tatanasol?*"

Majij glanced down at the corner of a magazine protruding beneath the box spring. "And you are going to say you are doing God's work." Majij drew his legs up on the bed and leaned against the headboard. "How can I be of service?"

"Get a pen and paper."

Majij turned on the bedside lamp and took a pen from the nightstand. "Yes?"

"You will need to go to a phone, with push buttons. Better if it is not in your house. A payphone. Write down this number."

Majij hunched over the nightstand and wrote.

"You will hear a tone," Hakim said, "then you will need to enter these numbers as well, then press the pound key." Hakim recited a long code.

"Do I need to do this right now?"

"Of course not. Any time in the next six weeks. But do it after five. Otherwise you might end up talking to someone at a bank, and you wouldn't know what to say." The patter of the keyboard continued. "It would be better if you used a payphone in Portland. Better for you."

Majij sat silent for a few moments, indecisive, wondering if he should try again to pry through the armor his only living family member wore and search for something in common, however trivial or mundane, that they could talk about, just to laugh at the same joke.

"That is all." His brother interrupted the silence. "I need to get back to work now."

"Fine, fine," Majij said. "Goodnight." But the line was already dead before he finished. He tore off the paper, folded it, and put it in his wallet. To discard the paper or fail to make the call would be an admission that he only pretended to believe with the passion his brother did. Just pretending to see the world with the same polarity as his brother made Majij feel like they were a little closer. An older brother that showed his love harshly, like a strict father—Majij tried to force this concept to fill an empty space. A disquieting sense of isolation fell over him nonetheless, and he started to reconstruct the comfortable vision he'd enjoyed before the call had come.

He wondered if the girl was really curious about Islam. She was young, and there were things that she should not learn about until later, but there was an entire world he could speak of, and there would not be so many preconceptions to disentangle if he could explain, step by step. Perhaps her parents were some of those Christians so preoccupied with the crucifixion that they overlooked all of the rest of God's justice, talking always of eternity or hell. Teenagers here could be like that, with their silly youth groups, handing out pamphlets on street corners, leaving little Bibles in his waiting room, instead of working for their families, knowing nothing of the world but pretending to know everything about God. Or they were godless. He tried to imagine her father; he was from Andorra, she'd said. Probably a Catholic, living by the Vatican's word, with contempt for everything he did not understand. Perhaps Majij should avoid Erika altogether. These were foolish fantasies, not the manners of a good Muslim.

He pulled the magazine fully from beneath the bed and opened it to the centerfold, where a leggy blond offered all of herself with a gaze that promised inexhaustible gratification. He had schemed, in so many scenarios, how he could get a woman, any woman, to look at him with that same passion, and then it dawned on him, at that moment, that she made that look for a photographer—*a photographer who paid her for that look.* He wondered how much he should expect to pay to get a young woman to look at him like that. To love him.

He sat on the edge of the bed. Things took time. He would be another two years in this place before he could save enough money to buy a clinic, with an x-ray machine, in Shiraz. He would be her friend and foster an idea. She would be maybe seventeen by then. He was unsure of the law in Oregon, but he was sure, with their sordid values, that no one would care if a seventeen-year-old girl went away with a man of thirty-two. No, he would be thirty-four by then. But that would be such a long time. Some boy her own age could come along, and all would be wasted—some boy in a big hurry with a cheap new car and leather clothes. Some boy who could not offer her the knowledge that Majij could share, the world he could show her—this world that confused him sometimes but only because he had neglected his faith, his priorities, and all of this could be sorted out with her. My faith can save us, he thought. He thought again of her knee against his hand and the satin smoothness of her neck. The blonde still lay on the floor looking up at him, her legs obscured by the glare from the lamp. Majij closed the magazine with his foot and rolled onto his side and gathered a second pillow against himself, his arm about it, pulling it to his waist. A stack of similar magazines sat on the end of the dresser. They were a bad and irrational habit, he thought, like trying to appease hunger by looking at pictures of food, and so much money wasted. He decided he would throw them all out the next day.

6

While students seated themselves, Sam walked between the rows, a bundle of old tests in his hands. "I've covered the names of your classmates. I'd like you to read these and ask yourself if you could answer the question better." It was an exercise he'd used a few years before when it had become evident that his entire class had an understanding of the Vietnam War based largely on Chuck Norris movies. "Some of your answers were quite thorough, actually. But some are embarrassing." He sat at his desk, and a hush fell over the room, interrupted now and again with a muffled giggle. Forty minutes passed while he stared out the window. Finally he stood and opened a ring binder.

"To continue from where we left off, Chaing Kai-Shek did not represent the people, but he was the only one the United States had established reliable communications with. We might have been better,"

A student in the back raised a hand. "Dr. Etulain? Didn't we finish this chapter last week?"

Sam stopped, glanced at the student, then flipped a few pages of his outline. He ran his fingers along each bullet, across his own marginal ball-point pen marks, then looked up again at the quizzical student. "Just a little review, Robert."

"I just thought since we took the quiz on Friday."

"Sometimes review is the best place to start a new period. History is not simply..." Sam stood motionless for a moment. "Chapters." He closed the outline binder, sat at his desk, and placed his fingers over his brow.

"You okay, sir?"

Sam took a deep breath. "Perhaps we should examine Australia's relationship with Imperial Japan, beginning in nineteen thirty-eight." He scratched the assignment across the board. "Obscure period. I suggest you look in *Foreign Affairs* about that time. Plagiarize freely, but learn it." The class bell rang and Sam collapsed again into his chair like a boxer in the eleventh round.

The following morning, Sam sat at the dining room table, thumbing a paperback copy of *A Distant Mirror*. He read page eighty-nine, each word separately of its neighbors, then page eighty-eight, and then started to read them again. He had wanted a son and had almost forgotten this, but now it struck him that he would better know how to approach this if Erika were a boy. His first lecture on Tuesday did not start until one. On any other morning he would be at his classroom by now, clearing his desk and updating the lecture with a comparison to some contemporary event, but students usually found the period interesting enough, and motivational sleight of hand was not required. This morning was his, he had formulated a course of action and had convinced himself that his anger would not bias his judgment.

In the middle of World War II there was little his mother, by then a widow, could do to control his brother's behavior. James had the whole world at his disposal at age fourteen—drugs, wine, and French prostitutes. Black Algerian prostitutes too. James had disgraced them and his life had gone off the map of sensibility. At some level of austerity, Sam felt, a student could remain optimally focused on the goals at hand. It had been that way for him at Cambridge. Erika's room had become a kaleidoscope of distractions and the few occasions he had put his head in her door while her music was playing, he'd forgotten what he'd intended to tell her. If he couldn't concentrate, how could she?

This morning would be prophylactic. If he discussed it with Teresa, she would take a moderate position, a measured response. Erika would bargain around them, find a way to preserve the chaos and the barrier she had constructed, and deepen the abyss she was digging for herself. He would simply have to proceed alone.

He grasped her doorknob and hesitated for a moment, thinking he should knock, then opened the door. There was a stale dampness to the room and the bed was unmade, a knot of blanket and sheets shoved to the footboard. The sliding door of the closet was open and the lid of the hamper propped up. Not entirely full, it was surrounded by an irregular mound of crumpled jeans, socks with blackened soles, and dirty underwear, as if they had climbed out by their own will. The desk was awash in notebook paper, dog-eared spirals, several library books on India, *Valleys of the Assassins* by Freya Stark, *A History of Persia,* and his own copy of *Napoleon in Egypt*. He picked up the last volume and flipped it open. Why would she want to read this? Commendable. He would have to remember to talk to her about that period after all of this was settled. There was a copy of *Seventeen* and a copy of *Beat,* both of which he put into the trash can. He sorted through the notebook papers, discarding anything that did not look remotely academic. A note to M_____. He started to read it, something about lunch. Did she know that (couldn't read name) thought that she was "fine?" Into the can it went. Another penciled correspondence about borrowing notes from geometry. Why would she need to borrow notes? Was she skipping school? He pictured her in the back seat of a smoke-filled Camaro, cruising through town at midday with older boys and that awful music. He started to save the note then decided he had extrapolated too much. Into the can it went also.

A vicious-looking lad snarled at him from above the bed. He grasped the edge of the poster and gave it a snap. It curled down from the wall over his eyes, disorienting him for a moment. He wadded it up and pressed it into the waste can with his foot. Four insolent fragments remained, like weeds, anchored by thumbtacks. He stood on the mattress, steadied himself with one hand on the wall, and pried them from the plaster with his nails. The second poster on the opposite wall, its sweeping sensuality, captured his breath for a moment, but no, the girl was half-dressed. Down it came. The waste can was compacted to its rim. Sam went to the kitchen and pulled a black plastic garbage bag from under the sink. He took a small plastic bucket of spackle as well, setting it on Erika's desk. A dozen smaller posters came down, transparent tape denuding the paint here and there.

He searched the dresser, drawer by drawer, running his hands on the bottom surface beneath her clothes. A small plastic bag, or maybe a bottle of capsules. Nothing. A tank top with "Guns and Roses" emblazoned on the breasts. Into the bag.

He returned to the desk and emptied each drawer onto her mattress: Scotch tape, paper clips, fragments of pencils, dozens of erasers, more partially used notebooks, stale sticks of gum, highlighters, and two plastic rulers, one broken. *French in Six Weeks* cassette tapes, most out of their boxes, some Halloween-sized candy bars, an unopened tray of eye shadows, and several broken crayons—but no drugs. He refilled each drawer, discarding the useless. He absentmindedly ate one of the candy bars. Three rectangles of grit remained on the fitted sheet. She can't sleep in that, he thought, and stripped the bed, pushing the sheets into the hamper, gathering up the vagrant clothing as well. He carried the hamper to the back porch, loaded the washer and started it.

He returned to her doorway. The mattress! He lifted it first at one end and then the other. A diary sat on the box spring near the head of the bed. He opened it, but the last entry was 28th of July, 1985, her twelfth birthday, with a list of what she had received: water colors, View-Master cards of Japan from Helen, and the twenty-four-inch bike. He returned the book to its place and lowered the mattress on top of it.

He inspected the remaining half of the closet. A mountain of unpaired shoes obscured the floor, a few still in boxes, which he dumped out. A Nike bag sat behind the boxes, and he unzipped it. More shoes, mostly canvas, including a pair she had dyed yellow last summer, soles worn away, grass-stained. He fingered the pockets of two jackets on hangers. Something creaked in the living room and he stopped for a moment and looked over his shoulder, then went on. A tennis racket dove at his head from above, glancing off of his shoulder before it clattered to the floor. He stood on her desk chair and pondered the stacks of jigsaw puzzles and board games, all enshrouded in a patina of dust, but saw no recent finger marks. A solitary infant doll lay in state, one arm missing, an artifact from a far earlier time. He carefully replaced the tennis racket and stepped down.

A plastic milk crate of record albums sat by the dresser. He squatted and flipped through them, peering through his bifocals. The first record, most of the cellophane still intact, he recognized from Christmas just a month ago. Rachmaninoff, Rachmaninoff, Ellington, Ella, Vaughn Williams, Culture Club…what was this? A man, or a very ugly woman on the cover, painted like a geisha. He pulled it out and laid it on the floor beside him. Two Guns and Roses albums joined it, as well as several albums with unreadable cover art and more surly young men. *Folk Music of Iran,* property of The Dalles Public Library, and Teresa's soundtrack to *Doctor Zhivago* as well as several albums of renaissance flute music. A handful of his own jazz albums that he realized he had not missed. He gathered up the culled albums and stuffed them into the garbage bag.

Poised on four concrete blocks behind the garage sat a fifty-five-gallon oil drum, a foot of wet ashes in the bottom. Sam crunched through the virgin snow, carrying the bag at arm's length in one hand and a box of strike-anywhere matches in the other. With the third match, some crumpled note-book paper took flame, creeping around the inside of the barrel until it was ablaze in orange, the burning vinyl adding a thick, oily texture to the smoke that twisted into the sky and out over the Columbia River. Sam crossed his arms, stood back from the fire, and watched. There was a little bit of hell in the barrel now, expurgated from his daughter's room. He felt like it might smolder and stop if he stepped away too soon. She would be angry at first, but in six months or a year, when her grades were back in order, she would understand, she would be thankful. This was the sort of decision only a father could make. A father's discipline—it felt powerful and virtuous coursing through his chest.

He walked back to the house as the flames died down, stopping on the back porch to load the dryer. He stood in her doorway and looked around the walls, scarred by tacks and tape like bullet holes. It would need to be painted now. Erika could do that. It would make her feel more like she was included. She'd always wanted to be included. Above the light switch, a few of Erika's classmates had printed their names with magic markers, each a different font, a different color, a small rainbow now made conspicuous by the barren expanses that surrounded it. Melinda, Aaron, Amanda, Trish, Steve, Kirstin. Individually, he could not imagine any of them lighting, ah, whatever they called it and passing it to his daughter. Maybe Trish. Yes, she might, the little hooligan coming to their house at Christmas, stinking of cigarettes and perfume. Quite a tart, she was.

He looked at the clock radio on the nightstand. A quarter to eleven. He pried the lid off of the spackle and, using his thumbnail, slowly began to fill the holes.

*

Teresa arrived home at four. As she walked to her own bedroom, she noticed that a sign was missing from her daughter's door. She gathered together a bundle of her own blouses and four of Sam's shirts and carried them to the washing machine. In the dryer she was startled to find Erika's sheets, fresh and warm. The kitchen counters undisturbed since morning. She stood still. A clock ticked above the sink.

"Erika? Sweetheart?" She pulled the laundry through the dryer door. There was a sock, then another. The free end of a small bra and an indigo cuff of denim. She shook the sheets free of their static, draped them over her arm, and carried them to Erika's room. At the end of the bed, she stood and turned silently to each wall. The collage that had been the room, layer upon layer for fourteen years, an archive of her daughter's life, had vanished since the morning, as if she had moved out. As if she had died. She gasped involuntarily, as if the air had been taken as well. The kitchen door rattled.

"Sam...," she said weakly.

"Teresa, are you home?"

"Sam." Her voice quivered. "Come in here, please."

Sam stood in the doorway.

"I don't understand this, Sam. What happened?"

"I felt that something needed to be done."

"Done? About what?"

"I felt as if we were losing her, as if she were falling under too many other influences."

Teresa turned and faced him. "What in the world would you be referring to?"

Sam pulled an envelope from his shirt pocket, unfolded it, and tapped the fragment of burnt paper into his palm. Teresa squinted at it, then picked it up and walked to the window, still studying it.

"I found it on our bathroom floor yesterday morning. I've assumed it isn't yours."

Teresa held it up to the afternoon sunlight.

"It's marijuana. James used to smoke it; I suspect he still does."

"How do you know James didn't…"

"Hasn't been over in six months, at least."

Teresa slowly shook her head. "I'll admit, this isn't good. I never expected…" She looked around the walls slowly. "But this, Sam," her eyes grew large, and she wrinkled her nose. "This is bloody awful." She took his hand and dumped the fragment into his palm. "Couldn't we have decided something, between the two of us?"

"I was afraid we'd lose the impetus."

"You were afraid," she said, shaking her finger at him, "that I wouldn't take this seriously." She pried his fingers open and regarded the fragment again. "I just don't think that's hers."

"I just felt a clean sweep was needed, all of that rubbish. I know I did much better at that age with a simpler environment. I solved the issue the way my stepfather might have."

Teresa touched his cheek. "Eric was a widower, and an army captain till the day he died. He didn't know any other way. Your clean sweep, Sam, was the war."

Sam picked up the can of spackle from the floor and turned it in his hands. "I thought maybe we could let Erika paint her room. Let her pick the color."

Teresa put the clothes in the dresser. "You think letting her pick a paint color will make her see something positive in this?" She stepped around him and a moment later he could hear her in the kitchen. He didn't have her alliance. She returned, her arms full of more clothing. She didn't look at him.

"Bras and underpants wash on gentle. At fifty-four, you should know that."

*

At a quarter to six headlights flickered on the living room wall, a car door slammed, and a moment later, Erika stomped her feet on the mat and opened the front door.

"Good evening," her father said without looking up from the bundle of essays on the table before him.

"Oh, hi." She slipped off her coat and backpack and disappeared into the hallway. A light clicked. Sam's pen stopped moving. There was silence. Erika stood a few feet into the living room. "Is there something you guys are trying to tell me?" Her voice trembled.

Sam laid down his pen and looked at her. "I felt some changes..."

"Jeeesus..."

"Some *changes were necessary.*"

"Jeeesus Christ!"

"Mind your language, young lady. I felt some changes were necessary, for your own reclamation."

"My *what?* What's with you people?"

"I'll explain, if you can explain this." Sam pushed the folded envelope across the table. Erika stepped forward.

"Explain what?"

"Pick it up. Look inside."

She opened the envelope and peeked in and wrinkled her nose. She tapped it into her palm.

"You know what that is?"

"I have an idea. It's no big deal. I've seen kids..."

"What kids?"

"I don't know. Just kids."

"It was in our bathroom, Erika. *Our bathroom.* How do you suppose it got there?"

"I don't know. I don't do that stuff." She vacantly turned her hand over, and the burnt fragment fluttered to the white tablecloth.

"Well, it wasn't your mother and I."

"So that makes it me, huh? How do you know it wasn't creepy Uncle Jim?"

"He hasn't been over since last April. Why would you say that?"

"He asked me where he could buy some, like I'd know."

Teresa, in the kitchen, relinquished her silence. "When did he ask you that, dear?"

"I don't know. Sometime last summer."

"Well, I'm having a word with him right now." She began to dial the phone.

Erika looked forlornly at her father again. "Daddy, all my posters…"

He felt momentarily apologetic, but stared at the table. "I decided your room needed painting. Some of them tore coming down." The phone returned to the cradle.

Erika turned down the hallway again. Her bedroom door slammed. Closet doors rolled first to one side, then the other. Drawers opened and closed. *What could she be searching for?* Sam wondered if he'd overlooked something.

She reappeared at the hallway and planted her feet. "My records. What did you do with my music?"

Sam continued to write impassively.

Erika raised her voice "I deserve an answer here."

An essay flopped from one pile to another.

Teresa came from the kitchen and placed three plates on the table. A fork tumbled to the floor. "Sam."

He leaned back and laid his pen down. "Some of that wasn't music at all, by anyone's definition. It's gone."

"Daddy, some of those weren't mine. One was Melinda's. Two belonged to Trish."

"I guess they'll think twice before they lend you any of that tripe again." He picked up his pen. "You've still got a lot to listen to."

Erika stood facing the hallway, staring at the floor.

"Erika." He spoke deliberately. "I despise a liar."

She pivoted. "So, you think I'm a liar now, huh?" She stared at him for the instant of a breath then turned and marched back to her room. "Shhhhit on you," she hissed as she disappeared into the hallway. The door slammed again. Natasha darted into the living room, then stopped and looked behind her, dumbfounded.

"You clean up your language, young lady. Do you hear me?"

A door creaked open. "Hey," Erika leered around the corner at her father. "I can't believe I'm related to you. I can't believe you're my dad. You're like the God-damned pope."

"Don't lower yourself any further."

"Okay." She stopped abruptly, but remained at the mouth of the hallway, swaying with an arm on each wall. She lifted the frame of antique stamps from its hook. "Hey," she hissed at him again, "watch this." With a snap of her wrist, the frame disintegrated on the floor, the glass bursting in a hundred shards.

Sam was out of the chair and across the room in a half second, his hand drawn back. Erika withdrew too slowly, his knuckles crushing her skin just below the eye, and she slipped as a scatter rug skidded, falling against the opposite hall corner. Sam stuck the plaster with the flat of his hand as Erika's jaw struck the floor. She was up and over him as quickly, her door slammed and locked.

"Did you hit her?" Teresa pushed his fist down to his waist.

"She slipped."

"But you would have."

Sam looked at the floor.

Teresa tried the doorknob. "Are you Okay?" She tapped with her knuckles. "Erika?"

"Go away."

Sam had returned to the table and sat rubbing his temples.

"Where are the records, Sam?"

"You should have seen them. I stopped believing in the devil long ago, until I saw..." He paused and looked at his knuckles in disbelief.

"What did you do with them, Sam?"

"Out in the barrel." He looked at her. "Burned."

"Oh, Sam."

Erika had locked her door. There were sobs and then silence. Something kicked. A chair knocked over. Sam watched passively while Teresa made more attempts to lure her from her room.

"I'm not hungry," she announced. "I'm still not hungry," she repeated later, followed by a louder, "Why would you want to eat with a liar?"

She noticed she had bitten her tongue, and it hurt to open her mouth. The right side of her face throbbed and felt bigger than the left. It was sticky where the skin had torn, and in the mirror above the vanity she could see a cut there. She leaned forward and pulled a needle of clear glass from her lower eyelid. A bruise was forming. The Kleenex and Band-Aids were across the hall in the bathroom. She took a white sock from her dresser and held it to her face, then sat on the bed with only the nightstand lamp on, the nakedness of the walls softened in the subdued light. She held the base of the globe pinched between her knees, twirling it, each time letting it slow to a stop before spinning it again. She looked at one portion of the room and then another, trying to remember exactly what had been there, trying to make an inventory of the injustice in her mind, but only the rectangular shapes in the tone of the paint where posters had been remained. The thought of something Trish had said about her own dad came back to her, but she could not remember the details.

Later that week, her parents opened a discussion about painting her room.

"Black," she said. She wanted to paint it black.

7

In the weeks that followed brief conversation reemerged, the minimum necessary for civility, small green shoots here and there, but spring never seemed to arrive. Sam initiated a conversation about Napoleon one afternoon. Erika arose midsentence and went to her room, returning with the volume from her desk. She placed it on the table, beyond his reach.

"Done with your book," she said in a perfunctory tone, then slipped on her jacket and went outside. She stood for a few minutes, close enough to the house that her father could not see her, then walked up the street and stared across the highway at the dead gray hills beneath the winter sky on the Washington side of the river, arms crossed, fists clenched. No traffic passed, in front of her or on the opposite shore, the water was absent of any craft and the sky without birds. The entire universe conspired in her isolation.

"I feel like a prisoner in the third world," she blurted out one evening after supper, "like I'm being punished ever since I started at Wilson, and I don't know why!" She coughed and blew her nose in her napkin. "When are you going to search my cell again? Have you tapped the phone?" Her chair fell over as she pushed it away from the table. She ran into her room, crying. Sam looked at Teresa, but she looked away and stood to clear the table.

Erika agreed to paint her room. Her parents believed this a concession; Erika understood it as the only means to end a discussion she'd grown tired of. She would not paint over her friend's signatures, she announced, and was surprised by their indifference. Feigned enthusiasm, and more feigned indecision over choosing a color. Feigned congeniality. Three gallons of a pale gray-rose came home, two flat, one satin enamel.

She arose each morning an hour before her parents and stalked about the kitchen, heating water in the microwave for tea, leaning against the counter to chew an Oreo, watching the heat rise from the toaster. Her mother got up morning after morning and stood in the door to the kitchen in her bathrobe and offered to help, but Erika kept her back to her, moving quickly to disappear into the bathroom and then to her own room, door closed. She would emerge dressed and leave the house early, declining her mother's offers to drive her, riding her bicycle over the frozen gravel on the warmer days. She started to look thinner, and halos of darkness surrounded her eyes.

Restlessness smoldered long into the night, unseen embers in darkness, until three thirty or four, when she would die dreamlessly for a few hours. When she awoke at sunrise before her alarm, the sparks were still warm beneath the ash. A hypothetical action would be rehearsed, its consequence, its outcome, and its cost. Lying in her bed, staring into the corner where the intersection of the walls and the ceiling became a tangle of blood vessels, in that indeterminate blackness, a dozen possibilities played out. Silence, starvation, arson, even suicide—none would restore her dignity. She had no value to these people. Somewhere, she told herself, someone respected her.

She would turn on the light at two or three and try to read, but could not lose herself in a story as she had done the year before and would seldom finish a chapter and couldn't focus on where she had left off the previous night. She would pull the Rand-McNally Atlas from the bottom shelf in her room, open it to Iran, and run her fingers over the glossy five-by-seven of "Majij Aziz, MD."

"What else will you teach me?" she said one night and wished she could talk to him, nose to nose. He respects me, she thought, he would understand.

Fatigue weighed upon her like concrete, until the last hours of darkness in the third week when, eyes crushed by the ache of four sleepless nights, the groundwork for a plan and a new paradigm materialized. She breathed deeply and relaxed, intoxicated by its simplicity. She slept deeply for an hour and a half, then slipped out of bed at six fourteen, quietly rolled aside a closet door, and removed a small duffel bag that had been filled with old athletic shoes. She removed each shoe until it was empty, folded it flat, and pressed it into her backpack.

*

"How was school?" They would ask each evening. *Still there,* she would respond. "How is Melinda?" *Fine.* "How is Steven?" *Don't know, haven't seen him much.* "Did you try out for basketball like we suggested?" This always irritated her, the idea that someone should want to play a stupid game just because of their body shape. *No.* "What did you learn in class today?" *To keep my thoughts to myself.*

"Anything special at the hospital this afternoon?" She sensed her parents felt ill at ease with her hospital duties but were too proud, too committed to their previous encouragement, to voice an objection now. This delighted her. "It's the best part of my day," and she would elaborate about shit-stained sheets, pools of blood on the floor, and women screaming in childbirth, all of it made up.

"That's enough," her mother would say.

She wedged the duffel into the bottom of her school locker, steel and impregnable, which she locked. The morning following its arrival, she brought a pair of jeans and some underwear, moving them to the bag after Melinda had trotted away to her own side of the hall. Melinda would not deliberately betray her, but Erika thought it better she not be placed in such a position. Two blouses and a sweat shirt arrived the following day, with more underwear and socks the next. She brought a spare pair of shoes, and a black aluminum flashlight. From the cabinet beneath the bathroom sink, she took a tube of toothpaste, two bars of green soap, and her mother's old curling iron. Finally came the tray of makeup. The bag swelled to its full dimensions.

*

"This will be fine, right here," she would say to Mrs. Mathews as they would approach the corner of her street. The Subaru would slow onto the shoulder, and Erika would hop out. Waving as the car U-turned, she would wait until the taillights were out of sight, then walk quickly back to Trish's street and down to her house. Trish remained in Portland, Erika knew, and hoped her mother had heard from her. Each night the windows were dark and the driveway empty. The house was not vacant; a chest freezer where Mrs. Curtiss kept cartons of cigarettes and a few rolls of freezer-burnt ground beef was still visible on the porch.

March approached, muddy and chill, the snow that remained in the shade of picket fences shrank each day. She stood looking between the two houses one evening, at the hole in the fence surrounded by brown leafless vines, once dense with blackberries, the secret route of her childhood. It was too small for her now.

Two weeks passed, then on a late Saturday morning, a green Ford Maverick was parked in the driveway. The inner door lock rattled, and Mrs. Curtiss appeared in a pink chenille bathrobe and greasy deerskin slippers, a cigarette between her lips, her peroxide hair rising in fronds, static from the pillow it had known just moments earlier. She moved slowly, automatically, too sleepy to be angry at her awakening. She flipped the latch on the screen and turned her back, speaking as she returned to the front door. "Haven't seen you in a coon's age, Emily."

"I'm Erika." She followed the somnolent pink robe. A box of kitty litter had overturned, and she stepped around it but still felt the grit beneath her shoes.

"Erika, yeah. I'm sorry. Trish ain't here, you know. Shut that door, will you?"

Erika closed the door and looked around the room as her eyes adjusted. There was more disorder than she remembered. The place still had the same smell she'd been aware of as a little girl, and something she didn't recognize, a little more sour. A stack of unread newspapers and unopened mail filled the seat of an overstuffed orange recliner near the door. Two sketches of doe-eyed Indians hung on the wall above the sofa, the bottom edge of the frames layered with dust. A gold ashtray the size of a hubcap sat in the middle of the coffee table, two brands of cigarette butts to the rim, with a trio of beer cans nearby, lipstick on the edge of one. A throaty little growl rose up from Erika's feet, and she stooped down. Beneath the coffee table was an ugly little brown creature with bulging eyes and a crushed face with an underbite. A pug, she thought initially, but its hair was too long, the body badly drawn on outturned legs. *If I ask about its pedigree,* she thought, *it'll take all morning.* The dog growled again and stepped forward near her ankle. She swung the backpack casually down to her side, striking it in the side of the head. "You got a dog. What happened to Tiger?"

"Got run over last year." Mrs. Curtiss glanced over her shoulder. "Was Trish's cat, anyhow. That there's Champ. You still in school?"

"Yes, ma'am." Erika was startled at how Mrs. Curtiss's shoulders drooped, as if some vital bones had dissolved away.

"I think Trish is still in school, she talks about vocational school."

"You've talked to her?"

"Not real recent. We don't see exactly eye to eye, got a lot of her old man in her, I guess." She sat down and crushed the cigarette into the pie pan. "That boy, he's a strong one, though." She picked up a lighter from the table and looked around as she spoke, spotted the red-and-white pack on the dining table, and stood up again. The dog had retreated under a chair and now spouted random alarms, insecure little barks, threatening only in their quality of coming from a creature that felt cornered. "Shut the fuck up, Champ."

"So, do you have her phone number, or an address?"

"Like I said, he's a strong one, he'll keep her in line." She tapped another cigarette, pinched it between her teeth, and sucked until the tip crackled and flared. She exhaled and paused. "I got her number…let's see." She pulled a ratty phone book from the top of the refrigerator just inside the kitchen door and peeled back the cover. "Got a pen?"

Erika nodded and printed the numbers down in a notebook as Trish's mother read them. She stood up. The dog crept out from its shelter, sniffed at her ankle, then crouched and dragged its anus across the carpet for several yards.

"You talk to her, you tell her I'm standin' behind her, all the way. You hear?"

Erika looked around the room a final time. "Yes, ma'am."

The air was bright and sweet as she walked away, the narrow rutted gravel street the first steps of a magnificent new freedom. At the end of the block, she stopped and looked back at the little house with its muddy yard beneath the bare trees, and realized for the first time how badly the paint had peeled and how the roof sagged, in contrast to the cottages that flanked it. Kitty litter on the porch, for a cat that isn't coming back, she thought. And Jesus, that dog! Mrs. Curtiss had trouble just standing by herself; she could not imagine any benefit having her standing behind you. Trish, in her gritty, knowing way, had done the right thing.

*

The two girls came and went at the hospital, Majij watching them climb into the same station wagon each night. One afternoon, Erika's face had been bruised and swollen, but he could not manipulate their paths to cross, she almost seemed to be avoiding him, and then she was gone for over a week. When he saw her again, something about her was broken, exposed, that made her all the more precious. Erika waved to him a few times, hesitating as if she had something to say, then she would be gone again. In the corridor, she would smile if Melinda's back was turned, then reoccupy herself with her duties. She had stopped wearing makeup, he noticed, but every angle of her face still captivated him. He started taking his coffee from the dining room, in a chair at the table where they had once sat, adjusting his tie, picking lint from his jacket, making certain his socks were up and his trousers hung properly, hoping she would wander in with a question or some declaration about her life. Even a long, silent moment of membership in her world would restore him.

Always hesitant, stumbling on the second or third word, he tried initiating small talk with the young brunette who clerked the convenience store where he bought his gasoline. Her responses were diplomatic, detached, never revealing any interest in knowing him. She did not smile so richly as Erika, there was something rough in the way she walked, a coarseness to her complexion, a dullness in her eyes. A round-faced girl with copper hair in his apartment building was equally aloof and smelled of cigarettes. He had been insincere in each case and was quietly relieved.

Erika remained foremost in his thoughts throughout his day, and he talked to her as if she were in his car as soon as he left the office, a thousand questions formed, their conversations unfolded. They were driving again, with no finite destination initially, but later it would be to San Francisco, still later to Montreal, and finally on a road to the Caspian Sea, to the beach. He would tell her of medicine, how bodies worked and how they became sick, how he could help people. He would speak of Persia, its history, the birthplace of mankind. In his apartment he would talk to her, lean over the kitchen counter, introducing her to new tastes, new foods, new music, all from a life he had never shared. He intoxicated himself with all that he wanted to give her, designed all of her dreams and fulfilled them. Entangled at night. He would awaken with her lying on his arm. He could not remember being so gravid with visions of any one girl in all of his lifetime. He would find his mother and introduce her, and she would not like Erika, and that would be good because it was finally time for his recognition as a man grown and married, but she would eventually worship her and respect her as he did. They would lie on his bed, their faces near, and talk some more. He would teach her about Islam. Each topic rehearsed over and over on his mind's stage, each summarized in a beautiful finale, Erika would feel richer and closer to him for this. He would slip his arm around her waist, and she would wrap her legs around his.

Home in his apartment, his fantasy exhausted, his faith would reemerge, incomplete, a skeletal outline, his soliloquies would uncover a flaw, then another in his own knowledge of the religion, and he would try to ignore these. She would have questions he couldn't answer. Islam changed form continuously while the world watched, a revolution birthed on the eve of his departure, and Majij knew he had been sitting in the audience for too long.

Manners of dress, which hand to extend, how to bathe and when, a rule of conduct for every waking minute—all of these he could recite for Erika, but he would be unable to justify them. Already he could hear her challenges.

His parents communists, his father did not come home one night when he was fourteen. Such things happened, and neighbors would notice and divert their gaze, one did not speak of it the next day, and did not inquire. Even to wonder in the privacy of twilight was to invite the same fate. To that point, he had been raised agnostic. His brother, Hakim, always more just, quick to accuse and judge, decided that atheism had been their downfall, and preached this at the table each night and again each morning, until they vanished in separate directions in the streets. After his father's disappearance, his mother grew less vocal, falling into her husband's vacuum until at times she would not answer for days, neither bathing nor eating, staring catatonically at the door where she had seen their father last.

Majij loitered at the periphery of the mosque, participating in the discussions of the faithful, imitating but never fully understanding their actions, he indulged in their hospitality wherever it was offered. At some point, his entire comprehension of the faith consisted only of its prohibitions, but he was admonished less and less by the faithful. He had acquired little since. By contrast, Hakim threw himself into the faith as a man into a well, with the conviction that only garments of burning pitch would enfold him should he remain among the worldly.

Other interests stirred in young Majij. Girls, certain girls, were available. A neighbor who owned a cab taught him to drive. He worked for a while in a tobacco shop frequented by tourists. Dunhill cigarettes left him giddy but euphoric and empowered. He watched CNN at every opportunity and learned English, reciting folksy idioms if the customer was American. "Early to bed, early to rise," he would say, or phrases of virtue, prefacing his monolog with, "I have a dream," or "The only thing we have to fear is fear itself," phrases that became a part of him, natural enough to convince a passenger of his character. Eventually he convinced himself.

Science made sense to him and biology came easily. He finished secondary school a year late and was accepted at the university. He still sat near the gate of the courtyards of the mosque when food was provided, usually reading a textbook, listening with token interest. Hakim sat closer to the speaker, deeper in the crowd. Majij would point at his watch when he could catch his brother's attention, then rise and slip away. Hakim would frown momentarily and listen all the more intently. Majij daydreamed of a future of money and its commensurate respect, a Ferrari, or a Mercedes Benz, perhaps, and perfumed girls with pale, smooth skin. Hakim lived in the injustice of the past. The chasm between them expanded until they no longer spoke if they passed on campus, Hakim would not even look at Majij if he was in the company of a young woman. More clerics invaded the university. So much depended upon absolute faith in a revealed truth spoken by a cleric, a man who didn't know and didn't care which direction the blood flowed through the heart or how the kidney worked. At a point in life where his academic survival depended on an attitude of constant inquiry, he found himself instead required to memorize more dictates of Haddith. In May of 1982, Majij boarded a bus for Turkey and then a plane for the United States. Hakim boarded a truck for Afghanistan.

The atmosphere at home had only grown more dogmatic since he'd left, but they remained desperate for doctors. Western training, vocally denounced, would still elicit an approving nod at the right door of entry. He could arrive at those doors with a young Western wife, properly attired, versed in proper decorum, and create few ripples.

A wife with perfect English, she would be the envy of the staff, and he would unequivocally belong in their midst. She'd be a wife of Western ways in their privacy, who would understand what had in secret become a part of him. Welcome in the circles of the other wives, she would never fully understand Farsi and all of its nuances and would be thus always at a small disadvantage. However inept, she would be unable to compromise him.

*

Erika stood in the cafeteria alone, at one end of the long row of windows, looking out on the fading light of a March evening. She had not been visible from the hallway and Majij was surprised to find her there, dressed in blue jeans and a pink angora sweater, her navy wool coat draped over her shoulder. At her feet sat her backpack and a small, plump duffel. It was almost six thirty.

"Did you miss your ride, with your friend?"

Erika turned. "Oh, hi...no, she's trying out for the high school yell team."

He glanced at the bag. "Your parents, they will come for you? You are not late now?" She was wearing the sheerest of eye shadow and was more vividly beautiful than he could remember.

She pulled a chair away from a table and sat down. "I've got other stuff to do tonight." She looked out the window again and exhaled as if she had a cigarette. "I'm just waiting for it to get darker."

Majij placed his cup on the table and sat down across from her. She smiled a quick smile, looked again to the window and then at the surface of the table, and rubbed her temples in a way Majij thought a child would pantomime an adult.

They sat quietly. Majij had watched her earlier as she worked the hallway alone, hurried, never looking his way. Already certain he would miss a chance to be near her, here she was, and all of his rehearsed conversations of the previous weeks, books returned to a mental library, were temporarily inaccessible.

She chewed her lower lip and looked into his eyes. "I need a favor. A really big favor."

"Yes?"

"I need a ride downtown." She lowered her voice. "I was waiting till it got dark outside."

"Just anywhere downtown?"

"The Conoco station by the interstate. The bus station."

"You are traveling?"

"Just for the weekend. I've got an aunt in Portland."

"Why not just ask your mother or father?" He leaned back in the chair, tilting it on two legs.

"They're real busy tonight. My dad's got a class to teach, and Mom, she's got some meeting at the church."

He'd recognized an air of intrigue the moment she'd spoken. He lowered his head and looked at her with subtle condescension. Close enough in age, both recognized the deceit; there could be no hiding it between them.

She bowed her head. "They wouldn't approve. They don't know I'm going."

Majij remained balanced on the two legs. He could compel her to return to her parents now, drive her to that same lonely intersection at the edge of town. She could lie to them as well, explain away the lost hour, and they would forget. He could hide her bag for her, or she could hide it outside her house. Or he could take her, where she wanted to go, indulge her beauty, and refuel all of his fantasy. He leaned forward and the chair returned to earth. "Do you remember my car?"

She nodded.

"The passenger door does not lock. Go to it now, and do not let anyone see you," he whispered. "I will come out after a few minutes."

She touched his hand. "Thanks." She picked up the duffel and hurried out of the room without looking back.

Majij's car was gone when he walked out to the parking lot, and he registered a stab of paranoia, then realized it was merely concealed behind a

Suburban. Good—less likely anyone saw her get in. She had unlocked the driver's door for him and now lay on the reclining passenger seat with her jacket pulled over her head. She peeked at him, said nothing, and pulled the collar high over her straw hair again. At once comical and earnest, the gravity of the situation surprised him in the gut for a moment. *"In shah Allah,"* he mumbled, started the car, and sped out of the parking lot.

Night had settled over the interstate down close to the river, shaded deep in the river's gorge.

"I think you should sit up now. It is just across the freeway. It might look irregular if you pop up after we get there."

She raised the seat and blinked at the glare of the truck stop. No bus had arrived, but people had formed an uneven queue in front of the building, duct-taped luggage and plastic bags across the pavement at their feet. A younger man paced, smoking, weaving through the line without regard, spiked leather and chains hanging from his shoulder, his hair in a Mohawk. As the Saab passed slowly, he sneered at Majij, flicking his cigarette across the car's path. Majij accelerated, then slowed to a stop in partial darkness at the far end of the station. Erika kneeled up on the seat and looked out the back window, scanning the sea of vacant faces that loitered in crumpled, sweat-stained dresses and dirty overalls, some without teeth, some shivering, like refugees. She'd pictured some college students or maybe a confident young man to sit near. These people looked lost. They looked at the ground or into the night or into the headlights from the exit off I-84, desperate that the bus might bring them something that, temporarily, they had been stripped of.

She sat down again, pulled her duffel from the back seat into her lap, took a deep breath, and stared at the glove compartment. The engine idled.

"I would not feel good about leaving you here this night."

"Lots of people travel this way, but…" She cocked her neck and looked over the seat again. "But."

"I will take you to your house now, if you would like."

She did not acknowledge him, looking instead out of the side window, following the lights of a barge that moved on the water in the blackness below. For Erika, decisions, set in motion, were irrevocable. "It couldn't be all that bad," she said in a weak voice.

"How much will they charge you for a ticket to Portland?"

"Nineteen dollars."

"To go there and come back?"

"One-way."

Majij pondered the duffel, the backpack, the sullen girl. He felt moved to protect her, a new guardian for her welfare, and a greed for her proximity. He confused these two desires. He rubbed her shoulder affectionately. "You need to save your money. I will drive you."

"No, Maj…"

"Yes."

"No, I can't let you do that."

"It is done. I was going to go to Portland this weekend anyway." The car began to move. "And this way, I will have you to talk to."

They rolled out of the station and crossed the intersection, leaving the dispossessed to wait for their bus, entering the on-ramp and into the sea of taillights before them, all headed west.

*

Erika sat quietly, allowing the weight of the duffel on her lap to settle her into the bucket seat, a tenuous security. She watched the headlights on the Washington side of the river and wondered where they were going. She knew there were little towns over there, towns she had never visited, and she decided the headlights probably belonged to cars full of people going home for the night. She was being carried away from her own home now, only an abstraction an hour earlier. Already she was missed, she felt, and the impact would only compound by the minute. Salty liquid came up to the back of her jaw, and she hoped Majij would not want to talk, thinking that if she opened her mouth, it would pour onto her clothing. She told herself it was only hunger but thought then of eating at her own table, *at home*, and the tempest in her stomach doubled its fury. She clenched her teeth. Her father, the historian, would recognize the message with perfect clarity. This was her *declaration*. He would eventually understand the care and preparation she had made for this war, and it would be painful. Mom should have taken a stand, and I won't grow up to be like *that*. She grasped this rationale and repeated it in silence until the nausea passed.

She wondered if Trish would be home or if she'd have to sit by her door for hours. "You can crash here long as you like," she'd said, but their call had been cut short by a knock at Trish's door. She said she would call back, but didn't, two weeks ago. The phone call would appear on her parents' bill. Unknowns upon unknowns, her determination faltered, and the angst returned. They were approaching Hood River.

"What will you do about school?" Majij asked, his presence in the car illuminated once again by the lights of the exits.

"I'll just register next fall, I guess. I'm ahead in my classes." The car slowed. "I've heard Portland schools are easier, anyway. Why are we stopping?"

"I must pick up a chart at the clinic here. My clinic in The Dalles is a part of this clinic."

They turned back and crossed over the freeway and the railroad tracks and drove up the hill away from the river.

"Will anyone ask you who I am?"

"I don't think anyone will be there. Come in if you like."

They slowed before a one-story corner building, surfaced in pebbled stucco, ungroomed junipers in redwood planters beneath the windows. They parked in the shadow of the portico, an awkward vestige of the building's previous life as a Sinclair station. Majij peeked down the alley beside the building. All of the lights were off and not another car in sight.

He unlocked the front door and flipped a light switch, Erika in his shadow. "Mohammed Rashid, MD, Adult and Family Medicine" glittered in gold leaf on the door. "He is my partner, we share patients. The man I admitted to the hospital today, he was from here."

Erika walked slowly around the waiting room of maroon Naugahyde chairs and fingered their surface. A potted palm stood in one corner. It smelled clean here, of iodine, and something else she could not identify, something from the doctor visits of her childhood. Majij was behind the reception desk, flipping through chart tabs in a file cabinet. His world was perfect in order and purpose, so vast, so polished, like the chairs and counters of this room. A green linoleum floor, meant to look like marble, reflected her form when she looked at her shoes.

A metal drawer slammed. "Let's go." And he stepped to the door in three strides, turning out the light as she walked behind him. He held the door open for her, then locked the deadbolt.

They were silent as they drove through the town again, Erika studying the faces of the few people who remained on the sidewalks. Ronnie had friends in Hood River but she didn't know what they looked like. Soon they were back on the interstate. The Myers Park exit swept past. Trish and Ronnie didn't have to go there anymore. It was an ungraceful thought, the two of them entangled in a car.

"Is this your father's sister or your mother's sister we go to see?"

"She…" Erika paused. This would be the second lie she had told him. She admired him. Lying to him would only validate her father's accusation.

"You have an address for this aunt of yours?"

"She's not actually an aunt. She's like part of my family, really. She's just older than me, and I think of her as an aunt."

He glanced over at her, at her legs in the dark. "Because I want to take you to a house. See you go in a door safely. That is, I don't want to just leave you downtown somewhere. So what will this aunt of yours think if I bring you to her house?"

"Her boyfriend is older. Trish is cool, she'd think it was neat if I showed up with an older guy."

"I didn't know that Trish was your aunt. Your parents must be very young. Is this the Trish that ran away with Ron-nie? Why don't you just tell me that you go to visit a friend?" He paused. "How old do you think I am?"

She could not read him in the dark of the car, but felt him smile.

*

The exit for Multnomah Falls flickered by. She remembered her hand in her mother's, she had been three, perhaps. A giant pounding wall of water, the rhythm of it perceived in her chest. You didn't need to be afraid if your mom and dad were with you, if they weren't afraid. As they left, she waded into the stream of liquid ice to retrieve a coin, perfect and round beneath the surface, teasing her with a fragment of the sun. Her mother dried her feet with towels in the car, laughing, her father smiling, pulling off his wet shoes and socks. She remembered watching his bare toes grasp the pedals as they drove home. Now her parents were alone in that same house.

As the highway narrowed, they slowed, passing Gresham, broken trees and mounds of earth, big yellow machines, silent and still in the flash of passing headlights. They had to narrow a highway before they could make it wider. They had been making this one wider since she was a little girl. They were close to Portland.

She rolled down her window a few inches. The air was warmer here, bright and new and full of spring. High over the river, weightless, the skyline in the mist, she held her breath momentarily at the sense of arrival.

"I would like to come visit you here, if that is possible."

"Sure. That would be neat." Anything is possible here, she thought.

"To make sure you are being treated well." He turned left onto Burnside, driving west for a few minutes. The sidewalks, the crosswalks, the doorways to restaurants and taverns were alive with motion.

"Do they know you are coming?"

"It's been a coupla' weeks since we talked."

"I hope they have not gone out for the night." They turned on Twenty-first, looking for 2019 Everett, pulling over at a driveway. "I will wait for you here."

She took her backpack, leaving the duffel on the back seat. A young man in a black sweat shirt, bleached hair, was coming out as she reached the door and she caught it before it closed. Trish had said 2-A. The hallway was dim. Erika could smell food cooking, the humid smell of many people living closely, and a welcome feeling swept over her. A television played somewhere. To the right rose a broad staircase with bicycles chained to the bottom.. She ascended, looking around her as her eyes adjusted, her fingers sliding along a banister too large for her hand, grander than she had pictured. At the end of the mezzanine she looked down at the waiting Saab through an enormous round window. No light shone beneath the door at 2-A.

She knocked.

Quiet. She knocked again. Someone downstairs slammed a door, saying good-byes. She pounded now, with the base of her fist. She heard footsteps, voices, and a door unlocked behind her. Light poured into the hall and Erika turned.

A skinny Asian girl stood in the doorway, barefoot. A face with a beard looked briefly over her shoulder. "There's nobody there. They got evicted last week. I helped them pack some of their stuff."

She spoke quickly, and Erika just looked at her, unable to respond.

"I'm sorry," the girl went on. "They had a *lot* of parties. Too loud. People gotta work. Some people still finishing school."

"Yeah, that's what I was going to do," Erika said, her voice fading. The door closed gently and she stood in the dimness of the hall again. She descended, dazed, aware only that she would not be living there. She flopped into the seat of the car, placed her face in her hands, and sobbed.

Majij felt uneasy as they turned the corner, the euphoria of having her next to him outweighed now by the need to put her somewhere and knowing that he could not just put her somewhere, as distraught as she was. They turned again onto Burnside. In the distance up the hill, safely confined by the eastbound lanes, lay the bookshop he had visited just two months before, a lover chosen in desperate hours. He averted his gaze as they passed, as if it might wink at him or call his name. "Maybe we should just take you back to your house. You can say you went to a movie. They will be angry, yes. In a week or two, it will all be forgotten."

She wiped her eyes with her sleeves and shook her head. "No, they wouldn't let the question drop. Dad's a history freak. He can't stand having just a little piece of time missing. He'd make life hell, till he knew."

This was lost on Majij, for whom time, when promised to others, was always a pliable commodity. He pulled a handkerchief from his jacket and handed it to her. "How long did you plan to stay away?"

"I don't know. A year, maybe. A school year." She wiped her eyes again. "I was going to come here and go to school for all of next year and then go home. If I showed them I could do that…" She had stopped crying, filled now again with the nobility of her plan. "I'd make killer grades—they've got neat classes over here—I'd be away from all the creepy kids at Wilson. I wouldn't do drugs or get pregnant or any of the stuff my dad was sure would happen."

They completed the block and turned northbound on Twenty-first. The traffic crawled. The bistros, restaurants, and sidewalks were alive with people, some walking more quickly than the car, which edged forward in brief advances with the brake lights ahead of them. They had moved this way for a few blocks when a Volkswagen pulled away from the curb and Majij took the parking spot.

"Why are we stopping?"

"I am hungry. Are you not hungry?"

She shook her head.

"Come with me anyway. You need to learn about Persian food. We can talk, and you can think about what you want to do next."

They took a booth in the smoking section. Erika glanced around disapprovingly.

He sat across from her. "In Iran, everyone smokes. There is no option."

A bowl of *mast o khiyar* arrived. Erika pulled off a portion of flat bread and began to nibble at it, dipping it into the bowl, slouching, her elbow on the table. "I like the way this smells." She passed the bread under her nose. "It smells spicy in here."

"I know. I miss this. Most American restaurants, they do not smell so different from the hospital." Majij spread his napkin and did not mention her parents again. Twice he had offered to take her home, and this, he decided, fulfilled his moral obligation in that respect. She was meant to be with him tonight, at this table, in his car. There was a reason for this. He watched her quietly for a few minutes, her perfect fingers tearing off small pieces of bread for her perfect mouth, then spoke. "This has been a very busy day for you. You must be very tired."

"It was supposed to work. I've been planning this since February. Everything was perfect. It should have worked."

She spoke of the accusation. How in one day, her room and everything that represented her life had vanished, but did not mention the blow, which she thought would make her seem too helpless.

Sympathetic but half-interested, Majij listened. Some people, he thought, somewhere in the world, had to walk away from much more than that. After another minute, he was totally absorbed with the smooth curve of her clavicles where they flowed into the base of her neck, the small concavity there, pure, untouched, and wasn't listening to her at all.

"What's this stuff I'm eating?"

"Oh. Lavash."

"So." She looked at the menu. "You said Persian was different from Arabic, but this looks like Arabic."

"That's because you can't read. Iran and Arabia, they use mostly the same alphabet. Like Germany and England. Same letters, but different words, meanings."

"So what does this say?" She pointed to a character.

"Why ask me? It is written just below, in English."

"'Cause stuff always gets dropped in translation." She started to smirk, "Like, I've heard you guys eat sheep eyeballs. I bet you wouldn't write that part in English."

He started to frown at her, and his voice rose until it seemed to be the only sound in the restaurant. "You saw that in a movie. That is very unfair. People generalize…"

At his suddenness, she stopped chewing and put her fork down, their table the epicenter of a quiet that spread to the surrounding diners. Erika glanced around. People were looking at them. He took a deep breath, and his features softened.

"The eyeballs, in any case," he gestured at the empty plate, "were in that."

"No!"

"Oh yes, chopped up. Very fine, like a paste."

"I don't believe it."

"No, really. These words here? They do not translate into English so well, but French, in French it is said, *'oculare puree.'*"

She mouthed the syllables slowly to herself, and her eyes narrowed. He lifted the napkin to his mouth and patted gingerly, but behind it, she could see that he was beginning to smile. She felt him touch her foot with his shoe, and she did not move away, instead curling closer to him over the table. "So what is this letter here? I like the shape of it."

"That is *Zaid,* our letter 'Zee.'" He leaned over the candle, and she turned the menu toward him. The edge of her ear was close to his lip.

"So that means 'lamb' or 'with lamb'?"

"No, not really. Persian is written from the right to the left, so it is really part of the first word, but there is no translation for this, it is a mixture of things, of seasonings."

A stew arrived. She teased the garbanzos from the lamb and from the lentils, tasting each separately, with each part of her tongue and then together. She reached across the tablecloth and stroked his cufflink with the tip of her finger. "Are those real?"

"Real gold, I think. The stones are just crystals." He raised her chin with the tip of his finger. "Are you a girl who dreams of diamonds?"

She shook her head, smiling, covered her mouth and swallowed. "You'd die if you knew what I dreamed."

"*Shir berenji,* two," he said to the waiter. He looked at her. "I would like to find out." Two small dishes of pudding arrived. They talked on, Majij telling her of an idyllic childhood in another world, much of it borrowed from folk tales.

Erika's pudding disappeared in smaller and smaller spoonfuls. She yawned and turned her head to read his watch. It was ten forty-five, upside down. "Oh God, Maj, what am I going to do?" She pushed her fingers back through her hair, then excused herself.

The check arrived and he placed a credit card on the plastic tray. She was taking a long time. He began to wonder if she had left through the back door, if he had laughed wrong, if he had been too forward. He stood and looked down the narrow hall that led to the restrooms. She was coming at that moment. She picked up her jacket and glanced at the tray on the table.

"I guess I should help out." She started to open her backpack.

"No. It was really very little. You will be my date tonight, in any case. I have not had a date in a long time."

She pulled the backpack over her shoulder.

"Is that where you are keeping your money?"

"Yeah."

"That is unwise. I mean, to leave your pack here. What if I had stepped away?"

Majij put the receipt in his pocket and they stepped into the night air of springtime in the city full of possibilities. She was tired, but a good tired, she thought. She stretched and looked up into the sky. He opened her door and she got in.

"We need to stop at a grocery store, before we go wherever we go."

"You are still hungry?"

"No. Just something I forgot to pack."

"Really? I may have something…"

"It's girl stuff. Don't make me embarrass myself."

In the parking lot of the Thriftway, he watched for her and played with various scenarios in his mind. She appeared again in a few minutes, but stopped to dig in her backpack, then stepped over to a hooded payphone. She took out a pen, punched the keypad seven times, and a half minute later, slammed the receiver in the cradle. Then he remembered the number his brother had given him.

She flopped into the front seat. "Disconnected. No new listing."

"I am sorry. I need to make a call right now. Please stay here to watch the car. Okay?" And he ran over to the same phone, returning a minute later.

She imagined that he called the hospital. Something to save a life. "Everything all right?" she asked when he started the engine.

"Fine."

Left onto Twenty-third. Left again on Burnside. Cars slowed and something blocked the right lane farther down the hillside. Erika looked at the cars in the opposite lane, and ahead of them. Ronnie's car had been black with a white roof, big and square, she remembered, but she couldn't guess what it looked like from behind. Ronnie and Trish, with a gun under the seat. Pretty lowbrow, she thought. Living with them would have been just a little too weird.

Majij spoke without looking away from the traffic. "You are, you have chosen to be, an adult now. Right?"

"Yeah."

"When you are an adult, surprises come. Sometimes they are good surprises, but surprises still."

A man in fatigues was playing a saxophone on the corner, and she turned her head to watch him as they passed. His tones rose and fell, swallowed by the voice of the traffic.

"I don't know what you will decide, where you will go or who you will decide to be with. But I don't want you to have any bad surprises."

The light changed, and she looked at him. "I might not be with anybody."

"I think you should be taking the birth control pill."

"Is that all?" His comment struck her like a wave and she swallowed.

"It is just that in my office, I see sometimes young women who decided to be adult, for a night or two, and now they are very unhappy, with this baby, and no young man to stay with them, just angry mother and father. I do not want this to happen to you."

"You think like my dad."

"Your father, he speaks of these things?"

"No. But he thinks about it all the time. Like that's all girls my age want to do."

"I would not say this except that I am a doctor…"

"All right, all right…"

"And it is my duty…"

"Thanks. I appreciate that, but I've got a lot of other stuff to think about right now."

They turned onto Morrison and turned again at Sixth. Erika rolled down her window and looked on at dozens of girls her own age with older boys, black boys with loud radios and sun glasses and unshaven, disheveled men in tattered green army jackets and long ponytails. Some boys played with a hacky sack. A blond-haired man strummed a guitar that no one appeared to be listening to.

"Does he remind you of your boyfriend?" Majij spoke, it seemed, behind her.

"No." She turned to him. "I told you, I don't have a boyfriend." And she turned back to the window. She wondered where they all would sleep that night and if all of the girls were on the pill. She wanted to get out of the car and ask someone. She wanted Majij to get out of the car and walk through the crowd with her, but he wasn't dressed right. "Let's drive around it again."

This city, glorious and alive, in only an hour had become closed to her. Now she felt invisible to this private club, those lucky few who wandered about the square now, free and full of life.

*

At seven Teresa called the nurses' station at the hospital. Only one candy striper worked that afternoon, the tall one. Erika? Yes, somebody in the background thought that was who it was. She'd finished all her work. No one saw her leave. Nobody keeps track of that. We're in report right now, maybe if you call back tomorrow someone in the kitchen will know something.

Sam sat at the head of the table, mute and indecipherable as a block of granite. He hadn't anticipated this. He wasn't sure what he would say when she got home, and he bolted from one avenue of thought to another. She was certainly coming home. You couldn't thrash a child that age, not a girl. She didn't drive. You could take the car from a boy, if you had a boy.

Teresa called Mrs. Mathews. Melinda had tried out for cheerleading that afternoon, and they'd thought Teresa would pick up Erika. Melinda got on the other phone, but didn't speak at first. Yeah, Erika said she'd call her mom. No, nothing was wrong.

The fat hardened on the surface of the soup. Noodles grew cold and darkened at the edges where they dried to the edge of the plate. The screen door rattled. Sam leaned over and looked out the window. He got up and opened the oak door and Natasha scurried around his feet.

Mrs. Mathews called back at eight forty-five. Melinda told her that Erika had been looking at a Greyhound schedule several weeks ago. She put Melinda on the line.

"A coupla' weeks ago, she asked me if I thought it would be a good idea if she moved to Portland for a while. She didn't say she'd do it, like she didn't really have a plan or anything."

Teresa pressed the receiver more tightly against her ear and closed her eyes. "We don't have any family there." Then she thought of James.

"Trish lives there," Melinda interjected.

Mrs. Mathews got on the phone again. Could she do anything? Drive around?

Teresa hung up the phone and leafed through the phone book for the bus station number.

The mention of Trish gave Sam a target for his frustration. He paced slowly, reciting every transgression he could recall about the girl. "That time she almost burned down their garage? Erika came home with soot all over her clothes. And the time Trish gave her beer? Poor girl came home and spewed all over the kitchen." And he recalled a conversation he'd overheard, once, from his daughter's bedroom, Trish talking about what made her "horny."

Teresa gestured for him to hush. She had the phone to her ear. "Eight ten? No, I don't want to buy a ticket...I need to know if someone got on that bus...Is anyone there with the bus company?...Will there be any more buses going west tonight?...Thank you...I'll call then...Yes, thank you." She hung up.

"There's nobody but the boy selling petrol. The ticket office is closed. They'll open again at ten tomorrow." She leafed through the phone book again, finding Annie Curtiss' phone number and dialing, but there was no answer.

Sam only shook his head slowly and took off his glasses, sitting at the table with his face in his hands, as Teresa went down the hallway to get ready for bed.

She has just moved, Teresa told herself later that night, just moved. She hasn't run away. She's safe behind a locked door with people she knows. If they could just locate Trish, they would find Erika.

*

They drove on through the dark for almost an hour, eastbound on I-84, Majij struggling to articulate a proposal. He was most eloquent when preparing excuses, forging an alibi from fragments of previously unrelated truths or explaining the incongruent with an air of servitude that often left the inquisitor feeling guilty for asking. She appeared to be sleeping, and he looked at her in the green glow of each highway light, the arc of visibility passing over her silently. She lay on her side, facing him, the seat reclined, her coat a blanket. He placed his hand on the swell of her hip for a moment, then let it fall to her waist. She did not awaken and he kept it there for several minutes, euphoric. She was breathing softly, and his fingertips rose and fell, and he knew that beneath a few layers of fabric lay her warm skin. The thought of this redirected the flow of blood in his body in so many ways that he grew dizzy and put his hand back on the wheel.

"Where are we?" She sat up and blinked.

"We just passed through Hood River. The police might be looking for you by now. You have anyone else you can stay with tonight, any friends? Melinda?"

"It wasn't part of my plan." She thought for a moment of Melinda's frenzied schnauzer, as they had climbed once from her second floor window with a ladder. Her mother had discovered the vacant beds and locked the window, forcing their appearance at the doorway hours later.

"Then you will stay with me. It is after midnight."

"Why would the police be looking for me?"

"Because there is a law about running away. They would put you in a detention center." He paused. "They would go to your home and make an investigation of your parents. A big embarrassment for them. Jeopardize your father's job. They would be even angrier."

"I've got rights…"

"You only have your *rights* until you get caught or you become eighteen." He waved a finger at the sun visor. "In Iran, you have rights. Here, no rights!"

She put her seatback up. "I could become an emancipated minor."

"I do not know about this *e-man-see-pated* part." He looked over at her. "But if it is so easy, then there would be teenagers living independently *everywhere,* whole cities of them."

She smiled.

He stared down the highway somberly and went on. "And these detention centers, very bad. The other prisoners, girls, if they do not like you, maybe just because you are new, they may come in the night…"

"Yeah, I've heard about juvie." She tried to inject boredom in her voice but the scenario terrified her. She knew she would not be accepted by anybody important in a place like that; no one would protect her like Trish had. They could stab you. A girl she'd read about in the paper had hanged herself. Now it occurred to her that the girl might have been murdered.

"In any case, it would all be a terrible, terrible fiasco," he went on. "All of these plans, to show how you could do well, all would be lost. They would never listen to you again."

She was still pondering detention; Juvenile Hall, they called it. She had not given the possibility much thought, and now felt stupid and vulnerable. She had no contingency for this. Maybe there was no contingency for it, like a high cliff and gravity. Just stay away from the edge. Don't get caught. He was wise to point this out, and she felt suddenly more secure at his side. She reclined the seat again.

She had not answered his question. This perturbed him until he realized he hadn't actually asked a question. Had she heard him? If he asked now she might vacillate. Exit 85. He slowed and she sat up again. "If they are looking for you, it will be here in The Dalles," he said softly.

She laid down once more. She could see the roof of the police station and the sign for Burgerville. She sensed a right turn. The car climbed and growled in a lower gear.

Majij drove around the block. The apartment building, intended to look at a glance like a large, two-story rambler, was quiet, its windows black. No police cars awaited him. He pulled into the alley and turned into the parking lot behind his section and turned off the engine. He switched the dome light so it wouldn't come on, and opened his door. "Please stay here for a moment; it is not so tidy." He leapt up the staircase to his doorway. Inside, he tore two pinups from his living room wall, a third from his sliding shower door, and snatched a magazine from the nightstand, shoving them all into the brown sack beneath his kitchen sink. He rotated the dial of the thermostat and the baseboard heaters began to moan and pop.

When he returned to the car he opened her door for her and took her duffel, climbing the stairs behind her, watching over his shoulder for head-lights in the alley. Below his apartment was a storage room. The apartment next to his had been vacant for a month, and the windows were dark. What had once made him feel isolated was now a pleasing insulation.

Erika stepped into the darkness at the open door and he closed it behind her. A smell of heat filled the air, but the wall was cold where she reached for the switch. Majij pulled the curtains and turned on a light. Before her stood a bookcase with thin shelves that sagged and a plastic, wood-grained entertain-ment center with a disproportionately large television, a student desk piled with papers that might have been crumpled and were now flattened again, and a sofa, rectangular and plain, upholstered in a brown-and-gold western motif. A remote smell of human feet lingered. It was not the home for him that she had pictured.

"I'm sorry it is so cold. Sometimes I am not here for a long time, so I turn it off so not to be wasteful. I'll make it as warm as you need."

"I'm alright," she said, leaning over to look at the bookshelves, her arms crossed.

"You will sleep here," he said, gathering the pages of a newspaper from the sofa. "It folds out to make a bed."

"You don't have a Koran."

"It is in my bedroom. Do you want to see it?" He moved into the kitchen and opened the refrigerator. "Do you want a Coke?"

"No, thanks. It'll keep me awake. I haven't been sleeping too well lately." She lifted the cushions and stared at the handle and frame below.

Majij reached in front of her and pulled. Two springs groaned and a bed rose, serpentine, snapping into place before her. "The sheets are clean. I will get you a pillow."

In the bedroom, he pulled a pillow from his own bed, smelled the pillowcase, and brushed it with his hand. Pinching the pillow beneath his arm, he yanked open the drawer at the bedside, picked out a brown plastic pill bottle and opened it, tapping a red-and-white capsule into his palm. He put the capsule back into the bottle. She would be more trusting if she saw the container.

She sat on the mattress, shoes off, probing the duffel. He stepped around her and drew a glass of water from the kitchen.

"Take one of these," he said, sitting down beside her. "It will make you rest." He twisted open the cap while she looked on with uncertainty. "No, really, it is safe. I use them myself. I have trouble sleeping, like you. See, they were prescribed for me." He turned the label so she could read it, tossed the pillow behind her and took her hand, tapping out a capsule.

She took the glass and swallowed. "Thanks. I need to change now." She pulled a long T-shirt from her bag and went into the bathroom.

"Of course."

He stood and went into the bedroom. He pulled the door closed and stood in the dark, hesitant to make a sound or disturb her in any way. The light came on beneath the bathroom door. The lock button clicked. The fan went on. Water ran. A toilet flushed. Water ran again. Brushing teeth, *her teeth*—every sound excited him. He could sense the air her presence displaced on the other side of the door. The fan went off, and the far door opened.

She slid beneath the cold, stiff sheets and buried her neck in the pillow. He was before her again, seated on the edge of the mattress. He smiled.

"You have my special pillow. Enjoy it." He kissed the tip of his finger. Silently the finger came down and touched her forehead. *Beautiful man, beautiful, handsome man.* The bed bobbed. She closed her eyes. Bobbing like an air mattress, it slipped away from the edge of the pool, summer voices far away. *Beautiful, handsome, man…falling, falling, ten thousand feet.*

8

"...Spring sale on eighty-nine Fords, so come on down for March madness, half-ton F one-fifties, five point nine on approval...I can't believe it's not butter...exploded, killing two Israelis and a British tourist..." She opened her eyes. He crouched on the end of the bed, the television remote in one hand, wearing a long-sleeve white shirt and blue jeans.

"That thing's loud. What time is it?"

"One o'clock in the afternoon. Are you hungry?" He clicked through several more channels.

She blinked and rubbed her closed eyes with her fingertips. "I don't even remember coming here last night."

He looked over his shoulder. "You slept very soundly. I have been out to the hospital and back already." He clicked off the television.

"What was that you gave me?"

"Not much, really. Your body just wanted sleep." He turned around, leaning one elbow on the mattress near her ankle. "You will have black hair. I think that will be best if you are going to stay here."

She yawned, only covering her mouth after the fact. "I don't know if that's a good idea."

He stiffened a bit. "If you are not going to stay here with me, then tell me now."

"No, what I mean is staying *here,* in The Dalles. Hiding in your house." She didn't register his sharpness, a pleasant glaze hung over her thoughts, and she had difficulty teasing them apart. Simply going home and having breakfast, momentarily, seemed like a feasible option.

"So you would want to stay with me, if we were not in this town?"

"Yeah, I'd stay with you." She nodded, while the invitation sank in shallow water. "But the whole idea was to go to school."

"School, yes." He searched her face for the acceptance he had dreamed of for months, but it was bewildered, adolescent, full of indecision. "Sometimes it is better to take a break from school."

"Maybe you're right." She reached out and stroked the back of his hand. "I'm not able to go anywhere else right now anyway."

He stood and went into the kitchen. "Oh," he said, "you wanted to see the Koran. This is my copy." He tossed a thick paperback on the mattress. He opened the refrigerator. "So, are you hungry? We have eggs, yogurt…"

"Yuck."

"Rice." He snapped the lid off of a plastic container of rice he'd cooked the week before. A few pea-sized colonies of mold dotted the snowy surface. He scooped them off with a spoon and flicked them into the throat of the garbage disposal.

She didn't answer. She turned the television back on to CNN. Some people were skiing somewhere, and a girl fell down laughing in the foreground. A dreamy composure enveloped her, the events of the previous day already at the other end of a telescope. She yawned again and the sound of the television evaporated for a moment. Her jeans were at the bedside, and she scooted over and pulled them on quickly, damp and cold, tugged the waist of her sweater down, and crossed her arms. She stood and the floor swayed gently like a small boat. She grasped the end table and sat down again. A placid geniality radiated within, for the room, the town around the room, for the people on television, for the man in the kitchen. She felt a twinge of embarrassment that her careful plans could have been derailed so readily and that he had witnessed it but did not say, 'Let's be sensible,' or 'I told you so.' He was so, and she fumbled within for the right word, so, so generous. Yes, generous.

She stood again and went over to the table, picking up the box. *Clairol Ebony*. "Why black? I still won't be able to go outside." She stooped and spoke through the pass to the kitchen. "People will say, 'There goes Erika Etulain. She's dyed her hair black.'" She staggered and caught herself.

"So it will look like mine, if we go anywhere else. So maybe if you are seen, it will seem as if you are my sister, or my wife."

"If I stay here." *Wife*. God, did he just say 'wife?'

"If you stay with me." He dumped the rice into a pan of hot oil, and it sizzled. "If you go away, I don't care what color your hair is."

"Wife." She turned the Clairol box in her hand and started to read the instructions. "Sounds like you want me to stay."

He halted for a moment and stared at the burners. What he wanted he dared not speak, nothing so direct, to invite rejection and self-doubt. Instead he would ignore one option, delight in another, and indulge her opinion on the equivocal, manipulating options the way one manipulates a breeze on a hot night, opening and closing windows in critical locations. Eventually the desired outcome is the only obvious path. Still he would not speak it, even to himself. At some point, these things occurred without conscious effort. To pretend devotion to one cause while promoting another agenda had been central to survival since childhood. One could convince those around you easily if you convinced yourself first. He lifted the pan from the heat and folded the rice with a spatula. "Yes, I would like you to stay. I like you." He set the pan down, wiped his hands, and stepped around the counter. He drew her against him. "I like having you here, and all of your questions." He could feel the delicacy of her shoulder blades beneath the warm angora. She took a deep breath and relaxed against him. His arms fell around her waist, and he kissed her temple.

Giddy and stunned in his embrace, she held him, buried her ear against his chest, and could hear his heart. Embarrassed that he might feel hers, she wanted to pull away, but it was too wonderful, feeling that if she let go, she might collapse. She waited for him to kiss her again.

"The rice," he said, releasing her, and turned back into the kitchen.

She followed and leaned against the stove.

"One of these days, I will go back to Iran. For a visit." He took four eggs from the refrigerator. "Do you think you would like to see Iran?"

"Sure. Yeah." She frowned. "Is it safe there right now?"

"For you, with me, of course, yes. It is a very different world from here."

"How so?"

"It is a careful way of life, not so wasteful. People are good there. They do not waste a lot of time doing silly, selfish things."

"Like here?"

"Like here and many other parts of the world where people have a lot of money."

"But you make a lot of money. I mean, like, more than my dad. Being a doctor and everything."

He cracked the eggs, dropping each onto the oily heat that had started to smoke. The third yolk tore and ran between the first two. He stared at this for a moment, then took a fork and scrambled the pan, breaking the fourth egg with less finesse, then picked a shell fragment from the gelling white.

"Could we go to Africa? I've always wanted to go there."

"So you could wear a pith helmet and shoot things? Have black people carry your trunks?"

"No, so I could be a nurse there." She hopped up on the counter. "I can't even believe we're talking about this."

He glanced at the denim where it clung to every feminine contour between her legs. "Do not sit up there like that. It is not proper." He smiled as he scrambled the eggs. He turned the rice again. "You want to be a *proper* nurse, don't you?"

She hopped down and picked up the glossy box from the kitchen table with casual disinterest, studying it like an autographed baseball. "Ortho-Novum seven, seven, seven. You really think I should take these, huh?"

"Yes."

"Do they really make your boobs bigger?"

"Some women believe so. They also say it keeps them from being so angry at certain times of the month." He was not looking at her. "But I cannot imagine you angry."

"So I have to take these if I stay here?"

"If you stay here. If you go away. It makes no difference. You are old enough now." He placed two plates of fried rice and scrambled eggs on the table. "I think it is a very good idea."

"Thanks." She felt herself sway and balanced herself with the tips of her fingers on the table's surface. Someone knowledgeable wanted an answer to a question she had not yet seriously asked herself. A year before, the entire prospect would have disgusted her. Now it tingled, this flattery, that she might be desired, chosen someday, by someone. "Yeah, okay." She sat down at one of the plates and pulled a foil wrapper from the box. She started to tear it at the corner.

"No. Not now. Tomorrow. You must always start them on Sunday." He took the package from her.

"I just wanted to look at them."

"So look. Look." He pushed them back across the table.

She pulled the disk out and studied it, stroking her fingers over the four different colors, half expecting something to radiate through the plastic between her fingertips. She glowed at him. "Trish says they make her acne better."

"Your skin is already beautiful. Eat." He went into the kitchen and returned with two cups of coffee and sat down. "And they don't really work for a month. You should know that. Very important."

Her cheeks flushed and she opened her mouth but said nothing, and looked into her cup instead. She took a sip and curled her lips. "Do you have any tea?"

"I'm sorry. I did not know you were going to be my guest today." He laid his napkin on the table. "I will go out this afternoon and buy you everything you need to make you happy here. What kind of tea do you want? Green? Jasmine?"

"I dunno. Teabag tea, I guess. You know, like they have at the hospital."

"Oh, that. That is terrible tea. 'Cousin Farmers' or whatever they call it. I think they put in the roots and everything. I will find you some good black or Kashmiri Green." He rambled on, dizzy with his own generosity. "You stay here with me, I can show you so many things. To cook Persian food. To speak my language. You want to improve your speaking of French? I speak French better than Frenchman. There is so much history I could tell you." He leaned forward in his chair. "I could teach you much about our bodies." He cleared his throat. "Medicine, I mean. How bodies work. You want to be a nurse? You go to nursing school, I can help there a lot also. You will graduate at the top of your class!"

He had planned to meter out his assets to her gradually, always having something in reserve should she grow restless or disappointed. Now, in an unplanned demonstration, he had dumped them all, like a boy, beautiful marbles across the floor.

*

A puddle of rainwater had collected at the bottom of the stairs a few days later, and Majij stooped and picked up the soggy newspaper and shook it open. In the right lower corner, a bold heading read, "Wilson Junior Student Missing," with a postage-stamp-sized picture of Erika already half eradicated by the disintegrating newsprint. He looked up at Mrs. Greyson's window. The curtains were closed. He hesitated; surely she couldn't focus on anything more than three feet away with those glasses, and it tore at him to be unfaithful to her, to himself, but he turned finally and threw the paper into the dumpster.

On the third morning, while she was asleep, Majij cut the television cable with a pocketknife, leaning at arm's length on the outside of the building, after a story aired on CNN about a missing girl from Chino. He pretended that the tuner had failed on the television and made up a story of how it had been repaired once before and how he was unwilling to spend any more money on it, American news being filled with so many lies and exaggerations anyway. He searched each subsequent copy of the newspaper for any mention of her before bringing them home.

Rashid had taken the occasion of Aguilar's death to rain down greater humiliations than usual, first in the presence of his receptionist and a roomful of patients that waited just beyond a thin partition, and later in the doctors' lounge at The Dalles hospital, while three other physicians pretended to watch television. Rashid stood just a few feet behind them, sputtering in his best English for their benefit, thumping his finger into a worn copy of *The New England Journal of Medicine.* Majij stood facing him, arms crossed, looking at his shoes. When Rashid finished, he pivoted and crashed out of the door, throwing the journal on the end table. It had been an odd choice, Majij thought, looking down at the crumpled white cover; neither one of them subscribed to it.

Through some casual attitude of the hospital's business office, welfare eligibility had not been established before Aguilar died, and all of his bills went unpaid. Rashid regarded this with the same indignation as someone who has been pick-pocketed, and he subtracted all of the physician fees from Majij's check.

"Just like any other business," Rashid told Majij, who could not argue this point. Still, while he had visited the office in Hood River only a few times, Majij came away with the impression that the patients in the waiting room there could pay with little misgiving. His own waiting room looked more like the crowd at the bus station.

Majij began to peruse the listings in the back of the journals each week, most of the positions requiring board certification or eligibility he could not claim. Some clinics in Texas and Kansas were looking for general practitioners. More money was offered in Texas, but during his exodus from Chicago four summers before, it had looked so much like Saudi Arabia, what little he had seen from the bus window along Interstate 30, with hellish heat at each stop.

Kansas. He opened the map of his desktop encyclopedia to be certain he knew where it was. It was brown, like a desert. He wondered what group of American doctors, probably old men, would let him care for their patients while they vacationed. Salinas. An *oasis,* he thought, in a great state of sand, the last place anyone would look, a place Americans didn't like to go themselves unless they lived there. No one he had met in Oregon seemed angry about the embassy hostages anymore. Could it be any worse in such a provincial part of the country?

Hakim lived in Topeka now. A solitary job, Majij imagined, working in a bank. His brother could be very harsh, but no action was ever a compromise.

He could bless as well. Perhaps he could locate a place for them to live and conceal the papers. Sublet, they called it. Perhaps he would help with new papers for Erika.

He sensed Hakim's dissatisfaction with him had softened since his brother's arrival in the United States. Hakim had written a single letter, ripe with memories of childhood and a reference to their mother but not her name, with a cryptic quotation, phrased as some kind of encouragement, added as a postscript: *Act according to your capacity, I too am acting. Surely the unjust shall not be successful.* Hakim had called Majij twice, just after his arrival at his new job, and asked questions about unrelated things. When Rashid had been audited, Hakim begged Majij to obtain copies of the audit. Did Portland get its water from the mountains? When he wanted *Yellow Pages* for the city and a map, Majij had torn a set from a phone booth in Beaverton. He'd rented a post office box for him in Salem and had mailed him the key, as Hakim had requested, to an address in Topeka. Then, until the phone call after Christmas, Hakim had been silent for almost a year.

*

They stepped around each other awkwardly, the first few days, the peculiar waltz of new roommates, neither certain when they could embrace, each wanting to.

The second afternoon, she waited until four thirty, when her father would still be at the college, then sat down on her pillow by the phone and punched in the numbers of her home. The phone rang louder, closer than she expected. A second ring, a third. She drew her knees up to her chin and put her hand over the mouthpiece.

"Hello?"

She did not breathe.

"Hello?"

Erika closed her eyes.

"Erika? Is that you?" A small sob followed.

She put the handset gently in the cradle. Her mother's voice, familiar but foreign, was now the voice of someone she had injured but for whom Erika had no apology in a language that would be understood.

From the bedroom window, she could see a portion of an intersection with Second, but did not know the name of the street that passed beneath the window, nor could she remember ever walking on it or riding her bike there. The gutters were full of trash, the sidewalk heaved and dipped where broken, and one morning, a man slept in a doorway, wrapped in a blanket. Above the roof of the stone building across the street, she could see the sooty brick spire of the Masonic lodge a few blocks away, and she made a guess at what part of town she now lived in, and it was nowhere she had ever gone, as if it had been invisible. Now, merely by being here, she was invisible also. The phone call had felt like a glimpse of another dimension.

Erika dwelled on Trish, calling Portland again one morning after Majij had left, then Ashland, where one of Trish's aunts lived. Life took people away, and that could be a good thing for them but not for old friends who needed to talk, to touch one solid familiar person. How everything in life just seemed like a straight line, she thought, everything associated with something else, just because we walk past it from a particular point of view.

Six days passed. They had just finished eating supper when Majij answered the phone. "A man with chest pain," he said after hanging up. Before she could object, he was out of the door and into the blackness. She watched from the window as his headlights backed away below. It had not occurred to her at all that this might happen, that he could leave, that anything might be more important to him than her presence. The silence was suffocating, the noise of the dishes as she moved them to the sink, explosive. She went from one window to the other, looking for his car in the parking lot, then to the view of the street from the window, searching for some comfort. She clicked on the clock radio.

"...in other words, hold my hand..."

Old Blue Eyes, dad would say. Dad. And her heart pounded, and she was aware that something shaped her fate now that she could not temporize. The walls were too close, she wobbled on a tightrope over an abyss; looking back was looking down. Her father spied on her but would not extend a hand. She turned the radio off. She lifted the phone but put it down, then ran to the kitchen and lifted the receiver there, but her punishment must have compounded daily, she thought, and put it back in the cradle. "What have I done?" she said and went back to the bedroom. "What have I done what have I done what have I done?" She dashed into the bathroom and opened the cabinet above the sink, looking for the brown bottle. She looked under the vanity, then the cabinet above the toilet. She went into the bedroom and pulled open the nightstand. Pens and a phone book and little pads of paper and nose spray and coins and the little brown bottle. She ran her finger across the label: 'Flurazepam 30 mg.' She dumped two into her palm, then put one back. She swallowed the other dry, chasing it down with tepid tea in the kitchen, and fell asleep in her clothes, the table still cluttered, the lights on.

*

In the week that followed, Erika tried to read a chapter of the Koran each morning, looking for some comfort, discovering after a few minutes that it was printed from back to front, but still it made little sense. Some chapters related some sort of history, inconcise, with characters undeveloped or even anonymous and without the continuity she expected, certainly nothing like the Old Testament. Her father had spent a week of dinnertime conversation rehearsing his lecture on the Ottoman Empire, but she could not dovetail it with what she read. Arcane chapters were scattered through the book, like *runes,* she thought: '*And you see the mountains you think to be solid but they shall pass away as a cloud.*'

She recalled standing in a park on a hillside with her father when she was six, it must have been in Portland, watching the gray plumes of ash drift across the Washington horizon across the river. Her father bent down to her and said, "It's a volcano, Erika. The earth just belched." And he had wiped her nose and tried to cheer her, because she must have been crying, thinking the world would end. A lot of volcanoes have gone off since the seventh century, she thought. How sad for all of the Muslims who had believed it was the end of time. '*And when the word shall come to pass, we shall bring forth for them a creature from the sea that shall wound them because people did not believe our words.*' It all sounded like Revelation, punctuated with warnings of the fate of unbelievers. What believers were to believe remained elusive.

She asked Majij, but he shrugged, pretending his mind was engaged elsewhere, and said, "That is the subject of long debate among the mullahs."

An irregular pile of *US News and World Report,* six or seven inches deep, sat under the desk, all addressed to the hospital, along with several magazines in Arabic and one copy of *Playboy.* She reread the *US News* until she might claim expertise about the world from July 17, 1988 to January 2, 1989. The Arabic magazines had mostly pictures of men, none of them smiling, and every other page or two bore a picture of the ayatollah or someone who looked like him. She read a story in *Playboy,* full of teasing, intimate words, and practiced them out loud, mimicking the photographs near the center-fold, kneeling on all fours in her socks and underwear, looking back between her knees at an imaginary camera, pouting her lips, then elevating her chin and trying to toss her hair back. Then she flopped all of her hair forward over her eyes, imagining Majij helpless but willing, trapped beneath her, wanting her, as undressed as a boy in an underwear ad.

She practiced kissing him each night when he came through the door, an arm around his neck or waist, and clung to him until she felt him wobble, losing his balance.

He tried to sound cheerful and asked, "Did you call anyone today?" or "Did you answer the phone?" or "Did you stay here, like I told you?" And sometimes, casually, "Do you think of your boyfriend, Steven, today?" And she'd say no, and add that she hadn't gone anywhere because she wanted to stay.

She came finally to a decision about him, an Erika decision, something she felt sure she could do, and tried to stay drunk with anticipation.

*

The sofa bed remained extended throughout the day, and she'd lie on it in the afternoons and the evenings while she read. Majij would join her and pretend to read also, his calf against hers or her buttocks in the small of his back, or behind her with his arm around her waist, her back pressed into his chest, always touching like spoons in a drawer. They would watch VCR tapes like this, travel shows about Persia and Iran, subtitled French films or film noir, Majij losing track of the story line repeatedly as he tempted himself with fantasy, his face by her ear, breathing her in, longing to bury himself in her. Each sought the presence of the other if they moved apart, passing the night partially dressed on top of the covers, the end table lamp still on at sunrise. Majij told himself she was a good girl; he pictured her making his house in Iran ready someday, where he would direct a hospital while all of the men in his neighborhood envied him, also aware that four weeks of abstinence was recommended with birth control pills, pregnancy would mean discovery and losing her. It would mean prison.

*

One morning at the end of the second week, he stubbed his toe badly on the outstretched frame and the *thump* woke her up. He pivoted and flopped down on her mattress, still holding his foot tightly in his fist, cursing. "We should sleep in the bedroom, like normal people," he snarled. "This is foolishness."

She crawled forward in her nightshirt.

"It is fine," he grunted and glanced for a moment at her nipples before her shirt fell across them again.

"No. Let me see. Move your hand."

He relaxed his fingers and looked away. His fingers were sticky with blood, the great toenail pulled away from its base.

"Oow, geez…let me get a washcloth." She stood and went into the bathroom. Sometime during the night, she had removed her jeans, and at the glimpse of her briefs and her buttocks and legs, he closed his eyes and floated in an erotic ether. His toe stopped throbbing.

"Where are your Band-Aids?" she called out.

"Top left shelf in the cabinet."

She returned a moment later with a washcloth in one hand and a bandage in the other. He took the cloth from her and pressed it without looking between his toes, instead taking in the whiteness of her thighs, their perfect symmetry. She unwrapped the Band-Aid, and after he pressed the torn nail back to its position, she stretched it tightly around the toe.

He sighed and pulled her hip against him. "Thank you."

She felt the stubble of his chin penetrate the cotton of her briefs, against the rim of her pelvis. She placed her hands in his hair and drew him more tightly against her, still unsteady from the medication, and watched the bandage, which slowly grew red in the center.

Erika had come to think of the living room as her own space, her books, a cassette player, a bottle of *Anais Anais*, and a small incense burner Majij had given her, all precisely arranged on the end table. These things she moved into the bedroom, taking the nightstand without a lamp nearest the window. She brought several of his medical books that she had adopted and petitioned him for a lamp, citing her need to continue her studies. The following afternoon, he brought her a stainless gooseneck lamp from the office, its shroud loose, a sterile looking thing designed for pelvic exams, which she put behind the nightstand. As she settled under the covers and rolled onto her side, she looked around. What had once been his territory was now *theirs,* and the warmth of the lamp and the weight of the comforter on his king bed kindled a strange new sense of belonging.

When night came, a new ballet took form, a dance where only one or the other would change clothes in the room, after a shower, back carefully turned. When his breathing settled, she would roll over incrementally until she faced his back, silhouetted in the light of the window, and draw herself slowly toward him until she could put an arm around his waist, smell the cleanness and the heat of his skin, and slip into the dreamless sleep of the red-and-white capsule.

A few days later, as Majij finished his breakfast, a knock came at the door. Erika had just gone into the bathroom. Majij peered through the door lens at a policeman who appeared to be looking directly at him. Another knock and then five loud raps. He panicked for a moment. If he ran to the bathroom to warn her, it might take too long and would arouse suspicion. Maybe there was already suspicion. Maybe they knew, maybe he was to be arrested. Steel on his wrists, he would never see her again. Another knock.

"Yes, yes...one moment please." He rotated the deadbolt and opened the door, remaining slightly behind it, his foot planted in the carpet, imagining it would prevent the door from being forced further.

"Mister *Ah-zis? May-jidge Ah-siz?*"

"*Doctor* Aziz, actually. Yes?"

"Sergeant Warren Haynes, Dalles Police department."

"Is something wrong?" A prayer swelled like a tumor in his esophagus.

"Is it correct that you work at, how should I say this? Take care of patients, at the hospital here?"

The policeman looked through him, at the room behind him, Majij felt certain. He tried to take a mental inventory without turning around. Had she left anything out that could be seen?

"We're looking for a young girl, this young lady here." He opened a folder and turned it toward Majij.

Erika's photograph, a school portrait about a year old, was paper clipped at the top. Majij locked his knees and sank his fingertips into the door frame.

"She was a volunteer at the hospital. She's missing. Run away maybe, gone about two weeks. Does she look familiar?"

Majij cocked his head and leaned closer to the picture. "Yes, I do remember her. Very nice little girl."

"We're contacting anyone we think might be familiar with her. One of her classmates said you talked to her sometimes at the hospital."

"Yes, sometimes she asked...medical questions." *Please don't flush the toilet.*

"Have you seen this girl anywhere recently?"

Did she put her dishes in the kitchen? "No. No, I have not seen this girl since several months ago."

"Well, if you see her, anywhere, please give me a call or call the department." The officer pulled a blue-and-white business card from the pocket beneath his badge and extended it. "Her folks are good people, and they're real worried about her."

As quickly as he had arrived, he was walking away, down the wooden stairs. Majij watched as he got into his white patrol car, parked behind the Saab. Majij closed the door and the bolt and pressed his back against it. The toilet flushed.

On the kitchen table, her teacup remained, her plate could not be seen. Two teacups. Had he noticed this? They could see something and not say anything, but you knew, and they knew you knew. They would play with someone for a while. Like that little hunchback detective on television. There would be surveillance. A rich country had more money for police, for things that listened, for cameras that could watch through walls. He went into the bedroom and peeked between the curtains at the street below. SAVAK had cameras like that, from America. Now he was *in* America.

"Maj, what are you doing?" She stood in her underwear and a long gray T-shirt, drying her hands. "Who was at the door?"

You might not know who is police, who is not. "A policeman. The police are looking for you." He handed her the business card. "He said you are in a lot of trouble for running away." He walked past her into the living room without looking her in the eyes.

"Shit. What should we do?" Erika turned the card in her fingertips, feeling the raised ink of the letters. "Why'd they come here?"

He put a hand on her shoulder and looked at the card. "Maybe it is time to move. Somewhere it is harder for them to find us." The mention of *we* had, for years, triggered an instinct to distance himself. Now it was alluring; this wonderful, fair girl whose life he controlled considered him a partner. In thirteen more days, a month of birth control pills completed. He kissed her.

She stepped back. "But your office."

"It is Rashid's. It is not paying so well now."

She shimmied up onto the dresser. "Can we go to New York?"

"I don't have a license there."

She toyed with the package of unopened hair dye and then stood up and opened her drawer and withdrew a pair of jeans. She pulled them up and snapped them beneath her nightshirt. "You gotta have a license for each state?"

"That is the way they do it here, like it is not one country."

She settled on his lap and cupped his face in her hands and looked down at him. "So where do you have a license?"

"Washington, Illinois…Oregon, of course. And Kansas."

"Kansas." She let his face go and stood. "Can't we just go to Portland?"

"If the police are looking for you in this town, then they look for you all over the state. The police, they talk to each other with computers."

"Washington?"

"I do not have insurance there."

"Illinois? I'd like to see Chicago."

He thought of the incident. It would be known everywhere. "I cannot get insurance there either."

She sat down on the bed next to him and leaned into his shoulder.

"But I am willing to move to Kansas to protect you." His hand slid into the waistband of her jeans.

"Kan-sas." The two syllables felt dissonant, off-center. It was one kind of independence to know your mom and dad and all of your previous life were just a few miles away, and another to go to Kan-sas. She struggled to articulate this but could not, and in the end, the Flurazepam erased the initial terror, and the sight of the policeman's card was already forgotten, replaced with a labyrinth encircling the very core of her life as she understood it. "It's far. Really far, isn't it?"

He felt her tremble, her eyes scanning his. He closed her eyes with his fingertips and hugged her to his chest. "Only three, maybe four hours, by plane." He kissed her forehead.

In the security of his hands, her face against his chest, any course of action seemed inviting, any direction that did not lead to conflict, back to her father, back to J. G. Wilson Junior High. She mustered a smile, stood drunkenly, and picking up the bottle of Ebony Black, went into the bathroom and began to cut her hair.

*

The following Monday when Majij sat at his desk, he found an envelope and unfolded the note inside. Rashid was taking a four-week sabbatical to Iraq. "Salaries will not be advanced," the memorandum stated. Majij had anticipated this, and in turn, kept all of the cash at his clinic, erased portions of the ledger, and omitted chart notes for the corresponding visits. His receptionist was thrilled to take the two weeks off he offered.

All of these violations he justified with the knowledge that a real purpose for his life had arrived, a purpose that towered high above the mundane formalities of his contract with Rashid, an abrupt polarization of what had been to that point in his life only random acts of self-gratification. Rashid was Iraqi after all, a Ba'athist, and probably an apostate as well. Allah had given him this marvelous satin-smooth, mistreated American female who waited for him each day, who waited for the blessed time and place that she could give all of herself to him. She needed him, and he would save her from a life of useless distractions and the unhappiness of greed. He must make the way right, arrange every step of their new path together, and that would require money.

*

Erika startled herself each time she passed the mirror over the dresser, her hair so black, a blue gloss in motion when the sun came through the window, as if she had taken the body of another, her spirit beneath another more sophisticated girl's skin. Not knowing how Iranian women wore their hair (their hair was always covered with a scarf in *National Geographic)*, she sculpted it in the shape she'd seen on Egyptian servants, in books about pharaohs, her bangs to her eyebrows, bobbed above the collar. She had never worn her hair so short, and the bare skin of her neck felt foreign, sensual and free. Free of those pressures, those requisite postures of deference in the humiliating hierarchy of the ninth grade.

She missed talking to Melinda and spent afternoons imagining how she could call her and not have the number traced. Majij had described how the police probably had tapped everyone's phone by this time, especially her parents', and contacting anyone seemed terribly risky. She admitted to herself that it was mostly her own satisfaction she wanted to wave like a flag. Steven wouldn't be able to ignore her now, god, no; he'd have to go to confession every day just for the thoughts he'd have.

Romping around the apartment, sometimes in one of Majij's shirts and a pair of his sunglasses with round brass frames, she would look out the window with a new boldness, draw up the blinds, and imagine walking about town, passing her old enemies completely incognito. Flipping through the

Rand McNally Atlas of the United States, she would plot various routes for their exodus with a pink highlighter, hearing herself introduced as his wife, *Mrs.* Erika *Aziz,* trembling at the thrill of it. Talking, whispering, with him so intimately, in a restaurant, in French.

They would have sex eventually, she decided. It was inevitable, it was what women did, even enjoyed, everyone said so, but she could not picture how that would proceed. Fuck. It sounded abrupt and painful, something selfish. Even if Trish were so casually familiar, telling her once of straddling Ronnie in the front seat of his Dodge, each fantasy Erika envisioned, taking off all of her clothes in Majij's full view, or being undressed by him, left her weak and embarrassed. Twisting out of her T-shirt, dropping her jeans before the mirror, she was bony, misshapen, pasty. He would see this and be so grossed out. She would do something clumsy and hurt him. He would hurt her, maybe because she wasn't made right. No. No, no, no, they were going to *make love,* something faded to soft focus with these words. She wondered if they needed to be married, if Majij would insist upon it, and she wondered how Muslims did that when there wasn't a mosque around or anyone to perform a ceremony.

Majij left the apartment early one Sunday morning, "to make rounds," he said, and was back by one, removing his shoes and crawling onto the bed for a nap. Erika watched him from the doorway for a few minutes, then crept closer to the bed, resting her chin on the edge of the mattress near his cherubic, benign face, and imagined how exhausted he must be after struggling with disease and cancer, and how defeated he must feel when someone died anyway. Did that kind of struggle make a person hard? She stroked his fingers and his arms and chest until he murmured.

Her new reality had evolved in those weeks, sleeping more than she could remember since childhood. Thoughts of her mother came less and less frequently. She could walk away and be home in twenty minutes, she calculated; after all, truly, she wasn't *dead,* or in any danger. Being this close absolved any guilt. She was taking care of herself as she had been taught, and if the truth were known to them, they would be proud. They had believed what they wanted to believe before she left, and it was their own goddamned fault if they got their panties in a wad now for believing something else.

At eleven she would get up and shower for the day, standing for long minutes motionless while the heat and steam melted away the residual fog of the medication, until the water started to cool. Wiping the condensation from the mirror, she would admire her breasts, at least those were pretty, larger, rounder, she was sure. She would dress and then wash her clothes from the previous day and hang them over the shower door. Majij snapped at her the first time he came home to a bathroom still damp with her underthings, but he allowed her to continue.

The television received nothing after her third night there. She had watched the Discovery Channel the first two days, and then it was gone. Majij promised to call the cable company each evening, but they never arrived. She ate all of his canned soup, several frozen dinners, and a box of saltines in the first week. Oblivious to her hunger, he had arrived home one night of the second week with only a gallon of milk, two boxes of corn flakes, and a carton of oatmeal.

A single cookbook, *Recipes of Southern France,* lay in a top drawer in the kitchen, a circular burn on the cover betraying its use, once, as a trivet. In the cabinet were rice, Crisco, a partially used package of lentils, and an assortment of seasonings, none of them except the pepper called for in the south of France. Two freezer-burnt chicken breasts became 'Blanc de Volaille à la Goudaliere,' almost every ingredient substituted, laid cautiously one evening before Majij, who ate with the courtesy expected of a guest or perhaps with courtesy because he was tired. Another morning, she gave him a list, required ingredients for another recipe. He forgot this, and went back out for a bucket of chicken instead. The following day, he arrived home with only a few things from the list, saying that the others were too expensive.

She would awaken some mornings after he had gone and lie in bed with a book open, staring at the pages, then sleep for a few more minutes. She grew frustrated with the Koran, and turned to a set of tall, thin, green books with beautiful illustrations, one on the heart and another on the digestive system, spending an entire morning reading a chapter on cirrhosis. Pictures showed scars inside each cell of the liver, blood pooling in the wrong places, bilirubin oozing into the skin. Alcohol could do that to a person, it explained, and the Islamic prohibition Majij had mentioned once now made sense.

One volume was dedicated to reproduction, filled with cross-sections of vaginas and penises, with blue vessels, red vessels, and pink flesh, healthy but disinterested looking men and women. All just slightly flabby, forty maybe, and faintly distressed at being partially dissected by the illustrator. Sex was just like lungs and kidneys and livers, she thought, something people did. Majij at least had nicer muscles.

One afternoon, she noticed an old book protruding from the skirt of the sofa, evidently shoved there to replace a broken leg. She tugged it out and carried it back to the bedroom and laid down again. It was *Cecil's Textbook of Medicine, third edition,* yellow at the edges, the blue fabric of the cover frayed at the corners, 'C. Waterbury, DO,' inscribed inside the loose binding. The doctor who delivered me, she thought. A general practitioner with a thinning rug of red-and-gray hair, he had always looked angry, even when he'd draw a puppy face on her Band-Aid after a shot.

She closed the volume and pushed it across the mattress and looked at it, then stroked the cover with her fingertips. He had died eight or nine years ago, and suddenly she was glad that he was gone.

*

Majij stumbled in the door one evening, his arms full of empty cardboard boxes, and announced that he had resigned. No real resignation had been composed, just a curt note left on the appointment book at his own office. The receptionist would find it and the rest would unfold as he expected. They were moving.

"Not to Iran," she said, a plea in its suddenness.

"No. Kansas. My brother has arranged everything."

"To, like, a little town?" She pictured a place people had left in the depression. At one time or another in her daydreaming, she had imagined living in almost every city in the country, none of them in Kansas. There were only little towns there.

"Salinas, near Topeka. A city, like Portland. You will like it. I need to be there no later than the beginning of September." It was a locum position, he went on. Some doctors would be gone, sick, or retired, and he would be needed for seven months. They were desperate and board certification was not necessary.

It made Majij feel more confident saying his brother had arranged things, but his brother had done little. He'd mentioned a place to stay and had acknowledged that Majij was coming, and he hadn't openly objected. "Come later rather than sooner, that would be better." He had seemed detached at the time of their phone conversation, which had come in spurts and pauses, he was doing God's work, he said, in a house Majij had never visited in Topeka. Majij hadn't mentioned that he would be bringing someone.

"We need to leave right away?"

"We still have two days to pack."

"The furniture too?"

"It was here, with the apartment, so really, there is very little." He stood surveying the surface of his desk. "We will only need the car."

"If you don't have to be there for four months, we could stay here a little longer, couldn't we?" She hugged him from behind.

He turned and held her. "But you are like in a jail here. Don't you want to be able to go outside? And the police, they are still looking for you. They will not stop."

"But wouldn't they look for me in Kansas, too?"

"My brother, he can help with that. He can get you papers, passport, that say you are somebody else. You want to be eighteen, have your rights? A tall girl like you he can make eighteen." He stepped around her with a fistful of envelopes from the desktop and went into the kitchen, still talking. "You were not going to go back to school until next September, correct?" He brought the trash can back and placed it beside the desk. "So now you have four months' vacation with me, if I am not so bad to be with. We will take time."

"Could we go to San Francisco?"

"Why?" He paused, searching the desktop. "What is there?" In every spare moment for months, he had dwelt on a vision of the two of them, removed from critical eyes, undressing her in afternoon light in a motel in a small town, no telephone, no clinic, to draw him away. It was a private world he had invented, a vision he could not reconstruct in a large city. Too many eyes, too many police.

*

The following morning she awakened to a clatter in the living room, a thump, a murmur, a curse. Another thump. She pulled on her jeans and opened the bedroom door. Majij struggled with the television, trying to hold it with one arm against his leg while he attempted to open the door, the television slipping slowly away from him. She crossed the room and caught the edge of it, then opened the door behind him.

"I'm going to sell it," he said apologetically. "It is too big to take with us in the car."

She followed him. "Why don't you just give it to Goodwill? It hasn't worked since I got here."

They were halfway down the stairs when he realized how visible she was. "Go back," he hissed, "people will see you." A door at the opposite end of the complex slammed.

She sat on the sofa and pulled her T-shirt over her knees, drawn up before her. The stereo went out the door. I still have my Walkman, she thought. Was there a cassette player in the car? She couldn't remember. It had been winter, over a month ago. Now they were really leaving, this was the *real* beginning. The script they had played with, bantered about, had come to life, and retreat was suddenly untenable. Kids at Wilson would be out on spring break now. Her own spring break was going to be a little longer. She smiled. This journey was different, but far greater than she had ever planned, two months before in her bedroom. It was the sign she had waited for. When she heard his car start she rose and retrieved a bottle of red nail polish from the bathroom, resumed her position, and began to paint her toes.

Majij did not reappear until late that afternoon, laden with cartons of Chinese food from the Golden Pheasant. He had been at the office, he said, emptying drawers, taking some books that were his. There were books to return to the hospital as well; leaving them in the apartment would reflect poorly on him. "The pawnshop gave me two hundred and fifty dollars for the stereo and television," he said with an upbeat note. "Just a small problem with the tuner, easily fixed."

He showered, emerging from the bedroom a few minutes later dressed in a clean white shirt and the black slacks of his only suit, wearing musk she could smell across the table, over the garlic chicken and the moogoo gaipan.

She had painted her fingernails, curled her hair into a pageboy, and wore a white blouse with ruffles at the cuff. No skirt had been packed that week in February, so black shorts, high and tight from seventh grade, were worn instead. She had shaved her legs with his electric razor. Disposable chopsticks deft between her fingers, she thought of Aunt Helen showing her how to use them. She must have been about ten at the time. It had been a frustrating exercise, but she had insisted on eating everything with them for a month, her mother puzzled, her father amused and proud. She and Majij ate quietly at first. A decision she had made earlier that afternoon intruded with every bite, she couldn't get away from the image it spawned and could not put two words together for a sentence. She couldn't just tell him, you didn't blurt out that sort of thing while you were eating. *He'll find out when he turns out the lights.*

He looked around the room at the bare shelf where the stereo had been, unaccustomed to the quiet. "This should be a special night for us."

"I know. Probably the last time we'll eat here. I sort of wanted to fix something special."

"You fixed yourself, you look very pretty. Enchanting, tonight. This is the beginning of a good time, for me and you." He smiled at her with a reverence that she couldn't immediately reciprocate. "Oh." He leaned back, reached into a trouser pocket and withdrew a glossy white cardboard box. "For you."

A gold chain, slender as woven hair, draped over the cotton batten inside, and near the center hung a small golden crescent. She draped it across her fingertips. "Thank you." She slipped it around her neck and wrinkled her nose as she struggled with the clasp. Her decision, so easily and abstractly made that afternoon, was unsettled by the expectation she read in his eyes. She didn't know how to respond, and scanned his expression with the faintest panic.

Majij fumbled with his chopsticks for a few minutes, trying to spear his chicken with one of them, grew frustrated, then laid them on the edge of his plate and used a fork.

*

Erika lay on her back, rigid, holding the covers beneath her jaw with each hand, unconscious of the force with which she pressed her head into the pillow. Legs straight, parallel as a ruler, she shivered and could not control it. She'd entertained the notion of keeping her socks on but had finally taken them off, wanting him to see her painted nails, but now wished she'd left them on. It was too dark for him to see. She couldn't warm the place where her feet were, and rubbed them one over the other, scratching one sole and then the other with her toenails, a temporary pain to deter the dread. The room had not been cold just a few minutes before, but now it was frigid, damp, and inescapable as a well. She tried to abate her angst with the self-affirmation that everything would be beautiful, no, it would at least be bearable, and it would not be painful, well, at least not as painful, that none of what was about to *unfold*...God what an awful word! Positioned at the far edge of the mattress, she watched as his silhouette entered the room, then watched his reflection instead in the mirror over the dresser as he removed his robe and sat down on the edge of the bed. Escape would require running around him, but now she could barely move her pelvis.

"This is a very special night for us," he whispered as he drew back the covers. "Special in our memories for many years."

The mattress sagged as he lay down, and she rolled on her side to face him, the blanket drawn more tightly around her. He drew her close and tugged the blanket away until she could feel his cold thighs against her own. Her jaw trembled. He held her more tightly, like a constrictor, until she could not tremble, nor inhale, nor think. After a long moment he relaxed and she took a breath. He kissed her, wetting her lips, her neck, the crest of each shoulder. Her nightshirt rose and he circled each breast, tickling in an awful, paralyzing sort of way, and she gasped. She shivered again. Forcing one knee between her thighs, then the other, he pulled her beneath him, exploring her, trying to guide himself, finally pressing against her, dry, unforgiving, relentless.

"No...Maj...this doesn't...stop...oh God!" And then her face stung.

He rose up on one arm and tried to slap her again, but she had closed her eyes and covered her face with her hands.

He was out of bed. When she opened her eyes, he stood with his back to her, narrow buttocks visible now that she had acclimated to the dark. He held his face in his hands.

"Do not...*blaspheme.*"

"I..."

"You blasphemed." He stepped to the window and separated the curtains a few inches. "You have ruined this time, this night."

She touched her face, and it no longer stung, it had been little more than a token blow. Red neon from the street flickered on and off, painting his body the color of blood, every muscle defined perfectly, his posture a renaissance sculpture, nothing like the forlorn, flabby illustrations in the green books. Erect, he was enormous, disproportionate, and his body perfect but nearly elfish. She watched from the dark, hypnotized, as with each flicker he withered, like time lapse photography, it occurred to her. She was not shivering any more.

*

When she awoke it was light in the room, and he was lying on his side looking at her, his face pliant, apologetic. The air smelled of coffee.

"I do not want to be angry with you. It is not respect."

"I just didn't know, I've never done that." She pulled his hand to her mouth and bit a knuckle softly. "But I'm pretty sure you're not supposed to slap me."

"I am sorry. I was angry." He rubbed his eyes and sighed. "Never? Not even with a boy at school?"

She shook her head.

"I want you to stay with me, more than anything else. We need *sigheh*, I think."

"What's that?" She separated his fingers with her own.

"A contract, to be married to each other for as long as we want. It is Iranian -Islam custom. When two people do not know each other so well…"

"But I'm only fifteen."

"…very legal in Iran."

She recoiled slightly, pulling a pillow under her arm. "You ever going to hit me again?"

"Never. I swear."

"My dad hit me once." She rolled onto her back and stared at the ceiling. "Don't we need a judge or a priest or something? What if you change your mind?"

"No priest. We just make contract, for however long we both agree, and promise to each other. When we find a mullah, we can get his blessing. In Iran, this is done often."

A telephone rang in another apartment, and they both stopped for a moment and looked at the wall. The ringing ended after the eleventh ring, both of them realizing they had silently counted to themselves.

"I dreamed of you, one time. I think." Her face grew serious. "Three years ago, before I met you. Weird, huh?"

"Then maybe it is right you are here." They both rolled onto their backs and stared at the textured ceiling.

"You said once this was your special pillow. Why?"

"I did? When?"

"I dunno', sometime. I just remember it, I think. So did you say it, or did I just dream it?"

"I remember. The first night you were here."

"So why's it special? Looks just like the other one."

"Because sometimes, before, in the winter, I would pretend that it was you."

9

Fog hung over the river, filling the gorge and draping the town in a pale glare that leaked around the Venetian blinds of the apartment. When Majij looked out, he could only see the outline of the roof of the Saab and could barely discern the dumpster at all. Erika packed all of her things in twenty minutes, leaving only a pair of socks and underwear to dry in the bathroom. Majij ventured down to the car at forty-five minute intervals with a small box or bag, thinking consecutive trips would arouse suspicion, and he made several trips to the dumpster as well, throwing away magazines, most of what remained in the refrigerator, and great bundles of old notes and receipts off his desk, watching carefully that none of her small sketches or handwriting went into the bin. By eleven, the fog had lifted and the apartment had begun to look vacant.

It would get dark around seven thirty; he decided they would leave about an hour later. He considered leaving her coat behind, she would be less likely to stray, but it was probably part of a 'missing persons' report by now, and he hadn't a means of destroying it. Maybe she would lose it later. At nightfall he would bring down his suitcases.

Erika napped intermittently, curled up on the bed most of the afternoon, and thought of what had and had not happened, still chilled by his nakedness but compelled at the same time to think of it, again and again. The nakedness of it all. 'Sig-hey,' he had explained, a contract that would recognize the holiness of their devotion to each other. Holy. *In the eyes of Allah.* Didn't Allah realize they had ended up together by accident, her fear of riding the bus? But how would I have gotten home? No, he was sent. But God, Allah, could see that beforehand, because he was God. Or was that why they said *it is written?* It wasn't chance alone. She had been wishing for them to be together, and it happened, just not the way she had pictured. She hadn't planned a way into his apartment. 'The Lord acts in strange ways,' her father liked to say, usually when he was pissed off about something. Did the God at Saint Mark's know about *sigheh?* All of these thoughts floated around in her head as she curled to one side and then the other on the bed, grasping at small images of his skin near hers and the brief heat of his body, while Majij thumped around in the living room.

Sitting in the car, finally, it was emptier than she expected. His two suitcases and her duffel sat in the back behind his seat. The rest, he said, was in the trunk. She reclined her seat, but sat up on her elbow as they accelerated onto the freeway and the streetlights faded. As they drove east, she watched the glitter of the lights on the hill to the right of her grow scant, knowing that one of them was her home, knowing that she was missed up there in one of those houses. If she could only talk to her mother, tell her she was sorry, that she was safe, this educated man loved her. Dad—she pictured him in her room and what might be left behind for him to take and burn. Majij had traveled more than Dad. He was a doctor, *a doctor,* and she repeated this to herself silently in the dark. He cared about people. He would care for her now; her parents had wasted their chance. Then the lights were gone, and the idea of talking to her mother grew more and more implausible. To the left, the long row of lights on The Dalles dam appeared, the eastern boundary of the world as she had understood it only a few years before. The lights folded to a single point as they passed, and then that point was gone also, and they rode on in darkness while Erika quelled her uneasiness with a new theory, that her actions were driven by a divine benevolence, leading them both to a better life together.

She lay down again, pressing her ear against the seat cushion, settling into the rhythm of the tires over the asphalt. She lingered in twilight, reawakening repeatedly, alive with a thousand thoughts, wondering if she would get back to school or if it was even necessary. A birth certificate, a driver's license—Majij's brother could provide those, whatever his name was.

She knew her mother was crying, and an awareness settled over her that no one knew where she was. This had only been an abstraction while she lived in his apartment; at any moment she could have just stepped outside. Now they were on the road, and her action struck home with finality, a feeling of cold-steel daring dancing in her mind like a sparkler, but disconcerting with no audience, tugging her away from deep sleep. "Where did you put those capsules?" She rolled her head and opened one eye at him.

"We are in Washington now," Majij said. "We cross the Columbia. It comes all the way from the Coulee Dam."

Erika opened both eyes and looked out the window. "I think it starts in Canada, in the Rockies. Can you ever step in the same river twice?" she asked him.

"Of course you can." He answered without looking away from the bridge railing. "Why couldn't you?"

High above the bridge over the water, the moon cast a yellow path across the blackness below. Stars speckled a coal sky. Headlights approached, and she lay down again to avoid the glare. Steven could shine a flashlight into the sky, like a light saber, revealing the Pleiades, Orion, Gemini, and Leo. Steven would squeeze her hand in the dark and whisper, "There you are," only last summer. She dozed on this memory.

The car came to a stop and a truck engine rumbled behind them. The car was full of light.

"Huh?"

"We are in Kennewick. It is not so far from Hanford, where US government made the first atomic bomb."

She yawned and thought for a moment. "I don't think so."

"I am wrong?"

She looked at his resolute jaw, fine stubble silhouetted in the passing traffic. "It was in New Mexico. Los Alamos. I learned that in sixth grade."

"They teach you these things in sixth grade?"

"Yeah." She yawned again. "Or maybe my dad told me…"

"You believe everything your father tells you?"

She took a deep breath and sighed. "Look, they made a movie about it…"

"So you believe what they say in movies also?"

"Okay. They made part of the bomb there, the part they put inside."

"So what is the difference?"

But she pretended to fall asleep, turning away from him. She was anxious to get back to Steve and his flashlight and the stars. Fermi was there, Dad had said, Oppenheimer too. It was a gamble, it might set the atmosphere on fire, a chain reaction, consuming every molecule of oxygen on earth. It hadn't. Sometimes a decision needs to be made with some unknowns. It took courage to do that. Have faith in yourself, stop apologizing. Someday everybody leaves home, she thought, just not everybody agrees on the right time. The right time. Once again she pondered the weight of him, his hardness, his expectations, and distracted herself with the tip of a finger in the darkness.

During the night, she awoke again in a glare from above, they were still and the engine silent. The door opened and slammed, cold air fluttered around her legs, and she curled up tighter. She heard a clatter and a squeak, and smelled fuel flowing somewhere. She tucked her coat around her thighs and closed her eyes again. The driver's door opened and closed with more cold air, the engine purred and they were moving forward, a turn through a wide arc. She pressed into the seat, the gearshift, the touch of his leg. She would not fall away, he was there. Later she awoke to pressure in her ears and the deafness of altitude. She turned over in her seat and watched his profile, so absorbed, so relaxed in the glow of the instrument panel. Her ears popped and everything sounded like it should: the engine, the road, and the slipstream around the little car. The night seeped in.

The parking brake ratcheted to a stop, and Majij yawned. The heat, the motor, perhaps a dream, had risen to a crescendo and ended. Pink stratus above gray, grayer still over mountains to her right, sunrise approached. Erika sat forward and her coat fell away. A motor home was parked about fifty feet from her window. Before them a small cabin and a drinking fountain. Two brown painted garbage cans overflowed a few feet from the bumper. "Where are we?"

"It is a rest area. I need to rest. We are not far from Me-zow-la." He arched his back and stretched. "You need to use the toilet? Go, now."

The door swung open awkwardly, she straightened her legs and shut the car door behind her. A fresh coolness enveloped her and she breathed deeply, standing by the hood until he tapped on the window and made a curt gesture toward the bathrooms.

Empty and cold, her footsteps echoed, fluorescent lights hummed. When she was finished she inspected herself in the stainless steel mirror, rubbing frigid water over her face. A bulletin on the exit door warned not to feed the wildlife. Outside, a band of yellow light was stretching over the mountains, speckled with snow and trees at higher levels in the distance. A solitary truck was coming down the highway, still far away. She stretched each leg, every muscle in her body, with each deliberate step. It felt good, as if she had never really been awake before.

A green pickup displaying a round seal on its door rolled to a stop at the far end of the parking lot, a shovel behind the cab, a radio antenna, and an amber light on the roof. The man inside took a sip from a thermos, sat numbly for a moment, then held a microphone to his lips. When she looked back at Majij, he was gesturing to her with an urgency she had not seen before. When she got in he pressed down on her shoulder.

"That truck," he said. "You should hide yourself."

"It's just a maintenance guy."

"But he could see you."

She slouched beneath the pressure of his palm. "He's a *janitor,* Maj. Janitors don't arrest people."

"He has a radio…"

"To talk to the head janitor. Get your hand out of my face."

The man lifted two white plastic buckets from the back of the pickup and began walking toward the restrooms.

"What's with the back seat?" The seatback was folded forward, and a pile of boxes filled the floor and the rear deck.

"I have made a place for you to sleep while I sleep…"

"In the *trunk?*"

"It is not really trunk. It is very flat, more comfortable. It will be dark."

"I don't want to stick my head in there. Besides, I slept all night." She paused. "You could let me drive," inflecting the final word like a question.

"You know how to drive? Really!"

"Really. I've watched Melinda's mom."

"Oh, that is excellent. See one, do one, teach one."

"Is that yes?"

"It is a kind of joke we say in the hospital. Sometimes, the first time you do one, the patient dies. I am not so ready to be your first patient." He pulled his collar up, crossed his arms, and turned away from her. "No one should see you while I am asleep. Someone could look in. This is best. I am getting angry now, please go in the back and cover yourself."

Erika corkscrewed her face and hoped he would see her in the rearview mirror, but he was not watching, so she did as she was told, lying on her side, bending her legs and dangling her coat over the rear deck like a tent. The floor of the trunk pressed into her left knee and ankle. She would try to reposition herself periodically, conscious that the car moved slightly when she did, and she started to wonder if anyone, someone who might have silently driven up, was watching them now.

"Was there a telephone in the bathroom?"

"No. Why?"

"You would not try to call your parents, a boy maybe."

"No." She sensed him relax, and he shifted in his seat. Silence followed.

"Maybe you will take driving classes when we get to Kansas," he said softly, "when my brother makes you eighteen. Or maybe in Iran." His breathing slowed and he was asleep.

The whole cabin of the car grew stale and warm as the sun rose, and at the moment when Erika thought she might suffocate, she heard him stir and the door opened. She lifted the jacket. He stood next to the car, looking around, then looked down at her and shook his head, motioning that she should stay there. The door slammed and he walked away.

A few minutes later he was back, springing into the car and starting the engine in one motion.

She pulled the coat down. "What's the matter?"

"I feel better now. It is almost ten o'clock. We should drive further."

The car lurched in reverse, and she crawled forward from her cave. He snapped the lever into first gear and spoke loudly over the engine without looking back. "I think it is better for you to stay there, for a while. It is day-time."

"But no one knows what I look like now."

"I still think it is better. Do you understand?"

"Jeesus Christ, can't I just,"

"Do not *blaspheme*!" He waved a finger in the air. "I just need to think for a while."

He slowed to a crawl at the end of the on-ramp and looked in the mirror, but couldn't find her. "You make noises in your sleep. Do you think of other boys?"

She raised her head. "What?"

But he had already begun to accelerate and did not hear her over the engine. He steered with his left knee and unfolded a map of the western United States over the wheel. Missoula. No, it was not far enough away. But a university was there, that was good. Foreigners came to universities and were not noticed so much. Bozeman. It was a few hours further, with a university there also. Older men were seen with younger women, the faculty having sex with the students, this he had seen in movies. The two of them could go unnoticed among such busy, promiscuous people. An apartment would be cheap. He adjusted the mirror to look at her, at her small mop of black hair and her lower lip. She would be grateful to come sit in the seat after a while.

He began an inventory. Toilet paper, a hair dryer, there were some sheets in the boxes also. The Saab should not be seen. A garage was absolute. They needed a furnished apartment. A bed. He could have her that night, but sigheh first. But how to explain this? Like an engagement. Girls liked to know they were engaged, a promise was everything. Or she could refuse. There would be much ugliness, with the months to come full of anger. Would she want a priest? Someone official, a formality.

Friends he'd known simply prepared a document when they traveled in Iran with their girlfriends and had it ready if they were stopped or questioned. One could prepare sigheh and have it officiated later, if the situation came up, for a small fee. At least before the revolution—they were not so casual about it now.

American girls wanted some ceremony, someone official to preside, and a ring. *Bride Magazine*, he had picked it up once when he'd first arrived in Chicago, with the notion that he could find a girl there. Where would he find a ring? The pawnshops would be closed; better not to give money to Jews anyway. It was Sunday, an American holy day, so Kmart would be open! "Erika, are you awake?"

"All morning. Just awaiting your next command."

"Open my canvas bag, the brown one."

A zipper buzzed.

"On the side there is my Koran. Take it and read from it."

"Just anywhere?"

"Surah four."

She fluttered through the pages, forgetting for a moment that it was arranged from the back. "Oh people be careful of your lord, who created you from a single being and…"

"Quietly. Read to yourself." He looked at her again, at her downturned eyelashes. She leaned on one elbow. "In the side pocket of that same bag, take out the *chador*. It is not chador, really, only scarf. You must always wear it when reading Koran."

So that was why it didn't make any sense, she thought. "Can I sit up now?"

"Yes, yes, sit up. Put on the chador."

She folded the cloth into a triangle and laid it over her hair, tying it in a quick twist beneath her chin. It slipped loose a moment later, but she grabbed it and tied it again in a square knot. It stayed.

Erika read on in what seemed a monolog addressed to men of rules pertaining to the handling of women, how and why they could be punished, how to allocate their property, who was forbidden, and how many could be kept.

"Maj, do you have a sister?"

"No. Why do you ask?"

She read for a few more minutes, and then the sentences appeared more and more cryptic. She skipped ahead, looking for something to rivet her interest, but little more appeared regarding women. There were a lot of commandments on how to deal with enemies and nonbelievers, which Erika found herself skipping over also, having decided by sixth grade that it was best just to go around people like that or to walk away, as her mother had said. She skipped ahead to 'The Bee,' and started to read again, but lost interest and laid the book on the seat beside her.

Majij noticed this. He wanted her to read, to go through some motions at least, so she would feel like her decision, which he would make for her, had been informed. Sigheh was an Iranian invention and he knew, with only his own casual knowledge of the book, that there wasn't going to be anything pertinent there to the contract they would make. He wanted to scold her for finishing too quickly, but he could not think of another Surah she should read, having only the vague notion that she should appear to be a believer, a quality that would bear fruit when she met his brother, and when they arrived in Iran. But at the basest level of his desire, and with respect to all that he envisioned he would do to her, it had no bearing at all.

*

She was warm and she was awake. Range land rolled by, billboards, farmhouses, and a continuous fence just beyond the shoulder racing along, rising and falling with each hill and culvert, punctuated every few miles with a tangle of fence leading off to the foothills. Great tufts of grass near the road undulated forward, pointing them down the highway. The wind was at their backs and the sky was blue and enormous, as if they traveled at the top of the rim of the earth.

Majij looked forward down the highway, glancing in the rearview mirror periodically, which he had adjusted to watch her, but she was always looking to one side or the other, smiling about something. What did she have to be so happy about? He had awakened with a calm mind, but his body was starting to ache from sleeping in the seat. A hundred miles down the highway, intrusive thoughts, flies awakened by the sun, began to trouble him. Eventually someone would notice that she was younger than she should be for traveling with him, and they might ask her. He had already prepared his own answer, but what would *she* say? They would ask how they met, whether she was in school, and they would notice the difference in accents. She sounded English sometimes, and that was actually a good thing. People would be less perplexed by two foreigners.

A pale blue car had appeared in the side mirror, about two hundred meters behind them. Majij did not know how long it had been there. Had anyone noticed him packing the car yesterday or the girl who crept down the steps after dark, the girl no one had noticed before? No patients had been left in the hospital, and they would not find his note until tomorrow morning. Recalling this, he relaxed slightly.

The blue car was still there and didn't seem to be getting any closer. It was a sedan, square and dull, the common sort of car the police used. He would have to be with her all of the time, at least for a while, there for a quick explanation to dispel suspicion. Until she learned, until it came for her like a reflex, as it did for him. What if some official asked her for identification? If they were to be two foreigners, then someone would want to see a passport. They would just have to avoid official people until they were at Hakim's. He was certain she did not know how to lie. Could she simply be private about these things? Unanswered questions were always a potential source of conflict for Majij, who did not see manufacturing answers for them as deception but merely truths that needed to be adjusted. Now, by her simple presence in his car, he would have to be adjusting things every moment they were awake. How did she do this?

The blue car was suddenly beside them, a silver-haired woman at the wheel, dressed well. It passed. Montana license plate.

Erika watched Majij's head and wondered how he could go for so long without moving it. He is her driver of this limousine, and only a few minutes remain before the concert for her to collect herself. In Montreal an eight-foot grand had been substituted, and it had sounded cheap. She made it clear to her manager, nothing shy of a twelve-foot Steinway. Fleshy and damp, Mrs. Turner, her old piano tutor, is in the audience. It is the debut of the new album. Form-fitted tubular, black and studded with sequins, strapless, with satin gloves to her elbows, she glides onto the bench. She glances down at her small breasts. Too pretentious. I've grown beyond that; they come for my music alone. So it is faded denim, an old cardigan, and silver hoops.

Her stomach growled.

"Maj, can I get my ears pierced?"

"Of course. Do you want to get your ears pierced?" Anything, he thought, to help change her appearance.

She pinched her ear lobes simultaneously. "Aren't you getting hungry?"

They took the first Bozeman exit, stopping at a Denny's a few minutes later. She was aware again of the scarf, as people glanced and then glanced away. She could not have felt more unnatural with a duck sitting on her head. She played with the ends of fabric quietly, but had tied the knot too firmly to loosen. She would have to pull it off of her head without untying it and she knew that would look unusual.

In the restaurant doorway Majij had picked up a small newspaper of classifieds and now spread it out over the table before them, leaning over it with a black pen and the calculating intensity of a man disarming a bomb. One could sink into a college town like sand. Rents were lower, and a sea of faces changed from semester to semester. He remembered patients commenting that he looked too young to be a doctor. Motels were expensive; move every day, and you must pack, with a new registration every night and new people to be convinced.

Erika watched him, playing with her teabag but not drinking. He had wise, kind eyes, she thought, like those of a surgeon. He made a careful circle here, another there. He pulled a vinyl covered notebook from his pocket and lettered in it. "Can I see?" she asked.

He didn't answer and closed the paper when their food came. "We will stay here for a while."

Erika glanced around the restaurant, at men in mustard colored overalls, truckers in down vests, tired, heavy women with hair short and curled, seated like bookends, retaining squirming children in their booths and their husbands, detached, weatherworn. A cloud of cowboy hats and smoke hovered at one end of the dining room. "I thought we would travel more, first."

"The town I am sure, is different. There is a university. We will live near there."

*

At the first address the apartment sat above a frame shop, the stairway rising from the street, between the doorway to the frame shop and a beauty salon, where a garishly made-up woman looked from the counter at the two of them as they pulled open the stairwell door.

Her look stayed with him as they went up the stairs. They walked the length of the hallway, an unnatural light coming through the orange curtain at the end, at the apartment number listed. He could hear traffic on the street. A radio played somewhere. Such a nosy glare, so much gossip in a place like that.

"I don't think this is such a good place," he said, looking around. "There could be a fire. It is too noisy."

Erika pulled the curtain aside and looked down at the street. "It would feel odd to live in a place without grass." They both agreed on something and it felt good. They trotted down the stairs faster and Erika took a deep breath when they reached the sidewalk. It was a beautiful freedom to go looking for a place to live, stay with the man you loved. She liked the way it sounded in her mind. This was what it felt like to be older, what she had dreamed of.

Approaching the second address, they passed through a portion of the campus itself, with rows of dormitories alive with students clicking past on bicycles, some in small pickup trucks, downy-haired girls walking in twos and threes, whom he followed with his eyes. The apartment was at the edge of the campus, on Kagy Boulevard, in a long row of townhouses. It was just four thirty and most of the doors were open, and young men sat on the steps with plastic cups in their hands or wandered to the cacophony of electric music and rhythm that he could feel already in the door of the Saab where he rested his arm.

"Too many young men," he said, smiling, then made a U-turn. "They would steal you away from me."

The Greentree Apartments were on Montana Street at a point where it dead-ended into a spruce-shrouded hillside. It looked to Erika like a two-story motel without an office, with olive siding and weathered shake shingles, needles and cones scattered across the roof. When Majij shut off the engine, the sound of air moving though branches smothered any noise from the downtown district just a few blocks away. A squirrel ran along the handrail of the second story, then stopped and stared at her in a solicitous posture.

"I like it here," she said.

They got out and walked up the stairs and looked into the window of the vacant apartment. Behind the building was an alley and a carport for each address, each stall concealed by a gate. Not perfect, Majij thought, but close enough.

A few minutes later they were parked in front of the realty office. Majij scribbled on the edge of a map and handed it to her. "this will be your name." He pulled the door latch.

"Aisa?"

"Ais-ha. It is a good Muslim name. You want to be a good Muslim, don't you?"

She thought about this for a moment. "Can't I be a bad Muslim?"

He shut the door. "What is the problem, with Aisha?"

"I don't know. It sounds Chinese. I just want to pick my own name. You know any other names?"

"I knew a girl named Fatima."

"No thank you. People would call me 'Fat' for short."

He flinched but added, "Aisha was the prophet's youngest, wisest wife."

"You gonna tell me you've got a couple of old wives around I'm going to meet?"

"Don't joke with me on this. If anyone asks your name, say it is Aisha. It will help us be more private."

"Aisha Erika Aziz?"

"Aisha Aziz."

"Aisha Aziz," she repeated, with a tone of defeat, and looked out the window. It did have a pretty sound.

A bronze Cadillac pulled in next to them, and a middle-aged woman stepped out wearing a flannel blouse, jeans, and pink western boots.

Majij unsnapped his seat belt. "You have darkness under your eyes today, you do not look so young." He got out. "This is good." And he shut the door.

Erika watched from the Saab as the two of them sat at opposite sides of a metal desk and talked. Majij smiled a lot and the woman laughed. He laid out his wallet. He filled out some papers. He smiled some more. He gave her a card, which she copied. He pulled an envelope from his jacket and counted out some cash. The woman recounted it. Some forms were separated. Majij stood. The woman stood.

The woman glanced and smiled at Erika before turning to get into the Cadillac, and then she was gone. Majij tossed a folded yellow paper onto the dashboard and backed out of the parking spot. Erika unfolded the sheet.

"You told them our name was *Aguilar*?"

"I did not say to look at that."

She felt suddenly criminal. They drove in a few blocks in silence. *Aisha Aguilar.* "So how do I answer the phone?"

"We don't need a phone." He drove on, not looking at her. "And only God needs to know our names."

*

The living room, painted a pale pink gloss, had been repaired with small patches of flat paint of a slightly different hue. Spider webs encrusted the ends of the curtain rod. Dust and a few fly carcasses covered the end table that sat next to a small love seat upholstered in brown vinyl. A half wall separated the kitchenette from the living room. Erika dragged her finger across the kitchen table, gathering a wad of greasy lint, which she flicked onto the stained linoleum. The hallway ended at the bathroom, its fan, connected to the light, sounding like a damaged plane in a steep dive. Erika turned it off. To the left a single bedroom with a swaybacked double mattress and on the far wall, a great trapezoid of light from the afternoon sun. She turned and looked at Majij, who was staring into a refrigerator with no shelves. "We're just moving on up, aren't we?"

Later that evening Majij left Erika in the apartment, with instructions to unpack the few boxes and make up the sagging bed. He returned an hour later with four brown grocery sacks: a miscellany of frozen dinners, several frozen pizzas, a small sack of rice, two dozen eggs, a pound of lentils, coffee, and sugar. He didn't pull any tea out of the bags, and Erika pointed out, in a retaliatory tone, that there was no coffee maker. This irritated him enough that he did not speak to her for another thirty minutes. The oven baked too hot, and they picked and scraped the tarry contents of their aluminum trays in silence.

While Majij was in the bathroom, the fan running, Erika gently passed her fingers through the folds of his clothing in his suitcase until she found the flurazepam and took one. She was in bed lying on her side when he came out and had turned out the single overhead light. He slid into bed behind her and put his arm around her waist, drawing his hand up over her breast and kissing her weakly on the neck. She had been, in her weariness, prepared, by way of surrender, for anything to happen; she even wished that it would happen, having decided that the first time was going to hurt and that there would be blood, no matter when or who, and it was better to just get it over with. Instead, he flopped back onto his pillow, his hand falling away, and was asleep a moment later.

The following morning he was up before her, clattering in the kitchen, cursing in Farsi at an aluminum pan that had lost most of its Teflon and now tenaciously held his fried eggs. She stood in her underwear and a faded lavender T-shirt with her arms crossed and leaned toward the heat of the stove. He had already boiled a saucepan of coffee.

"Here." She placed her hand over his, inverted the plastic spatula, and taking the pan from him, gently nudged the eggs onto a plate, "Mom taught me that." She soaked a washcloth with hot soapy water and wiped off the top of the table.

The chromed steel and red Formica kitchen set sat too far from the living room window, and the bulb in the fixture above it, which had no glass, was blackened and dead. They ate quietly in the silver shadows of morning light, speaking in low voices. No sounds came from the next apartment. Small feet scampered over the roof periodically.

After breakfast, they walked three blocks past other apartments and duplexes, where it seemed most of the occupants had left for the day. Erika untethered, drenching herself in emancipation, while Majij examined each dark window quietly, for someone who might notice. They crossed Clinton. At the next block, Main, they turned left onto the broad sidewalks. They passed a bookstore. A barber shop that was closed. A sewing machine and vacuum shop. A hardware store where they stopped and Majij bought some light bulbs. She tried to guide him down an aisle to look at a vacuum cleaner. "Just a small one," she said, but he would not listen.

"There is a broom already at the apartment. You can sweep a carpet in as little time as a vacuum."

"But how do you scoop it up?"

"Just open the door. Sweep it out. The wind will blow it away."

When they returned to the apartment, Majij installed a light bulb in the kitchen and then sat down with a yellow legal pad and began to carefully print, filling about half of the page before he stopped. Erika leaned over his shoulder.

"It is sigheh," he said. "Now you must write what I have written just below. Leave a place for me to sign."

She took the chair next to him, pulled the pad in front of her and began to write. Majij stood and walked slowly around the table like a teacher.

One year. "Just one year?"

"We can make it longer at any time, but we must put down for how long."

She looked down and continued to write in tall, willowy, meticulous letters. When she had finished she read it to herself.

> *In the name of Allah, Most Gracious, Most Merciful*
> *With his help and guidance;*
> *With all my trust put in Him:*
> *With my free choice and freedom of will,*
> *I (here he had written 'Aisha Aziz') propose to marry Doctor*
> *Majij Aziz, and take him as my husband, for a period of one year,*
> *In accordance with the teachings of the Qur'an,*
> *Before the present witnesses.*

She glanced around.

"*We* are the witnesses, for each other," he said.

It was something plain, she thought, too purposeful. It lacked the romance she expected, and Majij read this on her face.

"It is just a contract," he said. "We will have to make the poetry ourselves."

He leaned over and kissed her on the neck, and a thrill ran the length of her. She signed her name and dated it, April 30, 1989.

When she was finished, he took the pen and placed his own signature.

It was delicate and commanding, like Arabic, she thought. She had opened a hospital chart once to see what it looked like, running her fingers over it, enchanted by its grace. Now here it was on a document, for her. He folded the paper in thirds and slipped it into his jacket pocket.

"Isn't that mine?"

"I am just keeping it for you. I have a place to put it, to keep it nice." She looked at him, full of doubt, wrinkling one side of her mouth. "Where would you put it? In your pack? It would get all dirty."

She looked at him earnestly. "We could get a copy tomorrow."

"Where?"

"Where you got the light bulbs."

"I saw no copy machine…"

"Next to a file cabinet, behind the counter. Between the file cabinet and the case with the binoculars."

"Oh yes." He pretended to remember. "But that is theirs, for their business."

"They'd probably make a copy for a dime."

He scowled. "They would read it then. It is very private."

He was growing annoyed and more annoyed that he needed to conceal it. He had plans for her. He shut his eyes and rubbed his temples, then went into the bathroom to interrupt the discussion. Did she remember all of that, at the hardware store? It was disquieting. He took a drink of water. He would go back to the hardware store tomorrow to look.

He came out of the bathroom. "We should eat something. It is after five."

They baked a frozen pizza and the apartment smelled warm, like a home. Erika pictured him, smarter than the smartest boy in her class, sitting in the library at Wilson with an enormous medical book open in front of him. One or another faculty approached timidly and asked him questions. Somehow he was her age. She held her finger up to obscure his moustache in her line of vision.

Majij looked over at the wall. "What are you pointing at?" he asked.

"Just imagining you, young."

"I was traveling quite a lot by your age." He talked of the Caspian shoreline, of sunshine and sand and warm wind over the rocks, a rugged beauty he had seen in a movie, actually, but merged the images with his own memory of a single trip he had made there at fifteen with an older, heavier woman who had paid him to sleep with her.

The light from the window faded, and they were drawn closer to the orbit of the light over the table.

She told him about Seaside, summers that all ran together now, digging after mussels, and her mother's laughter. She spoke of driftwood fires in a hollow in the sand and her father roasting marshmallows one at a time. They were there again, her parents in her mind's eye, center stage, and her life with them had an unexpected glow. She realized she was smiling, an insuppressible radiance from the heart of her, and he was looking at her, puzzled. Disgusted with herself, her enthusiasm faded and she stopped midsentence. As if he had grasped her sudden phantom of guilt, Majij said, "It is okay," but they both ate in silence for the rest of the meal.

She went into the bathroom and brushed her teeth, thinking briefly of a path that ran into the dark trees from the ocean beach, which she had never been brave enough to explore.

She took a flurazepam, turned out the light, lay down and waited for him, determined to stay awake, confident that she could release herself at any moment from consciousness should he get angry again. She had signed the contract, had she not? It was her own decision, independent proof that she had made the right choice. Erika decisions, she vowed, were irrevocable. She was going somewhere, toward some greatness, and this was the beginning.

He brushed his teeth for an absurdly long time. She watched the light beneath the bathroom door, alternately watching the shadow of the pine boughs on the wall from the security light over the parking lot. The door opened finally, and he was there, crawling onto the bed behind her.

He took her hand in his own and kissed her behind the ear and along her jaw, finding her mouth; their teeth touched for a moment.

Don't kiss a guy hard, Trish had told her once. *They don't like that.* She traced his lips with the tip of her tongue, drawing her fingertips up his back. She grew sleepy, holding onto consciousness, holding the back of his neck with her arms, playing with his curls in her fingers, unsure what to do or if she should do anything at all, taking deep gulps of air and exhaling slowly, trying to calm herself, thinking all of the time, *I am married now.*

He followed the course of her shoulder, kissing her and licking gently, to each breast, drawing her into his mouth. His arm was now between her legs, his hand in the small of her back, pushing her underwear down to her ankles and away, his fingers exploring, seeking her moisture. Then he was over her, holding each arm extended across the crisp white cotton sheets, his lips against hers again. Cool firm bed and soft, warm, powerful man, moving shadows and light, the wall, the wind outside. Briefly abrasive, a fullness, he was inside of her now.

Thrusting slowly, a pleasant friction, he rocked over her in another world, staring into the pillow. She tried to pull his mouth to hers, but he pulled away, rocking more urgently. "Everything's okay," she whispered to herself. "Fine, just fine."

Dreams tugged at her each time she closed her eyes, rhythmic, wonderful dreams on the verge of understanding, all mixed up with the stories he had told, and she thought about waves on the Caspian, and struggled to stay awake. She bit her lower lip, heels pressed into the mattress, the headboard creaked and pounded and she slipped into an image, the surf of the Pacific against the rocks, sun on the sand at Seaside, her parents miles away. She pressed herself to him, into the wetness between them, until no space remained for air. Her hands slid across the expanse of his shoulders, fearful she would slip away, locking her calves behind his, drawing him further into her, a madness of want occupying every muscle of her body.

He gave a small cry, stopping abruptly, and relaxed. At this, she was fully awake. His breathing slowed, his weight fully upon her, perspiration between them like thin oil, his head sideways, away from her.

"Maj?" She wanted him to move again, she wanted the rhythm, as if a pretty song on the radio had ended too abruptly. "You alright?" She pulled at his waist, then his buttocks, but he melted away, snoring softly. She wondered for a moment if something had happened to his heart or if he had had a stroke, and she lay there passively for a long time until he felt so heavy that she could not take another breath. She rocked from side to side, the heels of her hands in his shoulders, until he rolled off her. He grumbled something she didn't understand, then snored again.

The sweat on her body soaked slowly into the cold sheets; the pressure of his calf against hers grew more remote until she had forgotten he was there.

Scrimshaw light and shadow moved gently on the ceiling, and she thought of Melinda, of Aaron, downhill on Fourteenth, pedals rotating in reverse, the hillside falling away from them, the floating river above the town. Summer? No, spring quarter of seventh grade. Steve ahead of them all, hunched over the handlebars of his twenty-one speed, looking left and right, entering each intersection in a serious, protective way. Taking point, he called it, the four of them sliding effortlessly though the air like an arrow of geese. She moved her arms outward, feeling the wind beneath them, and touched Majij.

Startled, then proud, pleased that she had dared. No one in class could ever even dream of this. Not one of them would ever go so far. She thought of Candice Chilton, who had goaded her, saying she talked "like a Canuck," standing with those girls by her locker, announcing above the talk, "I don't know; I'll have to check my *Shed-jewel.*" Then all the girls started using "shed-jewel" around her in the weeks that passed, and she grew oblivious to it. Finally, they were using the enunciation in class, to the teachers, unconsciously. It had become something vogue and was no longer delivered with cruel emphasis.

Now she lay next to a man, her man, her husband in the laws of another world. A man who spoke Arabic, Farsi, French, and English, a man whose knowledge would surely dwarf the minds of those little people at J. G Wilson, even the principal. Devil take them, she thought, in her father's voice. I can learn anything, go anywhere, with him.

She drew her fingers through the fine hair between her legs. Something unfulfilled, just beyond her grasp, eluded her. It had not eluded *him,* she thought, rolling onto her side. This I will learn also.

*

Sam had been awake since daybreak, finding Teresa fully alert but mute, staring at the ceiling, both of them having gone to bed after a great exercise in blaming each other and the subsequent shame that followed. It had been a violation of their vows, he'd realized, as he drove the four miles along East Nineteenth to the college. He let himself in through a door near the registrar's, and a few minutes later, sat in his own office, looking out the deeply tinted plate window over the still vacant campus. She had ignored his apology. He rummaged around his desk for a teabag but found none. He phoned the house, but she hung up as soon as he spoke. He could call again, he knew, and she would answer every time the phone rang, thinking it might be news, but it would only be harassment at this point. They had addressed one another in words he'd never thought they'd use. He walked down the hall to the faculty lounge, a fresh janitorial cleanliness in the air, and wondered if he had missed some wiser perspective in not seeing his world so early in the day, all of these years. He found a bag of Lipton's and tossed it into a cup of water in the microwave. Footsteps tapped in the hall, and another office door opened, then closed.

A stack of essays on the Boer War sat on the desk before him, but he could not bring himself to lift the top binder from the pile. Someone stopped in his doorway and Sam swiveled his chair. It was Robert Wellborn.

"Good morning, Bob. What can I do for my president that he can't do alone?"

"I saw your car. Everything okay?"

"Thank you, yes." Sam turned his chair full away from the desk.

"How is Teresa handling it?"

"She's not."

"I can't begin to imagine how you must feel." A standstill settled over the conversation for a moment, and neither looked at the other.

"I feel," Sam began, "like Yamamoto, in December, after that first blow."

"You can't blame yourself."

Sam stroked the knuckles of his right fist, still wondering if he had really struck his daughter. "We're all responsible, all of the time. For what happens to us and the ones we love. Every teacher knows that."

Wellborn stepped into the room a few feet, leaned against a four-drawer file, and glanced at the stacks on Sam's desk. "Staying ahead of it?"

"Word out I've gone crackers?"

"No. We all understand. It can slow a man down, that's all." Wellborn tapped the file a few times, unable to slap Sam's shoulder without feeling inadequate.

"I know. Just thought I'd get an early start." Sam wanted to add that the longer the day wore on, the more intruding thoughts would arrive, the loss magnified through the lens of his own preoccupation. A word or a gesture or some comment of a student would remind him again of his daughter, and he'd lose his way. There were some things you could not tell your superiors, even one as affable and as inept as Wellborn. "Thanks." Sam rotated to face his desk and the rest of his morning.

10

Light came and he awakened her, kissing her neck and face, sour breath floating between them. She rolled away, trying to reach a package of mints on the nightstand, then sat up and went into the bathroom. A stickiness persisted between her legs, and looking down, she saw the blood and wondered if it was her period, but no, that had ended a week ago. She slipped back into the bedroom and lifted the sheets to look at the stain and then realized what it signified. A loss or a trade for another joy, she was not certain, but she was relieved by the finality. This would at least convince him to stop asking about other boys. As she stood brushing her teeth, she glanced down at her purse, open, on the top of the toilet, and could not remember putting it there. She gripped the brush in her teeth and spread the top of her purse with her fingers. He had searched it.

Some people were hard to read, and it was better not to judge, she reminded herself. His world was like a vast castle; some of the rooms remained dark, and there were chapters of his life in those rooms. He had entered her world completely, she thought, last night. She slipped back under the covers and listened to him tinkering in the kitchen, then the long zipper of his hanging bag. A few minutes later he was back, wearing blue polyester trousers and a fresh white shirt, wrinkled from the suitcase.

He flopped onto the bed next to her, smiling like a man with amnesia. "You have such a good memory, I think maybe you should learn some Farsi."

"But you speak English so well."

"My brother, he is a difficult man to impress favorably. He will like this, if you have tried, and also," he stared at the ceiling, "if, when, you go to Iran with me, you will speak like other Iranian women. And gossip."

"Iran?" She rolled up on one elbow. "When are we going there?"

He ignored the question and pointed at the bathroom. "*Dast shuyi.* Can you say that?"

She thought of Mr. Rogers, with an accent. "Dast shoo-see," she recited slowly.

"No. Dast *shu-yi*,"

"Dast shuyi."

"Better." He pointed at the window. "*Panjere.*"

"Pan-Jeer." She said. "The window?"

"What else would I mean?"

"Maybe the trees or the sunshine."

"No. But sunshine is *aftab nur*. A tree is *derakht.*" He picked up his shoes and held them before her. "*Kafsh.*"

"And doctor?"

"It is the same. Doktor." He put the shoes back on the floor and then, pushing her hair behind her ears with his fingertips, cupped her face with both hands and leaned forward. "*Ma' shuge.*" He spoke softly.

"And what is 'ma' shuge'?"

"Lover."

And so it went the rest of the morning. Each thing she touched, he would translate: door, refrigerator, table, kitchen. She made dry toast for them in the *ojagh.* They sat at the table, crunching their toast, Erika with one leg folded beneath her, each of them believing, for the moment, their lives had only begun the night before.

*

She flipped through the Koran each morning after he left, mostly for something, anything to read, constructing her own haphazard interpretations but usually ended up picturing panoramas from old movies. She tried to engage Majij each time when he returned, assuming that he was an authority, but he showed little interest in pursuing a debate. She entertained the notion of making a notebook, but the only paper in the house was an accumulation of the local swap paper, and each day she would close the book earlier than the day before and read the listings of garage sales and used cars for sale and the job opportunities, wondering how it would feel to make 'up to a thousand dollars a week without leaving your home' and imagining the CD player she could buy, a whole stereo to go with it, and a new television for Majij. It would be two in the afternoon when she closed the papers and shoved them under the coffee table again.

After a week, she folded the papers into the garbage and, in spite of his warnings, ventured outside after he left, walking up the hillside over the soft, rotting pine needles, inhaling the mountain scent. She picked up a piece of moss-covered granite, then a dry branch, and examined their surfaces. She looked down at the pine cones on the shake shingles of the roof and marveled at the notion that it was all part of the same planet, the same world, as the town of her parents, only a long day's travel, really, just over a curved horizon that she had left behind, seemingly decades before. The next morning she climbed to the top of the hill, where the pines grew thin and outcropping slabs of lichen-speckled granite formed a seat, from which she could look down at the rooftops and the backyards with toddlers and mothers and barking dogs and elderly men trundling out to the street with garbage cans. Beyond the traffic and the streets and the edge of town, a river could be seen. The wind carried all of the sounds to her in small whispers and fluttered her scarf around her ears. It became a daily religion. Some mornings, she would take a few crackers with her and sit on the steps after she came down, tossing fragments to a squadron of squirrels and eating a cracker or two herself. The squirrels grew less cautious each day. Her hips would ache gently and remind her of Majij and the closeness between them. She would hug herself and draw her jacket tight and want to be held again. The rocks, the bark of the trees, the parched surface of the wooden stairs, the cold breeze, and the warm sun all parts of a rough but harmonious world, which she felt a part of for the first time.

After two weeks she stopped wearing the scarf, deciding it was inauthentic anyway, and the mornings were getting warmer. Except for the sound of the wind through the pines, it was quiet, the building almost vacant. At a quarter to ten each morning, a man with a backpack and a bicycle helmet would roll away from the lower level at the far end of the building. She noticed his arms and legs were very thin, even his shoulders and head seemed narrow, as if pressed flatter by the helmet, so she christened him "the thin man" in her mind and referred to him as such in her one-sided conversations with the squirrels. One morning after he left, she explored the gravel alley behind the apartments. A few cars remained, near a long row of garbage cans, one of them with a small stack of books on its lid: a paperback copy of *Nineteen Eighty Four* with its front cover torn off, *Basic Calculus,* and *Introduction to Economics.* She smoothed the corners of the paperback and put it beneath her arm and picked up the economics text, leafing through it as the wind fluttered the pages. It had been highlighted in several colors and notations made in pencil and ballpoint in the margins. She took both volumes back to the apartment, and in the afternoon lay down on the bed with *Introduction to Economics,* reading the first six pages before falling asleep.

When she awoke Majij was standing at the edge of the bed, flipping through the book. It was late afternoon. "Where did you get this?"

"Maj, I…"

"Did I not tell you not to leave the apartment? Never, without me?" He snapped the book closed like a trap.

"I found them by the trash can, when I took the garbage out."

"You did not go up to the bookstore?"

"No."

He moved over to the bathroom door and turned on the light and leafed through the book more carefully. "This is about *Western* economics, making loans and taking interest…*usury*. A moral crime. The Jew economics that has raped the Arab world. Just so you know that." He closed the book and tossed it on the mattress next to her and turned in to the bathroom.

She heard him urinating, then a long wet fart that startled her, sounding like her father; she hadn't expected that he was capable of such a sound. It occurred to her that she hadn't actually taken out the garbage, and he would discover this, that she had lied to avoid injury she did not know for sure would follow, and she wondered if she would lie again to explain the first inconsistency. Must one explain at all, if someone really loves you? The toilet flushed and he came out, but turned and went into the living room. She knew he hadn't washed his hands, and waited to hear the kitchen water go on. Maybe men could urinate without touching themselves.

Majij flopped onto the sofa and pulled the curtain back to view the Saab at the curb where he had parked it, after a full tank of gas and a free carwash, to which he had added the one dollar wax option. It sparkled symmetrically, purposefully, in the final sun of the afternoon, as fine an instrument as any man might want to command. The day he'd bought it, he had placed eleven hundred dollars down and signed a note at 8 percent, even as another twenty-four hundred dollars lay folded in his pocket. "Use that cash to make your life sweeter," the salesman, Duke, had said. "You'll never beat eight percent." And so Majij had driven off the lot, intoxicated with the leather wheel in his palms, the tenacious radial tires obeying his very thoughts as he poured down one hillside and up the next on a scenic drive just above Hood River, the engine's perfect libretto moving one chord to another as he shifted, all the time still remotely aware that, because he had not paid in full, the car was not entirely his. Thus, he did not deserve the car at that moment, but in the weeks and months that followed, he decided to behave as if he did, staying at his desk after the last patients had left the office to look through a textbook for a better explanation of their symptoms, or double-check the remedy he'd pre-scribed, and struggling with his own limited understanding of the language, to appear more compassionate. Before the year was up, he had paid the car off in full, having calculated the deferred cost over three years as absurd. But the habits of diligence remained. It was growing dark outside, but he could still see the grill of the Saab and wondered if the car had made him a better man. *Usury.* It was a term his brother had taught him at age sixteen, with a scowl on his face, his brother who now worked in a bank.

Majij let go of the edge of the curtain and grappled with all of the incongruence he had unveiled. The Escort would never have come this far. Perhaps she would not have even climbed in, that snowy night. Buying on credit was no different, he reasoned, than stocking up on extra food before a famine. Or was it a means to gain access to an unearned luxury, yielding to a fantasy? Contrary to all of his apprehension, life now was good, with a fine car, a solid space in which to cook and live, and that delicious girl in the other room. It was as if he had acquired her on credit as well. Would she make him a better man? He felt as if he had taken a Valium, and a fleeting guilt at feeling so good came and went, nearly unnoticed. It was a backward notion, this prohibition on lending, but one they could live with as long as they lived well now. He stood up and washed his hands at the kitchen sink, dried them on his pants, and went back to the bedroom. He was calm when he sat next to her, pushing the book behind him. "So what else do you do while I am gone? Do you talk to anyone?"

"On the invisible phone?"

"There are other people here. When you take out the garbage. Times like that."

"I feed the squirrels. I talk to them sometimes."

"So you feed the squirrels. That is good, being kind to the animals. You will be a good Muslim." He stood again and went into the kitchen. "I have brought food. Come, eat."

An orange-and-red fast-food sack sat on the table, and Erika stuck her nose in it. Three sliced roast beef sandwiches. Curly fries, cold, some of them loose in the bag. Two crumpled sandwich wrappers. No horsy sauce. "You kinda' got a head start, huh?"

"There were five. I know you do not want to grow fat. So I save you."

"That's not the point. You started without me." She clicked the knob of the oven. "Maybe I can heat these up." She dumped the remaining fries onto the broiler pan and pushed them under the glowing element. She turned and sat down, her chin in hand. "Drinks?"

He handed her a thirty-two ounce cup, a single straw from its lid. She swirled it like a chemist. Ice rattled.

"I saved half of it for you."

"Maj..."

"It is more economical that I get the large cup, that we share."

"Maj, it's more economical for me to walk to the store, the store that's not three blocks away, and buy something to cook for us."

He sat down across from her and tilted his chair back, his face withdrawn from the light. "And if someone asks you your name?"

"Eri...*Aisha*. Aisha Aziz."

"Aisha Aguilar."

"But that's lying. Besides, I'm not the one that looks Mexican."

"It doesn't matter how the woman looks. You think I look Mexican?" He put a finger on his chest.

"You must think you can pull it off. You told the lady at the realty company..." She stopped and her eyes narrowed. "Did you, did you tell her I was your *wife*, or your *sister*?"

"It doesn't matter."

"Maj?"

"We were not married then."

"Jesus! So first I'm your sister, then I'm your wife. Too complicated for me, Doctor Aziz." She slid her chair back, teeth clenched, dragging the last syllable like a terrier. She stood and started to step around him. "Or is it Aguilar?"

She mocked him, his own name now from her lips, just like the nurses had played with it. He grabbed her arm and flung her back to the chair, nearly tipping it over. He rose over her and slapped his hand against the table. "I provide for you. This place where we live, this food." He shook the bag at her face. He halted, feeling foolish, angry at his own name. He wanted to smash her in the face; he could do this so easily, but, he thought, it would feel like he was hitting himself. He turned instead, snatched his jacket from the back of the chair, and slammed the door as he left.

She heard him gallop down the wooden steps and stared at the doorknob for an immeasurable time, then went to the window to look for him, into the gray evening that settled around the trees and the streetlight down the hill, but did not see him anywhere. The air in the kitchen was blue when she turned, smoke rising from the oven.

Majij marched to the end of the street, then turned and looked back to see if she was watching him. The curtain hung undisturbed at the window. Lights were on in the apartment below theirs, and several more on the second level; this startled him, and he understood that they really were not as alone in the building as he had thought. He turned and started walking again, into the wind, with his head tucked down, turning onto Main, passing one darkened business front after another, wondering who had heard them, wondering how much of their words might have made sense through the thickness of a carpeted floor, and with some element of shame, how the neighbors would think of them as quarrelsome and unhappy. They would think of him as a poor provider, not the way of a good Muslim. She had looked terrified when he left, and now his victory seemed selfish and trite.

He found himself in the sodium light of the Safeway parking lot. He estimated he had been walking only four or five minutes, and he looked back up the way he had just come. "I'm sorry," he said out loud to himself, "if I have frightened you," and he rehearsed the line two more times, each time accenting a different word, trying to decide how he would deliver them when he went back. He watched people come and go through the automatic doors for several minutes, and started to go in when he found he had left his wallet behind. He turned and started back to the apartment. He would give her ten dollars, three times a week, he decided, and she would follow this path exactly. He would walk it with her, once or twice, so she would understand.

*

Most mornings Majij left the apartment for a few hours to look for work, to sell clothes in a fine haberdashery, he imagined, though usually he'd wander around the men's stores, daydreaming, asking for an application only after a clerk grew suspicious of him. He had started with just over seventy-six thousand dollars American, including his last two weeks at the clinic, which had nearly doubled his little egg of hope, but he felt he should guard his money, reserve it for his passage home and his plans there. He would use Aguilar's driver's license initially, but he hadn't thought to look for a social security card. Maybe Aguilar didn't have one, the man's presence in this country more dubious than his own. He did have his own J-1 visa number, but they would see that the names did not match. Taking the license had been an impulse, and he was angry at himself now for his lack of foresight.

Majij had taken applications at Burger King and Jerry's Men's Wear, wanting to experiment with the credibility of his alias, but decided that without a social security number that matched his name it was simply too dangerous. A fuzzy logic loitered in his head, that Iraq had been at war with Iran and therefore, America would favor Iraq. Thus, if Rashid asked the FBI to locate him, they would. It was not an entirely sound theory, but it was congruent with his own sense of self-importance and helped feed the small thrill he enjoyed from his new clandestine existence.

He took a temporary position at a lumberyard instead, moving its inventory to a new location. Nine dollars an hour. "Off the books. The job won't last that long," they had said. It was physical labor he was unaccustomed to, and he tore the pocket of his khaki trousers the first day while moving some steel shelving. His shoes were filthy when he got back to the apartment, and his shoulders ached. Erika rubbed them without being asked, somehow sensing his stiffness.

The next day he stopped at the hardware store and purchased two pairs of generic denim work pants, some cheap athletic shoes, and a denim jacket. Now I dress like Aguilar, he thought, standing in line at the single cash register. Behind the counter he saw the copying machine, exactly where Erika had described it, cycling slowly, intermittent green light glaring from its lid, silent and freakish, as if she had conjured it into existence. He watched uneasily, wanting to touch it, stepping forward every few minutes until he was facing the woman behind the counter, who startled him when she asked for his money.

Through the mornings, his mind wandered with little focus on the assignment at hand, teaming up with a Nigerian exchange student who spoke politely but seldom. The rest of the crew were Montana teenagers, loud, foul-mouthed, swaggering boys who would grow up to be bullying and arrogant, like the men who controlled all things in America.

Erika occupied much of his thoughts, as he stacked boxes of light fixtures, electric drills, and cartons of nails. Erika beneath him, receptive and wet, but somehow never satisfied. Becoming like other American women, wanting more of him. *Je vous aime,* she had said. He had hesitated, feeling cornered. Pressured to respond, he finally answered with a quote, "The gift of lovers testify to invisible love." Still, he liked thinking about her thick hair, her bare shoulders, her nakedness in his private little world.

A chador, a real one—she must have this before they went to Hakim's. A *burka*? No, Hakim would laugh. An *abayah*, and he could watch the wind draw it around those hips, lifting its hem, he could stroke his fingers the length of her legs. She should be comfortable in putting it on and should know when to take it off. Overall, things had fallen into place as he had dreamed they would. After thirty-two years of loitering in stations and aborted journeys, he had boarded the train that was to be his life, approaching full speed.

Other mornings, he would grow uncertain; the days were too perfect, and it might all be enchantment, some seductive spell. It was she who had descended on him after all, stopping before his car that afternoon, her hair on his face, taking the place beside him, taking his breath, taking, taking, taking. Appearing without invitation, she might be a very clever *jinn,* a malevolent spirit targeting his carnal weakness, Fatima returned, laying a trap, scheming punishment for his indifference. Everything he had envied in his youth, the pale skin and blue eyes he'd longed for, he now must defend, this divine gift he did not deserve, that other men would fuck; she would invite them as soon as he turned his back. She would be taken away as soon as he committed his heart.

She knew a lot of things and maybe could see what he could not, castrating knowledge, when she willed it, like a witch. She might be centuries older than he. These ideas worried him, legends told by an ignorant people, aunts from the villages, toothless shopkeepers, *keshavarz.* All ghosts from his childhood, before he had learned the power attained by stepping outside oneself, outside of the authority that tried to make you obey—beyond the laws of Allah, and Majij shuddered invisibly when he thought this. Life by instinct. There lay a greater rhythm; one could feel this, things flowed as they should, automatically, unstoppable. It was a rhythm his brother, the *Faqih,* could not acknowledge, but Majij knew it was there, waiting.

"Aguilar! *Le gusta jugar trabajo?"* The foreman had shouted at him across the yard, paralyzing Majij momentarily before he finally responded with a nervous laugh. When he moved closer, Majij told him it was better that he speak English, and that he preferred it so as to not anger the other workers. He failed to respond to his adopted name several times the first day, but gradually the delay grew shorter before he would turn and answer, "Si," with a feigned Mexican accent. Think Mexican, he would tell himself, until at last, by the third week, he found himself lapsing into the idea that he was the reincarnation of Aguilar, a concept that both fascinated and disgusted him. This, too, he thought at times, was her fault.

It was during that week Mr. Gary had come through the yard, stopping at one group of workers and then another with a small book in his hand. When he stopped Majij at lunch, he opened the little book and asked him for his social security number. Majij faltered, then gave the phone number of his old clinic, deleting the last digit. He had rehearsed this and was ready to say, "Oh, I gave you my old phone number," should he be discovered.

But Mr. Gary did not care about the number. He wore brown, greasy overalls and a flannel shirt like Majij's own. He would give the number to someone else, who would not put a face with the number. Only at the end of the year would anyone notice. Then there would be a letter and a puzzled official somewhere. Majij always pictured the tired official working at night in a dark office with a solitary lamp and baskets of papers. *Aguilar in Bozeman. Better notify the FBI there. He is not real.*

*

The sun was higher in the sky each day he left the lumberyard, dismissed earlier as the pallets of unmoved inventory grew smaller and the days longer. Images haunted him some days of some college boy with muscles and a silly country voice, having discovered her loneliness and having now taken Majij's place, skipping classes, arriving at midmorning after he had gone. Some boy with clever talk, who knew all those musicians on television, kissing her, arms around her, on top of her, inside of her.

He took the driver's seat one morning and drove the five-ton van back to his apartment while Lateef spouted alarms, that they would be fired or arrested, pleading with him to return to the yard, Majij saying only, "Just a minute…it is not far…just a few blocks further," until they turned onto Fourteenth. The shade of the street, the quiet air, the softness of the pine needles absorbed the truck's sound as it rolled to a stop in front of the apartment.

Lateef sighed, hoping that since they had stopped, they would start their return soon. "This is very beautiful. This is where you live?"

"I forgot something. It will only be a moment."

As Majij came to the door, Erika pulled the curtain back, curling around the edge of the window so her bare legs couldn't be seen.

He opened the door with brutal deliberateness. "Where are you going?"

"I wasn't going anywhere. I'm not dressed. What happened?" She peeked through the curtain again. "Why do you have that truck?"

He walked through the apartment, not answering, every sense a loaded gun, prowling for the irregular creak, the breath of an intruder, the smell of bodies, the air of conspiracy. He looked in the closet. The bed was warm where she had tossed back the covers. *Nineteen Eighty-four* lay open, face down.

"You were reading?" He snatched up the book, closing it. "This is trash." He tossed the book back onto the bed.

In the bathroom, he saw his watch and lunged at it, slapping it on his wrist like lifesaving equipment. "I forgot my watch," he said, walking back to the front door and opening it. He stood there for half a minute, looking all around the room for any clue he might have missed on his first pass, then stretched and relaxed and beamed a smile at her. "I am home earlier, this afternoon. This is good, no?" He leaned out to take her hand, but she shied away from him and the open door.

She could see Lateef's puzzled face in the cab of the truck looking at her. "Yes."

"We do something fun. Go to a movie house maybe."

"Yeah, sure."

She watched through the window as the truck backed away, gears grinding before it lurched forward up the street. He had not worn his watch for over a month, telling her he was afraid he would break the crystal. Contention hung in the apartment now like poison gas, a rigor ran up her spine. She pulled on her blue jeans, wrapped her jacket around her, and took her paperback outside where it would be warmer. The chill followed her. She could not find her place in the book.

*

A test of will flared at the ticket office, Majij initially suggesting a film advertised by a poster of a blond girl in a bikini, holding an enormous pistol between her legs. But Erika screwed up her face and said "Barf!" and he finally agreed to *Empire of the Sun,* anxious to get out of the evening light and the small clusters of white-faced, blond-haired people strolling across the parking lot, worried that someone from the lumberyard might see him, all of the time aware of the police car that approached slowly from the street.

He took care that both of them had their own drinks, and he leaned over at the end of the previews to ask if she wanted anything else. After that, he was lost in the dark, in the central character on the huge screen, alone for two hours with his own youth.

Erika sat next to him, with his right hand in her left while she grazed popcorn slowly, absorbing the nearness of every other person, studying their silhouettes in the flicker to either side of them. She had started reading *Japan's Imperial Conspiracy* while her father was outlining it for a class the year before, and as she looked around, wondered if anyone else in the theater shared her perspective.

It was late evening when the film ended and they walked to the car, Majij solemnly quiet, tugging her hand across the parking lot like a small child. "He was an orphan." He said, almost to himself.

Headlights came on and engines started. A small plane buzzed across the darkening sky above them. As they pulled onto the street, she commented, "People say the Japanese, when they got to Nanking, threw the Chinese babies in the air and caught them on their bayonets."

Majij swerved the car across two lanes and pulled into a vacant bus loading station. He shuddered, then looked over at her, still clutching the wheel, with a terror that erased all of his features momentarily. "The Iraqis. They do that as well, to the people of my country."

His sudden disintegration took her unprepared, and she retreated against the door initially, studied his eyes, and deciding it was not anger, but grief, reached over and put her palm to the side of his face. He fell into her shoulder and she held him against her, afraid to let go, afraid he might break into pieces. The traffic shot by, car after car; no one would know, and no one would stop and help her figure out what to do next.

*

Majij came back to the apartment at one, the third Friday of June. He parked the Saab behind the building, walking around to the front, startling Erika, who sat on the stairs midway through her daily squirrel feeding ceremony. The squirrels shot up the trees at his appearance, Erika's first reflex to do the same. Instead she stood and backed up the stairs several steps.

"So I work to support these squirrels." He looked up at a branch where one remained, staring back at him. He walked up the steps, picking up the box of saltines, and put his arm around her waist. "Job is over. No more work to do there. I am home to be with you." He combed through her hair with his fingers spread. "You are uncovered." But he said it with a tone of seduction.

And they went to the bedroom without eating, and she unbuttoned his coarse blue twill shirt and unbuckled his belt and pulled down the blue denim, slowly, she had learned that he liked this. He seemed younger without the knot of the tie at his neck, like someone different, but she didn't say so, worried he might believe it an infidelity.

Afterward they lay on the twisted sheets, not sleepy, and listened to the sound of the daytime through the open window, the voices of birds, the traffic blocks away, the clatter of a garbage can and departing footsteps in the alley. It seemed to Erika there could be no purer freedom. Surely her parents had never felt this way. She thought it might be nice to have a baby, understanding now why people wanted to do that. She imagined it on the mattress between them, sleeping. A little girl.

Majij sat up after twenty minutes and pulled on his jeans, going into the living room and looking out through the curtain. He had intended to write a letter, a carefully worded letter, to his brother, explaining his new bride and his travel, alluding cleverly to his alias. Hakim would be impressed with his alias. Now his thoughts were scattered like an overturned table of dominoes. She did this. He opened the box of saltines and took out two of them, walking onto the deck and squatting, holding them near the first step, but the squirrels only leapt from one branch to another, glancing down at him with trepidation. He tossed the crackers into the yard and went back inside.

He looked in the bedroom again and she lay there, still looking out the window placidly, the afternoon sunlight playing across her long legs, the small mound of her pubis, her scalloped abdomen. He was drawn to go to her again, when a chill passed over him like an eagle's shadow over a rabbit. He did not really know her, where she had been, what seductions she may have woven in another life, this stunning, odd, strange girl or woman, and for a moment he could not remember where they were. What she did to him. A jinn, surely a jinn. He went back to the kitchen and called for her to get up.

11

At six thirty the next morning they left, cruising down East Main in the sun, still cool from the night. She glanced up as they passed the Safeway, then more of the city flickered by, and she thought of how little of it she had actually seen, cloistered in her apartment with an audience of squirrels. The school year was now over by three weeks, the lockers emptied at J. G. Wilson. Melinda would have turned her books in. The courses Erika had left unfinished now ran together in a great morass of trivial fragments, and she could not remember what the books had even looked like. The principal, maybe even the police, might sort through the papers she'd left behind, looking for clues. Her classmates would have no answers when questions were asked, but they would think later that maybe they could have teased her less, realized just how smart, and *tortured*, she really was. Or they would think she'd gone, like Trish, with better things to do. Or they would think she was dead. This last possibility troubled her. People eventually forgot the dead.

The town became warehouses and then truck stops, and then at the easternmost margin where the rangeland resumed, they accelerated onto I-90. Concentration had been so difficult in those last few months of classes. She had been on stage at Wilson, unable to remember her lines, every day in the glare of everyone's scrutiny. She was not leaving friends, so no bonds tugged her to reconsider. She had even stopped missing Melinda. All of that life and everyone who affronted her were far, so far away, that they became like a confusing dream that grew hazier with every passing minute of daylight.

Sleep came more easily now, the mornings clear and calm as a pond. She felt like she understood trade, the economy that adults talked about, had learned a hundred or so words of Farsi, read a science fiction novel that still resonated with her, and had learned things about her own body and what it was capable of. This was growth, learning of another kind, learning what she had *chosen* to learn. She looked over and felt close to him, they were equals in this capsule of steel and glass and black upholstery, moving across the land. She wanted to talk to him about the novel or Persia or the future of the planet, it did not matter. She stroked her palms over the contour of her abdomen beneath the seat belt and looked at him, troubled that it might become a silent morning. Already he seemed adrift. "Wouldn't it be neat if we had a baby?"

He looked at her as if struck by a dart.

"He could have your dark hair and my blue eyes. Wouldn't it be beautiful?"

"No," he said. She had actually hinted at this one morning two days prior, while she was yammering on and on about things that Majij dismissed as unimportant, things he thought most girls her age yammered about. Then he had heard the reference, 'baby.' "I mean later on. That would be nice. Much later on, don't you think? You want to finish high school, no?" He rubbed her knee affectionately.

She deflated.

"You have been taking your pill, haven't you? That is why I put you on them. I thought I made that perfectly clear. I have seen what happens to a girl when she has a baby when she is fifteen."

"I'm almost sixteen. And I'm not pregnant," she said. "I was just kind of thinking about the future."

Both of them were silent for a while. Majij noticed a billboard, 'Jerry's Gentleman's Club 44 Live Girls.' He had been to places like that when he first arrived in Chicago, after the shah fell. Long legs, high heels, a strand of yarn.

"Stupid sign," she said.

He looked at her and wondered if she had read his mind.

"I mean, who would want to go to that place if they had dead girls? Or stuffed girls?"

"You think too much," he said.

"I used to be the smartest kid in my class."

"Good," he said. "That means you will learn things faster."

"You're really smart, too."

He smiled.

"It would be a smart baby."

"Stop that! I don't want to hear any more about babies right now."

His tone, she decided, was theatrical, and she chose to believe that it was a false posture. He was right about the practicality of it all and how it would capsize any vision of her completing school, and her parents, God! He was always so, so...*logical*, but she wanted him to dream, just a little bit. "Later," she said.

"Much later." Majij stole a glance at her profile and imagined a tall, fair boy, someday, with blue eyes and black hair, as she had said. A superb tennis player, all of the girls would want him, but he would study, follow his father, even become a surgeon. Take over my work when I have worked enough, he thought, and he relaxed his grip on the wheel. He looked over at her again, and she looked into his eyes, this fine girl who would have his children, and glimpsed a future full of the families of their friends and their children's children. He sought out her fingers and took her hand.

Between the seats, Majij had shoved that morning's copy of *The Bozeman Chronicle*, taken from another apartment doorstep before they left, and she unfolded it. 'Van Cliburn to play in Chicago.' Another article alluded to the killing of students by tanks in Tiananmen Square, sometime earlier that month. And in the right front page column, "Supreme Court: Approves to Execute Minors and Mentally Retarded."

She sighed. "The Chinese killed a bunch of students."

"So?"

"Maj, they were students. Unarmed. College kids. Maybe high school kids. Just protesting."

Majij snapped his sunglasses open without looking at her and put them on.

"Maybe they should not have protested."

"Is that all you think? Maj, c'mon…what if it had been me?"

"But it wasn't. They are Chinese students, in China. The Chinese have the right, to do whatever they like with their own people." His tone softened. "It is too bad, I agree. But those students, they knew the risk."

"They say if you kill one person, you kill a whole world."

"I don't believe that. What if the person is not important?"

"Important. Important to who?" She searched his face, but he was suddenly busy looking at the map, out of the window, or at the instruments, and it struck her that he was pretending. When he finally turned, he gave her an innocent, puzzled look. She folded the paper and turned in the seat. "So what about, like, in communist countries, where they come at night and arrest people. They just disappear?"

"You do not know that that happens."

"You know it does."

He started to reply when a bubble formed deep inside of him, gas of something decayed for eighteen years, rising through the bog. It stopped him, and he could not swallow it. Neighbors who had looked away, not daring to speak to his mother. The beginning of the time of emptiness.

"My dad said, when Stalin…"

"Why do you care what your father said? I am tired of this. Is it not because of your father you are here?"

"Well you're here because of your dad. What's that got to do with anything?"

The bubble choked him. The disciplinarian, detached, distracted, missing so long ago. The man his mother had worshipped. He took another deep breath, preparing to speak, then stopped himself.

Several mileposts passed. She looked at the classifieds for a few minutes and wondered if she could be a receptionist in a chiropractor's office. 'No experience necessary.' All of life was like that, and it didn't seem like such a bad thing. Reincarnation would be the scary part. She folded back to the front page. "Oh, this is great. The ayatollah has forbidden women to appear on TV. You sure you want us to go there?"

"Do you want to be on TV?"

"No, that's not the point. But if I did want to, say, be a news announcer…"

"But you don't."

"How do you know what I want?"

"Because you say you want to be nurse. Or do you lie to me because I am rich doctor?"

"No."

Majij puckered his lips in a pout and remained silent. The morning heat fluttered in the windows. Two more mileposts passed.

"So what else do they do to women?"

"They don't *do* anything *to* women."

"Like, why do they have to wear these?" And she flicked at the point of the scarf that had blown up over her head and now hung like a quail's bob just above her eyes.

"They do not have to. But *hejab* is proper."

"Hey-job?"

"Proper dress, hejab. It is women's armor, abayah and chador. When Iranian men see women so dressed, they do not bother them, pinch them."

"Nobody pinches me now. Guys aren't like that here. Decent guys are courteous."

"That's because you are young girl."

"Do young girls do what we did yesterday afternoon?"

Majij went on. "So the ayatollah, he decides what is best for the people…"

"Everybody, or just the Iranians?"

"For the believers. He is the voice of Allah on earth."

"Like the pope, huh?" She turned away from him and looked out across the fields. She tingled inside and wanted to be back in bed with him, but now there was this draconian attitude. She imagined the US Army firing machine gun bullets through all of her classmates at Wilson, and she could not put the image away. He didn't, couldn't, really believe those things. After a while, she pivoted in the seat again. "So if the big revolution was nine years ago, and it was God's will, how come God's just making up his mind on some stuff now?"

He snorted and did not look at her. "You are very disrespectful."

"You always say that when I don't agree. Anyway, I think the big head rush of having a revolution is getting to change everything. And once people, like, take over, they still want to keep changing things,' cause it gives them such a buzz." *These bureaucracies must keep moving forward, to survive.* She had read this, or her father had read it to her, and it remained cryptic in her memory, like hieroglyphics of a lost language. Now it made perfect sense. A society defined by its prohibitions instead of its rights. You would need to keep finding new things to forbid. He had stopped talking, so she turned away again, into her own thoughts.

The sky was blue and the clouds white, the midmorning sun brilliant. She wiped her sunglasses on the edge of her T-shirt. One lens was scratched, and there was a little bar across the top like she had seen on mountain explorers in *National Geographic*. She had bent them so markedly that Majij couldn't wear them anymore. She slipped them on and leaned forward, facing the heavens through the windshield, and the sky was even bluer. She untied the chador and tossed it unceremoniously into the back seat; it wasn't protecting her from anything. She rolled the window completely down and stuck her head out, far enough that the wind thundered in both of her ears, while Majij shouted at her, words she could not distinguish from the roar of the summer heat.

*

At one o'clock, they pulled over at a Pilot truck stop in Billings. Majij demanded she use the bathroom, forbidding her to tarry in the store, angry that she would have to go through the store at all to use the toilets, which he thought should be, properly, behind the building. "When you come back, walk past my car, out around that truck there, before coming here, then get into the car quickly."

"But what if that truck's not…"

"Go, go." He glanced at the speaker on the post above the pumping instructions and waved her away, feeling like their conversation had already been recorded. When she returned, he told her to wait and ran into the store to pay. He tossed a paper sack into her lap when he got back, and two twist-top plastic bottles of Pepsi. They pulled onto the frontage road and up the ramp.

"I like Dr. Pepper." She pulled the cellophane apart and spread the two slabs of soggy bread. "Why cheese and ham?"

"Why not? You are not hungry?"

"Not for ham."

"You don't eat pork? Are you becoming good Muslim? Finally? Good Jew, maybe?"

She twisted open her bottle and it hissed. "No. Just trying to cut down on meat in general."

"Oh. So you become Hindi now." He tried to sound jovial.

"What kind of sandwich did you get?" She reached over between his legs and started to unwrap it.

"It is turkey." He swatted her hand away.

She gave him a cheated look.

"It was the only one they had."

The ham looked subtly different at the edges; instead of pink, it was brown, and after deciding this wasn't caused by the color of the sunlight through the tinted windshield, she flipped it out the window. "Marry a doctor. Die of food poisoning," she singsonged.

He frowned at her.

"It didn't get on the car, if that's what you're thinking." She set the two pieces of bread on the dashboard, glistening side up. "Maj, don't you wish sometimes I was older?"

"How much older would you like to be?"

"Old enough to pick my own damn sandwich."

"I am sorry you are unhappy about that." He inspected his fingernails while he thought. "You are runaway. I don't want you to be caught and punished." He looked over at her. "Also, I don't think people, here, people in that gas station, would understand what is special between us." He looked forward down the highway. "In Iran, it is not so unusual. The ayatollah recently decreed girls may be married at nine."

"Whoa." Erika cringed. "Doesn't it hurt, the girl, I mean?"

"Oh no. It is not like that. They are not to have sex until she is ready to have children, until the menses comes, you know." He felt her stare. "It is so a good girl from a good family is assured she will be taken care of." He rolled up his window to think more clearly. How assured would her parents feel now? So her father was a *professor*, hard and critical. It might have taken a year to convince the man of his worthiness. Perhaps forever. His own dishonesty bit him on the nose and he wrestled with it, trying to rationalize their elopement. "The girl's father and mother, they are quite happy, for they have picked the man."

"Am I a good girl?"

He ignored this. "And the girl, she learns very early, what pleases her husband."

And that's what you're doing with me. "So don't you think, I mean, what's to stop the man if he wants to have sex with her before it's time?"

"It is not *Sirat alMustaqeem*. How do I say? It is not the way of good Muslim. So do not even think of such things. You are not a good Muslim for even seeing this in your mind." But as quickly as he spoke, his mind grew into a tangle of young limbs, perspiration, the smell of adolescence, the face of Fatima. Hakim had made it clear, by means of telling Majij repeatedly to stay out of theaters of Western films, that Hakim knew those men with the locks and chains and gasoline; Hakim might have been one of them. But Majij had not known Fatima's parents, so he could not have warned them, could he? And so, with her parents gone, Fatima had become his, her full lips, willowy legs, narrow hips, and nearly hairless pubis. So many little urchin girls back then, virgin children of the war or the revolution, clinging to life with the only currency they had. He might have kept her. Maybe God had sent her to him. She would be about twenty now, maybe full of babies, but he had not kept her, and he knew why now, and the shame of it turned his stomach. She might be dead; he wished she was dead, so she couldn't know, so she couldn't tell, and he felt a wrench of guilt tear through his chest again and looked at the palm of his hand. There was no scar, no mark. It had not been enough. He glanced over at Erika and believed she knew what he was thinking, as she looked out the window pretending innocence. Several minutes passed and he struggled to disentangle himself from the web she had lured him into.

Erika watched a farm approach on the right-hand side and wondered what it was like to live there, to come home from school and help your dad or an older brother, handling ropes and pitchforks and bags of oats, collecting eggs from the henhouse, feeding horses, bringing cows in, and maybe having to milk them. Or maybe she would have to do that in the morning before a school bus came. Kids on farms could drive; after all, they had to. They were needed to drive pickups and tractors or maybe those big things that picked wheat. Kids were important on a farm.

"That was a very dirty thing to say." He spoke loudly and slapped her shoulder with the back of his hand.

"Ouch!" She put her other hand on the shoulder and twisted away from him. "What was that for?"

"I strike you to clear your mind of this."

"Like shaking an Etch-a-Sketch? Do I have to go sit in the back seat now, too?"

"You are very insolent girl. So sarcastic."

"I'm not being sarcastic. Just don't want to get hit again." She sat forward, shook her hair, and brushed it away from her face. "It's just that," she began again, cautiously, "there's men in this country that like to hurt, have sex, with little kids."

"This country, yes," he said authoritatively. "The United States is a degenerate place. The Saudis, they do that terrible thing also, with little boys." He shook a finger in the air. "And the Turks also…"

He was about to add the Iraqis to his list when she spoke again. "What about the Jews? In Israel, I mean."

Majij hesitated. They would have to be worse, far worse. He remembered a neighbor woman from his childhood who had terrified him. "When they catch the Palestinian children, they eat them."

"Bullshit. It would be on the news by now."

"Do not talk like that. The Jews, they control the television!"

"That's just conspiracy thinking. Every group in the world has said that. We told kids the Germans did that, in World War One."

"Who is *we*? Were you there?"

"I still don't believe it. I don't think you believe it either."

"Do not pretend to know what I believe." He slapped his fingers on the edge of the steering wheel and the car shimmied slightly.

"Okay, okay. So what exactly does the *ayatollah* believe?"

Majij weighed her question, looking for some trap, realizing the possibility that he might fall into his own machination. She could do that. He smiled and glanced over at her, cautious and firm. "What the ayatollah, what everyone wants, is for the West to be gone, or not so big, everywhere, in our Iran.

So that when we go down street, there is not McDonald's, Sony, Coca-Cola sign everywhere, taking money,"

"Sony is Japanese, isn't it?"

"So?"

"So that isn't Western."

"It is Western inventions. All of these things the shah brings, buys with the people's money, technology that brings evil, tempts people away from the faith. Dance, movies, television, music that makes young people want to…" but he stopped there, knowing it was the voice of his brother and knowing what his brother would say next. "It is just that we have not been our own people, for one hundred years or more. Always, someone else tells us, takes the best of our country."

"So if TV is so evil, how come the ayatollah is always using it to get people all jazzed? Would be kinda' like the gun-control people using guns to get rid of all the gun owners."

Majij furrowed his brow and puckered. "And bad jets. The US, they sell us bad jets, they all crash. Very expensive. The Americans take important pieces with them. Sabotage."

"So is it sabotage or bad American jets? The Libyans crash their jets too. They have Russian jets I believe."

"When is this? How do you know this?"

"It was in the paper. Just before, you know, I moved in. Qaddafi sent two MiGs…"

"But the Jews control the papers…"

"Right, the Jewish pope. Come off it. Wanna know what I think?"

"No, I do not want to know what you think."

"I don't think Arabs know how to fly."

He took his foot from the accelerator, abruptly. "I could put you out of this car, right here, right now."

"What are you so bent about? You're not even Arab."

He started to slow the car onto the shoulder.

"People would want to know how I got out here, huh?" She took the remaining piece of bread and smeared mayonnaise garishly around her lips, leaning forward and puckering. "We're fugitives, Maj. Just like Bonnie and Clyde."

He recoiled. "Don't do that." He accelerated back into traffic.

"I'm sorry. It's a generalization. I still don't understand, though, what Khomeini is trying to do."

"Islam, it is very old culture, much science and astronomy. Though not so much recently, due to this noisy Western culture that crushes everything it touches. There is no reason, given time, Iran cannot build own jets, Islamic design. Anyway, this is what some people in Iran think should be done."

"Huh." Erika twisted a strand of her hair thoughtfully. "So you guys are gonna start from like, nothing? Reinvent physics and science?"

No answer.

She rocked about in her seat and turned to face him again. "You're a doctor, right? Is everything you learned, is it like already written in some Muslim book somewhere? What if somebody's got pneumonia? You only going to give them medicine from Iran?"

"Knowledge, it is from God, from Allah. It is for all people to use." His brother chanted with him, inside his head.

"So sometimes Allah makes knowledge pop up in some American chemical company somewhere?" She went on. "It's like the Russians. They hated the Nazis, all that belief in genetics and a superior race and stuff. So the Russians burned all their books on genetics, for like, *growing things*, and set their farming back hundreds of years. People starved."

Majij spoke though his teeth. "Look. I do not know where you go with this. You try to make fool of me? Of Islam? I do not know all that the ayatollah intends. Only that they believe things were more just, one hundred, two hundred years ago. No one starves." He shook his head from side to side and squinted, as if she had hung crepe before his eyes.

She was silent for a while and then spoke in a small careful voice. "So what part do you keep? What part do you throw away? We should know before we go there."

*

What part of her would need to be erased? Only the obvious influence of Western inequity, clear to those they might pass in public in Tehran, he thought. No one would listen to all of that pointless history she had memorized. To whoever she might meet or talk to, close to her own age, it would mean nothing. There was no family. Hakim would have no reason to visit; he might not even come back to Iran for a decade. There would be no one to report them. One only had to pretend to throw away, in public, this much he understood from the magazines and the journalists and the papers. Just pretend, and the morals police will drive on by to bother someone else who is more arrogant, someone they can make an example of. But will she understand, *to pretend?* She will call it *lying*, simpleminded girl. A Jinn? No, an empty vessel. She is not evil, just the reflection of it.

Always, there is something to give up. She is starting to understand this. But not the sex. She likes that. She must like it more. Girls give all to their first lover. A bed of black satin, a hotel built by the French, the contrast of her, her hair blond as the day he first saw her, the thought pours down through him. He feels himself rise. So she does this to him. Who controls whom?

He had forgotten, momentarily, what highway they were on; for a while, they were driving toward Tabriz. He watched the shoulder, alarmed that he had let this happen, and he wondered once more if she had powers to do this. "I am a physician," he thought. "I control, I can control what I choose." Finally, a road sign appeared, 'Miles City, 22 miles.' They were on Interstate 94, heading east as planned.

*

The Saab crested a high point between several buttes and began a long descent into a valley of pastureland dotted with dark cattle and scattered, rusting automobile bodies, doors open and hoods up. A gravel frontage road swung near the highway, and mobile homes, sides of oxidized tin and faded pastels, branched off it at irregular distances with dirt driveways. At one, a red tricycle sat near the ruts in the muddy yard, and a black-haired girl of four or five stood alone on the front steps and pointed directly at Erika, and Erika turned her head, holding her gaze as they passed. She shifted in her seat and looked out the rear window as the row of trailers grew smaller. Somewhere outside of The Dalles, there were people living like that, she thought. Someone at school might have even grown up there, and she contemplated this with the attention given to small epiphanies, a fleeting compassion for the child she could no longer see. She watched Majij as he drove for several minutes and wondered if he had ever lived in such a place.

"Maj."

"What?" he asked without looking at her.

"Maj," she repeated, "why exactly can't you get a license, anywhere you want?"

"It is political. Mostly because I am not board certified yet."

"But you're a doctor in Iran, aren't you?"

"Yes, yes. I am doctor in Iran. I told you that, you know that."

"How do you get certified?"

"You take an examination, after you finish residency."

"Did you finish residency?"

He felt his face grow warm. "It is long story. Things happened, and I did not have time." He felt her pass her fingertip over the tip of his ear. He rolled down the window and the wind roared past, and he thought of the pediatrics clinic where he had been assigned at the time, serving an urban poor where mothers brought their children for simple things—colds, allergies, bladder infections, immunizations. More interesting cases, surgeries or congenital malformations, were handled at the university hospital. He felt misused, relegated to the urban clinic, as if he lacked some esoteric wisdom essential for the complex cases, cases where he might actually learn something. The girl seemed old for the clinic, eleven according to the chart, but breasts already like halves of oranges. A pure, delicate abdomen.

"My stomach hurts" was all she would volunteer, her mother adding that there had been "blood in her poop." The mother, not the girl, he was certain, smelled of cigarettes, like all American women, and she left the room to go to the adult walk-in clinic, coughing as the door closed behind her. He was left with the nurse at his side and the girl, the perfect little girl, before him. The gloves were all size eight, even the boxes crammed below the sink with the bottles of iodine and spray bottles of bleach. Nothing for his small, intelligent hands. Purposely overlooked again.

"Size seven," he reminded the nurse as she left the room.

He waited so long for the nurse to return. He waited too long, he thought, to examine the girl. Surely she was cold. Surely she wanted this to be over. He had been very gentle, and the girl did not complain, did not say anything. If the mother was so concerned, she would not have left the room. Each time he looked at the girl, she was looking at him. With hope? She was moist, then cool and damp, and felt feverish. She did not speak as he ran his fingers over her abdomen and pressed gently at each pelvic rim. He placed a finger inside of her. A uterus there, a cervix, full, ready.

Still no nurse, no gloves.

The girl looked at him in continued wonderment. Her hymen was perforated. Was he the first to examine her, as her mother had said? The girl said nothing to the nurse, who seemed so alarmed when she returned, a box of seven and a box of seven and a half beneath her arm, which she dropped. She had submitted a horrible report.

The meeting in the chairman's office was brief, but the most terrible moment of his life. Dr. Funderburk, stoic behind his desk, said little to him, all of their friendship gone. Harry Freeman, the school's legal counsel, on the far side of the desk, would not look at him at all. A Jew. He would get money from this, no matter what happened.

Erika was speaking, but the roar in the window drowned all but her inflection. She was still questioning him.

The girl's parents entered, the Kreiters, he remembered—the greasy, bullish father, the mother, crying, her brown makeup running like thin dirty water down her cheeks. The details of the rest of the meeting raced by in a blur, voices rose, accusations and a fist, the finality of that afternoon struck as solidly as any physical blow. Majij's head swam, and for a moment, his vision faded to gray.

"Jesus!" Erika grabbed the wheel and the car lunged back into the lane from the shoulder.

Majij focused and took the wheel and glanced at her. "Thank you." He stretched his fingers over the wheel. There was no part of this recollection he could share with her that would not trigger the same disgust. Funderburk had stared at Majij for a very long time, and Majij had searched the face for something familiar, some offer, some promise, but found none.

"Maj?"

His contract had not been renewed. Other programs where he applied the following year universally told him they had no openings.

"You okay?" Erika stroked the back of his hand. "So what exactly is a *residency?*"

"It is where you spend many hours at the hospital for extra training. I already do this, in Iranian hospital."

"So why do one here?"

"More money can be made in American hospitals, but I must have American residency. Like I said, very political. Iran, America, used to be good friends. Now that the shah is gone, Iranian doctors are not wanted so much."

"Oh, I understand." And she turned away from him again.

There was a pause in her attention, a long silence that seemed to fill the rest of the afternoon and begged him to try answering the question differently, but he would not, for in retelling his plight repeatedly, it had become the only truth he knew.

*

At Miles City, they turned south on 59, and in forty-five minutes passed through Volburg, the sun now lower in the sky. The approach of night always comforted Majij, who believed that, as in his own country, the further into the rural outlands one traveled, the less informed the police. For reasons he hadn't fully identified, he felt sure his license number was wanted by now, and toyed with various schemes to steal someone else's. When parked for any length of time, he started draping an old towel casually out of the hatchback so it obscured their plate, and several times forgot it was there until he saw it as they drove on the highway, behind them the next morning, fluttering like a banner in the rearview mirror.

Several nights they slept in the reclining seats of the Saab in the cool air of the foothills of the Rocky Mountains. Once in a campground, where they managed a fire in an iron box intended for picnickers, near a concrete table, feeding it twigs, leaves, wastepaper, and cups from the trash barrels until it died away, the heat vanishing with the flame, only a ghostly white column rising into the light of infinite stars powdered across the moonless sky above them. She pulled him against herself and felt a tingle and wanted him, there, but the interior of the car was so cramped and irregular. Majij looked into the sky through the open sunroof with a wonder that bordered on fear, utterly lost. She wanted to pull him from that and into herself and keep him there until morning, but he remained distant, hypervigilant, and turned away from her.

On another night they pulled over at ten thirty into a rest area where Majij tried to build a fire, but the matches were damp from the perspiration of his shirt pocket, and one after another they crumbled until he wadded the book of them and threw them into the charcoal pit.

"C'mon. It's not that cold anyway." She tugged him toward the car. She had opened both of the car doors.

"People could steal our things."

"Not with us right here." She ran over and turned the ignition switch partway. The radio blared with clarinet, an arrangement she had danced to with her father. 'Bewitched, Bothered, Bewildered.' She took both of his hands. "Let's dance. It'll keep us warm."

Majij studied her moonlit face, full of sincerity, made an awkward step, then another sideways, then stopped and looked across the parking lot where a row of eighteen-wheelers sat at idle.

"Don't stop. Look, I'll show you." She tried to move him again. "It's a slow song. Nobody's watching." She slipped an arm around his waist. He felt brittle.

He allowed her to steer him, stiffly, to the left, to the right. His feet dragged in the wet grass and he lost his balance, but she caught him and pulled him back. Her closeness, momentarily so arousing, was now a force to resist. He let go of her and stood away. "No, not here. I just cannot do this."

The melody faded away. "You were doing fine." She took his hands again and pressed her lips into his neck and began to sway her hips against his, but he had become as fixed to the earth as one of the pines. An ad for Sominex came on. They both sat on the edge of a picnic table.

"There are just some things I have not learned," he said in a fragile voice. "I've been very busy in my life."

"You've taught me a lot of things. Just let me teach you this."

"Maybe I will learn later. In Iran."

"Is that allowed?"

"Anything can be done in one's own house."

"But will there be music?"

"I don't know," he said. "So you dance like this, rub your body, with boys?"

"At school? No. My father taught…"

"Your father." He stood up.

She took his hand and jerked it. "I was little. We didn't 'rub bodies.' He just taught me." She reached across and took his other hand and he relaxed. "Didn't your dad teach you anything?"

"My father." And he stopped, and his thought sank into the shadow at their feet.

She watched his lips, waiting, and finally squeezed his fingers. "Did you have a dad?"

He inhaled deeply. "My father," he said with a quaver in his voice. "My father," he repeated, "was taken away, was killed. When I was young." He looked her in the eyes. "About your age. For believing too much in an idea." He stood up, went over to the car, and turned off the radio. "So the lesson *he* taught me was never to believe too much in one thing." A moving van, yellow and green in the moonlight, pulled into the far side of the lot and turned off its lights. They both looked at it. "We should sleep now," he said. He rummaged in the glove compartment, producing the medicine bottle. He placed a red-and-white capsule in his mouth and pressed another into her palm.

*

They drove past long blocks of motels in each town as they waxed and waned along the roadsides, ill-repaired places of peeling pastels and stonework from another decade, cracked, empty pools, and pools filled in with geraniums and mums, all of them bearing at least one incomplete neon sign. One announced, "...ancy," and Erika commented that only very nervous people would be welcome there. Another read, "MOTE," to which Erika responded that it pretty well described the whole village. Her favorite, and she always asked Majij to look for another, as if they were a national chain, was "UN... DERBIRD LO...GE," which she chose to interpret, combining German and French, to mean "under the bird box." She laughed each time she tried to say this and expected Majij at least to see part of her pun, in French, but he was absorbed elsewhere and only looked at her blankly before resuming his search for a place to have her for the night.

Majij had quietly fabricated a pathetic story to tell the motel clerks, of financial ruin involving his lost sister, who had come to America to work as a maid and was certainly nearby, and he had several variations of this in which a mother or father had died (certainly true) or someone still needed to escape from Iran, which was truest, as Majij saw it, in a very philosophical sense. Majij would eventually obtain a lower rate after agreeing to take the room for six or seven days while he explored the surrounding communities for the sister he'd always dreamed of. Only the Pakistani owners closed the registration book while he still spoke, turning away from him in midsentence, as if he were retelling an old, distasteful joke. He returned to the car at one office as soon as he smelled the curry.

"They are full," he said as they turned in a semicircle around the nearly vacant parking lot.

Each week or so, this ceremony was repeated, finding the motel row of each sand-worn settlement, the gateway for the weary vacationers of past decades, on old highways to places no one in North America dreamed of going anymore. Parking lot to parking lot, he would study the diners, the Indian jewelry shops nearby, the other cars backed into the spaces on the uneven pavement (too many meant too many curious onlookers, too few meant it was too expensive or too dirty), and the alleys behind the motels, should they have to leave quickly. He knew you could bribe a policeman in towns this small, but wasn't sure just how much it would require or what to say or at what point you should show the money, a scene he had rehearsed in his mind and now prayed would never come up. More and more he found the natives staring at him or his bride. It was not so easy to be lost into the wild west of America. Each week the ceremony of finding that special place, so special after she was sitting on the bed and the door locked, grew a little longer.

One evening in southern Wyoming they silently watched CNN as the casket of Khomeini bobbed along, held high by the arms of wailing, turbaned men in a swarm of thousands, suspended like a leaf in a brook. At one point the casket fell and the body tumbled onto the pavement and the crowds engulfed it, dozens of hands tearing away strands of linen.

"Wow," Erika said finally. "Is that how they bury everyone in Iran?"

"No," Majij said, embarrassed. "Those people are ignorant. They are, how would you say? 'Hill-a-billies.'" He rose abruptly and turned off the television and went out onto to the second-level walkway, closing the door behind him. He went down the steel steps, leaned against a rusty support, and stared at the insect-crusted grille of the Saab, feeling embarrassed by the scene that had just unfolded. It was good while the ayatollah was sick; nothing changed. But all sick people, old sick people, die eventually, and now he felt stupid for not anticipating this. The administration could change, they could forbid any foreign-born women entering. They could forbid his own return. They might allow both of them in and then execute them both. They might even reestablish relations with the United States, and they might both be extradited. He only knew that until a few minutes before, he had felt happier than he had in his entire lifetime, and now none of it could be relied upon. Oh, how seductive women were, making a man blind to any danger. He walked around the car slowly. In the back seat lay a copy of *Newsweek* with Khomeini's picture on the cover. She was smarter than he had expected. Just last week she had read it to him, how the old man was dying. A smart girl from America would not be welcomed by people like that in Iran.

A strip mall stretched half the length of the block across the street, above and behind that the interstate, and above that, on a grassy hillside a mile or two distant, someone had built a ranch home. It faced west, to enjoy the sunsets, Majij supposed. He was beneath them, whoever they were; they looked over and beyond his misery, safe from the frustrations of the itinerant. How to get a house like *that* and stay there forever, apart from Islam, the police, her parents, and his brother, with this wonderful satin girl—the question taunted him to the brink of contempt.

It was not her fault. He'd seen her and taken her, and no one could ever pry her away. She was his. Life on this earth was beautiful enough and they belonged together. He would push on with his plan.

When he returned he watched her through the window, seated on the bed. She held the remote and had turned the television back on, where waves of devout Iranians swayed in the street, a turbulent tide, *an ocean of God,* his brother would say. But his brother would not be down there, crushed by the mass of their ignorant passion. He would be on the roof with a radio in hand, directing it all. If you looked closely, there were always men on the roofs, but Majij could only imagine himself one of them until his infidelity to his faith and his counterfeit soul betrayed him.

12

They were just north of Denver and the sun was at its zenith. Erika stroked the insides of her thighs, the smoothness that seemed at times to command his every breath, and thought of the previous night's moon, their last in Wyoming, then squirmed and broke her legs free of the perspiration that had glued her skin to the bucket seat. The chador stuck to the skin above her upper lip from the moisture of her breath and it smelled bad, a cheesy odor that grew stronger at the tails, stiffer with accumulated dried saliva. She pulled it loose and it fluttered at the suction of the partially rolled down window.

"All of this will end. God cannot ignore indecency his punishment is coming." He swept his hand before him across the windshield, both lanes of traffic, and the Plymouth minivan with the "Baby on Board" sign in the rear window just ahead of them.

These apocalyptic visions erupted from him every week or so with such regularity that Erika started to sense when the tide of anxiety was rising. He'd become quiet, usually in the late morning, his thoughts subterranean, then pop up somewhere distant from her, God's warrior. Guessing what triggered the eventual outbursts became a morbid little game she played with herself.

Once in Montana, it had been a billboard for a casino. In Sheridan, he had gone into a bank to cash a check and had exploded after getting into the car. When she mentioned the disaster of the Exxon Valdez, showing him a photo of a grease-laden duck, and said, "It's summer there. We could go help out for a month or two," he had responded with a long diatribe about how easy it was to be wasteful with that which was stolen.

Erika looked out the window at the brown terrain. They had been falling downhill all morning, like Moses descending from Sinai at seventy miles per hour upon the golden calf; this had gone on for hours since they left Cheyenne. Factory Outlet Mall, destroyed by God's flames. Denny's and La Quinta, into the burning pitch. Billy Dee's Steak House, seventy-two ounces free, if you can eat it before the rapture, she thought. Regular unleaded, self-serve, $1.05 per gallon, cash or credit. *Would gasoline make hell hotter?*

"Do we need any gas?"

He looked at her, puzzled. "We filled up in Cheyenne." He glanced at the gauge. "You haven't been listening to me, have you?"

"I have too."

"So what was the last thing I said to you? Can you tell me that?"

"You were trying to decide what to get me for my birthday."

He scowled. "You know that isn't true."

"Aren't there places you'd think God would destroy first? Like Bangkok? I've read that, like, half the people there have AIDS. All kinds of prostitutes and stuff."

He rubbed his chin thoughtfully. He had two theories, both proposed originally by his brother: one, that AIDS had been invented by Jewish scientists to destroy black people. Another, that it was one of God's scourges on the faithless. He knew that the two theories weren't compatible, so he hadn't voiced them yet.

"You can't be too careful with your company,…" she sang.

He seemed lost in thought.

"I can feel the devil *sitting* next to me." She poked a finger beneath his armpit.

"What is this? You think I am the devil?"

"It's just a song."

"On the radio? A song about the devil? For the devil?"

"It's about Bangkok."

"Bangkok," he said finally. He glanced around the floor as if he had dropped his script. "It has become that way because the Orient has been sodomized by the West. Now," he said, reaching across and tugging at the far side of her scarf. "*Purdah*. Cover yourself."

He would come back after a few hours or by tomorrow morning. "In a sec." She took off the scarf off and held it tightly in the flutter of the wind, hoping some fraction of its odor would dissipate, then refolded it so the freshest edge circled her face.

*

Majij crossed through the center of Denver with an agonizing vision, shifting uncomfortably in his seat, troubled by and enjoying a memory of a girl in a magazine he had discarded, and the sight of Erika that morning pulling on her socks. At West Sixth, he exited, and after a few minutes, stopped the car in the parking lot of the largest mall Erika had ever seen. As an afterthought, he rolled down the windows and instructed her not to speak to a soul, to pretend to be asleep if anyone approached.

"If I don't talk, they're going to think I'm dead," she told him. But he was off and through the double doors a minute later.

He wandered through a Nieman Marcus and then Saks before he stopped at a Victoria's Secret, wandering about the store, both aroused and enfeebled by his own ignorance until a girl, a blond whisper of a girl whose perfume made him dizzy, led him to the undergarments, providing him affirmation along the way.

"Can I assume this is all for the same special someone?" the girl asked.

Majij blushed. "Of course."

"I only asked because you picked up D-sized hose, and the lingerie is 'Small.' Do you know her size?"

Majij started to gesture the dimensions of an imaginary Erika next to him, stammering, correcting himself.

The girl nodded several times and finally asked. "How old is she?"

"Fifteen," Majij answered, aware as quickly that the girl stood silent, slack-jawed. "What I mean is that I have known her since, for, fifteen years."

"Right," she said, stepping around him, swapping the 'D' hose for 'B,' but she didn't look him in the eye for the rest of the purchase. She handed him his receipt and sent him out of the door with a pair of sparkling black thigh-high stockings and a bra and panty set, charcoal, as thin as a fine layer of ash.

He waited over a week, thinking Erika would reject them, finally presenting them to her on her birthday, at a cabin they rented at Ogallala. She put them on in the locked bathroom, gazing in the mirror at her small nipples that showed through, embarrassed at how the ensemble only made her skin more pale. She pulled her nightshirt over them.

He had purchased an abayah for her as well in Colorado Springs, demanding she put it on every morning, acquiescing each afternoon with less protest when she would slip out of it as they traveled some remote two-lane, twisting left and right, thumping about the unairconditioned Saab, sitting for a while in only her underwear before pulling a T-shirt over her head.

Majij spoke in long soliloquies, rambling through the gastrointestinal tract, then the nervous system, and told her of the very peculiar behavior of a man in Tehran who'd had a brain tumor that they had only discovered after his death, when Majij and some other medical students had dissected him. Or he and Erika would banter in French, Majij correcting her where he could. He talked about the Russians and how foolish it was for America to worry that the Russians could come through Persia, that Persians were very fierce and had not been conquered in over two thousand years. Americans only drove badly and were remembered by the elders as having run over a lot of people.

In a few towns the streets were gravel, and fine dust rose up into the car, settling onto the black dashboard, irritating Majij, who was afraid to display his temper when he noticed many of the men along the street wore those brimmed hats. Those men were volatile, he knew, and Majij had the notion they still hung men in towns like these and were more likely to hang a stranger. He looked up each street for gallows, and trying to sound casual, asked Erika.

"You're weird," she said.

"But in Iran, there are villages that have not changed for three hundred years. And they stone people."

"It's all just for tourists."

"No. In Iran, there are not so many tourists. And they could not watch…"

"I meant here," she said, gesturing at the storefronts.

He had bought a third pair of blue jeans, '501's' she'd demanded, and they fit him well, tightly. And even though more and more he asked her to stay with the hot car, the sunroof and windows open, she didn't mind because she liked watching him walk away. Just the shape of him, thinner than Ronnie, smaller-waisted but broad and strong through the chest in his white shirts, made her want to show him off to Trish, wherever she was. Other girls on the sidewalk would turn as well sometimes, as he passed. When he returned she would get out, pulling him against her as he unlocked the trunk, when his hands were full and he couldn't push her away without appearing obvious, and she knew she had him. And she would pretend to search his front pockets, straying daringly toward his midline with her fingertips.

In Lander, Wyoming, they parked against a curb in front of a Baskin-Robbins.

Majij rolled down the window. "I must go over to the bank. Do not go far," he said. "They have cameras in there. It is better I am alone."

When he was out of sight, she took five dollars from her backpack and opened the door. She stood on the boardwalk, both hands behind her back, swaying, aglow and impish, when he reappeared.

"Yes?"

When he had stepped close enough, she lunged her lips into his, pushing a melting mass of cherry ice cream into his mouth with her tongue, an arm around his neck. When they fell away from each other, she held a waffle cone in each hand and gave him one. He looked at it, full of wonder and happy in a way he could not translate, beautiful insanity he was at last part of. She stood before him, smug, confident, drawing the top of her own cone into her mouth. "And you love me as well," he added.

*

She watched his hands as he drove, knowing when he was angry by the whiteness of his knuckles and how tightly he pressed his fingers into the wheel. At other times, when he grasped the gearshift as delicately as a Da Vinci drawing, he seemed a paragon of understanding. Sometimes he would hold her hand in his own, resting in her lap as they drove for spells of contentment, the weight of his hand comfortably between her legs, and she would want him and feel like she could never get enough of him. Too often this was in the afternoons, hours before Majij found a motel he was willing to stop at, and she wished they could stop then, anywhere, so she could have him until she screamed, until something deep in her, something she thought biological, was full.

He would pull his hand away eventually, to say something, his hands and his mouth seemingly synchronized by some mechanical absolute if something important needed to be said, and everything Majij said was important. She would drift away from him then, out of the window and across the fields, Majij fluttering his fingers in the air, reiterating in dissonant tones one injustice or another that had never been rectified. Things could be unfair, she agreed with him, sharing his outrage at the first telling, but through the summer, she noticed that he revisited these wounds until she started to know what he would say next. Some points, she noticed, were inconsistent with her own understanding of the history of Persia, but decided it was only what she had read and what her father had read. Majij had lived there.

On days he was happy, he was full of curiosity like a child, stopping at every roadside plaque, the Corn Place, Mount Rushmore, the dinosaur farms. She loved him the most then, his voice melodious and hypnotic, and every word spoken was sweet stories of poppies, his father's hand in his when he was small, wonderful recipes of honey, the love of another lifetime, the ingredients that had created this perfect man, and she counted herself very lucky.

But the days he was happy grew farther and farther apart, and the mornings that he did not speak at all, sullen and withdrawn, multiplied.

By August, they were in Nebraska, having crossed portions of South Dakota, Wyoming, and Colorado, following old US highways, two-lane journeys over hills and through washes, roads flanked by hundreds of miles of undulating telephone wires strung from one crossarm of blue glass insulators to the next, pavement cracks of black strings of pitch laced across the bone white concrete that stretched before them.

They would stop several times each day to buy gasoline, but never again, it seemed, at a restaurant. Instead he would bring her a Slurpee or a strawberry milkshake, and a paper boat of chicken wings. She would sit cross-legged while he drove and they ate, tossing the small bones out of the open windows, leaving a convoluted trail of them across the western states and into the plains.

*

Sam walked away from the counter knowing that everyone in the drugstore had listened, prurient, parasitic, though only an elderly couple waited on the bench behind him.

"I'm sorry," the pharmacist had said. "I heard what happened."

"Nothing *happened,*" Sam replied. "Nothing at all." He took the pill bottle out of its fresh paper sack and shoved the bottle into his trousers. "You don't know shit."

"I hope Teresa…" But the pharmacist stopped; Sam was nearly to the door.

He sat in the car for a moment before starting the engine and wondered if he'd been unfair to the man. A gauntlet of interrogators had appeared over five months, the last of them well-wishers, people who had been invisible before but now appeared like apparitions, offering limp handshakes, imbecilic, unsolicited theories, and promises to "keep her in their prayers." A woman outside Saint Mark's one Sunday morning, some acquaintance of Teresa's, offered to "pray for Erika's soul," and he was tempted to hit her, break her nose on the first blow, but Teresa had his arm at the time, and feeling his bicep tighten, led him away. The implication of it all! Pompous old bitch.

The police had arrived first, the initial officer impersonal, polite but brief, disinterested, cutting him short, standing ominously in their front doorway while late winter blew in. Chest bulging, a dozen black devices in their pouches hanging from his belt, he clattered as he ascended the porch, writing notes in a ridiculously small notepad. Asking an American policeman into your house was like inviting an armored car into your living room.

The detective, Haynes, had been far too personal. He wanted to look at Erika's room, and commented that it looked rather barren. Had she ever left the house during the night? Gone through the window? Did she come home after her curfew? Did she even have a curfew? Boyfriends, older boyfriends? How did she get money? Who did she know who had a car? Did she take any medicines? Was she on birth control pills? Did they think she needed to be on birth control pills? Lots of girls her age were, he said. He slid the closet doors to one side, then the other, but didn't really look into the closet. Had there been fights in the home? Drugs? Sam and Teresa looked at each other, then shook their heads.

Haynes appeared at the school the following afternoon, closing Teresa's office door after him as he came in. He picked up a framed snapshot of Erika and Sam from her desk and turned it over in his hand as he spoke. "Did Sam ever *touch his daughter,* mishandle her?"

"He taught her to dance."

"But…was he ever alone with her, in some way that you're aware of, that was…"

"He's her *father.*" She interrupted him. She rose and opened the door and stood by it. "Just find my daughter." She picked up the photograph when he was clearly out of the office and noticed a thumbprint over Erika's face. She breathed on it and rubbed it clean with a tissue.

"Mrs. Etulain?" Mary Farnsworth, the school switchboard operator, a woman Teresa did not think was very bright, trotted over. "I hope that wasn't bad news."

"No, Mary. He just thought he had some leads. Sounds positive." Teresa tried to look chipper.

She told Sam about the conversation with Haynes a week later, as if it had given her cause for reflection, cataloging the time he had spent with her, reviewing every mental transcript of their discussions.

Sam, in turn, now weighed everything he had said to her, careful of each phrase, aware he was guilty of making certain *corrections* to Erika's room. By extension, he would eventually be held accountable for everything that would happen to Erika, even, God forbid, her death. Someone sounded a horn, and he looked up and saw that the light had changed. Teresa was no longer his ally. When had she abandoned him—the day she had walked in as he spackled Erika's room, or was it before that? Some monstrous presence had grown between them since April, consuming Teresa like leprosy.

His first instinct was to call Haynes and challenge his innuendo, but it was difficult to challenge what hadn't actually been said, and his initiative withered as he realized he could very well lose the interest of the police and they could move the case to the bottom of their priorities. They already insisted on referring to the case as a *runaway*, so Sam resolved to endure whatever humiliation arose, telling himself that these were standard questions they asked of all parents, that however insulting, it was at least fair. Still, he felt disempowered.

A woman had come from Portland after that who wanted a good photograph of Erika. They would reproduce it, she said, putting different colored hair, different cuts, different makeup, so they might understand all the ways "…she might appear. Sometimes they wear wigs," she said.

"When?" Sam asked. "Why would she wear a wig if she never wanted to do that at home?"

"Sometimes," she answered, lowering her voice, speaking slowly as if to a foreign visitor, "they make movies. Young girls with boys or with other girls." Did she have tattoos? Any scars?

Sam began to speak, leveling a finger at her.

"They're forced to," she added. "It's not a choice. But only if she's been taken by those people, the ones who make video movies." She sat up and spoke with confidence. "Volunteers will look, scan over these movies, they can be bought or rented, maybe even here in this town. They'll look for"—she paused and stole a glance at the folder in her lap—"Erika."

Sam pulled away from the curb, eastbound on Third. He had been unable to pass a video store since that day without reliving the conversation with that woman. He wanted to look himself. He'd gone into one store and walked straight to the adult section in a small room separated by a curtain. Nothing on the smudged plastic boxes suggested little girls or young teenage girls, though certainly a lot of 'college freshmen co-eds' were being promoted. He wondered if there was a secret code or sign he would have to show to gain access to tapes of younger girls. He was determined that he would rent them all and have them loaded into a box when he found them, watching them one after another till he found her. Now nothing on the shelf looked suspicious enough to risk the embarrassment, or worse, the heightened interest of Haynes.

He stepped out of the closet. "Is this all there is?"

"That ain't enough, man?"

Sam scowled at him.

"You got a title? I could search." He drummed his fingers by the keyboard of the computer.

But Sam walked out. He had not stepped into a video store since.

Every other week for two months, they had driven into Gresham to meet with a support group, where they would listen to an angry alcoholic woman whose daughter had, more probably than not, been taken by her natural father, and a couple in their late twenties whose three-year-old had disappeared from a day-care center. Bill and Shirley, whose son had run away to San Francisco in 1968. They hadn't heard from him since.

"He would be thirty-four now," Bill said and took a folded paper from his jacket, an artist's rendition of what he might look like.

Sam was disturbed most by Bill and Shirley, and found himself thinking about them the entire next week. They had done something wrong, missed some sign, failed their boy in some way. He didn't want to be found, and they were just too dense to recognize the truth. Erika would want to be found, when she grew weary of this little exercise.

Each interloper was of less influence, but with each he felt incrementally greater contempt. With Teresa's retreat into herself he felt more and more alone, and well-wishing from inconsequential people, however well-intentioned in their shallow understanding of his dilemma, only reminded him how impotent he had become. Each of these encounters he turned over in his mind on a daily basis. While he lay in bed in the darkness before sunup, while he was making tea, or paying the bills, sorting through the junk mail settled like silt on the table, or driving to the Thriftway, or waiting while an attendant put petrol in his car, a continuous replay of every minute of his life since Erika vanished tumbled by until his consciousness functioned on two completely independent channels, one devoted to an imitation of his previous life, the other devoted solely to scrutinizing the past five months.

Two Friday nights in a row they had driven to Portland, both knowing as soon as they were westbound how vast the city was, ten cities, one upon the other, the maze of streets infinite convolutions on a landscape where their daughter was a speck of dust. The absurdity was not lost on them, but each harbored a fragment of magical thinking that happenstance would place Erika in a crosswalk just as they approached an intersection. They argued, they fought, they accused, and were silent. Then, after a while, one or the other would say in as calm and neutral a voice as possible, "Perhaps the mall in Tigard," or, "Janzen Beach; there's an amusement park there." They circled the downtown district and drove around the university. The second weekend, they drove until their eyes burned, and Sam got a motel room in Beaverton. The following morning, they drove for two more hours until Sam noticed they were retracing a neighborhood they'd surveyed the night before and said so out loud. Teresa began to cry.

Sam felt intuitively that Erika was still in The Dalles. He began driving alone around the city each evening, stopping regularly at two video arcades, knowing she'd never really been interested in them before but thinking she might be with someone who was. He slowed to pass Burgerville, Arby's, and every fast food restaurant where he saw teenagers in cars, getting in or out or sitting on fenders, windows rolled down, music playing. When he had exhausted the downtown, he would crisscross the residential streets, driving at a crawl, sometimes with his lights off, listening. A light in a kitchen or a living room, and he would stop, trying to interpret the body language of the forms moving inside, sometimes only a midriff or a shoulder passing behind the nearly shuttered blinds. He would be home by midnight and Teresa would be awake. He had extended the cord on the phone from his desk, and usually she lay in bed with it resting on her abdomen in the dark.

As the weeks had unfolded, Teresa decompensated by inches. One night a half-eaten pork roast was wrapped in foil with care and placed in a cabinet. On a different evening, she thawed a chicken in the microwave and then prepared a completely different meal. At the end of the school year, it was as if she had let go of something. His patrols grew briefer and briefer, the gradual loss of his wife pulling him farther and farther from his quest for his daughter. Any thought of pursuing Erika beyond the city limits became tethered to Teresa, and he began to resent her for needing him, and hated himself.

At the Texaco he made a left turn. He had reached Juniper before he realized he was just two blocks from his house, traveling twenty-six miles per hours in a fifty zone. Had a herd of zebras galloped in the pasture beside him, he would not have noticed. The pharmacist was forgotten. He pulled over at the row of mailboxes before turning onto Lottie, a small, silent prayer offered once again for a note, a letter, or card of any size from Erika. Not for himself. He had already decided she was alive, and his only dilemma was designing a penance for her. He prayed for something to show Teresa, some scrap of data that would prove in a glance that it had all been a foolish self-deception. Something that would promise Erika's return by the next school year. Something that would obviate his guilt.

Two small catalogs were folded into the box, one addressed to Teresa Etu-lain but clearly promoting products for the new mother. A statement from The Dalles County PUD. He pulled *The Oregonian* from the box as well.

At his front door, he twisted the knob and pulled the door against the frame before turning the key in the deadbolt, opening the door without making a sound.

He sat down at the head of the table, slipped off his shoes, and unfolded the still warm paper. An American, Col. Higgins, had been hanged in Beirut. An observer, observing too closely, he thought. Barbaric people. More forest fires in Canada. He turned the page. Some medical clinic was closing, the address somewhere on the other side of the railroad tracks, owned by a Dr. Rashid. Charges were to be filed against another doctor, Majij Aziz, who allegedly embezzled "…in excess of a hundred thousand dollars," Rashid was quoted. There was a picture of the alleged embezzler, a handsome little man with dark skin and a moustache, like a photo from a driver's license. A nurse at The Dalles General Hospital said no one had known him well. Missing since April.

A month after Erika moved out. A habit had grown of indexing every event according to its proximity to Erika's leaving. Sam imagined the hospital and wished suddenly that he had gone to watch her, at least one time, performing her duties in her striped uniform, so smart and lovely like his mother. "Someone who worked there," Erika had said one evening, had given her a ride home.

He walked down the hallway slowly, rolling on the sides of his socked feet, and peeked through the partially closed bedroom door where Teresa lay with her eyes closed. He went to Erika's room and stood at the end of the bed and looked around. The names of her classmates still lettered on the wall in 3-D, paisley, striped and graphic, he wondered where they all were now. The globe sat on her desk and next to it a stack of unopened mail. On the wall near the head of her bed, Peter O'Toole and Omar Sharif. Omar Sharif.

He went back to the dining room and spread the paper out flat on the table and looked at the second page again. He went back to her room. There had been something else. A letter, perhaps, or a note from school. He had burned them all. No, something bigger, something so proper at the time, something odd now. He turned the globe absently, then stopped and stared at the desktop. A book. *Freya Stark in Persia*. It had been right there, and he'd dropped it back at the public library. But there wasn't any attention to the Middle East in the ninth-grade curriculum. He remembered this because he'd made a point of it at a faculty meeting, how incoming freshmen were so igno-rant about the most controversial real estate in the world. What had made her check out that book? He went into the kitchen and, cradling the handset on his shoulder, began to leaf through the phone book.

13

'Welcome to Kansas, THE SUNFLOWER STATE. Speed limits strictly enforced.'

Majij drove straight-armed, deeply absorbed in his favorite authority role, 'Harry' the underdog detective, ignoring the 'Dirty' prefix, not understanding how Americans could create such a noble hero struggling against every conceivable betrayal and still regard him as *dirty*. He loved the name, *Cal-ah-han*. First hard, then soft, like an American name should be, capable of laceration or embrace—his own two soft syllables lacking exactitude, even turgor, the object of derision since he had arrived in Chicago, the nurses first calling him "Ah Sneeze" and for a while, "Dr. Sneeze," and then just "Sneeze," and finally, though never directly in his presence, only from hearsay via chatter in the residents' lounge when he entered once before anyone noticed him, "Sleaze." Now he raced across the Midwest in an armored bus, his blond lover beside him, through the gauntlet certain to appear as he neared his dream. He looked over at her and wished she had not dyed her hair.

"What are you thinking?" she asked. "You were smiling."

"I was thinking." He flushed at his heroic fantasy. "I am proud, to be protecting you, taking you to a better place."

"Yeah. Isn't that a euphemism for being dead?"

"You will see," he said. "You must learn to be patient." Plans seldom emerged entirely as he envisioned, and the closer he drew to his brother's presence, the greater was his angst over one detail or another that Hakim would object to, some small gesture that might offend. They would abstain while at his house; even the smallest sound, a glance, a touch on the hand, would detonate all of the fury Hakim possessed, the accrued interest of his self-denial. Hakim had not lain with a woman, he did not know how they smelled, how smooth they could be, the perfectness of the world in the warm security of their total embrace. Majij looked at her silhouette again, the round richness of her lips, the tip of her tongue as she wet them, the magical angle of her jaw, the heavenly purity of her skin. An oblique shift, a blur of brown, quite close, passed in the mirror beyond her. Something was pursuing them. He checked the rearview mirror, but the road was empty for a thousand meters.

Hakim had a right to spiritual condescendence. He would demand a penance they could not pay—abstinence or perhaps a small mutilation. All of these scenarios had shadowed the Saab for a week now, initially far on the horizon to either side, but each night they had further closed the margin, and now something paced them just beyond the first row of wheat, where he could not look at it directly but could feel its breath. Did it come for her, or had she summoned it? *Aicha Kandicha*, the image occurred to him, and he found himself watching the windrows.

Erika turned the radio knob.

"*...it's late September and I really should be back in school...*"

"That man has an ugly voice." Majij twisted the tuner.

An announcer emerged, followed by a telephone voice with a question about hybrid seed. They both listened to this comfortable, warm voice for several minutes without retaining any of it.

"It would be good to be a farmer," Majij said. "Easier to be a good Muslim. Each year you plant, you are rewarded. Not so many temptations."

"Sometimes farmers plant and they lose their ass. I should be back in school."

"Circumstances change."

"Do they really? When are you gonna work again?" She slouched in her seat and drew her knees up, wrapping her arms around them. "You're doing exactly what you planned, aren't you?"

"You worry about money? Like all women." He took her hand. "We have plenty of money."

"I still need to be in school." She pulled her hand away and wiped her nose with her palm. "Don't want to be twenty when I graduate."

"Stop thinking of school. Just two more weeks. We will find what there is fun to do in Kansas."

She watched a row of poplars race past, some flecked with yellow, some already bare, birds like specks darting from limb to limb. It looked cold, for September. "Tornados." She sniffed. "Don't we have any Kleenex in here?"

"Think maybe of this. I will be in Salinas, just an hour away from my brother's. You go back to school in Topeka. New name. New papers. You become"—he waved his hand in the air—"*trade student*, and go to Iran with me. Go to school there, for a year. I have friends at the university."

"You mean *exchange student*. I don't think Americans are allowed to travel to Iran right now."

"So? We go to Turkey, take a bus to Iran. You finally get to ride the bus, okay?" He paused. "Maybe my brother will make you Canadian, like himself."

"Beats being Mexican."

"And we were not discovered, were we?" He thought all American teenagers wanted to be out of school. The freedom he offered now was currency shrinking in his wallet, his presence in her life diminishing in value. She wanted to go back to school. This puzzled and was beginning to irritate him, such devotion to a trivial idea. Better she might study Islam as earnestly, become a good Muslim, better than he. He squeezed her hand more firmly. "You are married to me now. We will do this together."

She did not respond to his grasp in kind, and when he looked over, she stared down the highway with an air of indifference, searching for some target very different than his own, and he felt a distance between them and wondered if she was thinking of someone else. Majij tightened his abdomen, and a tension born in his youth settled over him like a static charge. The requisite sacrifices of Islam never justified in his own conscience, now he would have to be her model. Eventually she would be chained to the fourth pillar. Could she go ten or twelve hours without eating? It was difficult imagining her not giggling, making some inane observation or an irreverent gesture. His brother rode invisibly with them, watching her, and found her wanting. She did not have the appearance or behavior of a good Muslim, and her carnival of expressions, her liquid laughter, the motion of her hips, everything about her that had drawn him so passionately, he wanted now to hide. He had not told Hakim enough about her. He didn't like to hear of women at all, nor what one did with them, how a girl could make you feel, and so Majij had said little.

Eight more weeks until Topeka, six weeks of work, two weeks that he could live in accordance with his brother's expectations. He must indulge her like he had not before until she was bonded to him in the heat, dreading the hours of daylight when he was not inside of her. This would keep her through the months to come, sustain her through her Christmas they would not be permitted to recognize, through any test Hakim might devise. And slowly, during this time, he would take away the unneeded. She would forget about those silly things from her life as a child.

Hakim, defined by the laws of the prophets, was all that Majij should have been. He had followed the undefiled path. He was of the same blood, the same earth. Majij had no excuse, he had left the path of obedience and found himself wanting as well. He could not talk or listen to Hakim without staring at his shoes. He could not picture Hakim's face, only his own. He could see Hakim as an adult only in the photograph he'd once held, Hakim bearded and dusty, squatting near some stone building, clutching an Enfield. One must look in a mirror to view a volatile god.

'Sex, Lies, and Videotape' hung out over the sidewalk on a movie marquee in the last town they'd passed through in Nebraska, and Majij could not get the words out of his head. Discard the gluttony! So many things to repent. *Tawba*, Hakim would demand tawba, ask him to sacrifice something. Hakim was just. Majij had lived with the unjust for too long, neglecting *zakat*, with food, credit cards, and pornography, there would be a price—restitution. He must feel remorse, but this was the essential problem. He could say to Hakim, "I feel remorse," but Hakim would see that he did not.

He had succumbed to his loneliness, his desire, and now his whole little world in Oregon was gone, a price paid already. Majij struggled to remember how his world had been imperfectly grounded in Rashid's clinic, but it did not seem now that it had been so bad; he had been rewarded with money, if not respect, for his training. He was ashamed that he was afraid, and ashamed of what he had lost, taken away by this girl. It would be better again, in Tehran, in a clinic where he was needed by people of the faith. *But I will have her.* He should be able to keep her for such a trade, that was fair. He would point this out to Hakim, "See, it is for her that I return to Iran. It is for her I repent to my faith." No, Hakim would say what was fair. He would create the papers. Beyond Salinas, beyond Ramadan, beyond Hakim, these trials they must pass through. He reached across and took her hand and touched her cheek, the back of his fingers to her lips.

"You okay?" she asked.

He nodded.

A scene from a movie occurred to Erika, where the jungle grows silent before some great predator arrives. Something palpable in his touch, more than the substance of his skin, an uncertainty emanated from him, a fear. It was greater than his fleeting paranoid ideations, his resentment of a glance from a waitress in South Dakota, a discourtesy on the highway in Wyoming, or a curt farewell from a motel clerk. Such things he forgot quickly, sometimes midsentence. Now he said nothing, but it radiated from him in every breath, his posture, the clearing of his throat, his constant readjustment of the mirrors. The very light around him changed, less forgiving of small flaws over his cheeks, the bridge of his nose more hawklike, the joy of his laughter in Portland, his thoughtful gaze as he read the news, his careful grip of the wheel, all reduced to mere wrinkles and shadow. He smelled frightened. It rode in the car with them like a third presence that had joined them that morning. Intuition whispered that she was not going back to school, that she was going somewhere in this car she did not want to go, some-place she would be terrified, as much as he was. She wanted to help him, leap into this great void that had opened in him, but could not grasp its origin. Her helplessness to do so unsettled her more. People were supposed to be there for each other.

The news was on. Irving Berlin had died. She turned the volume up but nothing more was said of the composer. She drifted perilous, unanchored for a moment, a notion that she was not where she belonged, floating headlong over Multnomah Falls. The feeling passed and she turned the tuner again. The frequencies flickered through the entire scale of the band, then stopped at a weak signal.

'*...now you've given me, given me, nothing but shattered dreams,*'

"Do you know Christmas songs?" he interrupted.

"Yeah." She leaned forward and listened closer.

'*... I could run away, run away...*'

"Sing one for me."

"Why? It's not even Halloween yet."

'*...on this empty highway...*'

"They are all happy songs. There is not much happy on the radio here."

She turned off the radio and thought for a moment.

"There was a song, in Iran before I left. Very popular. Two boys love the same girl. She cannot decide, so they crash their motorbikes into each other. Both die. All the girls, they cry and cry about this, then they listen to it again." He looked at her pathetically. "I will miss Christmas songs when we are there."

"Okay, okay. Dashing through the snow, in a one horse open sleigh, over fields we go, laughing all the way..."

He sang along with her, humming mostly or mouthing the words. The intruder slipped out of the car, but by the time they reached a truck stop near Grainfield, it was back. He told her to stay in the car while he filled the tank.

After he had paid, she watched him go into the bathrooms. He returned a few minutes later, drying his hands. He sat in the car and started the engine.

"I need to go, too."

He reached into the inner pocket of his jacket and took out a silk rose and handed it to her. "I got this for you."

"It's nice. Can I use the bathroom?"

"Please, not here. It is very dirty. We will stop at the rest area. Just ten, fifteen miles up the highway. It will be cleaner."

They crossed the interstate, Majij preferring the two-lane roads. Her rest area had been vandalized when they arrived. She took a wad of paper towel and waded into the wheat, just beyond two fallen strands of barbed wire, where a baby's diaper lay crumpled in a furrow just a few feet from her shoes. He was hopelessly apologetic when she returned and handed her a moist towelette he had fished from the glove compartment, kissing her and holding her against him until the console pressed into her ribs. That afternoon the scene was repeated near Liebenthal, Majij insisting she stay in the car, looking in every direction before turning off the engine, then smothering her with desperate affection when he reappeared.

When they'd returned to the highway, Erika tried singing, "Santa Claus is Coming to Town," but Majij stopped her in midverse, pointing out that mythical deities would hardly come back to the same place every year. It was a silly, stupid song; any god that could see all of the evil men did wouldn't come back at all.

"But God and Santa aren't the same thing. Santa's just kind of a symbol."

"For what?" He glared at her.

"For, I don't know…hope, I guess." She sat with the stem of the rose between her fingers, smelling it from time to time, forgetting temporarily that it had no fragrance.

The sun shifted and their shadow on the road stretched far before them when she spoke again. "I've been wondering how come, on TV, when you see the Syrians or the Palestinians with their guns, they always have bags over their heads."

"Bags?"

"Okay, ski masks."

"It is so they won't be recognized."

"But if they're doing something they believe in…"

"…by the Jew-police, the Massad."

"But if they really believe what they're doing is right, they shouldn't hide. The rest of the world will think they're chickenshit."

"But the rest of the world respects them."

"Like you'd respect a bank robber."

"Like"—and he mustered some paternal authority—"like you respect God."

"I don't think I'm afraid of God."

"You should be."

"Why? Have I done something wrong? Does God have an automatic rifle he shoots in the air when he's happy?" She crushed her eyes tight in thought. "It's like, here I am, I'm a soldier, and I believe in this, so I'm marching about, but I'm going to cover up my face. Nobody knows who I am. It's like a lie. They take the 'I' out of 'I believe.'"

He tossed her a condescending scowl.

"You've never worn one of those, have you?"

"Why should I? I'm Persian. Besides, I'm a doctor."

"I think it's braver if you always see a man's face." And she stroked his shoulder. "If you claim to believe something, people should see who you are. Otherwise it doesn't mean shit."

It struck him as a platitude, something his dead father might have said, the voice of his father from the mouth of this girl. He snorted and looked again at the road, but cooled as the next thirty miles passed. A few minutes after the sun dropped below the fields behind them, they rolled into the parking lot of a one-story motel, the Dew Drop Inn.

"Jesus, that's corny," Erika said, but all of the letters of the sign were illuminated, and she divined this to be an improvement. She lunged over and kissed him on the ear. "Let's celebrate."

At the end of the parking lot stood Big Jimmy's Burgers, a mural on the side of the concrete diner portraying Big Jimmy as a football-shaped caricature, leering as he pushed a burger into his mouth, and beyond that a small market. A hundred yards farther, the interstate climbed a small grade to an overpass, where the sound of traffic trailed off over the horizon.

After they had checked in Majij left her in the room, returning twenty minutes later with two burger baskets and a separate brown sack. He pulled out three forty-ounce bottles of Old English 800.

"You don't drink," she said.

"You don't know half of what I do. Besides, in Iran, there is no beer. So we drink beer here." He sang and did a little dance as he said this and twisted the caps off of two of them, placing one on her side of the table. He considered the mouth of his own bottle for a moment, then peeled the cellophane from two plastic glasses and poured clumsily, Erika's foaming over onto the tabletop.

"You gonna start smoking cigarettes too?"

"I quit. When I came to America, in Chicago. Too windy to smoke." He leaned back in his chair. "There's still plenty of cigarettes in Iran, though."

"They call Chicago 'windy' because of politicians, talking all the time."

"Still, very windy. From the lake." He smirked. "But I like that, you say 'windy.' You think Tehran will be 'windy' too?" He slouched forward, drank half of his glass, then unwrapped one of the burgers, lifted the edge of the dripping bun to look under it, and shoved it into his mouth. Erika thought for a moment he would swallow it whole. He tried to speak with his mouth full, just mumbling, and motioned that she should drink also. She sipped timidly at first and unwrapped her own burger. Majij finished his beer and poured himself a second. Mayonnaise escaped over his fingers as he wolfed through the rest of the burger, finishing his second glass and pouring a third. He opened the second bottle, picked up her rose, and placed it in the neck of the empty one. In twenty minutes, he became another man, self-possessed, limber and comfortable.

"What exactly does he do, your brother?" She refilled her cup but stopped before it frothed over. It was bitter, cold and jubilant.

Majij drew a paper napkin through his fingers and leaned back again, picking up the glass, holding it limp-wristed. "I think, he works in a bank. He has never actually told me this." He took another sip, as if he had drank daily, all of his life. "He works for our country, my country, well, *our country*"—waving the glass between himself and Erika—"when we go there. He does things with money."

He took another drink, and Erika, trying to catch up, finished hers. Her own bottle was empty. She belched, startling herself, and Majij did also, almost simultaneously.

"Good wife. Harmony!" And he raised his glass. Erika twisted open the third bottle and refilled her glass. He paused for a moment. "My brother, he does things with money, but he *works* for God. Not so many Muslims, good, good Muslims, are so lucky." He poured a fourth glass, then emptied the last few ounces into Erika's. "We will not be able to drink at my brother's house. That would not be *working for God*. There are many things we will be expected *not* to do." He rose from the chair, wadded up the wrapper from his burger, and hooked it into the trash can.

"Wow." She smiled, taken with everything fluid and free about him.

He stepped behind her, bent down, and softly kissed her neck. "So some things, we must do here."

"I see you wearing black, a black turban. You're a prince and come for me on a white horse across the sand." She stood, giddy, and held his face between her hands and kissed him, and with her arms around his neck, pulled herself up, wrapping her legs around his waist. He carried her to the bed, and she imagined a black tunic blowing around her face and was unsettled momentarily, that her focus blurred, that she might be dropped, that she might vomit. But her ears felt warm, the room gyrated, and she embraced the incoherence; an easiness followed, a luxuriant tide bearing her away.

"I never dreamed, I never thought, that I would allow such a gift into my..." His beer voice faded as his hands moved up the small of her back, beneath each shoulder blade and down again, to the orbit of her hips, and unsnapping her jeans, pulled them down slowly, his hands passing the length of her legs. What had haunted him in the wheat was forgotten, and for the moment he did not know how he had even come into her life, only that he wanted to be lost in her. Kneeling, he kissed her navel, drawing his lips in every direction away from it, kissing her right thigh, then the left, each one in turn until he kissed her knees, which she had drawn together. He nudged gently with his chin and kissed the inside of her legs, and drawing her legs apart, slowly kissed his way up, passing his tongue slowly the length of her.

She stiffened, unbearably tense, but with each stroke, each light passage, she would take a breath. She placed a relaxed calf on his back and then the other, still distrusting her instinct.

He could feel the tiny coldness of her ankle bracelet.

She raised her pelvis and he drew his hands beneath her, exploring deeper, his upper lip upon the firm mound of her, and always his tongue, moving, rising, and with each stroke, another sparkle the length of her spine, another breath, a current inside of her. Her hips rose and fell with the rhythm of his tongue, and she tried to speak but could only whimper, her arms powerless, her head swimming. Still her hips rose into him, to take him inside if she could, finally the rhythm sweeping through her like a long arc of lighting, her back a crescent, she gasped and could not exhale, all thought suspended they were motionless, her vision her prince her rider evaporating in brilliance.

He raised himself onto the bed and slid into her, to another rhythm, gripping the edge of the mattress with her nails for an eternity, the bed frame drumming against the wall. He gasped and she heard him cry, and she cried out also.

Already the colors of the ceiling and the color inside her eyes when she closed them ran together and she fell asleep. She slept fitfully, tangled in the sheets with him, turning away only to roll back, every inch of his skin new and strange and full of some seductive androgyny, mixed with images that came and went, something in the desert, a worm beneath the sand, terrible and imminent and just out of view. She awoke nauseated and thirsty. She had done something with her mouth that she had not done before. She rinsed one of the beer cups and drank water from the tap and felt better, and went back to sleep.

*

Cream-colored light leaked below the edge of faded white privacy curtains and through a few pinprick holes in the fabric. The fan of the heater rumbled on, and Erika could see the fine layer of lint, dust, a few cigarette butts and a chewing gum wrapper lying on the grid beneath the grill where they had fallen and never been cleaned away. She wondered who had smoked them, imagining another couple in their very spot. The wall was dirty pale yellow, and near the heater controls at one end became a mural of hand marks and smudges she had not noticed when they'd arrived. Another tiny beam of light shone through the peephole in the door. The blanket smelled of stale smoke, and she floated in the notion that they had both been moved to a different, dirtier motel while they were unconscious, a punishment for their transgression. "Girls like that must pay the piper," her mother had said, a dozen times at least. Erika's head hurt. The mere essence of a dream flitted by, something erotic, rich but cruel, a horse and rider approaching across the sand, a black flag. Her hand tingled and had become numb under the pillow beneath his head. She rolled gently and pulled her arm free. From the cadence of his breathing, he was still asleep, so gentle now. She curled into his back. Another fragment of the dream fluttered past, something under the sand. Steven was there. It took him and tore him apart, and she felt an odd guilt.

There was an ache between her legs and a river above it. She tightened her buttocks, slid one leg over the edge of the mattress, and placed her foot in the shag carpeting, taking care not to allow the blanket to move from his neck. Her pulse rose into her temples. He groaned softly but his breathing continued unchanged. Three tall empty bottles remained on the table in a yellow puddle, drips of mayonnaise everywhere. The doorknob of the bathroom was loose and someone had punched a hole about fist level in the mahogany veneer. She pressed her fingers against its surface and closed it, slowly releasing the knob until the latch clicked. September light, cool and silent, fell from the frosted glass high above the toilet. She sat down, took a deep breath and relieved herself. Majij had told her that the authorities in Iran were replacing all of the Western toilets with *Arab* toilets "that did not waste so much water." She would have to get used to them, he said. He would not say anything when she asked him about Arab toilet paper, and this troubled her more. She looked in her purse and realized he had searched it again. She found the circular package, put a pill in her mouth, placed her lips beneath the faucet and swallowed. She wiped the chill water over her face, then stared dumbfounded at her reflection for several minutes. Her hair had parted down the center, revealing a half inch of blond roots. "Jesus," she said. "I look like a skunk."

When she returned he had turned his head toward the window and his arm lay across the place where she had been. He was waking up. She sat down on the edge of the mattress. He slid up on one elbow.

"Where were you?" He rubbed his forehead and groaned.

"Bathroom."

"Oh." He seemed satisfied and closed his eyes again, flopping back onto the pillow. "We should be traveling now, we need to pack our things." He sat up again, squinting, and stared across the room, then started to gather his clothes, which were everywhere.

The parking lot was gray with the shade of the morning, and the motel lights were off except for the pink vacancy sign near the curb. The cold of the sidewalk reached up through her thin sandals and between her toes. The windows of the Saab were down about an inch, and fine condensation coated the glass on the inside. As Majij loaded the bags into the hatchback, she wrote 'Natasha' with her finger in the moisture, then tried writing it in Cyrillic but could not remember how.

Majij closed the motel door quietly and climbed into the front seat. He frowned at her disturbance on the glass, then wiped away a letter-slot patch of his own and peeked at the window of the room next to theirs, where the curtains remained drawn. He shoved the key into the console and started the engine.

They rose up the on-ramp and onto the interstate, into the nascent light. A truck approached in the westbound lane, almost on the horizon, reflecting the face of the sunrise they could not yet see. A few miles passed, and then, where the lanes seemed to join where earth touched the sky, the sun was rising.

Majij turned the fan of the heater on. "This should be warm now."

Erika sat up in her seat and pulled down the visor, wrapping her chador over her head. She turned the fan to high and the roar gave privacy to her thoughts. An hour of the night came back to her, disentangled from a dream: She had drawn him into her mouth until he was firm, then straddled him. The rhythm had been her own, his arms pressed to the pillow, his face foreign to her. Slowing as his eyes betrayed some crescendo, she would stop, then resume her journey. Even in his drunken grasp she had sensed a familiarity, and in the barest way, an ascending empowerment. She understood now that she had indeed led him. So this was what it was like to belong to a man. In initiative or submission, there was power. She repeated this to herself softly, a new mantra.

Majij drove with his eyes into the sunrise, his thoughts halfway around the globe, oblivious to her faint smile. Approaching the next exit, a large Texaco sign caught his attention, and just beyond it a red 'K' inside a red circle. The Saab drifted down the exit ramp and squealed to a stop at the sign. "Are you hungry yet?" He poked her knee.

Her equilibrium wavered, her head throbbed, and nausea pulsed briefly into her throat. "Not much." She cast him a sour grimace. "I don't think I've ever really drank before."

They crossed over the highway and he turned onto the frontage road. He stopped at the self-service island and filled up the car, washing the windshield and measuring the oil, his head always turned to the Circle-K parking lot. A rusty white Toyota, an oxidized Pinto—no police cars. When he had paid they drove over to the store. He turned off the engine. "Would you like to come in?"

"Sure." In abayah and chador, she followed him. "Look for some more Clairol."

A tarnished, silver-haired woman smiled at them from behind the counter. "Howdy," she nodded. "Good to see a young couple up and about in the morning."

Erika returned the woman's smile, and in the same moment, felt another tired ache between her legs and imagined the language of her steps had revealed her night. They were sisters who knew, she and this grizzled woman.

Country-western fiddled from a small radio somewhere. Erika explored each aisle, wafting of powdered sugar, warm grease, coffee brewing, rows of cookies in packages, small bags of nuts, boxes of candy bars, and sacks and sacks of chips; the sight of it all made her want to vomit. Her stomach ached and she could still taste the beer. Milk would make this feel better. She walked along the refrigerator case, passing racks of beer, like bottles of urine, she thought, *None Sold Before Noon*. At the dairy section she opened the door and picked up a pint, letting he door slammed behind her. In a few steps, she was next to Majij. "Can we get this?"

He was leafing through a new road atlas and took the milk from her without looking.

Another fragment of the dream passed. But no, it was not the dream but an element of the present, stunning in an unsettling way, like realizing that a familiar landmark had disappeared. She turned and walked, each step careful and deliberate, back to the dairy case and opened the door.

A young man about her age was in the space behind the racks, filling each angled track with more containers. He smiled with crooked teeth and a tangle of red hair. "Hi!" he said. "Where are you guys from?"

She did not answer but stood transfixed, staring through him, at the rows of cartons, the chrome and glass door in her right hand, the wave of cold air falling through her gown, across her abdomen and down her legs.

"Come!" Majij grasped her wrist like a wrench and snapped her arm.

She lost her balance and the glass door slammed shut. He pulled her behind him with one hand, a brown sack crushed in the other. At the car, he slid the bag across the roof, opened her door, shoved the seat forward, and pushed her into the back. He climbed into his own seat, over-revved the engine and slapped the lever into reverse. His knuckles white and jaw clenched, they roared beneath the overpass and onto the ramp. He glanced at her in the rearview mirror. She could see his nostrils flare.

"Did you want that boy?"

"What boy?"

"Did you want him to kiss you? Put his hands on your bottom?"

"Maj."

"It is always this way with you American girls. Always you look, always for something that is better."

"No, Maj…"

"Because I do not know, not know about your stupid music, your stupid movies." He gripped the wheel even tighter and slammed his shoulders against the seat. "I think last night I make you happy. I was going to trust you. And you give me this!" He swung his arm behind him and slapped her smartly on the thigh. "Do you not know, have I not shown you? In the Koran…have you not learned, that by our thoughts we come to act?"

He was trying to reason now, with her, with himself, but he was shouting. She recoiled to the farthest corner of the seat. He slapped again but could only brush her foot. He took a deep breath and snorted, put both hands back on the wheel, and glared at her again in the mirror.

"Our thoughts, huh?" How condescending, like a parent. She saw her opportunity and slid forward again on the seat and hissed, "So what thoughts made Majij, the good good doctor, wanna fuck a fifteen-year-old?"

His fist shot back, striking for her jaw, missing, but penetrating her chest like a cannon shot. The blow knocked her against the seat. She gasped but could only make a little squeak, the pain burned through her back and her arm seemed useless. He continued to flail at her, grunting, arching his back and burying his foot into the accelerator, flailing blindly, beyond all reason, trying to scratch or capture a fold of skin or a breast, to tear away, it did not matter. The little black car traveled faster and faster, then swerved to the left shoulder, he overcorrected and it swerved to the right, raising some dust from the shoulder before crossing the centerline again. They sped beneath an overpass, past a white Ford sedan in the tall grass of the median. The Ford roared out of the gravel and spun onto the pavement after them.

"Shit! Maj…stop it, look!"

Majij looked. "*Na!*" He swallowed and looked again. "*Gom shadom.*" Erika straightened her chador and pulled it over her nose, then put on her seat belt. He checked his own. He slowed to seventy, but the white car remained behind them, sparkling rotating beacons of blue, its headlights blinking from side to side. Another mile, and he slowed to sixty. The patrol car remained. They were very alone on this highway. American policemen could be very cruel. They hated black skin and hated foreigners in the South. The bright white headlight pulsated in his side mirror. Was this the South? He tried to think of the civil war he had read about, but could not remember where the line was drawn. He had seen *In the Heat of the Night*. But I am not black, he thought, and then remembered they hated Mexicans also. Suddenly he couldn't remember if he had covered his own license in his wallet with Aguilar's.

Erika tested how far she could pry open her window, popping it open on its hinge. The vacuum hissed, and a small receipt was sucked out of the ash tray. She pushed further. It was clearly too small.

Majij, preoccupied, unconscious of the rising roar of air from the back seat, hunched forward, his grip tighter, fixated on the side mirror and the enormous Ford grill that oscillated there.

She studied the lever on the side of the bucket seat in front of her and wondered how fast she could open the passenger door. Her chest still burned. She reached for the lever, but leaning forward felt like she would tear out a rib.

Majij finally pulled over onto the right shoulder where he had seen other cars stopped. The police car pulled over behind them and just sat there. Majij could see the policeman handling the microphone in his car, looking up, then looking down again. Calling for other policemen, Majij thought. This is going to be terrible, I am going to lose my visa. He then pondered what Southern men might do to a dark man like himself with a pale young American girl in his car. Too young. Suddenly he needed badly to empty his bladder. The door of the patrol car swung open and a giant stepped out, placed a wide-brimmed hat on, but stayed behind the door. He raised the microphone again. "Turn off your engine. Keep both of your hands on the wheel."

Majij did as he was told. Footsteps approached on the gravel, the giant was just over his shoulder now, probably surveying the back seat, the motion-less girl, the sack of spilled doughnuts, empty beverage cups, a crumpled map, a dog-eared *People* magazine. Majij felt powerless to turn his head, but watched the officer in the side mirror, a hand on the butt of a pistol, the leather strap hanging free, like a little goat's ear. In the other hand he held a flashlight. The officer tapped the glass of the window, then slid the flashlight into a loop on his belt.

The window came down in nervous little jerks.

"License and registration please."

Majij surrendered the documents, searching the glove compartment, dumping most of its contents in the process.

Erika noticed the policeman's name tag, above the left pocket. Sergeant Damien.

"Keep your hands on the wheel." The officer walked back to his car and resumed some dialog on the radio.

Majij remained half-paralyzed, facing the wheel, but captured her gaze in the mirror. They stared at each other in equal measures of rage and panic.

"You! Say nothing. Nothing!" he whispered hoarsely, as if the officer might hear them from behind in his patrol car. "Me, I will go to jail, and then probably back to my Iran," he went on, "but you, you will go to juvenile prison, until you are twenty-one, at least. A very long time." He wrinkled his nose and pursed his lips. "And the women there, I've been told they like to have very young…" The patrol car door slammed. The footsteps came back and Majij was silent again.

Erika continued to look at him, his exaggerated whispers orbiting in her head. She thought of the previous night. She thought of her parents and what they would think, all that they would ask, what they would have to know.

The officer stooped down, hands on his belt, "Can you explain to me just exactly what you were doing back there?"

Tiny beads of sweat had appeared at Majij's hairline. He did not answer. The officer leaned to one side and tried to look into his eyes.

Erika lurched forward between the seats. "My brother, he does not speak English very well, and he is very worried about his license," she said in her best Middle Eastern accent.

The officer remained stoic. "Well, he should be scared, that still doesn't explain his driving."

"It was a *bee*, a very large bee…"

The officer stood back a step, put a hand on each hip and looked up and down the highway as if waiting for a better answer or, it occurred to Erika, looking for bees. The radio on his belt crackled, "One-car rollover, Highway Twenty-five."

"Stay here." The officer disappeared again briefly, then reappeared at the driver's window. He peeled away his glasses and spoke to Erika, Erika alone, focused on a point inside of her. "Miss, is there anything else you have to say to me?"

She shook her head. She tried to look away from him but felt his stare. She looked at him again and saw that his eyes were blue, they *were her own eyes*. A chill rose through her neck.

"Are you sure, miss? Anything at all?"

She turned away and shook her head again. Majij appeared suspended in the moment, as if he were deaf, or frozen.

The patrolman put his glasses back on and tossed the license and registration into Majij's lap. "Try not to kill yourselves in the state of Kansas," then jogged back to his car and jumped in. The huge front tires turned and he roared around them. Erika watched and tried to see his face again, convinced she had only frightened herself, but he seemed to disappear behind the windshield of the Ford.

Majij said nothing but restarted the car after a few moments and pulled back onto the highway. Ahead, the white Ford grew smaller and smaller, its blue lights still sparkling. Its brake lights lit and it slowed, then disappeared into the median, only to reappear on the other side of the highway, passing them in the opposite direction a few seconds later.

Erika sat quietly and watched the brown fields race silently past in the midmorning glare. It might have been her only opportunity. She could have easily pushed the seat forward and opened the door when the policeman had gone back to his car. She would have kept her hands up. No, Maj was right; they would have believed *him,* not her. An adult's word was always more credible, and there would be the discipline to endure later.

She pondered her reasoning for a while but was dissatisfied with its simplicity. She could not identify all that she had felt in those few minutes while she shared a web of tension with Majij, his true vulnerability seen for the first time, the obverse of his arrogance. A peculiar loyalty had arisen within her, parallel to her love; the opportunity to rescue him from his speechless dilemma had been too seductive. In some way he was now indebted to her, and she was determined that she would not allow him to pay.

Majij spoke. "That voice, back there. What was that supposed to be?"

"The man asked a question," she said. "Somebody had to answer."

"You sounded like a Jew. Don't ever do that voice again. Certainly not at my brother's house. Do you understand me?"

"I could have gotten out. You know that?"

"I said, do you understand me?"

"Saved your bacon."

He screwed his face into a sidelong glance, as if she'd spoken German.

"But, I do not eat bacon."

She sighed and turned to the window again. Her stomach gnawed with greater ferocity, and she fumbled around on the floor for a few moments before carefully reaching on to the cushion of the front passenger seat and retrieving the carton of milk. Majij shot her a disparaging glance. She tore open the top of the carton, took a long swallow and it was heaven. A green Volvo passed them and it seemed to Erika that heads turned. 'They'd seen her in his car.' It was something she'd heard her mother say once to her father, about one of his colleagues who had become involved with a graduate student, in a conversation Erika had eavesdropped on one evening. She chuckled.

Majij turned, curious.

She laughed out loud.

"There is something you find about today funny? Our situation?"

"Our situation? No." She took another swallow of milk, but chortled, and it came out her nose. "I mean, yes!" And she laughed again, her face red. "It's just that law, you told me about. Nine-year-olds. In Iran." She was tearing now, still laughing, and she wiped her cheeks with the chador. "When we get there…" She chuckled and tried to choke it down. "When we get there. I just realized…" She took a few deep breaths but laughed again. "You might leave me for a younger woman!" And she howled and stomped her feet and howled some more. She spilled milk down the abayah. "Oh oh," she said, laughing, and pulled off the chador and wiped streaks of milk down her legs.

He drove and glanced back at her every few seconds, completely disarmed. It was frightening, like a laugh he'd heard from Aguilar once. "You laugh like a crazy person."

She didn't answer him but just giggled, in short fits that came less and less frequently. The miles slipped away beneath their tires, exits for more truck stops appeared and vanished behind them. She became aware again that she was hungry and finished what little milk remained in the carton, then folded the top shut and considered popping it on the floor, just to watch him jump. She thought of the dairy case and its cold air, and on the racks before her in row after row, in the same line the question that repeated itself halfway the down length of the store: 'HAVE YOU SEEN THIS CHILD?' With her eighth-grade picture printed above it, a grainy rendition in blue ink, she had stooped slightly to look into the window of the lens and feigned a smile at the insistence of the school photographer. No one had seen that child. She barely recognized herself these past six months, even if her hair recanted—the rhythm of her step, her cadence of speech, the bias of every thought now slowly transformed by the role she had elected—an Erika decision. She thought about the previous night once more. No one would ever see that child again.

14

By afternoon the lightning retreated before them, then fell off to their flanks, silent inside of the car but for the crackle of static from the radio, erratic flashes in an uneven sky drawing them forward over the black wet asphalt, until it was north and south of them. They pressed eastward toward a sun that had not risen that day. The asphalt became an appendage of the charcoal clouds, a dangling vortex in which they were held, defined at its margins by waves of brown grass shimmering, touched by the humid breath of something that would devour them.

Majij pinched a folded scrap of yellow paper in his hands as he drove, flicking it open as each exit ramp approached, looking to the left and right at each overpass, allowing the car to decelerate momentarily. Dissatisfied, he would put it back into his pocket and the engine would resume its monotone. In five or six minutes, he would have it out again. Erika watched him but could not read the paper from the back seat. She tried to remember when he had written anything down on a small scrap, if he had torn it from a page of a phone book, or if someone had given it to him. To the right, 'One Thousand Rattlesnakes' in faded reptile-green lettering on a billboard that had lost several of its panels, the rest of the sign oscillating in the fury of the coming storm. Her chest hurt once more with each inhalation. She coughed, just a small cough to clear her throat, and it burned as if she'd been hit again.

The car finally coasted down an exit, paused for a stop sign, and turned left. She glanced back at a truck stop illuminated against the caliginous sky. They had turned north and ascended an overpass. Majij, silent, was focused on a building at the horizon on the left. In another two minutes they slowed to a stop in the parking lot of a motel. The sign frame was entirely empty, a steel oval atop two rusty poles, positioned in such a way to invite travelers from the road that ran behind the building, not the road they had just exited. A small mustard Mercedes was parked near the office, its trunk blackened with diesel residue, and next to it, an old American station wagon with a flat tire. The rest of the length of the parking lot was empty, cracked and broken, tufts of cheatgrass growing randomly through the pavement.

They parked on the far side of the station wagon.

"Stay here."

The door slammed and he walked around the front of the car to the office door. A dark-skinned man appeared and Majij went inside without hesitating, the swarthy face, stony and obtuse as a Mayan carving, looking over Majij's shoulder at her as the door closed.

The paint was peeling on the narrow siding directly in front of her. A rusty airconditioner drooped from the window of the first unit, surrounded by bare, weathered plywood holding it in place. Next to it a door, faded violet, an outline of the numeral 'one' at eye level. The 'two' on the next door hung upside down. *No one has stayed here in a long time.* The entire motel was draped in the pall of a ghost town.

Rising from the grass in the field across the road she could see a long low oval of concrete with twisted conduit protruding at each end, all that remained of a two-pump gas station. She looked again at the row of dark windows stretching off to her left. Lighting flickered to the earth on the horizon, but she heard no thunder. A row of poplars a half mile away bent in the wind, but here it was still. Things are sucked away from here, she thought. *Living things don't come to this place.* She rolled down the window and gulped the thick, ozone-laden air and turned as far as she could, looking back, the form of a semi passing there on the interstate, two miles away. Life flowed there, and she had been cut away from it.

"What are you doing?" Majij sat down and slammed the car door. He held a plastic tabbed room key in his hand. She looked at him and he was a stranger; he had the same severe facade as the dark-skinned man. He backed the Saab, moving it to a spot at the end of the parking lot near the last unit, and turned off the engine. He opened the trunk, carried two bags to the door, and fumbled with the room key. "Why do you wait?" he called to her, then disappeared into the room.

She looked down at the console where the ignition key remained, then straddled it, slipping into the driver's seat. Thrusting the left pedal to the floor she twisted the key, the engine whined and the starter shrieked. Ramming the stick to the 'R,' she pulled her left foot away and the car lurched backward, the trunk lid flapping in the rear window. She mashed the center pedal and her neck snapped back, Majij screaming at her, holding on to the locked driver's door. She pressed the accelerator and the engine whined higher, the tachometer needle spinning around. Frantically jerking the stick left to right, she pulled it back and released the clutch, lurching forward. Majij ran around the front of the car and she struck him at the hip, but the passenger door snapped open and he was upon her. The engine stalled, unable to move the car in fourth gear.

Grunting, gnashing his teeth, he grabbed her ear and right arm, dragging her over the console, over the passenger seat and onto the pavement. She gasped, a long cry, and was slammed against the hot hood of the car, an elbow pressed into her back. His blows fell against her ears, her ribs, her shoulder, her buttocks, hard enough that her pelvis found the metal grill of the Saab, and she tried to cry out again but could not take a breath against the weight of him. With one eye she could see two small children beneath his arm at the end of the parking lot, pointing at her. A woman in a burka came after them, taking them by the wrists and pulling them back to the office, and the door closed. He was still striking her but she did not feel it, pressing her face all of the time harder and harder into the metal of the hood, drawing the heat, pulling it into herself, her cheek and her breasts, the last of the life brought with them from the highway.

*

She lay on the bed for a long time on her side, every joint that she moved aching, taking rapid, shallow breaths, wishing her heart would slow down. She pulled the blanket up over her shoulder cautiously. She was cold remaining so motionless, and believed that if he hit her again, it would protect her. He did not hit her, but paced around the room, rearranging their bags, opening and closing drawers. Periodically he would snap the blanket off of her, then walk away.

The gray light outside had faded and the window filled with blackness when she awakened. "Are we going to eat?" she asked finally in a hoarse whisper.

He walked around the room a few more times and then sat across from her in a plastic lawn chair. "So you are hungry. That is all you do. Eat. What are you hungry for? Your freedom? Or food? I have already eaten." He stood up and began to pace again. "You are hungry for that boy at the store?" He stopped and shook a finger at her. "We are partners, we eat together, no? But you try to steal my car. Then we are not partners so well." He turned away from her. "Steal a car in Iran, they cut off your right hand." He took some things from the top of the dresser and put them in his pocket, then went out, locking the door behind him.

She looked around the dim, silent room, rolling over cautiously to the nightstand behind her. There was no telephone. She stared at the door, at the cylinder lock, and realized it had no turn bolt, only a keyhole. She was locked in.

*

When she awoke again there was light at the window. Majij was nowhere to be seen. She lay very still but heard only a dripping faucet. She sat up in small increments of lacerating pain and took a long, slow breath. For a moment, she believed she was in Bozeman and was startled to see, as she approached the window, that she was almost at ground level. The pavement in the parking lot was as wet and dark as the sky above it, the grass bent eastward in the wind. Clouds hung level and flat to the horizon, where a brilliant band of yellow light separated them from the earth. The world was there, and she imagined herself a mouse or a lost toy, far beneath an immense sofa, watching for footfalls in the room beyond. The brightest of the light came from the left, and it had been, she sensed, from the right before, above the perennial ceiling of gray. Which was east, which was west? It was a different time, and she tried to calculate if it was a day or a week beyond the time it had been before. A lost toy. *The longer I am here, the less anyone will remember to look.*

She slid the glass to one side and the cold wind buffeted her. The Saab was gone. She pressed against the mesh with her fingers, then thought about cutting it, and looked around the room for anything with a sharp edge or a point. She tried to shove the screen sideways. At the bottom of the screen, two small tabs protruded. Once pulled, the screen popped out of its frame and slipped away from her, floating to the wet grass five feet below. She shoved the glass panel shut and stared at the screen where it lay and tried to judge the height. Looking off again toward the highway, the top of a truck passed. There were cars there, there must be. She just couldn't see them. Maybe the state trooper. The screen lay in the grass. Maybe Majij would think the storm blew it out.

She looked around for her bag and her coat, but could find only her backpack. Majij must have left everything else in the car. She stopped before the mirror and looked at herself in her T-shirt; then took an olive green manteau from the drawer and slipped it over her head. She tied her chador beneath her chin, knotting it twice, and reexamined herself in the mirror. In the backpack she found three quarters and a nickel; her paper money, about eighty dollars, was gone. She sat on the edge of the bed and pulled on a pair of dirty socks and her tennis shoes. She opened the window again, straddled the sill for a moment, and dropped to the ground. The cold wet of the grass soaked through the ankles of her socks. She ran across the parking lot and an uneven lawn, and in less than a minute had reached a furrowed field, sinking several steps into the muddy row. She turned without slowing her pace and sprinted to the edge of the road and up to the shoulder, where she slowed to a quick walk, her sides aching and her shoes heavy with mud. She stomped with each step in an effort to lighten them, and with each stomp a paroxysm of pain plunged through her chest.

The wind fluttered through every seam and fold and stuck the damp cloth to her legs. She wondered again how long she had slept, thinking that it only seemed a few weeks ago that they had been riding in the car and it had been hot. Could someone sleep away a month or more? School had started, and she had not been there. She walked more quickly. Majij knew this, she had told him. He knew it and ignored it. She started to jog and then ran again. Her chest burned more fiercely and she slowed, her legs growing heavier.

She pushed the mosaic of the previous week around in her mind, first one rationale and then another. Things could be better if he found a place to be a doctor, he must be frustrated about the license hassles and just got mad at the way things were. But nothing could justify the beating. She clutched the coins all the more tightly until her palms hurt. Her throat grew raw, then numb.

The overpass rose before her, only a narrow lip of concrete with a short guard rail at each side. She stood up on the lip and walked a few yards as if it were a sidewalk, but the wind pressed between her shoulder blades, trying to pitch her over the rail, so she stepped down onto the pavement again. As she crossed the crest of the overpass, the sign of the truck stop came into view, several letters were missing. Descending another fifty feet, she could see the illuminated interior, vast and dirty and empty, a large 'For Lease' sign in the window. She stopped and stared, not trusting her memory, wanting to see people, any people. She began shivering.

A pickup truck appeared at the crest of the overpass and swerved slightly as it passed her, blowing its horn. She ran the rest of the distance down to the frontage road, looking all of the time for someone, anyone inside, someone cleaning or repairing something. She slowed when she reached the parking lot. A small Plymouth sat behind the building, shaped like her father's car, its windows filthy and the tires flat. She walked around to the front. A phone booth stood close to the frontage road, its door accordioned open, a window shattered. Inside, the black and chrome phone remained, the entrails of the handset dangling mutely. She stepped into the booth, the wind could not find her there, pressed her head against the useless phone and closed her eyes.

A motor approached and she looked up. The pickup, powder blue and primer gray, rolled to a stop beside her. Eyes dancing, a face of stubble, young, dirty hands on the wheel, two other heads bobbed beyond him in the cab. "You dumb bitch, why'd ya just stand in the road?"

She bolted from the booth and across the pavement. A horn blared. The door of the pickup slammed. She ran down the median and across the culvert before looking back. He stood there, arms akimbo, yelling something over the roar of the passing diesels and looking for a gap in the long convoy of trucks that had appeared. She ran up the other side, slipping in the wet, rotting weeds, falling forward. Something stung. She drew up her hand and looked at the mud impacted there with a long shard of green glass. She plucked it away and red welled up, pulsing through the skin and down her wet wrist. She pinched it with the other hand, running across the opposite lane and under the far side of the overpass. She looked back again and the pickup had started to move through the arc of a U-turn.

She scrambled up the embankment, reaching the shoulder of the road returning to the motel, and started running, her left palm still bleeding. Looking at it made it hurt more, made her run faster, made her forget the pain in her chest.

The motor was behind her now, speeding, grating, shifting, then slowing. She ran in leaps, down off of the shoulder. *I can go off the road. They won't go off the road.*

"Hey, where you going such a hurry?" The horn tooted. "Hey you. You fast. You fast at everything?" Laughter in the truck.

"Hey! You wanna fuck me?" A fist thumped on the side of the door. They matched her speed.

Another voice. "What's that she's wearin'?"

"You want a ride? I'll give you a ride if you give me a ride." More laughter.

The fence dipped to the ground and she was over it, into the rows of furrowed mud, where she drew up her gown above her ankles, her feet leaden. A drop touched her face, spittle, or urine, then another drop. It was raining. She veered far from the road. The pickup was there at the edge of her vision; it sped, decelerated, then sped once again, with a holler from the cab, then receded in the distance.

She slowed until she stood still, rain pouring steadily on her, chador and manteau soaked to her like a second skin. She did not feel cold so much as sleepy, and so tired, her muscles all ached equally so that she could not tell where she hurt, only that she would become stone if she did not move again. She was grasping the fabric in her left hand and tried to let go of it but it stuck to her palm. One step followed another. A cough. A deep breath and more pain. She stopped again and looked around. The horizon and the highway and the pickup truck had vanished into a blanket of gray fog, descended from the sky.

She tromped on, automatically, mindless of each step in the ooze. When she finally looked up again the motel was before her, but no Saab. She crossed the grass, stomping her feet, finally reaching the lost screen. She picked it up and pushed it through the open window, then placed her hands on the sill and pulled, but her hands could not close on the edge, and she slipped off. She failed a second time, leaving a long, bloody streak on the white trim, and wondered if her arms, dull and numb, were paralyzed. Her back against the wall, she stared up at the soffit until it was the building that moved behind her, she was falling away backward from the zinc sky. She found herself before the door of the office, her fist moving mechanically. After several minutes of pounding the door opened and an unveiled woman stood before her, but slammed the door shut. Erika struck it again and again with both frozen fists, three, four times.

"That is all! Stop that! What do you want?" The woman glared, looking up and down the length of her. A small, silent boy came next to the woman, and she pushed him back protectively without looking down at him.

"I'm locked out."

"My husband manages those things. Come back later." She started to close the door.

"In the name of the merciful…"

The woman turned.

"Please," Erika said.

The woman left the door half-open, went behind the desk, pulled open a drawer and withdrew a key. *"Mundan,"* she snapped at the boy and bustled past Erika.

Erika trailed behind her the length of the motel. The woman stopped at the end unit and unlocked it, then turned and glared at Erika. "You are not"—she hesitated, searching for harsher repudiation—"a good Muslim."

Erika closed the door as she marched away and looked around the room. It was undisturbed except for the tangled, rain-soaked curtains and the wet carpet. She slid the screen under the bed, wiped her blood off the sill, and shut the window. She laid the coins on the dresser and stared at the jagged opening in her hand. Her palm had stopped bleeding.

She began to shake, shivering so violently she could not untie the wet chador. Mud caked the manteau to above the knee and she tugged at it, leaving a trail of dirt into the bathroom, where she pulled off all of her clothing, putting them in the tub and then, still shivering, stepped in herself. She turned on the shower and stood there for a long time until she stopped shaking, pushing her clothes around with her feet, coughing, watching her shoes fill like little buckets. The steam made it difficult to breathe. Little drops of red fell again from her hand and swirled toward the drain.

Hunger became nausea. She hung the wet clothes on the coat hook above the heater. She coughed again and felt something move in her chest. Another cough and it was in her throat. Over the sink she coughed again and propelled a rusty mass against the porcelain.

Less light came through the windows and it was raining again, drops driven against the glass like a thousand little feet. She crawled under the covers naked, curled up, and shivered until she fell asleep.

*

"The floor is very dirty here." His voice arrived in a dream. Something poked her.

"My little Aisha, I said, the floor is very dirty here." He sat before her again in the plastic chair, his tie and his white shirt loosened, his trousers rolled up. He picked something from the sole of his bare foot and tossed it at her face. "So what does my little Aisha desire?"

She struggled, trying to decide if he was real. His question held an element of truth.

"You have been out walking. You've made a big mess. You desire your freedom?" He stood and walked around the bed. "The woman, they say, has most of the desire. Nine parts of ten." He snapped away the covers and sat down across her left leg, driving her knee into the mattress so she could not move away from him. "Maybe you want another man. Maybe I am not so big for you, no?" He seized her thigh and pressed a thumb deep between her legs, deep into her.

She gasped and choked on something in her throat.

"In some places, some countries, they keep the woman from wandering by taking away some of the desire. Just a little piece of her." He stroked her with the tips of his fingers, then pulled a lock-knife from his other pocket, a knife she had not seen before, and flipped it open. "Maybe I need to do that." He wiggled his thumb inside of her. "Better myself, a doctor, than in some village." He brought the blade closer, until she could not see where it was. "That is right. Be very still." He stared into her, leaning forward, the cold flat of the blade against her labia. He kissed her.

"But in Iran, we do not do this thing. We are civilized." He closed the blade against his leg. "And I love my little Jinn just the way she is." He pinched her as he said this, then withdrew his thumb. He touched her abdomen and then her breast. "You are hot. You like this game? Maybe we will play it again sometime. Or do you have fever?" He stroked her face. "Yes, I think you are sick. You deserve what you get."

He stood up and she felt the blood flow back into her leg. He went into the bathroom, and not closing the door completely, urinated.

When she awakened again the room was dark and smoke burned her throat, her arms sticking to wet canvas, a blue flame consuming every strand of her, filling her lungs, she could not take in enough air to scream. I can move my head, she thought, and snapped her head from side to side, extinguishing the flames until a column of gray was to her left, smoke rising from her bedroom desk. Her arms and her hands were there, and she pressed them though her wet hair. She lunged to the right in the darkness where the globe had stood, striking Majij in the head.

He grumbled, then sat up, turning the lamp on. "What is it now? You are wet. The bed…did you piss the bed?"

She rubbed her eyes and it was clearer. Her eyes hurt to touch them.

"Get up." He stepped around the bed and pulled at her arm and it scalded where he touched her. She stood and the room reeled.

"Come, into the bathroom."

She followed him and saw herself naked in the mirror when the light went on and was surprised that nothing was burned. She slumped onto the toilet, leaned forward, and vomited.

"In the tub. Do that in the tub," he said, and cursed in Farsi.

She was empty and retched instead and shook on the cold porcelain.

Majij took the still damp muddy towel from the wall and threw it onto the puddle before her. "You will need to clean that up. I will not." Then went into the bedroom and sniffed the mattress.

Erika could only stare at the towel, which, against the yellow linoleum, had become a little mound of snow.

He reappeared with a stethoscope and moved it about her back. "I have nothing for you. It is four o'clock. You have pneumonia in there." He thumped her back. "It got in when you went for your little walk." He wiped her down with a warm, damp cloth and wiped her face. "Rinse your mouth." He held a plastic cup to her lips. He wiped up the puddle of vomit and threw the towel under the sink, then led her back to bed where she sat shivering. Majij pulled a long T-shirt from his duffel on the floor and handed it to her. "This is dry. Put it on." He laid down and turned off the lamp. "Tomorrow I will get medicine. You are expensive girl. I should send a bill to your father."

She fell over onto the mattress and pulled the blankets around her, shivering until every muscle was exhausted. A column of gray light at the window began to sway and curl like smoke and she turned away. When she looked again, it was her mother, next to her desk, still and mute.

*

At midmorning the door slammed and he was back, walking through the glare, a small paper sack in his hand. She remembered fragments of his leaving, tangled up with the memory of her own chest of drawers in brilliant purple, waltzing across the room, talking to her. Majij stripped the seal from a glass vial and injected it with the fluid from another. He inverted it a few times and drew the milky mixture back into the syringe.

"Roll over," he said.

"What's that...oow!"

"It is antibiotic. Streptomycin."

"What if I'm allergic to it?" She coughed. "My mom says I'm allergic to penicillin."

"You want to die of an allergy or die of pneumonia? Next time maybe you don't try to go away."

The ache flowed down her left leg. "Jeee-sus shit, that hurts. I've never had a shot hurt so much in my life."

Majij wadded the small sack from Ranch and Home with the six dollar receipt, put them in the trash, and sat on the bed next to her. He had guessed at her weight, about a hundred and thirty pounds, the same dose for a young calf. He leaned over her with one arm. "You make me very angry sometimes.

To do angry things. You will be better about this. So will I." She sipped on ice and 7-Up he brought to her for the rest of the day and slept.

The following morning, he awakened her with a kiss on the forehead. "Two more days, it will be your Thanksgiving. It is on Thursday this year."

"It's always on Thursday." And under her breath, she added, *"Asshole."* Her leg still ached, but was becoming numb. Tuesday. She had tried to leave on a Sunday, she thought. A day was missing. Was he lying? Sometimes he just didn't know and made things up. "Maj, are there any televisions in this motel?"

"I can ask to borrow. Why do you want one?"

"Oh, I thought you might want to watch football on Thanksgiving."

He cupped the side of her face with one hand. "I do not care about football." He ran his fingers up through her hair, noticed the blond, and tousled it. "You are becoming someone else."

"Huh?"

"Erika the Nurse comes back."

There was nothing else to say. She felt she had drained away all of the words that were left between them, even commenting on football seemed false.

The next two days he did not look at her for more than a glance at a time and spoke in brief courtesies, while he injected her each morning, his voice monochromatic, compressed, as if he feared that someone in the next room could hear. Twice as he spoke, he began hesitant, apologetic, but ended in sarcasm. He helped her dye her hair, holding her head under the faucet longer than she thought necessary, and she thought she could sense some hatred in his fingertips, some hesitancy to let her up at all. When they spoke again, it was in simple platitudes. She did not mention the knife again, and he did not speak of her day in the rain. It was a mutually agreed upon amnesia. Erika would lie with her arms still at her side for an hour or longer after he had turned out the light, waiting for his breathing to tell her he was asleep, before allowing herself to relax.

*

They sat on the edge of the bed with the television balanced on the nightstand, its antenna bent forward first, then in various positions as the images of floats, marching bands, and balloons vanished into a zigzag of buzzing snow, to triplicates of ghosts marching past Macy's, each a separate color. Finally the antennae were pushed back away from them like the ears of a humiliated cat. The image was still unsteady unless Majij held onto one of them, which he would not do.

"That really is snow," she said. "They're having a blizzard."

"It is the north, isn't it?" He thought of a glass globe his father had given him, with the Statue of Liberty, a sawtooth of miniature skyscrapers, and two towers at the right. When you shook it, snow swirled around the tiny city. "It snows there often."

"Not like this. Not in November. Those kids must be freezing."

He sat next to her, looking at the girls' legs, amused by the fanfare on the screen. As Erika became more animated, pointing out Rocky and Bullwinkle, trying to draw him into her enthusiasm, he grew more disinterested.

"Foolishness," he murmured.

"Beats Khomeini's funeral."

"That was different. Serious."

"Isn't there any time in Iran where people get dressed up, have fun?" She emphasized the last word. "Not everything's gotta' be serious as a heart attack."

"There was a holiday, very old," he reflected, puzzled, "when people got dressed like your Halloween. We were boys, and we used to jump over a fire. But not since the revolution."

"What did they call it?"

"I don't remember. It surprises me." After thirty minutes, he felt alien and small and angry at his own amnesia and at the stupid, fuzzy people on the screen—so much hilarity about nothing. Hakim watched him. Just one hundred miles away, he drew Majij's moral compass out of its random arc and provided him direction. Obscene displays of young virgins' legs, the glitter of their bodies down to the crotch—not virgins at all, no; all those boys blowing in horns had them, last night, the night before, and now they marched down the street proud of it, so proud in their glitter, girls twirling the long, stiff, shiny rods in the air with the ball at each end, smiling into the camera for the world to see, so proud of their indecency, proud that no one else dared do this before God. It was right that they should be cold. They all should die.

He pulled the plug from the wall, and the picture vanished.

She snapped away from him on the mattress, back to the headboard and pulled a pillow to her chest, but he just stared at her.

"I'm sorry," he said. He leaned forward and rubbed his temples, then his closed eyes with the tips of his fingers.

"Hey, maybe we could go somewhere for Thanksgiving dinner?" She poked the tip of her socked toe at the edge of his leg.

"I will go. Bring something back." He was up, jacket on and keys in hand in one motion.

When he returned carrying two sacks, his entire posture had relaxed. "I bought a turkey," he said, "and pumpkin pie."

Erika laid a towel on the bed between them, and Majij emptied the sacks, one item at a time. A foil pie pan with a plastic cover. A tub of mashed potatoes. A black plastic tray with a small bird.

"That's not a turkey."

"It is a small turkey."

"It's a chicken."

Majij took the knife from his pocket and opened it, cutting away a leg and thigh. He placed it on a paper plate and handed it to her.

*

A week passed. He would hold her, put his lips on her neck, and breathe into her ear until she would reluctantly drape her arms about him, allowing gravity to form an embrace. She put her ear against his chest while she listened to his heart, and wondered what it would be like if it simply stopped beating.

Each night there was the flurazepam, but she had grown accustomed to them and did not sleep, but looked forward nonetheless to the dreamy forgetting that they brought, the glide downward, a comfortable apathy. Every third or fourth night he would roll over upon her and smother her with his mouth, but he was not really looking at her, she thought, and she would close her eyes while he took her, moistening herself with her saliva to lessen the pain. Nonnegotiable, a due she paid, perhaps to keep her life, and neither of them spoke. He would have to navigate on his own, masturbate within her; she would not lead him now. She imagined Steven one night, surprising herself with a memory of a July day in the city swimming pool, when he had pulled her against him, close enough that the water was pressed away. They were both laughing, and some younger boys were splashing them, and she'd wanted to kiss him then but only realized it now, and had kept laughing because that was what everyone did, while she felt him grow firm in his swimming suit. He had kissed her but only on the neck because she turned her head.

But now she didn't, and they were alone, and he'd loosened her two-piece and she pulled away his trunks, and everything good, powerful, and true about him flooded into her, and her chance was there to return all of his attention that she had almost cheated him of.

*

"Someone is taking children from this town," Teresa thought. The people she thought she knew said nothing when she was in Albertson's; they came and went like machines, and she wondered if this was happening everywhere. Someone takes your child and then you forget about it. They gave you medicines that made you constipated, and then the thoughts stopped moving too. The girls have stopped coming to her office because they have been taken. She mentioned it to Mr. Hathaway, the principal, who only smiled and squeezed her arm gently and told her to get more rest. He is part of it as well.

She has looked for Erika's friends, but they are not to be seen in the park, at the public swimming pool, at the cinema where she parks the car sometimes when she is free of Sam. They have also been taken. Until the end of the year, she would linger in the school bus loading zone like a post in a stream, surrounded by a sea of turbulent, shouting students, looking for a glimpse of her daughter, believing that her disappearance was a weak hoax, that she was going to class with a different name, staying with another family. She just had to catch her at it. Someone must be helping her; she's not that bright a girl, after all.

A late summer afternoon, nine years earlier, overtakes her, a recurring, intrusive memory, she has even dreamed of it. Sometimes the dream tumbles over and follows her through her day, and here it is again. The sounds of the students wane.

Erika, almost six, stands on the back of her red tricycle in dusty patent leather shoes and a yellow cotton dress, watching something on the highway. The pavement banks steeply as it passes a bend near the house. The sun shines after a rain, the air damp and smelling of earth. The wind flutters her dress.

Teresa smiled at this. An onlooker might have thought she had spotted her child.

Erika has found a piece of rusty baling wire on the shoulder and holds it in her right hand, such a thing can be useful. She stands higher on her toes, mesmerized.

Crossing the centerline, folding, expanding forward, is a snake. A diesel growls upgrade, the blast of an air horn, a gust follows, sand and particles of dry wheat blow against her cheek, her blond hair dancing around her face. The snake writhes aimlessly for a few seconds, then stops moving. Erika steps down from her tricycle, looks and listens in each direction, then scrambles forward and squats in front of her discovery. It is beautiful, easily as long as Erika is tall, its back an elaborate pattern of gold and brown diamonds, a little spot of blood where its head has been pressed into the coarse surface of the asphalt. She pokes at it several times with the wire, but it does not move. She lifts its tail, but it is much heavier than she expects. She pulls the wire beneath its head and manages to separate it from the pavement, making a twist around the place where it is flat, hooking the other end of the wire beneath the seat of her tricycle.

She pedals down the gravel back to her house, looking over her shoulder, the snake tumbling over the rough surface. Squeals, terror, the illusion of being pursued. Teresa slices cabbage by the kitchen sink while tiny militant Iranians shake their fists at her from a black-and-white television on the counter. She looks up to watch her daughter as she pedals up the driveway. Is that a stick? An old belt? She prepares to look amazed when Erika bursts into the kitchen with the dead reptile in hand.

Last night, the dream had taken a different course, and she had sounded different explanations against what she knew of dreams and what she had read, but did not mention it to Sam. The snake had been alive.

"Mrs. Etulain, you all right?" It was Melinda.

Teresa seized the girl, hugged her, pulled her head against her chest until the pressure of her ring began to cut the girl's ear. The girl struggled and pushed, her books fell to the ground, other students slowed, began to form a circle of stares. One of the bus drivers was approaching through the crowd.

"I'm sorry, I'm so sorry," Teresa said. "The snake…"

Melinda backed away from her, then squatted down and picked up her books, never breaking her gaze. "It's okay, Mrs. Etulain," she said. "It's okay."

15

Ramadan would not arrive until April, but Majij felt Erika should experience the sacrifice before she met his brother, it would acclimate her, he thought, to the realities of their life abroad, and so he told her that it had begun, one morning late in November, admonishing her after she took a sip from an abandoned can of Coke. She swallowed rapidly before putting it down, like a dog with a captured hamburger.

Each morning, Majij would leave while the sky was black, pulling on his suit, knotting his tie, with all of the lamps on in the room.

"Aisha, Aaai-sha." He would awaken her, leaning over her ear, "Nine more days until my brother's house," or "seven more nights we enjoy each other," in a voice Erika thought sarcastic, as if it were to be a relief. "Read," he would say, and thump on the Koran on the bedside table, "Read it, make notes. My brother will ask you. If you are not…earnest, he will make no papers, no passport for you."

Some mornings he would quiz her in Farsi, but taught her mostly nouns. After he left she would try to imagine herself speaking on the telephone, or in a market, and always felt that she would have to point at things stupidly. She would never be able to give a command, tell a story, or ask for help. She paced, reciting until she had committed it all to a temporary memory, adequate to regurgitate when he asked her the next morning, but believing the whole exercise as pointless as counting spots on a leopard. She hoped another opportunity to escape would come, but tried not to dwell on it.

The cylinder lock would click in the door, his footsteps subside, the Saab would start, and then he would be gone, taking her coat and shoes in the car as well. Her own watch had stopped, leaving the only instrument of time the Seiko on his arm, which he took with him.

Fasting was absolute, he would remind her, and took all of the leftovers from the previous night out to the dumpster. He had a weakness for cocoa puffs, however, and bought large generic sacks of them. She would try to estimate how many she could eat without his noticing, sometimes putting ten or fifteen back. The water in the bathroom had a slippery taste and never satisfied her. By the time he would return, in the dark, her stomach would ache, digesting itself.

Night did not vanish with the dawn but receded incrementally until noon, when the concrete skies were the thinnest, as if the whole state was shrouded by a gray eggshell. She scrutinized every piece of paper she could find, receipts, food wrappers, fragments of newspaper, anything that might be dated, an anchor in time for her to grasp. It seemed essential that if only she could get a fix on the date, she would have a handhold, regaining control of one small aspect of her life. Her cough lingered, and her grip on her toothbrush, and on her buttons as she dressed, seemed barely able to overcome gravity. "If the door were opened tomorrow," she thought, "I could barely run to the office."

He left his small day planner on top of the dresser while he showered one evening, and she thumbed through it. It Single-word entries in English, longer notes in Persian or Arabic, dotted the pages. Two slips of paper from fortune cookies: 'All that you have planned for is about to unfold' and 'Happiness is wanting what you have.' When had they eaten Chinese? Somewhere in South Dakota. The second one had been hers. Fourth of July. A circle on her birthday, the twenty-eighth. Thanksgiving. Christmas. No Ramadan was marked at all. A New Year's Eve fantasy she had dreamt of her first month in his apartment came back to her, of heels, leather, Majij in a tuxedo, dancing until midnight, and the kiss. She could picture none of it, now as remote as a swim with dolphins. Only his knuckles and his knife remained—no embrace, only his grasp. The adhesive that paralyzed his feet, his thoughts, this religious glue that he could not communicate beyond its prohibitions, now held her immobile by association. She slumped to the edge of the bed, clutched her arms around herself, and rocked. "Fuck Iran," she whispered to herself. "Fuck him."

*

Majij packed all of their clothes one morning while Erika still lay half-asleep, her face buried in the pillow. "My work in Salinas is finished," he announced.

She sat slowly upright in bed, floating on the tails of the flurazepam.

He placed her blue jeans, two pair of sheer satin underwear, and a pair of thigh-high stockings in a separate paper sack that he dropped in the dumpster when he went outside. An abayah, a chador, several pairs of black socks, a pair of white, and some white cotton underwear were all that remained, hanging over the shower rod, when she slipped into the bathroom to dress while he packed the car. He had left the door open.

Majij sat in the driver's seat with the engine off, staring at the open door. The wind blew around the windows of the Saab, rocking it gently, erratically. He looked over one shoulder, then the other, certain another police car somewhere was descending on him. Rashid knew now of all the dinar missing, knows he was right to suspect a Persian, a filthy thieving Iranian, and that he should have been wiser than to trust him with the receipts. Minutes were being counted, *his minutes,* until he was taken down. *Hakim does not know all that follows me; he may not make the papers at all. Why should he? bringing shame to his house. Righteous anger, is all that I deserve. And the laws for young girls here,* and then he felt the black sticks of the police, of the prisons, of her family, striking his every joint, breaking his bones, shattering his spleen, blood leaking from its capsule, his life draining into his belly.

He took a deep breath and exhaled slowly.

One must think, be, all that is expected. Path of the righteous. Or the righteous path? Become the idea. Carry the idea with you, at all times, keep it in your heart, and all around you will believe. I must believe for her, conceal her hypocrisy. A stray thought, motion below the surface, would betray both of us. She respects me now, loves me in honor, just a little afraid, but that is good, to keep the respect. The knife was a mistake, I should have just told her. But Hakim will frighten, better that she be accustomed. There are far worse men in the world. Hakim can change what a man thinks, gently, or violently, with a word, a look, or a gesture. I could not even get fat people to stop eating.

Erika appeared at the door and set her backpack on the cement. "I don't have a key. Should I close it?"

Majij nodded and watched her as she picked up the pack, then looked across the field to the west and hesitated. "Minutes are passing."

"Huh?"

"Hurry up, damn you."

She bowed her head, opened the passenger door, and sat down, pulling it shut.

As they crossed the overpass, Erika thought again of the afternoon in the rain, the pickup truck, and as they passed the derelict phone booth, her parents. She leaned forward and looked at her reflection in the rearview mirror, through the grimy glass. *I have become what I have become. They would not know me now.* Patches of snow, round, thawed, and refrozen, dotted the shoulder and the fields beyond, broken stubble rising though coffee ground earth to the horizon, with no tractor or machine for as far as she could see, abandoned to the futility of the cold months to come. She watched for a long time for a farm house. Finally there was a small cluster of buildings, a contour like a fortress a mile or so away, but no windows were lighted. She could not remember now why she had left her own home.

I've got to stop letting him fuck me. There would be more beatings, probably. *Could you beat someone for his or her love?* She wondered if his entire religion was like that. It stunned her. *Love given sought is good, love given unsought is better. But love after having the shit beat out of you, well now…*

Majij was poking her in the thigh with his finger.

She gave him a wintry look. "What did you do with my clothes?"

"It will be different there, for a while." He tried to sound positive.

"How?"

"Just different. If you think it is going to be bad, then it will seem bad to you. You should keep hejab at all times." He reached over and tugged the chador slightly.

"Why? Is your brother," she scowled, trying to find the most offensive phrase, "kinda' horny?"

"Do not say that. No, just proper."

"But we're *married*, Maj, Married. You've got the paper to prove it. Show him that."

Majij said nothing.

"It's kind of a bullshit paper, isn't it?"

"It is as bullshit as you believe. You talk very dirty today."

She positioned herself farther from his reach, reflexively. "It's a bullshit marriage, *Aguilar.*" She poked him beneath his armpit, hard enough, she hoped, that it would hurt. "I'm just your *pootah pinocha.*"

"It is important that my brother like you."

"I may not like him…"

"You must respect him. You will be in his house. He does not care if you like him, but to show you do not like him, that is disrespectful."

She ran her fingers over her palm where the green glass had been, the scar never completely closed. She had scrubbed it after their every intimacy, keeping it open, picturing the glass over and over again, emerging from her flesh like a birth. The memory gave her comfort. She picked away the scab and a drop of blood seeped out of the fissure. She touched it and placed it on her lips and looked in the vanity mirror on the back of the visor. She took a second and third drop and swirled them on her cheeks and admired the effect. He was squeamish, antiseptically so, about her periods. She wondered how much she could bleed before he put her out of the car.

She gathered her hair into two pigtails with her fingers and bobbed her head to one side, then the other, prancing her feet on the floor. "Oh," she sang, "we're off to see the brother, the wonderful brother of Maj. Because because because because, because of the creepy stuff he does," but when she looked over at him he had softened.

"I like it when you sing," he said.

He was just too ignorant to insult, she thought. They could not talk about the news on the radio because it never said what he wanted to hear. She could not talk to him about books because, she had gradually realized, he hadn't read any. Now, when she most wanted to make him angry, he was too stupid to notice. He gets mad, she thought, when he misunderstands things. And he doesn't understand shit. "I don't want to go to Iran."

"You don't know what you want."

The past eight months were too near to talk about. Every part of the future Majij controlled, its focus changing from minute to minute with no sense of certainty. Sometimes one thing was obviously a lie, the next day some portion of it would come true, but some other detail would fail to materialize. She tried to silently enumerate everything he had promised that had not come to pass. Returning to school, learning medicine, understanding a religion it now seemed obvious he did not understand himself. She lifted a dog-eared road atlas from the floor of the back seat and began to thumb through it. "Did you ever read *The Ransom of Red Chief*?"

"No. It is an Indian story?"

"It's about a little kid that gets kidnapped. In the end, the guys that took him want to take him back."

"You came because you wanted to." And in a voice he felt full of sincerity, added, "You are too dear to me to take back."

She turned away from his leer and ran her fingertips over the dirty pages. The days and nights and weeks muddled together now with the dozens of dusty little rural towns. He had taken her to these places to *hide* and fuck, not to make love to her. All of these places she thought she had chosen, tracing a nail along one state road or another, serpentine gray lines, which dot she stopped at did not matter, as long as they were hollow dots. Eight months. She looked at her stomach. Thank Allah for the pill. Now they were on an interstate, the car pulled along relentlessly in some magnetic field, Majij pulled as well by something she could not see. It is the end of something, she thought, and it has come after many, many illusions.

"They're not going to let us in," she said.

"Let us in where?"

"To Iran, stupid."

"And why not?"

"Because you're a lying fuck."

He drew back his fist and she dodged, but made fists herself, her arms braced to block. "A fat lip wouldn't look good to your brother, would it? Would look like you're not in control."

"You will learn respect."

"That's hilarious. Know what I used to think? I used to think that's what your religion was all about. But it's really control, isn't it? And you can't say you respect someone if you're trying to control them, can you?" She tweaked his ear and he swatted her away. "And you can't love someone you don't respect."

He rested his hand on the wheel again and bit his tongue until it nearly bled.

"You don't love me. Nobody likes liars, anywhere. Even revolutionaries."

*

It was after three when they reached Topeka, turning north and skirting the city on the west side on a different highway, crossing overpasses above train tracks, stark and steel against the snow beneath them. Past grain elevators and long, windowless warehouses, the yellow arc lights above the road grew brighter than the sky, and they passed from one pool of light to the next. Majij took an exit to a frontage road, turning into the parking lot of a Kmart. She started to whistle the Kmart jingle. He looked at her and she stopped. He parked at the red curb and trotted over to a payphone that stood next to a child-sized sports car on a motorized pedestal. Behind the plate glass windows people handed over money or waved credit cards, with their children in the seats of shopping carts, bundles of plastic sacks, a Tonka box, a white-and-silver Christmas tree, or a fluorescent pink plastic sled. Bobbing and weaving in caps and down jackets, looking side to side, moving together, but alone, forward slowly, crowded beyond the cashiers, they were water behind a dam. Someday all of this will be gone, he had told her once. Take away the water in them and they are dust. She imagined she saw Melinda and her mother in the crowd but dismissed the thought. The people in the store seemed distant and irrelevant, like extras in a movie. If they all died tomorrow, it would mean nothing; they weren't like her. Sucked into the stratosphere by a flash of heat, a Chinese missile, painless and sudden. *As for the unbelievers, neither their money or their children will in the least save them from God's judgment. They shall become coal for the inferno!* She dwelt on the thought for half a minute and it didn't seem just. What could these simple people in their greasy work clothes have done to deserve the wrath of all of the poorer nations of the world, the dark-skinned people, as Majij had called them? Someday all of this might really be gone, empty houses, broken windows, streets of dust, and corpses. Perhaps Majij *did* know things, she sensed, only terrible things, as much as he repelled her.

He was back in the car before she realized he had hung up. They rolled slowly between exiting shoppers, out of the parking lot and back onto the highway. At the next exit they turned onto a broad boulevard of traffic, strip malls, gas stations, Church's Chicken, and a Winn Dixie. Another right, a left, and the light fell away behind them. Snow and ice rumbled beneath the floor of the car as they moved down a block of one-story homes, every second or third house flickering or flashing with tiny bulbs, windows outlined in blue glow, plywood reindeer on a roof. Three plastic wise men worshiped in a floodlight with bales of hay, and at the corner, a house with three crosses lit in white. "Got their holidays mixed up," she said, but Majij said nothing. The car turned again, slowed, and pulled into a driveway bordered on one side by snow-encrusted junipers.

He turned off the engine. "Wait."

But she did not, opening her door as he did. He said nothing else, and she followed him to the front door, which rattled and opened before they touched it. A figure emerged.

How very much he looked like Majij! Or had Majij changed to look like him, as he had changed at the motel? Hakim's hair was cropped short enough to reveal an asymmetry of the skull, and even in the dim light, she could see a scar in the thick scalp above the right ear, the top of which was missing. A scant beard rimmed the jaw. She followed his eyes but he didn't look at her. Dull, inanimate, they absorbed the entire block, the street behind them, seeing into the dark, two lead bullets that failed to glint in the Christmas lights draped over the junipers by the door. The two men did not touch each other.

"Festive." Majij fondled a bulb.

"It is important, to appear…" Hakim stopped midsentence. "I will open the garage door. Put your car in there."

He went back into the house and slammed the door. The garage door hummed and rattled a moment later, rising to expose an unlit interior, only a chrome bumper, sterling letters, '560 SL,' and a three-pointed star visible in the colored lights. Majij started the Saab, his headlights illuminating Hakim standing in the passage of the dark garage like a figure in a wax museum. It chilled Erika, and Majij momentarily seemed as startled. He pulled forward and the door clattered shut behind them.

Hakim turned on the lights. "You've bought a new car. Is it Turbo?"

"No turbo. The Ford fell apart," Majij said apologetically.

Nearly nose to nose, Erika thought of a man looking into a mirror.

"But this"—Majij gestured at the Mercedes, of polished obsidian and easily a yard longer than the dripping Saab, the massive mirrored grill and bumper nearly touching their knees—"to do Allah's work."

"When one handles the money of others, it is important to appear to have no need of it yourself." Hakim looked at Erika then for the first time, regarding her as if she were a stray dog that had wandered into his garage.

"This is Aisha," Majij said.

Erika extended a hand. Hakim only stared at it, then turned and stepped into the house. "You have taken the name of the prophet's youngest wife. A most difficult girl. You should learn what became of her."

He limped slightly, as she followed behind him, Majij pulling the door closed. Hakim turned to her. "Come in, you are safe."

Her eyes widened in the low light of the hallway, smelling of damp, cold smoke, as if the house had burned at one time and was still wet after extinguishment. Hakim reached through an open doorway to the right and snapped a light on. The room was expansive in its emptiness. A large mattress and box spring lay on the floor with an unopened package of sheets. He turned to Erika. "You stay here."

She stepped into the room and stood cross-armed against the cold and looked around. A bathroom opened to the left, the fixtures dusty and still labeled by the manufacturer. Across the hallway was a living room with a large floral carpet and small cushions near the walls. She walked over and stood on the carpet, the room was a few degrees warmer. A computer sat on a coffee table at the window, the only embellishment a portrait on the wall of a stern, bearded, turbaned man. Hakim called to her from the end of the hall.

"Go into your room. I did not say to come out."

She stood where she was and leaned into the hall. "Can I get my stuff from the car?"

"Majij will get your things. Go into your room please, now."

She crossed the hall and sat down on the mattress, her arms still folded. Harsh whispers were exchanged at the end of the hall. A few minutes later, Majij appeared in the doorway, his hands on the frame above him.

"Is that your dad?" She pointed past him to the living room.

"No."

"Who is it?"

He turned and looked at the portrait, annoyed. "*Cue-tub.*" And offered no further explanation.

"Why does he keep it so cold?"

"So not to be wasteful."

"Is something wrong?"

"Make up the bed. Moving will keep you warm. I will bring your things later." He walked away.

They were in the kitchen, she thought, or some room beyond. Hakim's voice was shrill and emphatic from moment to moment. Majij's, if he answered at all, barely audible. She rocked gently on the mattress, and the floor squeaked in counterpoint. She stopped and held her breath to hear them more clearly. After a few minutes, she decided they were not speaking English, but here and there a word of French, and the rest Farsi, its speed and cadence something new to her ears, but at a pitch and a delivery that could only convey an argument. Hakim said something in Farsi. Silence. He said it again, slowly and more loudly, in a way someone might explain something to the mentally handicapped. Majij mumbled something, and Hakim shouted, a kind of shriek that jolted her, a chill traveling the length of her neck and into her hair.

"I cannot!" Majij shouted over his own footsteps.

A door was slammed. Majij appeared at the doorway momentarily but did not look at her. A door at the other end of the house creaked, and Hakim hissed an incantation of some kind. It sounded like a curse, and Majij stopped still. He did not move until the door slammed again, and then he turned out all of the lights in the living room, the bathroom, and the bedroom, lying down next to her on the mattress without removing his clothes. As her eyes adjusted, she could see his profile in yellow and then in blue, then in red, green, and then in red again, colors from the string of lights that encircled the roof of the house next door, studying him to verify that it was indeed her Majij and not Hakim, entertaining briefly the possibility that a trade had been made. It was Majij's smell, though, his weight and the terror of him, the terror measured and predictable, as well as his sparse kindness, and she settled into a perverse security.

She did not see his lips move and could not tell if his eyes were open or closed, or whether he had eyes at all. A voice came to her in half sleep, and she debated with herself whether it had been part of a dream or whether he had whispered or had just made the thought materialize by will: *Hakim will find you. He would kill you, if you leave here.*

*

Light filled the room. She sat up and looked around. Her duffel was by the door. Wind chimes tinkled somewhere outside, but there were no voices, no footsteps. She leaned on one elbow and then the other, focusing for voices, but she heard none. She pulled on her sandals and opened the door a few inches and peeked around. The house was empty.

The kitchen table was in disarray, chairs askew, two smudged bowls, a box of oatmeal, small handleless teacups, and a saucepan layered with cold, gelatinous cooked oats with a spoon anchored in its mass. She tugged the spoon loose and took a bite. She salted it and ate the rest in seven mouthfuls, stopping between chews to listen.

The back of the kitchen opened to a long porch stacked high with cardboard file boxes on one side covering most of the windows, which were frosted with winter. Closest to her, draped under a blanket, stood a large rectangular sheet of white plywood with 'State of Kansas Department of Licensing' lettered across the top and strips of white Velcro beneath, with an array of black plastic letters attached in random clumps. She let go of the blanket and turned to the pile of boxes, the top box of which was packed with evenly folded, pale blue-and-white computer paper with long columns of numbers. At one end of the box was a bundle of Polaroid snapshots, each of Hakim standing before the plywood sign. Trimmed, she realized, they would be driver's licenses. Each one had a different name. In the second box was more of the same paper, but a fold or rise in the stack made it sit unevenly. From the bottom of the box she withdrew a thick mailing envelope and opened it. Two bundles of bills were visible, with red rubber bands, faded and dirty at the edges. She paused, then pulled two bills from the center of the bundle and folded them without really looking at them, lifting her abayah and shoving them under the elastic of her panties. She returned the envelope and tried to quell her own panic at not marking the exact layer from which she'd taken it, and possibly putting it back in the wrong place.

The back door was dead-bolted like the front, but she twisted the knob instinctively anyway, and then in an act she felt immediate remorse for, wrote her name with her finger in the frost on the glass. She rubbed it away with her fingers, and it looked more obvious, so she blew on it, hoping she could mend the gap in the opacity, but this only formed droplets that coursed down the surface to the frame.

A closed door stood next to the refrigerator, and it occurred to her that she might not be alone after all, that Hakim might be there asleep. She stood still for a moment until she decided that the only breathing she heard was her own, then turned the knob and pushed it open. A twin mattress lay along one wall with two blankets folded at the foot, and parallel to it, a small rug with a greasy, rectangular block of wood at one end. A folded tripod with a Polaroid camera leaned in the corner. A nightstand sat by the door, on top of it a dagger in a pointed sheath, a few coins, and a paper box marked, *9x19mm Berdan Primed.* She backed out of the room and pulled the door shut.

The door to the garage was dead-bolted as well as the front door, the scarred bare wood and the shininess of the metal suggesting a recent installation. When she lifted the telephone receiver there was no dial tone. The entire house had a temporary feel about it, not the austerity of a home of people of limited means, but the transience of disorder, like a camp, someplace in a war movie that was used up while planning to move elsewhere, everything expendable.

She considered taking a chair from the kitchen and throwing it through the front window and crawling over the thicket of junipers and ice. But who would open a door to a crying girl dressed in a sheet? Hakim seemed as pervasive as the devil. He could find anyone. She went back to the sink and filled it with soapy water. The frost on the back window was not so noticeable, she would just tell them that she wanted to look outside.

*

Majij stood in the shower of the half-lit bathroom, hot water pouring over him. Hakim had recalled for him all of the details, in such astounding clarity that he wondered if some had not been embellished as they poured from his mouth, of an afternoon with a girl in the autumn when they had just turned fourteen. Majij had forgotten or had driven her name out of his memory, but that afternoon he had lain in the heat of the loft, on top of her, penetrating her, while Hakim created one story and then another to shield him from his mother, who scoured their house just twelve feet below. The girl was two years younger, the daughter of the woman who sold cloth a few blocks away, and while Majij had always recalled the girl as provocative, and the situation the outcome of a dare from his brother, Hakim retold it quite differently, with an authority that only compelled Majij to realize he had been lying to himself for nearly twenty years. A bastard came of it, and Majij and Hakim both unleashed a rumor that her own brother had fathered the child, refuting her every accusation. Eventually the cloth shop was boycotted, the girl and her mother had to move away. Her brother joined the army and they both feared he could come back armed, but they never saw him again either. The woman had been a friend to their mother, and had comforted her when their father was taken away six months earlier.

Hakim brought this up to emphasize how it had destroyed their mother. When Hakim had returned from Afghanistan she could not be located, and no one remembered her, as if she had never existed. Majij had remained awake the entire night, pondering exactly that, the destruction of his own mother, seeing her starve, being robbed as she loitered near a hospital, her decaying body in a culvert somewhere, unclaimed, eaten by birds.

"Believers do not befriend any but your own people. The infidel spares no pain to corrupt you," Hakim had read to him from the book. Now Majij could smell Erika on his skin, touch and see each place she had defiled him. He let the water pour over his head, his lips closed, his eyes closed. He cupped his hands, three times to the left, three times to the right. Hakim was right, all of this must stop. He must empty her from his life as one empties one's bowels.

Everything has come too easily for you. That which is most difficult is that worth achieving. You cannot love if it comes easily, because it has taken you. Release yourself. Do what is most difficult, become free of what has taken you; then you can know God's love. If love comes easily, it is not love. You are just yielding to carnal impulse. Nothing could be lower. "Mother, I did not know," he said aloud to himself and tasted bitter soap wash into his mouth.

Discard that! Destroy what you only think you love, and everything will be clearer. You will take the first step on the road to righteousness. "Mother, forgive me."

Everything will be clear, I promise you. Take the first step. You must. I cannot do it for you. Take the first step. Majij recapitulated these ideas for many minutes, until the shower ran cold. Then he stood there longer.

*

Sometime while it was still dark, she was aroused by a thump and heard the garage door rise a moment later, an engine started and retreated, then the door closed. She swept her foot farther under the covers. The sheets beside her were undisturbed. Not knowing where he was unsettled her and she awoke fully. Had he left with Hakim? Or had Hakim driven away, leaving Majij in the house? It occurred to her that Majij might have driven off, leaving her alone with Hakim. She held her breath and listened, then lifted the sheets and stood by the bed. At the door, she folded into herself, breathless, pulseless, no molecule in motion, fixed to the floor, invisible. Something living waited on the other side of the doorknob. She grasped the knob, pressed the center lock button, and backed away. Testing each step, she went into the bathroom, dragging a blanket with her, and locked herself in.

When it was light again, there were voices in the hall, footsteps still rapid with the energy of the outdoors. The door to the garage closed. The bedroom doorknob rattled. There came a curse in Farsi, in Majij's voice. "Aisha!"

She climbed out of the tub, opened the bathroom door, and panicked with the bedroom lock, jubilant at his voice and his familiarity, terrified it was him. Majij grasped the blanket with one hand and slapped her, but hit the wool beside her face.

"Why did you lock the door?"

"You left. You didn't come to bed." She sat down on the floor. "I thought I was alone," and she lowered her voice to a whisper, "with him."

He sat on the edge of the mattress and spoke to the back of her head. "I will never leave you alone." He stared at her for several minutes, the door drifted closed and she watched him askance in the full-length mirror on the back. He stared at the ceiling, his face expressionless, his entire countenance a posture of surrender, like a man who knew that soon he would drown and could do nothing to stop it. "With Allah you are never alone," he said finally and placed his face in his hands. "You should get dressed." He stood and left the room, leaving the door ajar.

At noon he returned to tell her she could come eat after the two men moved to the back of the room and spoke in harsh whispers. They left three ovals of lavash and something made of beans she could not identify. She went to her room afterward and fell asleep, her stomach in a gassy ache. In an hour he was back again, telling her she should *salat,* but suggested no prayer, only that she should prostrate herself and dwell on the damage she had caused and praise Allah. Allah knew, he said, when someone was simply staring at the floor, thinking of sex or new clothing.

A little while later, he returned once more, probed around in his own suitcase and produced his Koran. He tossed it on the bed by her and told her to read it. He closed the door and she lay on her side, leafing through the book, and thought of Melinda and snow and the handsome guy who had helped her to her feet, and her mother's pancakes. He had said, "The damage *you've* done." And she tried to retrace every moment of their time together, of every decision that, in the end, had always been *his,* and she had supported him, she thought, ignoring her doubts as she made their bed warmer. Until they had gone to that terrible motel. Until the beating. Something in him had died there; it had died in both of them. She turned the pages until the verse, 'On the care and feeding of women,' as she had privately come to call it, was between her fingers. She tugged at it gently, then more persistently, until the first edge of the page popped and slowly crackled like a tiny fabric until it was free, separated completely from the binding.

She stared at it, horrified, in her hand, then put it back and closed the book, but the edge stuck out just a fraction and she rubbed it with her fingers, trying to press it in further, but it only flattened and was more obvious. She took it out again, went into the bathroom and tore it into a dozen fragments, watching them drift around on the surface of the water in the toilet for a moment, and wondered if they would reassemble themselves. She pressed the lever and they swirled into a whirlpool and were gone.

16

Majij could see five of the houses across the street from his position at the living room window. At the second house, a robust man stepped onto the front porch for a moment, stooped stiffly, pulled an extension cord from the snow and plugged it in near the door. A string of green lights came on around the eaves. The muffled voice of a crow called somewhere on the other side of the glass. Evening. In five days he had slept no more than three hours. Hakim had forbidden him the flurazepam, snatching the bottle from his hand at the sink, Just another Western vice. He was amiss, behind in his studies. Hakim fixed him more black tea with brown sugar, taking away the cold sticky cup, putting the fresh one before him. He turned the light brighter, took the shade from the bulb. The light burned through Majij's eyelids.

Majij had sat at the chrome kitchen table while Hakim circled, relentless, vigilant. All of heaven would know. Hakim had said this, nudging him each time he would doze off. All of heaven would know. He would drift, seated in the kitchen chair, to his office, to a dying patient, to white cotton sheets, to Erika's legs, his head would nod. Hakim would pace clockwise, then counterclockwise. All of heaven would see. Their father, their dead mother, all of the martyrs who had died fighting Iraq watched while Majij screwed American girls. It was now established firmly, unquestionably, ashamedly, that he had not confronted the knowledge before: their mother was dead. Whatever had distracted him from this obvious conclusion? Heaven would know, but heaven could forgive, Hakim said. Heaven could see when malevolent forces, when unreasonable temptation, could overcome a man. Only a change in the heart was required, and all actions thereafter would be guided by God, just as they had been guided by temptation. "Hakim does not lie," Majij spoke aloud, expecting some feeling of validation, like a prayer, but his voice felt hollow.

Hakim knew the time and place to cleave away, he'd read the Haddith, the heretical and the faithful, where a life should begin and where it should end. He saw the trajectories of nations and the trajectories of the people that belonged to those nations, how each might be played out according to God's plan, how each could go asunder. Hakim possessed the mandate, the two men knew now, to correct by the most expedient means, whatever impeded God's will. Hakim saw, Hakim was relied upon by God. "I lie. Hakim does not."

How can I be relied upon? He turned and went into the bedroom.

Hakim had pointed out, was quite just to point out, that Erika's presence could compromise all of his work, an entire operation dedicated to returning Iranian funds to the people of Iran, assets now used unjustly by America.

Someone would be looking for her. How could he be so stupid not to realize that? Not just her parents—even American police could be very sentimental about these things. The FBI or the CIA might be involved. They would think she had been kidnapped, and she would only need to talk to one person. *What could I have been thinking?* America was giving poison gas and money to Iraq. He lifted one of her Nikes from the mattress and it felt foreign to him. His own people were starving in every hamlet. They relied on the Arab nations around the world to restore their wealth, taken by the Shah, usury by Jews and Americans everywhere. Hakim's work was essential in restoring these monies to Iranian accounts. Did Majij want to destroy this lifeline?

"Has she been unhappy?" Hakim asked. "She might have signaled someone. Made a phone call."

"No," Majij said. "I've treated her well. I've clothed her." And he paused, remembering his expedition into Victoria's Secret. "I've fed her, taught her, cared for her when she was sick. She has never been out of my sight."

He repeated this as he buttoned his shirt, looking down at her where she napped. Foolish girl. You didn't want to go to Iran after all. Where is your curiosity? She murmured and rolled her head deeper into the pillow.

But she loves me. No, you just like to fuck her and you have confused the two, Hakim had said. *You may love a thing although it is bad for you, and hate a thing although it is good for you. The Almighty knows but you do not.* Hakim was right, she did not love him but only planned to use him, for his money and rank. They all wanted to marry doctors. She had been insolent for weeks. She could never believe, was incapable of sacrifice.

When he looked at her again she had opened her eyes, and for a moment, he wondered if she could hear his thoughts. "Get up."

"What's wrong?"

"Just get dressed. We need to go get something."

She looked so apprehensive. He took a deep breath and slipped his hands into his pockets in a casual slouch. "We need to go shopping for some food and other things. The car needs gas. I just thought you'd like to come along. Hakim says he must work alone for a while."

"And if I try to get away again?"

"You won't. You won't try." He put his hands on his knees and leaned forward and spoke more softly. "We must trust each other if I am to protect you from him. He has friends in this city. Important people," he lied. "Even the police."

"Couldn't we just get a motel room? This place creeps me out."

He stood. "Come."

"What about my coat?"

"It is in the car."

When she was seated in the Saab he shut her door, then got into his own seat and turned the key. The starter cranked monotonously, hollowly, but the engine did not turn over. Erika crouched and shivered. He switched the key off and tried again, with the same result. When he looked up Hakim stood barefoot at the mouth of the hallway. Majij rolled down the window.

"Perhaps it is your battery."

Majij got out of the Saab.

"Take my car." Hakim threw him a ring of black keys.

Erika climbed over the console of the Saab and stepped out as well.

"The garage door opener is on the visor," Hakim smirked. "You might open it before you leave." He closed the door, leaving them alone in the garage.

Majij opened the passenger side and Erika slid on to the leather seat. "What about my coat?" She glanced back at the Saab.

"You won't need it." He closed the door and it latched like a vault. He closed his own door and stared at the burl before him, the leather-wrapped wheel, feeling in the dark until he found the ignition in the steering column. He turned the key, a few lights on the panel flickered, the car's body twisted almost imperceptibly, and far away in front of them something hummed. The heater poured forth a gentle flow of already warm air, air Majij thought smelled of leather and money. He pressed the button on the garage opener and the door rolled up and over them.

*

Hakim watched between the living room curtains, the big Mercedes passing in a ripple through the wet glass. A moment later, the Suburban followed, its headlights still dark. He had noticed the Suburban four days before, always at about the same place, within visual range of his front door. A very new vehicle, dark blue. If the seal of the United States had been painted on the door it would not have surprised him at all. He had driven past it four times now, always approaching it from behind. Always there were two men in it, not dressed like people from this neighborhood, not dressed like people who worked. The driver was a white man, the passenger was black. They never looked at him, he did not know their eyes. His first instinct had been to park on the next street or in the alley and go in his back door, but he had grown fond of the big German sedan and wasn't sure what might happen to it if he left it parked out of his sight.

And what would he say to his good, simple neighbors? Two years before, in a whispered conversation with old Mrs. Bartholomew over the back fence, Hakim explained how his whole family had been killed by revolutionaries in Iran. How he, a former colonel in the Iranian Army, still loyal to the Shah (now in Christian heaven) and to the United States, struggled to make a new life. A few weeks later an older man he didn't know passed on the sidewalk and said, "Good morning, Colonel," as Hakim backed his car from the garage, and it was clear that they all held him in the same reverent esteem.

He had been waiting for a sign that his work here was drawing to a close and the Suburban was that sign. It had been a comfortable time doing God's work.

Majij, he was pretty certain, would not kill the girl. Majij could waste an hour deciding if he needed to piss. Faced with a decision like the one before him now, he would wring his hands all night.

Hakim turned away from the window, picked up a bundle of floppy disks from the computer he'd erased earlier that evening, and went to his room off of the kitchen, where he placed them in a cowhide carpet bag. Passports, maroon, blue, black, green, ahh, the serpent and the condor. Was it better to be the serpent, or the condor? He took two thick envelopes from the top box on the back porch and placed them in the bag as well. On top of these he folded a corduroy sport coat. He snipped the price tag from a new Stetson, then crushed the hat and pushed it into the bag. In the bathroom he gathered a small mirror, a package of gold adhesive foil, and a theatric moustache. He lathered his face and shaved away his beard, admiring himself briefly when he finished.

So she loved Majij. He would go to jail, people there would love him also. It would be good for him. People were useful to Allah or they were not. One must decide, where there is apostasy, even if they have the same mother as yourself. He placed the metal wastebasket in the bathtub and turned on the fan.

Hakim slipped from room to room down the hallway, purposefully, mercury through a maze. Papers, a few photographs, receipts, a driver's license, and five credit cards he had replaced from his brother's wallet, all of these he gathered together and placed in the metal trash can and set them on fire. From Majij's room he took Erika's backpack and stuffed it with her remaining underclothes, a nightshirt, a single sock (no time to look for the other), and her toothbrush. No makeup? Majij had been preparing her well. He took Majij's remaining shirts and suit, checked the pockets, and hung them in his own room. He stopped in the hallway on the way to the garage and pulled the Stetson out of the bag and it popped back into shape. He stepped into the bathroom, gathered some soot from the edge of the trash can, smudged the crown and the rim, then shoved it back into the bag.

He placed the backpack and his own bag in the back of the Saab as well as a small thin screwdriver, a plastic box of battery acid, and a jar of metal fragments. He pulled the hood release, reattached a distributor wire, sat in the driver's seat, and started the engine. Seven twenty-one; only twenty-five minutes had passed. The engine idled while he reviewed a mental checklist. He climbed out of the car and returned to the kitchen, where he pushed the table to one side, lifted the crawl space door, and kneeling down, reached as far as he could into the dark cold and adjusted something. He gently replaced the door, slid the table back, and a moment later rolled into the street without touching his brakes. *Bismaillah al rahman Rahim,* he said to himself, and drove off.

*

As they stopped at Fairway Avenue, Erika glanced at the three white crosses, where a violet angel profile had been added to the display above the cross to the left. She looked over the seat, hoping there might be a blanket in the back, and was struck by the odd illusion that the vehicle behind them had only just turned on its lights. It was a truck, she thought. It slowed, maybe looking for an address, and remained about fifty feet behind them. She stared at it as it sat motionless on the packed snow of the street and decided it really had had its lights off. If only it could be a police car. She pulled the lock button up quietly and Majij didn't turn his head, absorbed as he was somewhere else. The grocery store would likely be in a strip mall with ten or twelve other little businesses, maybe a pizza restaurant full of little kids and half-drunk parents. She would only have to run from the car a hundred feet or so and fling herself into a crowd. No, he'd probably be close to her initially, on guard when they first got out of the car. She'd wait till they were inside, offer to go to another aisle to get something. But what did they need? He hadn't told her. She would say she needed tampons; he wouldn't follow her then.

Majij gunned the sedan into traffic and they turned, the tail of the car swerving slightly.

When she looked back again she realized the truck was a Suburban and had turned in behind them. She watched the traffic in front, looking into the passenger rearview mirror every few moments. Sometimes the Suburban was there, sometimes it wasn't. Maybe it was better not to leave the store at all, because he would assume she had. Hide in plain view, go into the back where there are pallets and boxes of fruit, maybe go into a freezer, it was safe enough for ten minutes or so, and there was always a handle to get out. Taillights blurred in the streak of the wiper blades and the drops that froze as they hit the glass. All of the traffic had slowed to twenty miles per hour, the street had grown smooth and reflective, the mist beneath the tires scant. In the center turn lane one small sedan had hit another, a blue-and-white police car had stopped, its light bar twinkling. The drivers faced each other in the rain, their arms gesturing, mouths moving, a policeman with plastic on his cap held a penlight in his teeth and wrote with mittens on.

On the left they approached a shopping mall with a Winn Dixie, but Majij pulled into the outside lane and stopped, waiting to turn onto the ramp to the freeway. Erika turned and a copper-colored station wagon was behind them, a tired woman at the wheel, the motion of arms and legs of misbehaving children bouncing in the seat behind her. Behind the station wagon idled the Suburban.

The Mercedes moved up the on-ramp tenaciously. The Buick turned as well, fish-tailing as it made the corner, then overcorrected. The Suburban followed.

Erika looked back at the shopping center they had passed. As she watched, the car behind them spun, a gentle half-circle pirouette, smashing into the Suburban behind it. The two doors of the Suburban opened almost simultaneously, two men jumping out. She pressed the button on the console and her window rolled down, letting in the sleet and clatter of the studded tires.

"What are you doing?" Majij scrambled his fingers over the console until he found her button and rolled the window up again.

"There was an accident. I just wanted to see better." It seemed, for a second, as if one of the men was pointing directly at her, a black man with a phone or walkie-talkie. She turned farther in her seat but her window kept fogging with her breath. She had been surprised that he had asked her to come along. Perhaps a debate of her worth had been waged, in the conversations she'd overheard, and even without an opportunity to demonstrate her qualities, she had prevailed. But as the Winn Dixie receded in the night and the weather, something sank in her stomach. They weren't going to buy anything. "We passed a grocery store back there."

"Where?"

"Just before we got on the freeway."

"It was not the right store."

She looked over at his silhouette. Jesus, how he looked like his brother. "We're not in the right car either."

"How do you mean?"

"You said we needed to get gas for the car. The car means the Saab. Then we changed cars. So we're not in the right car now, are we?"

He looked at her, then looked away. She turned on the radio.

"*...make the Yuletide gay, from now on our troubles will be miles away...*"

Out in the rain in the night, another strip mall appeared, then faded in the translucent fog that swept over the highway in sheets. "Maj?"

He said nothing.

"Maj. Just take me to a bus station."

He nodded without looking over. "That would certainly be fine. A bus station. That is how all of this started."

The rain stopped for a few minutes and the wipers burped their way across the glass. Ice crystals drifted like moths in the headlights.

"Just let me out. Take me to that gas station down there." She pointed beyond the rail at the overpass they began to cross. She tugged at the door latch and the door lurched open.

"Don't!" He grabbed her left wrist. "Don't do that. No one is going to hurt you."

*

Hakim pulled up to the gate at hourly parking, pressed the green button, took his ticket and drove up the spiral ramp. He parked on level three, crowded with other cars.

He removed his bag from the trunk, reached into the back seat, cracked the side of the jar with the handle of the screwdriver with one snap of his wrist, then shoved the blade of it into the plastic box of acid. He locked the door and walked away.

In the first restroom he encountered, he took the stall farthest from the door, removed his black overcoat, pulled off his white shirt and replaced it with an orange, green, and yellow striped shirt with pearl snaps. He pulled a belt with a horseshoe-shaped rhinestone buckle through the loops of his trousers. He balanced the hand mirror on the top of the seat cover dispenser and carefully applied the moustache. He bared his teeth and wrinkled his face into a broad smile, pressing a piece of the gold foil onto his front left incisor. It was crooked and he peeled it off, dried the tooth with toilet paper and applied a second piece. He stared down at his own plain black shoes. Boots would have been better, but these would work well enough. He took out the Stetson and pulled the jacket on.

At the ticket counter, he spread a miscellany of American bills on the counter with the passport. "Mehi-co Ceety, por favor." He watched the female ticket agent count off the price and feigned suspicion when she pushed the remainder of the money back to him. She was an ugly woman, he thought. A burka would suit her well.

"Mr. Aljandro Rojas?"

"Si."

"Do you have any bags to check?"

He just smiled at her benignly.

She repeated, *"No tiene maletas para revisar?"*

"Solemente una vista corta con mi familia para Navidad."

"Well, have a nice visit." She smiled and handed him the ticket. *"Fell-ece na-vehda,"* she added.

"Gracias," he said and touched the brim of his hat as he picked up his bag.

He sat in first class and took a Pacifico when the stewardess offered him one. He had not slept much himself in five days while clarifying things for Majij. He justified the alcohol, employed as a medication. The doors sealed shut. The air vents began their soft whistle, and the terminal started to move past the little windows of the plane, which undulated over the variations in the tarmac. He closed his eyes. When he opened them again, they were climbing steeply, sharply into thin clouds, from his seat he could see the strobes of the wings flashing in the vapor. Far below, two silent fire engines were converging on the parking garage, then they were absorbed by the clouds as well.

*

I can end this, Majij thought. Sometimes you just needed to discard the wrong path, go back to before it started. He could see in his wake, all of heaven could see, just how much he had jeopardized a far more worthy cause than his own trivial lust.

Majij knew what he should do. He knew also what he wanted to do and what his brother wanted him to do. Each of these options raced serially in his head, then in fragments, stumbling as one course precluded the execution of another. The revolver rested in his left coat pocket, he had placed it there, farthest from her. In the event that she should move against him in the seat, she would not feel it. Hakim had given it to him on the night of their arrival, for no specific purpose, he had said, beyond the general implication that he might need it, that crucial things transpired in the house, things important enough that enemies of Iran might want to disrupt. Hakim had emphasized the word *duty*. Majij fell asleep that night trying to picture such a scenario, wondering if he could shoot a policeman, if it was his *duty*. He examined the gun the next morning in the bathroom, sliding each of the five copper and silver bullets in and out of the cylinder, fascinated by the slipperiness of metal on metal, stainless steel like a surgical instrument, designed for one specific procedure. No hammer to cock, no safety; one's only interaction with such an instrument of solitary intent was to squeeze the trigger. Now it was perfectly clear why it was given to him; so it would seem familiar, his own. After five nights without sleep, his reasoning crushed, digested, indecipherable pulp, the simplicity stunned him: One object, one purpose. Like a wristwatch.

But I am a physician, no one can compel me to do such a thing. The sleet turned to snow again and he slowed the wipers. No one. The life of one for the lives of many—Hakim had phrased it as an irrefutable necessity. No one can make me do this, Majij reasoned and, thinking of his brother, tried to estimate how long Hakim would wait for them to come back before he would know that they were taking the big car to Mexico, or Florida maybe, anywhere. The snow sucked at his tires with growing impedance. Like a ball thrown skyward, he and Erika were reaching their zenith and would begin to fall. They would never rise higher; he knew now they had been to their own heaven and had turned away.

He imagined his mother's spirit watching him with a gun in his pocket. Like the men who killed her husband, she would think. He would instead place the decision in God's hands. He would choose a location, somewhere far from the city, sufficiently far from the lights or any houses or farms where refuge could be begged, and leave her there. It was cold and she had no cover. Were it God's will she should live, she would be shown a way. If not, so be it. Freezing, he had read, was quite painless. Delirium, euphoria, then sleep. The possibility that she might live to betray him was suddenly not troublesome. That too, was fair. *I have lived unrightously. In shah Allah.*

"Who was born first?"

Her voice fell through his thoughts, a downturned dagger through glass. She was looking at him, resolute. She had stopped shivering.

"You're twins, aren't you?"

He stared into the path created by his own headlights. It would not be much longer. "I told you that was foolishness, just an old woman's tale."

"Who's nobler, Majij? Who's going to do the right thing?"

He fondled the butt of the revolver and thought about Salinas, just taking her back to the motel. It would take about two hours to get there in this weather. Just lock her in a room and leave. No, Farouq was in contact with Hakim, and eventually he would find out. She was bolder now and would probably just go out the window again. He coursed along Loop 470 for seven or eight miles, following this train of thought, then chose an exit randomly, FM road 1265, and turned left, crossing up over the freeway, away from the city. The road felt coarser, the Mercedes seemed more certain of itself and he sped up. Nine miles later, the road abruptly turned to gravel and he brought the car to a rumbling halt. Except for white flakes in the glare of their headlights, they were surrounded by blackness.

"Are we lost?" she asked in a small voice.

He executed a three-point turn on the invisible terrain, Fatima giggling, naked on the floor of his apartment while his mother begged for garbage. At the first gate he came to on the left there was no mailbox. He opened his door and ran to the gate in the snow, lifting away the loop of wire that latched it. The cold air stung his eyes and his head ached.

"Maj, we're gonna get stuck. You know this isn't right." Corn stubble rose on each side of the car, scraping against the doors, the glass. She moved away from the window and rocked in her seat. "I'm cold. We don't have to do this. We don't. We don't, we don't."

He turned up the heater. At a second gate, the stubble pressed against the car door but he forced it wide enough to slip out, stepping high over the frozen vegetation, and dragged it open. He got back in the car. "There is something I think you need to see." He pressed the accelerator, and the back of the sedan skated sideways.

Erika braced herself with her hands on the dash. "Oh Jesus!"

The road became better defined, then ended abruptly in a small clearing about a hundred feet across, surrounded by taller corn, left unharvested, frozen ghosts of gray and white in their headlights.

"There is something that needs to end. Now." He shoved the gearshift in park. "Get out."

"But Maj."

The power door locks clicked open. He reached in front of her and pulled the door latch. The door swung open.

"Maj!"

He shoved her shoulder. She began to cry, and one foot sank into the partially frozen mud. He pushed her again and she lost her balance and nearly fell, but steadied herself with one hand on the fender, backing instinctively to the heat of the headlights. He stepped out of the car and around it, leaving his door open, then locked hers. "You need to appreciate something. Over there." He pointed across the clearing.

"I don't see anything." She sobbed and snorted, pulling the chador tighter.

It was a pig-like sound, he thought. "Over there." He pointed again.

She glanced back. "There's nothing there."

He advanced, shoving her with his palm, side to side, blocking her return to the car, his other hand deep in his coat, on the revolver.

She backed, stumbling in the headlights, and it seemed to him that she was trying to duck into his own shadow, trying to disappear. Raindrop after raindrop fell, tiny needles in his hair, down the side of his face.

"Can't we just talk?" she sobbed and pulled the chador more tightly beneath her chin. "In the car?"

"No. Just stop."

The abayah grew wet against her breasts. She shivered and they were all the more prominent in the glare of the headlights, and in the relief of the shadows as she turned, her abdomen protruded. Was she pregnant?

"Maj, just let me…"

"Just stop saying, anything." Was she pregnant? "You've tricked me. You always trick me."

"Oh God, Maj."

His foot cracked through a thin layer of ice and muddy water poured into his shoe, the mud tugging at his foot. He glanced down, then looked at her. "You've made me a fool." To suck something out of a man like that, let it grow into an embarrassment that could destroy him. He watched her gasping, her arms clutched around herself, clouds of breath visible in the headlights. Her back to the wall of cornstalks, he thought she might turn and run into them, but she did not. Her strength frightening, even now he could feel her force tugging at his genitals; all things filthy and weak that could befall a man emanated from her wet form. The engine of the Mercedes idled and he found he had backed up next to it. She was now about thirty feet away. He reached behind him for the door. *Drive away. I must just drive away.*

"Oh God, Maj. Please. Don't. I'll be good. I won't try to run."

Is she pregnant? The fabric woman's daughter, what was her name? She is pregnant, a baby, the badge of proof for the ruin she has caused. His head throbbed with each syllable.

"Let's just go to a motel," she gasped. "We'll stay up all night. You miss that, don't you?" She turned away from the lights. "Just hit me, you're, you're..." But she didn't finish and cried louder instead, and her cry became a scream, the voice of Fatima, the voice of his mother, the voice of every girl he had ever known, every girl that had rebuked him, ridiculed him, thrown his gift back into his face, summoning the whole world to witness, the scream of her unborn. The revolver was out of his pocket, aimed and squeezed in a single motion. The pop silenced the world, the flash erased her momentarily. She struck her hand against her neck as if swatting an insect, wavered, startled and indignant, but only said "Maj?"

He squeezed again, another pop, and the silence was restored. She stood facing him, looking puzzled, every other emotion washed away by the blue flash. Turning her head to the sky as if to watch the bullet, deflected, fly over her, her knees folded and she fell forward, making a wet sound as she struck the earth.

His ears hissed, but her voice was gone, Hakim's voice was gone, his own thoughts a blank page. He strode forward nearly over her. The black abayah, only moments before soaked to her, every curve of her, now fluttered in the wind, defiantly, as if having taken over her life. He aimed where he thought her heart should be and fired again. Flakes fell, enormous irregular wet fluff. He stood there for a time he did not register, entirely empty of purpose. Empty. His ears rang.

He began to shiver, motion first at the molecular level, then spreading though his torso and weakening his legs. He stumbled into the driver's seat and grasped the wheel to keep his arms still, bewildered that aside from his hair and one shoe, he was not very wet. His coat had sheltered him from everything. The ground before the car had grown white, the flakes settling, soaking up every sound, every sin, every speck of blood. The cornstalks stood like a row of newly flocked pines in a forest. Where was she? There she was, a little mound of darker irregular earth, covered equally in flakes.

Four amber lights glowed at him from the dashboard, the engine had stalled at some point and he hadn't noticed. He shivered more violently. His ears still rang and he could not hear the engine start, but the lights suddenly went from sepia to white, the needles of the gauges rising to attention. The cold in him came from his spine, from his bones out. He turned the thermostat to eighty-eight and the fan to high. The air felt tepid, a distant whisper.

He moved the gearshift and the car bounded forward toward the mass under the snow. He smashed both feet on the brakes and the hood plunged. He shifted to reverse and backed up carefully. The tracks in the snow stopped inches from running over her. It would be a desecration.

He turned the wheel hard to the left, circling the clearing twice, the car bobbing and skidding drunkenly over the frozen furrows until he spotted the wire fence, outlined with snow, the open gate. The path only defined now by the white stubble that bordered it, the car weaved and wound its way through the flurry-filled night, guided only by the deep ruts. He could not remember the road being so far away until he burst out of the field and crossed it, braking just short of diving into the culvert on the far side. He turned the sedan and accelerated, alight with fear, shame, and ecstatic self-renewal, all crossing through his thoughts like so many convergent rockets in blackness, convinced that if he could only go fast enough back to the city, to the light, to the velocity of his life before all of this had overtaken him, all things would be right and good again.

He stroked his hand over the empty, cold leather seat next to him. His brother, who had only killed through the anonymity of a rifle sight, would be proud. To pull the trigger, the second time, had empowered him. It was said that he who died without having taken part in a campaign died in a kind of disbelief. A new knowledge of himself materialized, revealed by this decisive act; having killed this jinn, he could as easily kill himself if called upon to do so. Free at last to do God's work, this placed him, for a brilliant moment, in league with his brother. These thoughts he would breathe in, holding his breath as he drove, rapturous, the crown of the road the blade of a knife. Then he would turn them loose, exhale, and nausea and horror would enshroud him, a terrible truth in the red glow of his own taillights that followed him in the rearview mirror. The snow continued to fall.

The bend in the road appeared like a spirit. He crushed the brakes and the sedan skidded, climbing the bank of the pavement until the right side of the hood sank. Snow-covered cheat grass stood just inches from the tri-star on the hood, the right headlight dim as if under water. He sat at the wheel in disbelief for half a minute, then put the lever in reverse. The rear tires whined and spun, but the car remained motionless. He put it in park, opened the door and immediately slid down and away from the car, which rested at the apex of a steeply banked curve, its right front tire planted firmly over the shoulder. He was on his hands and knees. He stood up and looked around. He could hear the passing of trucks. Perhaps the interstate was nearby. He stepped over the shoulder, grasped the right front bumper and grunted, but the car did not move. He stood and saw her, pale behind the passenger glass for just an instant. She bent forward—to tie a shoe? He snatched the passenger door open and the seat was empty. He opened the rear door. The car held no one.

He shifted to reverse, returned to the bumper and grunted again. The car groaned and tipped up slightly, the tires found the pavement, and slowly it drove back from him while he watched numbly, crossing the arc of the curve, stopping with a metallic crunch as it struck a fencepost. The post, set in the frozen ground at an angle, had spared the bumper but caved a crease into the trunk. The wheels still turned slowly against the ice. He opened the driver's door and stood there for a moment, looking at the interior. Confident there was no one in the vehicle, he took his seat and shifted to drive again.

The car wiggled aimlessly for a few seconds, then moved gently forward, gliding from one side of the crown of the road to the other. The on-ramp to 470 had been sanded, as had the freeway itself. He accelerated confidently to about fifty. '470 North.' Nothing looked familiar as he looked down from each overpass. He did not really know where he had just been, and thus had no idea where he was going. This temporarily became his new concern, alternating with what excuse he might construct for smashing the back of the car. He would tell Hakim it had happened when he had left it parked somewhere. Someone else had done it, that was enough. Over all of this remained the disquieting notion that at some point in the evening, he had committed an absolutely reprehensible, irrevocable act, and though he tried to concern himself with the problems at hand, it percolated just below the surface, slowing all of his thoughts, weakening his legs, the stillness of falling though the atmosphere, knowing already your parachute will never open.

A red light appeared on the panel, and after a few minutes he noticed it. *Oh yes, it is just the fuel.*

He took the next exit and in half a block rolled to a halt in the brightly lit portico of a Stop-N-Go, parking on the wrong side of the pumps. He dragged the hose over the deformed trunk lid and put the nozzle in the tank. A garbled voice said something over the intercom and the fuel began to flow. Then he saw her. She sat with two boys and another girl in a booth near the window. She looked out, saw him, then spoke to one of the boys and they laughed. And she had a cigarette! She turned her back to the window. He crossed the parking lot, never letting her out of his sight, but she was ignoring him now.

Inside it was warm. He wiped his feet. Everything could be better, he felt, if he did this right. He approached the booth.

"Hey, what's your problem, mister?"

"He's probably drunk."

"He's a drunk raghead."

"Where's his rag?"

"Ragheads don't drink."

"Maybe he's sick or something," Erika said.

"God, he's so creepy."

One of the boys stood up. "What's up, sandnigger?"

The attendant walked over. "Come on, you kids. Outta' here. You've been here long enough. The rain's stopped. Go home."

The other three teenagers stood up and left, mumbling, moving past Majij, who now stood staring, it seemed, at the tabletop in the booth, at a cigarette that smoldered in the ashtray.

"You want to pay up?"

"Yes?"

"Your pump just went off. You want to pay for your gas now?"

"Yes. That will be fine." Majij pulled twenty dollars from his wallet and laid it on the counter. But things were not fine. They would never be fine. He thought of an evening when she had played the piano for him, in the lobby of a motel somewhere. He had stopped the voice that sang to him. Halfway across the parking lot, he vomited.

*

Fairview, he thought, he must find an exit for Fairview. A car approached in the lane behind, but the road was still very icy and it did not pass. The gun was no longer in his pocket. He searched around on the seat for it and as far as he could reach on the floor. Perhaps there had never been a gun. A hallucination, too little sleep. The driver behind him brightened his lights, perhaps because of the snow, Majij thought. He adjusted the rearview mirror and wondered if she had even come with him; he could not remember her getting in the car and could not remember why he had driven out in the night to begin with. All he needed to do was find his way back to the house, find his way back to before the evening began. A truck passed him in the outer lane, turning up acres of snow in its wake, burying his windshield for a few seconds. He turned the wipers up and it cleared. Another pair of headlights approached in the outside lane and he waited for them to pass also. It was then that he saw her, only in his most peripheral vision, reach for the controls of the radio. "I will not look at you," he said, "because I know you will go away, and I do not want you to leave." The radio was still dark, she had withdrawn her hand.

"I will do that. Do you want to hear Christmas music?" The dial glowed, and he rotated the knob. "I had a terrible, terrible dream tonight."

The other headlights gained, drawing up beside him, a large dark vehicle, then moved ahead, falling in front of him, raising a continuous fury of snow.

"I have been, strict, I know. I was not like that, before I came…"

"…*there'll be snow, and mistletoe, and presents, under, the tree…*" The radio startled him.

The brake lights of the vehicle ahead flickered. Majij slowed also, slower still, a moment later they seemed to be coming to a stop. Majij changed lanes and saw briefly that there was nothing beyond but snowy highway. The vehicle, a dark blue, swerved in front of him and slid to a complete stop. Majij slammed the brakes. The interior of the Mercedes was flooded with brilliant blue light, and men jumped from the vehicle in front of him, shining lights, shouting. More shouting men came from behind. He turned and she sat there, red-and-white striped dress in a wave across the seat, her legs in white nylons, folded beneath her, eyes like opals.

The door wrenched open, someone grasped his arm, then a hand in his hair, his face struck the ice and sand and slush of the road, a knee pressed into his back, and his wrists were bolted together and he was up again like a puppet. He turned his head toward the Mercedes, someone twisted his head forward, and he was lifted into the back of the blue Suburban, where he was able to turn again, briefly, and look into the Mercedes which was silhouetted by the glare of the car with the flashing blue lights. She remained in the passenger seat, still looking at him. The Suburban surged forward, and he saw someone slip into his place in the Mercedes, then all of it vanished in a whirlwind of snow.

17

Majij did not look up. When he was dragged from the Suburban, the snow was gone from the sidewalk. They guided him on the shortest path into a building with glass doors in steel frames, down a yellow staircase and through more glass doors. Under the earth, Majij thought, SAVAK. The corridor was lit with fluorescent tubes, uncovered fixtures every six paces. He was surrounded by perhaps a dozen men, some of them young men in dark suits and others dressed like soldiers who clattered and made a whishing sound with each step as they walked. His own shoes squished with each step, his shoes, socks, collar, and jacket soaked. At the door where they eventually stopped, most of the men walked on. Majij was pushed into a room about thirty feet square where, with some gentle pressure, he was seated in an oak chair at a long folding table. Two empty chairs remained. A black man entered the room with him and sat down to his left. Two others stood on either side of the door. It was at this point that Majij began to accept the notion that he was being taken down to hell.

No one spoke. A digital clock on the wall read 11:34 Almost noon, Majij thought, but it had been nighttime earlier. At 11:54 the door opened, and a man in his mid-fifties entered, and the man who had been seated at his left stood up and went over to him with a large envelope. The two of them examined the contents and spoke in low voices to one another.

The two men sat down at the table, the new man across from him. "I'm Special Agent Robert Quigley," he extended his hand.

Majij stared at the knot of his tie.

"And this is Field Agent Cory Johnson." The black man nodded.

"You're in the federal building, Mister…" Quigley flipped through the papers from the envelope. A passport fell onto the table. "Seems we don't know what to call you."

Quigley sat forward in the chair, moved the glasses down on his nose, and fanned the papers across the tabletop. "You might recognize these. They're credit card statements. Are you Hiroshi Mikado? Or Hassan Hakim Malouf? Or…" He opened the passport. "Harvey McMann, clothing wholesaler from

Vancouver, BC. How did you get this one?" He thumped his finger on the maple leaf of the green cover.

Cory smiled. "Hell, Bob, Canadians probably issued him that one, aboveboard."

"What I don't see here is a passport for Lebanon. You and I met before. Do you remember?" Bob Quigley shook his head and dumped a handful of colored plastic cards onto the table. "So many credit accounts, but you never buy anything."

Majij had assimilated himself into the symmetry of the yellow room, his central seat at a table at the center of yellow lights. The two men near him, the two men on either side of the door. It was balanced and just. He belonged here.

"Mister…" Quigley singled out one paper and leaned back in his chair. "Hassan? I'm sorry. I just don't think you're Japanese. Or Irish." He laid the statement on the table. "Mr. Hassan, you're not actually under arrest yet. You're a person of interest. Cory and I here both think you are rather interesting. If you talk to us, maybe we can all go home and get a little bit of sleep. If you don't talk, we're just going to get more curious."

Majij closed his eyes and the chair floated.

"Mr. Hassan."

"Is that his first name? Maybe it's his last name."

"You're right. At First National, he's known as Mr. Malouf. Mr. Malouf, please open your eyes."

The two men came into focus again.

"Maybe you could just start by telling us your full name. Where did you go to school?"

Majij's arms felt as if they had become glued to the table.

"We're very curious about Marchan Industries in Los Angeles. Seems their only asset is a post office box."

Light was shining under the door across the room, Majij noticed. The light surrounded the door, leaking through, around all edges. He closed his eyes again.

"Get him some coffee. Bring enough for everybody."

Majij heard the door open and close. When he opened his eyes, Erika had slipped into the room unnoticed. She was barefoot, wearing only a yellow sundress he hadn't seen before. She was staring at him.

"Marchan Industries to this date has been the recipient of loan funds totaling"—Mr. Quigley looked down at one of the papers—"two hundred and fifty-four thousand, nine hundred sixteen dollars. Plus four dividend checks from a company that folded two years ago, another twenty-two thousand dollars." Mr. Quigley had moved around the table. "All of these loans were ultimately approved by you." He bent down behind Majij, next to his ear. "It's not your money. Why be so stoic?"

Erika had stepped away from the wall and lingered in a shadow, halfway to the table, her face passive and neutral.

"Your face turned up on a list at Langley. Seems you may have been a contact in Afghanistan a few years ago. Odd prerequisite for being a loan officer, wouldn't you say?" Quigley sat down again. "I guess that's why you didn't put it on your resume." Quigley lifted one typed sheet like a dead bird.

Erika was pulling the dress up, slowly, deliberately, as if she intended to pull it off over her head.

Majij laid his head forward on the table.

"Mr. Malouf. We need some information. We have only so much time. I can authorize Mr. Johnson here to use medication, if necessary, to help you remember." Quigley took a handkerchief from his hip and blew his nose. "You're not being held, understand. If someone comes for you, you'll be released. Understand?" He put the handkerchief back in his pocket. "But I don't get the feeling anyone is coming for you."

Erika had wadded nearly all of the dress beneath her chin and was otherwise naked. She explored a hole near her left nipple with her index finger.

*

Coarse, cool, smooth. Teal and aqua, sun through spirals. A jolt. Floods, a fluid sound, a thousand tiny stings, swarms of footsteps. Sinking, sinking, sinking, the sun recedes.

The tumbler struck the oak floor like a barbell, and Sam snapped his head out of a dream and stared at the brilliance of the Christmas tree, momentarily thinking it was on fire, or had fallen, or had been the slam of the door of his university flat, his parents standing in the hallway, small Erika between them, her arms upstretched to hold their hands. *She is dead and with them.* He tried to gather together the fading smudges of conversation with his biological father, who had spoken Spanish but was in some way Eric, and the college was in Andorra. "But I never went to school in Andorra," Sam spoke out loud, while Erika dashed around the flat, speechless, pulling books from his shelves. And then it all vanished. The briefest latent echo hovered in the room, as if she had just been there, all fifteen years of her, tugging at his arm, a hint of the perfume she'd worn, and then it was gone as well.

The Wellborn's house had been appointed to the finest detail with the holidays, garland and holly, the wreath at the door, cloves and nutmeg in the air when Sam and Teresa had rung the bell. He'd stayed by Teresa's side as she had moved among the faculty, her conversation calm, succinct, seemingly rational, if not a little simplistic, while choir voices sung carols on the stereo and people cupped their hands to hear her. She declined every hors d'oeuvre but finally lifted a glass of eggnog when Martin Cordova toasted the new high school gymnasium. And the Wellborn daughters, cherubic and polite, venturing to the bottommost step in their pajamas to say goodnight. Oh, when Erika was that age! He had wanted to spend the rest of the night there and fall asleep in an overstuffed chair surrounded by his friends, his dear, well-meaning colleagues. A fleeting notion had troubled him since; they could *adopt* a little girl. Teresa had rewoven herself, fierce little woman she had always been. African girls, Chinese girls, they were easy to come by, just a lot of fees and paperwork, even a mature couple like themselves could be parents again. They could use the college fund they'd saved for Erika.

A precious night that now, Sam thought, they'd had no right to. Inside their own front door, standing finally in the quiet of their living room, ember-orange with the light of their tree, Teresa had dropped her purse in the chair.

"Oh bugger!" she had said.

"What?"

"Trish. I didn't get a gift for little Patricia."

And he had almost said, "Little who?" when he understood that it was Trish, big cigarettes-fuck-in-the-car Trish. "Why? She's never going to be here again."

"Of course she will," Teresa said in her same calm, succinct way that suddenly didn't seem rational at all. "When Erika comes back, Trish will bring her."

"She isn't coming back." And he looked in her eyes and saw her disintegrate. "Trish, I mean."

"Of course she is. They've been together this whole time. It's perfectly logical."

"It's perfectly daft." And resentment rose up in him, and he was about to reiterate all of the hours they had spent driving to Portland, but she was upon him, a hurricane of blows with the butt of her fists on his chest, his ears, his face.

"Goddamn you—Goddamn you—Goddamn you—so Goddamned normal, how could you speak to those people? Didn't you know," and she heaved and sobbed and then screamed, "they were laughing at us!" And she slapped his glasses off.

Afterward, she had folded on her knees onto the sofa and he had carried her back to the bedroom. She would forget about it by morning, he hoped, or they would both be ashamed.

Sam put on his glasses and leaned over the arm of the chair, looking at the unbroken glass, the small puddle, and the tiny remnants of ice cubes. It was two twenty-five by his watch. The Dalmore bottle on the lamp table next to him was half-empty. He had surprised himself; a gift from another faculty he thought might be in the cabinet for another five years. He started to stand and then knelt, wiping up the spill with his handkerchief, muttering, "I can't believe I'm pissed." He pushed himself up with his arms on the chair, grasped the bottle by the neck and stuffed the stopper in, then pulled two of Churchill's volumes from the shelf and put the bottle behind them. He started to reach for the lamp to turn it on, but looked around the room and thought the tree was light enough. He could hear the rhythm of Teresa breathing down the hall.

Gifts were stacked beneath the tree, more than he could ever remember on any past Christmas, most of them for Erika. Teresa had bought them, including a doll he could only vaguely remember his daughter obsessing about when she had been nine or ten. Saint Vincent DePaul could use all of that, he thought. Sometime after the holiday he would just load them up quietly while she slept and put them in the boot. He adjusted a blue-and-white porcelain ornament that had rotated away from the room, then stood back from the tree. It was visible from the outside to anyone who might happen by. That was the important detail.

*

The table was gone, the walls closer, another room had moved around him and he lay on a cot. In the door, a small square window with wire. She couldn't get in. The men on the outside would keep her out. If the men were on the inside, they were there to keep him in. It worked that way. It worked. He slept.

His mother held him facing her, six years old, skinny as a stick, she tickled him and her laughter flowed around him like honey. There was no Hakim. Or was he Hakim? He awoke, a moment so long ago, so lost.

The lock clicked and the knob turned, a blond man looked in.

"You need to use the toilet? It's eight in the morning."

They lifted him by the arms, and he went down the hall with them beneath the same fluorescent lights.

In the bathroom he could not empty. Only his urine flowed. She was stopping his organs, one by one, from beneath the snow somewhere. He wondered when she would stop his heart.

In the hallway, back in the light, he burst away and clutched a steel drinking fountain.

"Come on."

"Let him drink."

"He'll just have to piss again."

"That's his problem."

He arrived at the room from the night before, with two men inside the door and Quigley sitting at the table waiting for him.

"Mr. Malouf. May I call you Hakim? I hope you got some rest. As we were talking, or I should say I was talking, you were being silent."

Majij moved his chair slightly to the left. Symmetry with the door.

"We picked up your counterpart in Los Angeles yesterday. Arif Talib. Does that name mean anything to you?"

The two men were on the inside of the door. That meant she could get in.

"He's actually under arrest. Seems he had a gun on him. You can't do that out in California." Quigley moved his own chair, trying better to capture Majij's gaze, and softened his voice in assuagement. "He gave you up, you know. You don't owe him anything."

Quigley pushed a Styrofoam cup of coffee before him. "Make it easy on yourself. You could be on a plane so easily back to"—he glanced down at the passports—"wherever you call home." Quigley wiped his face. "We'll be searching your house this afternoon. I'm sure you have more passports. You can take your pick."

The cup was too far left of center. If the room wasn't symmetric, she wouldn't come. He shoved it gently to align it.

"Goddammit." Quigley stood up, coffee dribbling down his slacks. He pulled out a handkerchief and padded coffee off of one bundle of papers, then another, and shook them gently over the floor. "Call Geri. Ask her to run another set of documents on the First National case. We can't take these to court."

His stand had disrupted the symmetry. Now she wouldn't come. He wanted her to come.

"Get a psychiatrist and get this guy back to his room. Find out if he's sick or faking or just crazy."

*

The two agents stood to either side of the door. Cory knocked firmly, four raps with his knuckles, then four more with the butt of his fist. Allen, the other agent, who kept the screen door open with his torso, held an envelope in his left hand, his right hand on the grip of his pistol inside his jacket. No footsteps or creaks or thumps of any kind could be heard coming from inside. Wind chimes from a neighboring house tinkled.

Parked at the curb behind the Suburban, sat a van, yellow with red lettering emblazoned on the side, 'Carl's Lock and Security Services.' The first agent motioned to the driver, a stocky fellow who climbed out and waddled over the snow-encrusted lawn, squinting in the glare. He wore overalls and carried a small toolbox in his right hand and puffed clouds of vapor from his nose, as if the box weighed a thousand pounds. He made a cursory glance at the warrant the second agent had unfolded, then knelt beside the door-knob and opened the box. A moment later, the door swung open. "Happy shopping, boys," he said. "Will you be needing me for anything else?"

"Better stick around. There might be more locks, or a safe. Wait in your van. We'll let you know."

The two agents moved through the house, leapfrogging room to room, weapons drawn. It was unoccupied.

"Start at the front?"

One agent turned off the bathroom fan.

"Yeah."

"Look." He pointed to the can of ashes in the bathtub.

"Figures."

Cory lifted the computer and placed it near the front door, marking the top with a felt pen, while Allen gathered three phone books, one from Topeka, another from Portland, Oregon, and the yellow pages for Los Angeles, placing them in a plastic bag. Allen opened the door to the garage and took a few steps to the center and surveyed the walls: Hoses, a hedge trimmer, several partially used plastic bottles of weed killer concentrate, and a sack of ammonium nitrate. He turned his shoe in the grit and looked down at the cement floor. Two small puddles of oil, one in each parking bay.

"Come in here."

Cory appeared.

"Two sets of tracks in the dirt too. One on the left has to be the Benz. Did he ever show up in anything else?"

"Not while we were watching. Check out the bedroom." The two men went back into the house.

"What? He's single, right?"

"It strikes me as odd that we've got a queen bed on the floor here. The bathroom's used. There's toothpaste splattered on the mirror, and yet there's the hermit-style cot off the kitchen."

"Maybe he liked to brush his teeth in here. Used the other bathroom for burnt sacrifices."

"I don't think Muslims do that."

"It's a joke."

Cory raised one side of the mattress, then the other, then let it drop. Allen pushed the box spring away from the wall.

"Hmmm." He bent down and picked up a sock, white, with a border of small blue hearts around the neck.

"Hassan doesn't seem like a blue hearts kind of a guy."

"That's a woman's sock."

"Exactly. Or a girl's."

"Bag it up."

The two men separated. When Allen finished with the bedroom, Cory was standing in the hall.

"Must be twenty or thirty boxes on the back porch. Will we have room for them?"

"I don't know."

Allen started to pass him.

"There's something else."

Allen turned.

"I think there was a woman in that car last night, or a teenager."

"When did you decide that?"

"I didn't exactly, till now. When they were getting on 470, right after the accident. The passenger window went down for a second, and there was a face. Something, the way the person moved, was female. I mean, it couldn't have been the driver, right? Then the window went up."

"Did you tell Quigley? Put it in your report?"

"No."

"He doesn't like that kind of revision, man. Looks in court like you've added facts for convenience."

"He doesn't like speculation either. I just couldn't be sure. You were busy losing your cool at that woman who hit us."

"I'll cover you on this."

"Thanks." Cory turned away, went onto the porch and lifted the closest box. Allen followed, but stopped in the kitchen to study the floor beneath the table. He grasped the table by the edges and moved it to one side.

Carl had poured a third cup of coffee from his thermos when he sensed a thump, a silver flash, and a great gust lifting the van. His ears sealed up. He looked through the passenger window at the expanding house rising above the foundation like a tumescent balloon, all of its features distorted, racing away from a furious gray cloud at its center. A hail of glass struck the side of the van. Something penetrated the passenger window like a missile.

*

Erika stood near the cot, her bare leg touching his thigh. He tried to speak but could not. She bent forward and pressed her fingertips into his shoulder. Oh, to feel her touch again.

Majij opened his eyes. Quigley stood over him like a projection in the shaft of light from the open door.

"Get up. You need to be awake for this." Quigley grasped his shirt and pulled him to a seated position. Majij stared off to a corner. Quigley grabbed his ear and pulled until their eyes met. "You're going to be moved to the county jail. Your house blew up. Two federal agents, two of my friends, were killed. Anything you say can be used…" Quigley stopped in midsentence and stood up. He walked to the door and another agent opened it for him. He turned. "One of them was Johnson, the man who was kind enough to suggest we let you sleep. Goddamn you. You people just don't make any sense to me."

The door closed and darkness folded over him. Majij sat in the vacuum of his thoughts, aware only that something more precious than all of his grandest visions had been within his grasp and had been taken away.

*

Penetrating her nose, her mouth—every cubic inch of her belonged to the wind. She could not inhale, for the wind was already there. Warm, blue, a cloud of blue grew in the darkness, borders soft, red nearby, violet where they overlapped, the blue became green, the red orange and then yellow, all moving through a black sky. East, to the right? No the left, swiftly. Lighting struck, a hook in her bowels, tearing through her ribs. The wind buried her cry, her instinct.

"Print that, will you?"

"It's just artifact. Two thirty-four is agitated again." A small hand, tethered with a canvas restraint waved in the window of the room across from the desk, partially obscured by the Christmas tree. The thin nurse rose from her seat behind the monitor and trotted into the medication room. The keys rattled in the lock of the narcotic cabinet. She returned with five milligrams of morphine.

"Now, sweetie, don't pull at that. You're just going to wear yourself out." She pushed the needle through the pliable port of the IV, and the viscid little bolus swirled in the junction of saline-filled tubing, then vanished upstream.

Magenta, all of the lights blended to magenta and spread in an ethereal horizon, beyond which she could hear a river.

18

Darkness saturated the ceiling of the ICU, the hush of the early morning, the whisper of the ventilation, the glow of the monitors, and rhythmic tiny beeps all combined to form a comfortable organic pulse, which could be turned down but never completely muted. Souly Farag sat beneath one of the dimmed lights and smiled, thumbing through pages, each corner embossed in violet print at irregular angles, 'Jane Doe, C female AGE: UNK.' Another member of the incredibly unfortunate Doe family. During his internship in Houston he'd been astounded at the number of Does carried through the door of the emergency department, disheveled, unconscious, or dead, smelling of alcohol or vomit. This one had been shot.

It was always John or Jane, brought by city ambulances, or sometimes just left by others unseen, on the ramparts. Does of every age, black, white, Mediterranean—sometimes the race was not clear. He had shared his amazement with Dr. Jennings, who only smiled and stroked his beard and repeated the inquiry to Sandy, the nursing director, who laughed out loud. Still he did not understand, deciding that the Does must be poor, like the Hamids of Cairo. He had explored this theory by looking in the Houston telephone directory, where he found only two listings for Doe. Obviously too poor to have telephones. The rest of the house staff had laughed behind him, or thought him dryly clever. Several weeks had passed before he realized his error. *Fulan* was the closest word in Arabic, *an unknown person.*

Now he carried the anecdote with him and humored himself each time, sharing it at some point each month with his next group of students. Oh, how an elaborate theory could grow from faulty logic! One needed an open mind to capture the unexpected diagnosis, and open-mindedness required an open heart. Stay humble.

"Doctor Farag, would you like some coffee?" He glanced up at the white plastic name tag on the bust of uniform. 'A. Tomlinson, RN,' parked a cup on the desk in front of him, as she had done unsolicited for the past two and half years, the act always simultaneous with the question. She never failed to put far more sugar in it than he thought any human could consume; she'd probably read something in National Geographic.

"Thank you," he said. It was a kindness. He knew she wanted his attention, and he knew she would never step beyond this formality she had constructed. "Abigail." He had heard one of the other nurses call her "Abby." A comely woman. *Abby Farag.* It sounded like a tide pool creature. He massaged his left ring finger for a moment and imagined her planted in bed next to him in a shapeless flannel nightgown, flipping the pages of *Nursing World.* He discarded the image as quickly and gazed through the window of the room across from the desk. Snow fell through the light of the arc lamps over Tenth Avenue. The sun would not be up for another two hours.

Souly stopped at the operative report, handwritten, a smudge of blood at the margin. The pages had been wet at some point and had dried like onion skin. Defibrillated, in the emergency room. He turned a page. Defibrillated again, during surgery. Anonymity was never a positive prognosticator, arriving from the surgical suite. One should be well prepared, have one's passport, all of one's contingencies identified, and one's papers in order prior to such a journey. Even electively planned procedures, choreographed from the textbook beginning to end, could take a dismal turn at predictable percentages— a stroke, an infarction of the heart, an embolism to the lung, the infection that eluded all antibiotics given beforehand. To arrive, having so many holes in a person, indiscriminate penetration through so many parts, was terrible enough. Being anonymous multiplied the horror tenfold. Those without their names balanced at the margin did not speak, and no one could speak for them. There was no context of a previous life, no trajectory from which one could extrapolate. One needed one's own people.

"Souly." Mitchell Brady, his intern, touched him on the shoulder. He looked like he had awakened in someone else's bed.

"Good morning, Mitchell." Souly closed the chart.

"You get some sleep?"

"Two hours. You and I have another patient. Andrews consulted us forty minutes ago." He left the chart at the desk and walked over to the glass that separated him from the girl. "Young girl with gunshot wounds. Abdomen, chest." He turned back to Mitchell. "There will be police. We need to keep students away from her, for privacy." He clasped his hands diplomatically behind his back. "And for the university."

Mitchell dragged the chart across the desk with his fingertip and turned a few pages. "Think she might be someone important?"

Farag inverted his smile. "Everyone's important, Mitchell."

"Looks like she was hypothermic, big-time. Great teaching case."

"It would be better if you start with Mrs. Stuckey in CCU. She is acidotic this morning." Farag moved the cup of coffee-syrup farther away from the chart on the desk. "Give the students an opportunity to figure out why."

"What if I don't know why?"

"You're a smart young doctor. You'll know why. Look at the blood gas."

The intern turned to go.

Souly twisted partially in his chair, looking at Mitchell's feet. His socks were inside out. "Mitchell. I'll meet you on the ward at ten. You can learn about this patient on rounds with me tonight."

Souly went into the room. He stood at the side of the bed and studied the motion of her breathing at a perfect rate of twelve, he studied the posture of her arms, neither internally rotated nor straining to rise in prayer, *decorticate,* each foot gently outturned. He stroked the sole of each, but there was no response. *Of course not, she is sedated.* He drew up an eyelid, blue as an evening sky. He raised each lid simultaneously. Tiny pupils, each directed up and away, to different corners of the room. *We will need to see this go away.* The lips were pale and chapped where the tube exited, milky and translucent, supported by the swing arm of the ventilator like a snake from the limb of a tree.

He seated the earpieces of his stethoscope; her heart was regular and rapid, like a bird's. No gallop. It did not stumble. At the base of the right chest, a hiss, and he stopped and bent over to look at the clear plastic water trap connected to her chest tube. It gurgled like an aquarium, each bubble made of air that had escaped from a hole in her lung on that side. Keep drawing them away, and the lung would stay inflated. Stop the suction, and the lung would be compressed by air it had lost to the chest cavity, and the girl would suffocate. The chest was warm, each lung clear, wind through so many tubules, driven by the machinery every five seconds; she was riding the ventilator, a girl too tired to breathe. A girl with morphine. Or had some central event occurred? The EMTs could find no pulse. Who could guess how far from the heart had it withered away—perhaps her arms or maybe the carotids? Probably their hands had been cold, so far out in the country, as they'd put her onto a gurney and into the aide car. She'd had thirteen units of blood and six units of frozen plasma since arrival; at some point, so little might have remained to circulate, neglecting the cerebral cortex. An eighth birthday, a summer day playing in a field of corn, all of the spelling words from the sixth grade, the faces of her parents—gone. Retrograde amnesia for a day, a week, even a month was almost a certainty, but would her brainstem remember how to breathe?

He placed the palm of his hand on her forehead. Dry. Fever. He stroked his hand upward to a whisper of pale at the scalp. He turned and followed the tubing of her catheter, lifting the sheets to see where it disappeared between her legs. So she had dyed her hair black. Why? Nice farm girls in Kansas did not do this. Girls in the big cities, the west coast, San Francisco, or Los Angeles, girls in underwear advertisements in young people's magazines in the residents' lounge dyed their hair. The paleness of her skin made the hair of her head so much blacker, monochromatic in a room of pale green, mauve, and stainless steel. What was this? A deep scratch, ragged, encircling her neck. He stroked the scratch and it rolled, a fine, yellow braid of chain, overlooked by the trauma team, encased in the Betadyne that still clung like orange syrup to her neck. He disconnected the clasp and dragged the crescent through her tangle of hair.

He held her fingertips in the palms of his hand and stroked them with his thumb. They were not yellowed or dirty but freshly trimmed, no polish or paint. He smelled them; a punk girl who did not smoke. A nulliparous cervix had been noted by Rowe on the second page of the surgical procedure note, before he took it all out. She had not carried a child to term. Now she would never do this.

Vaginal swabs had been taken in the ER for sexually transmitted diseases, and a rape kit sent to the state lab. He looked at her again in her totality, backing away from the bed, knowing already that the swabs and the kit would tell him nothing. He took a wooden tongue blade from his clinic coat pocket, peeled away the paper wrapper, and wet it in the sink by the bed. He pressed the blade along the endotracheal tube at an angle, teasing away a curtain of mucous beneath the lip, and peered in, holding a penlight in the other hand. Some residual blood gelled around the teeth, which were otherwise, as far as he could see, sound and straight. No fillings, no cavities; a child of discipline. Someone taught her these things, someone who was looking for her.

Tomlinson walked into the room.

He turned. "Have you bandage scissors?"

"Somewhere." She rummaged in her pockets and handed him a pair.

He leaned forward over the girl and slipped the broad point of the blade near the scalp and snipped along the gauze. When he had gently pulled away the last strand, he stood back. The top of her right ear was missing, clearly a half-inch lower than the left, the edge blue and sticky like old fruit. No one had closed the wound, and now it was probably too late. It would just have to granulate slowly in on its own. He combed through her hair with his fingers, teasing it away from the right side of her scalp where it was encrusted. It fell to shoulder length, straight, and her bangs fell evenly across her brow.

"Well, now." He stood back again. "You look just like Ma'at."

"I beg your pardon?"

He knew she missed much of his humor, and this amused him more. "Our patient, she looks like Ma'at, Egyptian goddess of truth, don't you think?"

"I wouldn't know."

"You'd better find out. She may be judging you in the afterlife." He handed her the scissors.

Tomlinson shook her head and walked out.

He turned to the girl in the bed again. "Who are you, really? Where are your parents? Your brother? Sister?"

At the nurses' desk, he wrote his note, concise, trying to keep the tone optimistic. A dismal note could inspire dismal performance from others and become a self-fulfilling prophecy. He wrote orders: no valium, no morphine. He would return in four hours.

Four minutes after ten, he caught up with Mitchell, standing at the foot of a bed in room 2107. He waited in the hall until he filed out between his two medical students.

"Your patient has everyone talking." Brady spoke under his breath as his two students, young men in their twenties, walked several yards ahead of them in their short white clinic jackets. "The surgeons didn't think it was such a big secrecy thing."

"Is that so?" Souly asked.

"I think it was a student with the trauma team who spilled the beans," Brady added.

They all filled cups of coffee and sat around a table in the late morning sun at the vacant end of the dining room. Farag explained everything he knew of wound ballistics, from books by the US Army, papers published by Israeli doctors, and cases he had actually seen. He told them of kinetic energy and the hydrostatic shock that follows a bullet's path through soft tissue, fracturing organs and bones several centimeters away, tearing the skin before it exits, as he drew on the back of a paper menu.

"So you'd rather get shot with a small, slow bullet," one of the students said.

"I'd rather not get shot at all," Farag said.

The conversation drifted, to hunting squirrels, then pheasants, and an accidental shotgun injury that had been on the service two months earlier. Souly excused himself and wandered down the hall, stopping at the door of the physicians' lounge. He went in.

Robert Martin, the silver-haired faculty presence on their team who cosigned all of their notes, was constructing a pyramid of peanut butter on a saltine cracker.

"That's a sick girl we've got." He put the entire pyramid in his mouth.

Souly put his hands in the pockets of his clinic jacket and leaned against the back of a chair. "A lot of soft tissue injury. Very dirty wounds."

Martin mumbled, opened a diet Coke, rinsed his mouth vigorously, and seemed on the verge of spitting into the sink when he swallowed. "Detective from the state troopers called me, wanted to know if we thought it was drug or gang business."

"She doesn't look like that."

"What does 'that' look like?"

"She does not seem that old to me." Souly stooped over and looked in the under-counter refrigerator out of habit, then shut the door and stood again.

"I examined her awhile ago. Hard to say if she's fourteen or forty. You do a drug screen?"

"It didn't seem prudent. She'd already had her total blood volume replaced twice over when Andrews called me."

"Maybe she'll tell us when she comes around."

Souly opened his mouth as if to say something, but did not speak.

"Yes?"

"She was very cold, with a very slow pulse on arrival, and from the blood loss, I'd say she'd been injured four or five hours before. Probably she was anoxic. With so little blood to the brain for so long, I would be surprised if she can even remember how to talk."

"You're encouraging."

"My other concern is the bullet at T-12. She may not be able to walk either."

Martin shook his head. "Indigent medicine," he said. "We do what we've got to do."

The following morning Souly stood in X-ray, viewing the films alone as soon as they fell from the processor. He stepped back from the view box.

A rib had been broken, perhaps a few months before, delicate strands of bone knitting the uneven edges together. The rest of the girl's chest had become a snowstorm, tiny specks of white filling the ellipses of darkness that had been her lungs, obliterating the margins of her heart, erasing the shadows of her breasts. Each speck a confluence of water, of serum, of fluid not moving, settling in a space dedicated to the passage of air. Molecule by molecule, she was drowning. Her cells were leaking, each dying of its own rage.

Her blood chemistries would be discouraging this morning. He had not seen them yet, but he knew her kidney function would shift, her creatinine level would rise, the barometer of the body's capacity to rid itself of waste, of cellular death. Brady was right; she was a good teaching case, a resource to be consumed while instructing others.

A robust older man with a cauliflower nose, bald but for a halo of white hair, lay in her room, surrounded by ten or twelve visitors, most of whom talked to one another. The conversation stopped when Souly stepped between them.

A nurse came behind him with a breakfast tray. "We moved your girl to two thirty-six," she said without looking at him. "Mr. Knudsen has a lot of family."

Souly smiled as he backed away. The people smiled at him. They all had the same nose, he thought.

He stood and watched her chest rise and fall and watched the panel of the ventilator. Peak pressures had risen to thirty-two, they had been twenty the afternoon before, her lungs getting stiff, her airways immobilized like a straw in a thick milkshake. The inhaled oxygen had been turned up to 100 percent, five times the concentration of room air. She was requiring so much more to stay afloat. He listened to her lungs, to a sound like crumpled cellophane at every point on her chest. He asked himself who had broken her rib.

He opened her chart at the desk. Her blood count was unchanged, at least she was not bleeding. Her white count had risen to thirty-two thousand, she had an infection it could be assumed, and aside from his antibiotics, there was nothing else he could add. *Some things I can treat, some things I cannot treat.* Her creatinine had risen to 1.9. She was drifting away from him. He scribbled an order for diuretics. He thought again of the rib fracture. Perhaps it had been the same person who shot her.

At four minutes before twelve, he dashed into the university library. He stopped at the desk a moment later with eight copies of *Lung.*

"You can't check those out. Those are this year's," the girl said.

"I'll just be over in the auditorium. I'll have them back in an hour." The two knew each other. She mustered a scowl and turned her back on him.

He found a seat near the back under a dim light and waited for his eyes to adjust, his attendance expected as an example to others. At the podium, an intern and his resident from St. Anthony's presented a case of a rare soft tissue tumor, "one of only three in the literature," they said. They had made their diagnosis *before* the patient had died, a sort of minor victory among oncologists.

Souly opened the top journal to 'Acute Respiratory Distress Syndrome and the Utility of High-dose Steroids,' page thirty-seven. He scanned the abstract but it was equivocal. He opened a second volume to page 221, 'High-frequency Jet Ventilation: A Study of Nine Patients.' Interesting, but the nearest jet ventilator was in St. Louis. He searched each journal in turn, the editorials, the case studies. Two articles in favor of steroids and one against. One article documented four deaths and the injudicious use of diuretics. The lights went up. He pushed the journals back into his backpack.

In the afternoon her forearms were swollen, the white plastic identification bracelet pressing into her pale flesh. He pulled it toward the narrower angle of her wrist, and it loosened. What sense, he asked himself, was there in an identification bracelet for someone unidentified?

The following morning her wrist was more swollen. He carefully inserted his penknife underneath it and cut the band loose. Her creatinine had risen to 2.1 and only three hundred milliliters of urine had dribbled out of her catheter through the night. He doubled the dose of diuretic, then ordered two hundred and fifty milligrams of dexamethasone.

He wandered the wards until he found Brady and his students, and trailed them from bedside to bedside, pretending to listen to each student's presentation. He listened to half of what was said, looking out the window at the snow-covered lawn of the hospital, and pondered how death from renal failure or pneumonia, or probably ARDS, was thought to be an anesthetic experience. Certainly this girl was anesthetized, if for no other reason than the morphine. But did that count, or was it the last experience that someone saw or felt before they became unconscious that they would remember in whatever afterlife there was? He wondered if she had been afraid, or if the first bullet had taken her by surprise. She would just have to live longer, he thought, live long enough to reach adulthood, so that some other event would be on her mind when she died.

At noon he found a reason he could not eat with Brady's group, knowing he would not be able to think, and went to the doctors' lounge, but a conversation about golf was in the air. He took a quarter of a sandwich from a tray in the refrigerator, put it in his mouth, and went outside, looking over the doctor's parking lot. When the sandwich was gone, he pulled a hard pack from his shirt, took the remaining cigarette and lit it. Finest Turkish tobacco—he was allowing himself two per day. The Turks would just have to go back to growing poppies. The first he had smoked while using the toilet seven hours before, now he would have to wait seventeen hours until the next one. He stood shivering in his clinic jacket with his other hand in his pocket. A terrible example, he thought, to any student that might see him. When the cigarette was half-finished, he dropped it on the cement and crushed it with his foot. Tonight he would put two more cigarettes in the box before he went to bed.

In the afternoon Dr. Farag was paged to the lobby. Two policemen waited for him, one in plain clothes who introduced himself as Detective Wilson. They walked to the ICU and the detective asked questions. Had any visitors come? Did he think she was going to die? Had anyone called? They were anxious to speak to a man named Medina. When would she wake up? Always this question came, as if every critical patient's illness was something so simple as sleep, which would evaporate some morning like a headache. An awake patient, to the lay public, was a healthy patient.

They stood in the girl's room for a few minutes. The uniformed policeman commented that the room was at ground level, but seemed satisfied that the thick, tinted windows couldn't be opened. The detective walked to one side of the bed, then stood at the end of it, scanning over the ventilator, the tubing everywhere, and the small forest of plastic IV bags hanging from poles. He shook his head. "You'll let us know the moment she comes around."

"Of course."

The detective handed his card to the nurse, who taped it to the front of the girl's chart. The two men left.

*

In room 239, a twenty-year-old blond-haired boy who had taken too much methamphetamine laid attached to a ventilator. Remington Stansbury, but the nurses, in the absence of any visitors, had taken to calling him "Crack," for brevity's sake. In room 241 lay an unidentified woman also tethered to a ventilator, her breasts and arms a great schizoid tangle of tattooed images, who had been found beaten at a truck stop. Someone started calling her

"Tattoo." One of the evening shift nurses had begun calling the girl in 236 "Christmas Girl." For independent reasons, the Christmas tree in the ICU had been moved to stand outside her new smaller room, and remained there after the rest of the decorations in the ward had been taken down. Farag began to think of her as a cryptic, perhaps unwanted, gift. Tattoo bled to death on the twenty-eighth of December after an overwhelming infection consumed all of the cells needed to clot her blood. The following afternoon, Crack died after his heart digressed into a long, chaotic riot of irregular rhythm that no amount of electricity could extinguish. After that, Christmas Girl became simply "The Girl."

Late in the morning of the eighth day, Detective Wilson reappeared while Farag sat at the desk. "Excuse me for asking, but you're from over there? Arabia, I mean."

"I'm Egyptian, actually."

"I guess that's close."

"Not exactly. How can I be of assistance, Mr. Wilson?"

"Well, I took the liberty of bringing the girl's clothes, what she was wearing when she came to the emergency room." He placed a sack on the countertop. "I hoped you might be able to tell us if these were real, or some kind of costume." The detective pulled a mass of lightweight black fabric from the bottom of the bag as he spoke.

Souly took the fabric from him and, over the counter, pulled it apart where the blood had dried in a shiny crust in irregular patches. "Costume. Something someone wears when pretending to be someone else?" He fingered the small tag in Arabic near the collar. It was an abayah. He glanced across the ICU at his young patient and thought for a moment, then looked at Wilson. "It really seems rather lightweight for winter. I believe it is probably just a costume."

The detective seemed satisfied. He turned to leave, but stopped at the door. "We may be handing the case over to a female detective, if the girl comes around." Then he was gone.

Souly wrote orders for the tenth large dose of steroids, troubled by a rising gauntlet of incongruities. At her door he stood for several minutes, trying to picture her awake, talking, laughing, but could not imagine who she spoke to. He was off-call, and he would try to get home and sleep in his own apartment.

He awakened briefly during the night to the sound of the wind blowing hard around his windows, and asked himself, *Who will represent her in the court of the dead?* In the morning, he heard drops of water on the balcony, and when he turned on the light, the cement was bare and wet in places. The snow was melting, rivulets of water dribbling from the roof. A thin corona of turquoise rose above the horizon of the city. He repeated the question aloud that had come to him in the night. He went into the bathroom, loaded his toothbrush, and went to the balcony, sliding open the door and allowing the winter morning to wash over him. After he rinsed his mouth, he returned to the open door a third time, knelt to the rising sun, and for several minutes, struggled quietly for absolution.

In the X-Ray Department, he stood before the view box, convinced initially that he had picked up the wrong films. He clicked the lights from high to low, then lined up the previous week's films. The girl's lungs were clearing.

At the bedside, he listened to her chest and the sound of cellophane was gone. On the ventilator, the peak pressure was nineteen. Her respirations read '14', then '13', then '15.'. He watched the numbers flicker back and forth. The rate was still set at 12. Three of those breaths were her own. The needle on the gauge snapped irregularly, and the tube jiggled.

"That's been happening all night." A nurse had come in behind him, someone he did not recognize. "She's bucking the vent. I've got some more morphine."

"Who ordered morphine?"

"Dr. Martin."

"Did he come by? Look at her?"

"No."

"Let's hold that." He raised his hand. "She's only coughing." He clicked the rate down to zero. The girl's chest stopped moving. They both stood and watched the monitor. The girl's pulse started to rise. The nurse shifted on her feet, looked out through the glass at the rest of the unit, began to stammer, then stopped herself. After twenty seconds, the needle moved slightly and the girl's chest raised. Two hundred and seventy CCs of air registered on the screen, then it was gone. There was a shorter pause and the girl's chest rose again, and this time, five hundred CCs were drawn in. Another minute passed, and the rate rose to 6.

"This is really very good. The girl breathed six, so we will give her just six breaths from the ventilator." He moved the rate knob back up to six. "That way, the hospital saves electricity." He smiled at the nurse and stepped around her.

*

At midafternoon the following day, something tumbled with a hollow, muted sound, followed by the impact of something thrown.

"Two thirty-six." One of the nurses stood.

An electronic thermometer lay split in half like a melon in the doorway of the girl's room, and on the floor near her bed, a plastic washbasin and a box of gloves lay in a still expanding puddle of soapy water. She flailed her left arm over the bedside table, arched her neck and snapped her head from side to side. In another instant she grasped the tube near her mouth and tugged. It uncoupled just outside the mouth guard, leaving the end of the endotracheal protruding like a hollow tongue. The alarm of the ventilator sounded, a long, flat, mournful horn. One nurse tried to reconnect the tube while the other struggled to restrain the girl's arm. The girl continued to snap her head.

Farag appeared, stepped around the two nurses and touched the alarm's silence button. "Stop that," he said to the girl, and pressed his palm against her forehead, steadying it into the pillow. "Stop moving. You'll hurt yourself." He hovered over the girl until he had locked his gaze with hers. "You're in a hospital. You've been very sick."

The girl froze and stared at him.

"You can't talk right now," he went on. "You have a tube in your throat. We will take it out soon." He rubbed her hair away from her eyes.

The oxygen saturation read 92 percent. "Let's just leave her on pressure support." He turned the rate to zero. "Ask respiratory to be here in half an hour with a high-humidity mask."

A nurse stood in the door with the two halves of the broken thermometer, holding them up like evidence of a crime.

Farag took them from her. "Girls get angry when they can't talk," and dropped them in the waste can, then picked up the phone and called Martin. He wrote orders and left to find Brady and his students.

When he returned, the girl sat upright in bed with the bucket-shaped mask held to her face with an elastic strap. A mist blew out around the edges. The room was quiet and full of light without the ventilator, which had been taken away. The water trap of the chest tube continued to gurgle.

He listened to her lungs, then folded the stethoscope and put it in his pocket. "Can you speak?"

The girl turned her head to him, squeaked, then coughed.

"It will be better tomorrow. You rest now."

The girl took ice chips. She sucked water through a straw. She could move her legs and wiggle her toes. She raised her right hand when asked which side she wrote her name with, but she appeared to have a lot of pain when she moved her arm, which tugged at the chest tube where it emerged between her sixth and seventh ribs.

When two nurses attempted to stand her the following morning, she crumpled at the side of the bed. Speech came in coarse, one-syllable whispers. No, she wasn't in school. No, she wasn't from Topeka. Yes, she was from another state. No, she could not tell them which. No, she did not know her name. Farag ordered morphine, and she slept.

After her face was properly cleaned of tape residue and her hair was washed, the two policemen came and took her picture to be placed in missing children's bulletins. They asked a few questions she could not answer, debated between themselves, and said they would be back when she was feeling better.

*

She slept and awoke and slept again and again, without rhythm, without regard to lightness or dark, and on each awakening, the ceiling, the sheets, the rail of the bed, the clear tube driven into the back of her wrist, the glass of the windows on all sides, and the curtains were new textures to learn on a strange planet to be navigated with the eye and the tips of her fingers as far as she could strain. She would pluck away the tubes or the wires on her chest and look at them, as the high tone filled the air, and then women dressed in pajamas, new women each time, with plastic name tags and tubes and needles and detached purpose, would scurry into the room and reattach them. "Farag ordered this" or "Farag will be disappointed" or "Farag wants that in," they would say, but she thought they were saying "Frog," and began to imagine a trollish, evil little man, somewhere, who controlled her existence like a puppet. Sometimes they would shake their heads, then pinch her arm senseless and drive something sharp though her skin. She would cry, and they would rub her head and then go away, leaving her alone.

*

On a morning of hyper aesthetic brilliance, sterile and bright, she awoke to the touch of chilled metal on her chest. A slightly built man with olive skin and round tortoiseshell glasses was stooped over her, his gaze directed up over the top of the headboard at the monitor. He was clean-shaven and had an odor of sweet aftershave about him, heavy citrus, late summer. She strained to speak with every small muscle of her face, her eyes, and the rhythm, numb and remote, of her pulse.

He looked down. "Excuse me, and good morning."

"Sala'am," she whispered.

"Ah, so you speak Arabic. How convenient." He looked over her head again and moved the stethoscope to one side of her chest and then the other. He stepped back. "I do also. I am Dr. Souly Farag." And he squeezed her right hand firmly. "I have been looking after you for the last two weeks. Do you know where you are?"

Her voice began with the same hoarse squeak. "Car wreck?" She cleared her throat. The voice did not sound like herself.

"You're in Topeka, Kansas, in Stormont-Vail Hospital. But there was no car collision. Someone shot you. Do you remember who might have done such a thing?"

She looked past him at the snow on the lawn beyond the glass and for an instant could feel snow on her feet. She shook her head slowly.

"Can you tell me your name?"

"Ah-eesha." She looked at the clipboard in his left hand.

"Oh, this. This says your name is Jane Doe. You don't look very much like a Jane to me." He smiled benignly and looked over the top of his glasses.

"How long?"

"About two weeks. Some good surgeons took care of your wounds, but then you got very sick." He moved to the foot of the bed and hung the chart there. "Can you remember your name?"

"I don't think"—she frowned and shook her head—"Aisha is right. Could it have been an accident?"

"I think that unlikely. You see, you were shot once in the abdomen, once from behind, very close, and also through your ear."

He was mechanical, she thought, contrived from her own dreams. The frog. The troll. She stared into the foot of the bed and slowly raised her hand to her left ear, then to the remains of her right. She gasped and felt through the gown and fingered the tube.

"It's a chest tube. Right now, it keeps your lung from collapsing. Please, don't pull on it."

"Hurts." She let the tube drop. Evil. Smiling evil, looking so earnestly at her.

"I know. I'm sorry. It won't be there forever."

She pushed the sheets almost to her groin.

"That's healing very nicely," he said. "I'm sure your bowels and bladder should work fine."

She said nothing but ran her finger slowly over the thin red scar.

"They had to take some things out, I'm afraid. You were dying."

"I need to pee." And she reached down and lifted the catheter above the level of the sheets. "You do this?"

He turned away toward the window. "No. The nurses did. Or maybe in surgery. Would you like to have it out?" He turned back to her.

The violation was not lost on her, and she glared at him.

"I'm sorry. There are going to be some things you won't understand. You will need to be patient."

In the afternoon, he was back. He closed the door and pulled up a chair next to her bed. He had a small paperback in his hand, *Name Your Baby*. "So, Aisha, 'youngest wife of the prophet.' I don't think you are any more Arabic than I am Chinese." He opened the book. "So we are going to play a little game. I will read a name, and you will tell me if it's familiar."

She nodded.

"Abigail? Adel? Adine? Adrienne? You're not an Agnes. Amy? Andrea?" He looked up. She shook her head. "Barbara? Beatrice...no, you're not old enough to be a Beatrice. Beverly? Blythe? I've always thought Blythe was a pretty name. Bobbie? Camille? Candace? Carmen? Carol? Carrie? Catherine? Cheryl? Cindy?" He closed the book and looked at her. "Tell me your name isn't Zelma."

"My name isn't Zelma."

"Good." He opened the book again. "Shall we go on? Daisy? Darlene? Dawn? Deborah? Denise? Diane? Donna? Dorothy?" He paused and skipped over a whole column of names he felt certain hadn't been used in fifty years. "Elaine? Eleanor? Elizabeth? Ellen? Elissa? Emily? Erica? Erin?"

The girl opened her mouth and sat forward.

"So, it is Erin?"

She turned her head as if listening to some distant tone.

"Erica?" The girl did not speak, but put her index finger to her lips. Tears pooled in her eyes. "So it is Erica?"

"I think that's right. Erika. Erika Etulain."

He closed the book, anonymity abolished. "And where are you from, Erika Etulain?"

"The Dalles. It's in Oregon."

19

Souly arrived at the hospital just before sunup and went directly to the ICU. Abby Tomlinson was nowhere to be seen. Karen, a nurse he had known since her graduation and sometimes imagined as his own daughter, followed him into 236. Erika slept, her head to one side, mouth open, her hands on a pillow on her abdomen.

He squatted down near the water trap, which had stopped bubbling. "This is good. This can come out today."

"Shall I get some gauze?"

A gnome of a woman with a green apron came into the room and set a breakfast tray on the bedside table and left.

"No. Let her sleep." He glanced at the tray. "She's going to have a long day. Have her parents called here?"

"No one on night shift said anything."

"Well, they called me. At one o'clock in the morning. They are in Oregon. I pointed out the time difference, but I'm sure they'll call later this morning." Souly turned and the nurse followed.

"She doesn't have a bedside phone."

"Then you will need to set one up." Souly sat at the desk and took out a pen.

"Are they going to be difficult?"

"They are probably reasonable people. They were excited, of course. I could hear the mother crying in the background. The father, I think, was writing down everything I said."

Souly rounded through the rest of the ICU and then went to the wards. It was January third, and he had not smoked in three days. In a new deviation from his morning routine, he stopped in the cafeteria for a breakfast burrito. When he returned to Erika's room, it was sleeting, and tiny pellets tapped on the glass of her window. She was sitting halfway up in bed and had already pushed her tray away, but hadn't eaten more than a few bites.

"You aren't very hungry today. Are you Nauseated? Constipated?"

She looked away. "Maybe."

"The pain medicines will do both. Where do you hurt most?"

"My stomach hurts. And this thing." She pinched the chest tube.

"Well, we can take that out now."

The nurse helped Erika roll to one side and wedged a pillow behind her back. Souly picked away the dressing beneath her breast with a gloved hand, then cut the two thick black sutures buried in angry skin. "Take a deep breath." With a Vaseline gauze pressed over the wound, he pulled the tube straight out. She gasped. "Try not to cough."

The nurse cut long expanses of elastic tape and pressed more gauze over the site. Souly coiled the tube around the water trap and pressed it into the trash can. Erika repositioned herself, pushing herself higher in the bed, and grimaced.

"Does that still hurt?"

"Not as much. Just my stomach."

"Good. You can start walking this afternoon." He leaned against the windowsill. "Your parents called me last night."

"Oh my God." She put her hands on the edge of the bed and started to get up. "They're going to be crazy."

"Of course not. They're just worried. Your father said you have been gone since last March."

"What else did he say?"

"Mostly he just asked questions. I could only tell him about the last two weeks."

She grimaced again. "I don't remember. Right now, I don't even remember last night." Realizing this unnerved her. Panic stirred, an image, a river reflecting a full moon, fell to pieces.

"Who shot you?"

She wrestled with smoke, a square blue room, shreds of paper. "Huh?"

"Do you remember who shot you?"

She shook her head slowly.

He pulled a chair from the corner and sat facing her. "We know you were in a cornfield, near a pasture. What do you remember?"

"A motel. It rained a lot. I got sick in the rain."

"Where was that?"

"I don't know. It wasn't anywhere. We drove there. Majij and me."

A nurse walked in with a plastic phone, plugged it in and left.

"Majij. He is Arabic?"

"He's from Iran. Majij Aziz. He's a doctor, like you."

"A doctor." Souly buried his face in his hands and rubbed his eyes. "Wonderful. A doctor. Of medicine?"

"That's what I said. Like you, but younger."

"I doubt he was like me." He rubbed his eyes again. "And he slept with you?"

She nodded. "People do that."

"You went with him willingly?"

"We were married. Sigheh." And she said 'sigheh' again, with emphasis, as if it would explain everything.

"Ah, yes, those lucky Iranians." He smiled and tapped his pen to his temple. "Nowhere else in the world is there sigheh. Temporary marriage. So that the prostitutes and their customers do not get arrested."

"I'm not a prostitute."

"I know that. But shame on him." He put the pen in his pocket, aware that he had been waving it around like a pointer. "I spoke without thinking. Sometimes there is sigheh for simple economic reasons. Say an older woman wants to take in a man to help her with the house or her business." And while he spoke, it occurred to him that teenagers who had wrecked their parents' cars would feign more serious injuries in the emergency room, hoping for an element of pity. Her amnesia might be rehearsed, each morning before he arrived. "There's no reason to lie to me. I hope you know that."

"You sound like my dad."

He stood and walked to the window again and turned. "The issue at hand here is stewardship. Do you know what that means? Right now, for example, I am your steward. You are in the stewardship of this hospital." He raised his open hands. "Your father says you just turned sixteen in July. Did you know what kind of danger there might be when you ran away?"

She shook her head. "I helped him with lots of things. We were partners."

"You cannot be partners when one is so much older, so much more wise to the streets."

"But it wasn't all like that. He taught me stuff. I learned a lot."

"So tell me, what did he teach you?"

"I learned a lot of words in Farsi and French. I learned"—she sat forward and flinched, and her speech quickened—"some things about history that you don't learn here, about how the British really screwed up the Middle East. How the money here, in this country, is all controlled by…"

"It sounds like you learned his *opinion* on a lot of things."

"How to survive," she interjected, with a swagger in her voice, but she wasn't looking him in the eyes anymore.

Souly glanced down at the water trap in the trash can. "Right."

"I'm a mess, huh?"

"You'll get better."

"I wish I could hide for a hundred years."

"I know."

She grew sullen and stared at her feet. Souly walked to the far side of the bed.

"Maybe this Majij, he did not know the danger either. Maybe he did. Maybe he got shot also. But as an adult, he put you in harm's way."

The phone rang. Erika turned and looked at it, dumbfounded.

"Pick it up," Souly said, and excused himself. At the desk he could see her through the glass, sitting forward on the mattress, the handset to her ear. She spoke. She spoke again. She was listening. Her eyes teared. Souly looked down at the chart. When he looked up again, she had turned away from him completely, but still held the phone.

She awoke again when someone touched her leg. She slid her arm across the mattress next to her without opening her eyes, grasping for the familiar. "Erika?"

A tall blonde woman, hair frosted like someone's mother, stood at the side of her bed. She wore a blue suit beneath an open khaki raincoat. "I'm Patty Collins." She extended a hand. "I'm an investigator." She opened a small wallet with her picture and a gold shield and held it out. "How are you feeling?"

"Better, I guess. I had a tube in my chest until this morning." She made an effort to pull up her gown but stopped. "It still hurts if I try to move. You a detective?"

Patty pulled a chair up from behind her and sat down. "That's my title. I try to do more than detect things. When I can, I try to put all the pieces together for people." She set her purse on the floor and pulled a stenographer's pad from it. "Dr. Farag tells me you can't remember much. I'd like to help you with that." She opened the pad. "You're from Oregon, is that correct?"

"The Dalles. It's on the river."

"I spoke with your parents last night. They say Portland is fogged in."

"They're just mad at me."

"No one is mad at you. They sounded overjoyed."

"Am I going to juvie?" Erika gripped the edge of the blanket and pulled it up to her chin.

"I beg your pardon?"

"You know. Juvenile Hall. Jail for kids."

"Did you commit any crimes?"

"I don't think so."

"Then why would you go to jail? Running away isn't a felony, so far as I know. Not even a misdemeanor."

"It's not?" Erika released the edge of the blanket and folded her hands on her abdomen. "Are you from here?"

She set the pen down. "I'm from New Jersey, actually."

"You don't talk like it."

"I've been here a long time."

"Bruce Springsteen is from New Jersey."

"That's right. You remember that? Did you, do you like Springsteen?"

"He's got a good saxophone player."

"Do you play anything?"

"I play piano, I think. But not for a long time."

She wrote in the pad and then looked up. "For a year, maybe?"

"Yeah."

There was a pause. Patty leaned forward. "Erika, do you remember who you were with?"

"Majij."

"Was that Dr. Majij Aziz?"

"Yeah. I went with him."

"He didn't force you to go with him?"

"Nobody forced me. No."

"Why did you go?"

"He had a car. Things were really shit at home."

"Really? How so?"

"At school, nobody…God, I don't know."

"Your parents. Did they harm you?"

Erika stared at the back of her hand and stroked a bruise. "They didn't respect me. I think I wanted to prove something."

"It's easy to feel that way when you're young. Did Dr. Aziz respect you?"

"We got married. I loved him, I think."

"You married him." She wrote on the pad, pressing hard. "In what state?"

Erika closed her eyes and rubbed them. "We were in Bozeman, Wyoming, I think."

"Bozeman is in Montana." Patty scooted the chair forward. "Who witnessed this? How old did you tell them you were?"

"It was just a paper. A contract we made. There were squirrels there. It's legal in Iran for Muslims to get married like that."

"Is that what Dr. Aziz told you?"

She looked away. "Dr. Farag thought it was bullshit, too."

"Do you like Dr. Farag?"

"He's fair."

"Did you ever see a lot of money in the car with Dr. Aziz? A box or a briefcase?"

Erika looked surprised. "No. He acted all the time like we wouldn't have enough."

"Did he have packages in the car that you weren't allowed to look at? Things he picked up, or dropped somewhere?"

"I don't remember. I don't think so."

"Were there other people you visited, or stayed with?"

"I don't think so." She yawned and then started to search through the sheets. "I think I need another pain pill."

"In a few minutes, Erika. We really need to talk."

"It was Christmas, but it wasn't Christmas. There were people there, I think. I don't know."

"Were there drugs at the house?"

"I don't know."

"Did anyone give you drugs?"

"I don't think so. No."

"Does the name Medina mean anything to you?"

"It's a place in Arabia, where Mohammad…"

"No, I mean a person named Medina."

"I don't remember."

"Did Dr. Aziz, Majij, did he have any friends named Medina? Any Mexican friends?"

"I don't know. I don't think he liked Mexicans."

"And why was that?" She wrote more on the pad.

"I think sometimes people thought he was Mexican."

"Was this house you mentioned in town or out in the country?"

"It was more like a motel. In the country. It rained. But it wasn't Christmas." She rubbed her eyes again and her temples, then flinched. "I think it was Thanksgiving." She flinched again. "Look, I just don't know. I might have dreamed this, all of it, and I wouldn't know what"—she flinched again—"what was real and unreal." She found the call cord and started to trace it to its end. "I need another pain shot."

"Erika. The pain medicine keeps you from remembering. I can't help you if you can't remember. Just a few more questions."

"Erika Aguilar." The name had come to her like a flash card. "I think he told some people once that we were Mexicans, that our name was Aguilar."

"Think of Medina again."

Letters swam before her eyes and pain spread deep through her flanks. "No," she said, "Medina just doesn't mean anything."

The detective and the girl sat quietly for a few minutes. Finally Erika blinked several times as if she'd been asleep. "Have you seen Majij? Why isn't he here?"

"Do you expect him?"

"He loves me. He's angry. Some bad things happened to him, I think."

"What bad things?"

"I don't know. I just remember him being afraid." She put a hand to the side of her jaw. "But he never talked about it."

"We're trying to find him. We have a lot of questions for him, too. Do you remember what car you were in?"

"It was black inside, dark blue or black on the outside, I think. It was small. Bucket seats."

"Could it have been a Saab?"

"Yeah. Did you find it?"

"We found it. At the airport. Did Dr. Aziz talk about going anywhere?"

"He said we'd go to Iran."

"Did you want to go to Iran?"

"Yeah."

"Why?"

"It is where people have chosen to live as God intended."

The detective raised her eyebrows. "Do you really believe that?"

"Shit, no." Her own response, so unrehearsed, had startled her in its transparency. She was reflective for a moment, aware for the first time how evasive truth might be in the absence of any solid memory, her own inner voice a tangle of platitudes. "I just remember *he* said it a lot." She wondered if she should stop talking completely until everything was clear. The mattress jiggled and she realized Patty was shaking the edge of it with her hand, pen between her fingertips.

"Erika. Erika?"

Erika stared at her hesitantly, grasping for some known object to proceed from. "Was my coat in the car?"

"We don't know. The car had a fire in it. It was badly burned up." The girl was looking at her vacantly. "Erika, where did you go just now?"

"Do you think he's dead?"

"We don't know. We don't think so. We think he's left the country, though."

"He loved me. He wouldn't leave. I was all he had. Everybody else had taken advantage of him."

"Who took advantage of him? Did you see this?"

Erika closed her eyes and the highway stretched inexhaustable before them, fields, trees, fences, farms slipped past to either side, his hands gripped the wheel, his jaw tight against invisible leather, he turned to her. He had no eyes.

"Would he have allowed you to get shot if he loved you?"

"I'm really tired. I want my pain medicine now."

*

The head of the bed rose to the buzz of a motor. "You need to wake up. Your lunch is getting cold." The nurse's arms moved in a blur over the tray before her, taking away lids, removing foil, opening a milk carton, a straw, a napkin unraveled, the crash of knife-fork-spoon onto to the tray. Tomato-chicken-chocolate-rice, all of the colors and aromas rose in a vapor beneath her face. She lowered a spoon into the bowl, and a memory of eating oatmeal some-where raced past. The phone rang and she picked it up.

"Erika?"

"Yeah. Mom?"

"Erika. Your father and I have missed our plane. We're in Hood River right now. Are you listening? Erika."

"Yeah."

"Eighty-four is all covered with ice. A truck had an accident and blocked traffic for three hours. Didn't want you to think we'd forgotten."

"No, Mom." And the nervous voice far away, in Oregon, in the town, in the house that flickered in her mind's eye in silent footage, ran on and on in loops and turns that left Erika wordless.

"We're probably going to get a flight tomorrow." A pause. "Are you okay?"

"I'm just sleepy."

"You don't sound very well."

"I'm fine." She pushed herself higher on the mattress. The afternoon sun glared off the snow like a floodlight.

"We love you. Can't wait to see you."

"I love you too." A dial tone followed. She set the phone down. Across the distance of the snow the roofs of cars traveled back and forth on a street just below her line of vision. A white police car passed, and she waited for it to pass again in the other direction, but it never did.

Someone came and took the lunch tray. A few minutes later a young man in white, with curly black hair and a name tag, 'Alan,' arrived and unfolded an aluminum walker at the side of her bed. "Ready to go for a walk?" he asked, and took a wide rainbow belt from his own waist and slipped it around hers.

When she returned, an aide was placing her toiletries in a plastic tub and her chart lay in a wheelchair. They would need her room for a surgical patient. She was being moved upstairs.

*

Erika was sitting in the bathroom the following morning when there was a rap on the door.

"Miss Etulain? Honey, you know you're not supposed to go in there without help. You need help?"

"I'm fine."

"There's an older gentleman out here waiting to see you."

She imagined her father and stood and straightened her gown, retying it behind her neck, and checked her reflection in the steel plate around the light switch. She pulled her hair over the missing part of her ear. Each arm mottled with bruises and Band-Aids and needle marks, she crossed them one way, then the other. She flushed the toilet and opened the door.

"Miss Etulain?"

"Yes?"

"Dennis Wilson, Topeka Police." He stood with his hands in his pockets, a coat folded over one arm.

She pivoted onto the bed, crestfallen, and pulled a blanket around her waist.

"I hope you're feeling better."

She nodded. "I thought you might be somebody else."

"I realize Patty talked with you a long time yesterday, but a few things we're still not clear about."

"Like what?"

"I want you to think carefully." He sat down. "Did Doctor Aziz ever call himself Medina?"

"No. Or if he did, I don't know if I'd remember. Why?"

"The night you were shot, the caller on the 911 line identified himself as Jesus Medina, and he gave deputies perfect instructions on your location. Sometimes, a lot of the time actually, when a murder occurs, the perpetrator, well, he feels guilty or he wants to undo…"

"No. Majij wouldn't do this."

"I'm just explaining our concerns."

"I just know. He didn't do it. He couldn't harm anyone." As she said this, it occurred to her that Majij had been frightened, that she remembered him now as a soul lost. They had both been lost. There had been a knife somewhere. The policeman was speaking again.

"I know Patty asked you this yesterday, but maybe you're clearer now. Were you forced to go with Majij?"

"No." *A knife near my leg.*

"If you were forced, if he ever kept you from leaving, we could call it an abduction. We might be able to get the FBI to help us."

"I'm sure. We were close. We loved each other." He had a knife, now she was sure.

"Well if you really love him, you'd want the best people looking for him, wouldn't you?"

"And he'd get in a lot more trouble, wouldn't he?"

"Maybe."

She said nothing.

"There's one more matter."

"Yes?"

"When you were found, there were two hundred-dollar bills in your panties." He bowed his head as he said 'panties.' "Don't get me wrong. No one wants to prosecute you."

"Prosecute me?"

"Were you involved in, well, did you have sex for money?"

"No! I don't think so. I've never even imagined doing that."

"You could have been coerced. Think."

"I am thinking. And I don't think I've ever even touched two hundred dollars."

"I only asked because it helps us determine motives."

"That's good." But she retreated to the headboard a few inches, pulling the covers high to her shoulders. "I guess."

"I'm sure you'll remember more. Call me if you do, no matter how insignificant it seems." He placed one of his cards on her tray. "Thank you," he said, then turned and left.

She sat on the bed another thirty minutes, toiling with her thoughts like an archaeologist trying to organize two splinters of bone from an acre of earth.

She stood up, pulled on her robe, and stopped at the sink to comb her hair with her fingers. Above her right breast, she spread the robe wider and ran her fingers along an oval, faintly brown, dusty, coarse…she shut the door, opened the robe fully, and turned from side to side. A similar mark lay below her left arm, incomplete, a crescent, tender. Burned skin. At the light of the window she searched her entire trunk, touching, stroking, pulling what flesh she could not see into view, ignoring the sharp stretch of her new suture lines, but found no other marks. She retied her robe and wheeled her walker into the hall.

"Well, look at you," a nurse named Gracie called. "You be careful now."

"Is there a place where the babies are? In a window?"

"You mean a nursery? That's over in the new wing, on the second floor. That'd be a piece for you, I'm afraid."

"Okay." Erika said and turned the walker toward the sun-room instead. She coursed around the hallway four times and for a while, imagined the grip of the walker like the handlebars of her bicycle. When she sat on her bed again, she turned on the television and pressed the selector until it stopped on CNN. She watched transfixed for almost an hour. The world was in there and she had forgotten about it.

"Your parents called me again." Farag had settled in her doorway without her noticing him. He turned his head and looked up at the screen. A boy was lying motionless in a street, with blood pouring from the side of his head. The camera jiggled and panned to a street corner where hooded men crouched and fired machine guns.

"Lebanon?" he asked.

"Jerusalem." she said, without taking her eyes away from the screen.

"Why'd they call you?"

He moved sideways into the room, still watching the television, and sat down in the chair. "Reassurance, I suppose."

"Why didn't they just call me?" she asked, and in the same breath, was relieved they hadn't.

"Maybe they don't know how to start."

"They never did. Why is it," she asked, "that all of the Arabs and Jews hate each other?" Israeli tanks were rolling down a street of rubble.

"Some people say the Israelis have been heavy-handed." He sized up her question and frowned. "But that's like asking why everyone in the United States hates everyone in Russia." He turned the chair around to face her. "They don't. Not all of them. Certainly it is disputed territory. My father always resented the British, and he used to joke and ask, 'Why didn't the English put the Jews in Canada or Australia?' But I don't think he hated anyone about it." He shook his head. "When the wars came, everyone had to fight, but I don't think many really wanted to. That's why Egypt lost in sixty-seven."

"Were you in that war?"

"I just missed it. I was sixteen. My father was a pharmacist. He still is, in Cairo. He was attached to a medical unit; he lost the sight in one eye."

"I'm sorry."

"Things happen. I was at Al Azhar at that time," he went on. "I was to be a mullah."

"I can't see that."

"I was an intense student of the Koran for three years, but I believed, in a metaphoric sort of way, popular at the time among progressive Muslims, that it was consistent with science." He stood up and walked over to the window. "Some wished to view the teachings very harshly, very literally, sort of like some of the Christians on television here, believing the world was made in a week." He gestured at the television screen. "In poverty it is easy to lose sight of one's purpose. And young people..." He looked over the top of his glasses at her. "Always attracted to simple ideals."

Erika remembered stamps on the floor, shattered glass.

"It requires education to juggle all of the complexities of this world," he said. "Ignorance always inflates prejudice. And when someone happens along and tells you what to do, it absolves you from the labor of thinking." He sat down again. "I was too short, anyway. I would have to have stood on a box to be heard. In the hospital," and he gestured to her IV, "it is not such a problem. People have to listen to me. They're my prisoners."

"Will you go back? Maj was going back to Iran."

"I will visit sometimes, but it has changed since I was a boy." He stood up again and paced around the room. "There is no, no *tolerance*." No time was really ideal to address what had troubled him, and for a week he had struggled to articulate what really seemed to be several dilemmas—a nearly lethal misadventure while pretending to adopt another culture, her failure to recognize obvious danger, and her emotional vacancy, perhaps just an artifact of her hypothermia. Or was it the flaw that precipitated her truancy to begin with? *Some things I cannot mend.* Her parents would know, perhaps they could address it with a wiser perspective. He stopped at the end of her bed and rested his hands on the overhead bar. "You were wearing an abayah and chador, the night you were shot."

"I don't remember." But her answer was shadowed by the smell of it, the stiff, dirty fabric in the summer wind, hejab, a memory of entanglement. "Maybe he bought me those."

"I'm sure he did. They were made in Syria. I looked at them. Please…" And he stopped and drew his hands the length of his face, realizing how condescending he would sound. "Islam is a way of life, perhaps a good way, for that part of the world. But please, don't try to pretend that role again. What religion are your parents?"

"Episcopalian."

"Then go back to Oregon. Become a good Episcopalian. You seem bright enough." He took her palm, placed the chain and crescent there, and closed her fingers. "You want a moral compass? Listen to the one you have."

She knew the object in her hand without looking, staring at her closed fist at her side. "You get pretty preachy sometimes, you know."

"You would have died over there."

"I damn near died here."

"Did Dr. Aziz shoot you?"

"No." And she glanced about the room, and he watched her, following her eyes. She settled on his gaze and softened. "Am I going home soon?"

"Your parents are coming late tomorrow I think. You'll probably be ready for discharge by then, or the following morning." He looked at his watch and stood up. "I'm late for a staff meeting. I must go." He folded his stethoscope into his pocket, straightened his tie, and pivoted.

"Doctor Farag?"

He stopped at the door and turned.

"The idea that our thoughts can become our deeds, and so we should be careful what we think about, is that in the Koran?"

"No." He rocked on his heels for a moment, thoughtful. "Saint Augustine I think. He was Catholic. I think it is about owning your thoughts, being culpable about what we do. Why?"

"I don't know. Somebody just told me that once."

*

The next morning after her breakfast, her sixteenth day in the hospital she calculated, she put on her robe and took her walker to the elevator. She folded the walker as soon as she got into the car and lost her balance when it began to move, but caught herself. She stepped into the lobby and turned to watch the walker vanish behind the stainless doors behind her, then limped around for twenty minutes and briefly tried to decide how to reach the nursery, studying a sign with a red arrow and the words, 'You Are Here,' which was planted in the middle of a maze of lines in a glass case. Slush from foot traffic coming in the front doors soaked her rubber-ribbed socks. She went back to her room and took them off, laying them on the window sill. Her low back hurt like an abscessed tooth.

She stood at the window and let the warm air of the heater blow up the sleeves of her robe. A seamless, fluorescent gray cloud layer hung over the earth, and she watched cars come and go from the visitor's parking lot six stories below, knowing that her parents would arrive in a taxi or perhaps in a rental car, but still found herself waiting for her father's small maroon Chrysler.

Dr. Farag rapped on the door with his knuckle and walked in. She turned.

"So you are back. I came by earlier and you were not in bed." He walked up to where she stood and placed his stethoscope first on her back, then on her chest. He took the stethoscope off, placing it around his collar. "When I must chase the patient all around the hospital, it is time for them to go." She sat up on the ledge of the window near the wall and he did the same on the opposite end.

"What is going to happen to me?"

"I suppose you will go back to school, like most girls."

"What about the other kids, what do I say?"

"Tell them what you want to tell them." He stopped, reflective, engaged in a small personal memory. "But I wouldn't tell them anything at all. Very little of what they think or do will have any bearing on where you go in life. We all write our own history eventually."

She placed her toes in the updraft of warm air from the vent and looked out the window to the horizon. "Where, how far, was I out there, when they found me?"

"About eleven miles. It said in the ambulance report that you were in a pasture."

She looked at him. "And some guy named Medina just happened to be out walking around in the snow that night?"

"It seems he came home late, in his truck, and there was a cow in his driveway, and he knew, because of that, that a gate was open. When he took the cow back to where it belonged, he found you."

"I feel like I should thank him. Bake him cookies or something."

"Maybe you should thank the cow. In any case, he seems to be out of reach now, maybe in Mexico with family." He watched her as she exhaled against the glass, then wrote something he couldn't make out with her fingertip.

"Panjere," she said. She turned to him again. "He taught me that." She rubbed it away with her palm.

He looked out over the city. "At this time of day, in Cairo, you would hear the call to prayer, from the muezzin. I'm a little glad they don't do that in Kansas."

"Jesus, can you imagine? With all the different churches here?"

"It would be bedlam." They both laughed together for the moment and smiled privately as they watched the city streets illuminate to nightfall. An ambulance was approaching on Ninth Avenue, and they both fell silent until it disappeared somewhere below in the alley, where only the flicker of its lights could be seen across the snow in the parking lot.

Erika spoke. "Everything's a puzzle right now. And the Koran never made any sense."

"That is all you studied?"

"It was all he had. There was Arabic on one page, English on the other."

Farag shook his head. "He probably couldn't read Arabic either. In any case, you would need to get a book of the Haddith, if you're still curious. And finding one in English…" And he stopped midsentence, remembering it was his very intention to discourage her. "You don't remember being in that field at all?"

She sighed. "I wish."

"Maybe it is better that you don't. Those would not be good memories."

"You don't think I should just drop it?"

He leaned forward with a labored expression. "Whoever shot you shot you three times. They had no compunction about it at all. Dangerous people never become less dangerous."

"But if the police…"

"If they are caught, testify. By all means. But do not waste your life on an endless quest for justice."

*

At four thirty all the colors of a ripened peach burst over the horizon as the sun sank. Gracie appeared with a small bag of fluid. "More antibiotics," she said, hanging it on the pump next to Erika's bed, and shoved the needle through the port on the back of her hand. "Your mom and dad been here yet?" she asked.

"Not yet."

"I thought maybe they slipped in and out while I was in another room."

Erika muted the television. "I haven't figured out what I'm going to say to them when they come."

"You'll do fine, girl. Mamas always miss their children. She'll probably do all the talking. You just listen and be yourself."

Gracie left and a few minutes later, the sky sank into darkness, silent lights across Topeka glittering to life. Erika swung out of bed and wheeled the pole over to the window and resumed her vigil. Amber patches of illumination spotted the parking lot and the handful of cars that remained, amber snow falling and collecting on the windshields until all of them looked alike. A solitary car came down the avenue and turned, approaching the portico, its wipers sweeping an arc of darkness on the glass, a yellow-and-black taxi. The taxi stopped at the curb, the back door opened, and she knew.

She wheeled the pole over to the sink and ran a rag over her face with her free hand, then brushed her teeth, dipping her face to the faucet to rinse. When she stood, a weary looking woman was at the door, hair cropped short, gray, bewildered, regarding her uncertainly.

"Mom?"

"Erika, sweetheart." And her mother was upon her, holding her head to her chest, gasping in the long breaths of someone who weeps without sound. She finally pushed her back a few inches, taking her face in her hands and said, "What have you done to your hair?" but cried openly as she said this, smiling through her tears and pulling her daughter to her again.

Over her shoulder Erika could see her father, beaming, trying to remain somber. He held a black-and-white stuffed cat. She broke free of her mother's embrace after a minute. "Dad." And he pulled her against him. She fell into the folds of his cold leather coat, the wool of his cardigan, the warmth of his chest, the smell of his aftershave. "Dad," she whispered.

"Let me have a look at you, girl." And he turned her around slowly, as if looking for damage on a piece of art, then hugged her again and kissed her on the top of her head. "Natasha couldn't get a ticket, so she sent this in her place." He held out the cat as she stepped back from him.

"You must be tired," Teresa said.

Erika climbed back onto the bed, pulling one leg up beneath her, covering it with the robe. Teresa sat in the only chair in the room. Sam stood with his hands on his hips for a moment, then rested against the windowsill, and feeling embarrassed by his own wonderment and insatiable desire to stare at his daughter, looked up at the flickering silent television instead.

Teresa fingered through Erika's hair again.

Erika remembered the scissors, the dye, the chador, the accent she had feigned somewhere, once, to a policeman. "It's the style now," she said finally. "Black is cool."

Their conversation circled, waxed and waned, always tangential to the central topic no one wanted to mention.

Finally Sam asked, "So what became of that fellow, Aziz?"

"I don't know."

"Doctor Farag, he seems like a decent chap. He said you've been having some trouble with your memory."

"Sam…" Teresa interrupted.

He fell quiet, then, cued by something on the screen, said, "The Berlin wall. It's down now, you know." But his daughter sat with a puzzled, drunken expression and seemed to be reading Teresa's lips. It was not the response he'd anticipated. "Did you know the Rumanians killed that bastard, Ceausescu?"

"Sam."

""No," Erika said. "I've been out of the loop."

"You need to keep an eye on what's making history in the world, it's the world you're going to manage someday."

"She's got plenty to manage right now," Teresa said. "You take your time, dear."

A congenial voice overhead in the hallway announced the end of visiting hours. The hallway darkened. The three of them watched David Letterman for a few minutes. Erika yawned and tried to laugh at the man on the television when her father did, but half of the words sounded like another language.

"We'd best be back at the hotel," her mother said. Her father stood up, both of them kissed her, and Erika followed them to the door and listened as their footsteps whispered down the hallway. She looked at the toy cat, at its vacant plastic eyes, then studied her own eyes in the mirror above the sink. She tossed the cat in the chair, turned out the light, climbed into bed, and lay looking at the empty room. How odd it seemed, not to trust the idea that they had really been there just a few minutes ago. She fell asleep.

A presence, predatory and satanic, was at the end of her bed, just beyond her gaze, and was aware she could move neither her arms nor legs. She shook her head from side to side until she could shake it free, then her arms, and opened her mouth with a long, mournful wail. When she stopped she wasn't sure the sound had been her own voice. She sat up and took a deep breath. The heater hummed in the window sill. Pale yellow light from the parking lot illuminated the ceiling.

The lights went on. "You alright, girl?" Gracie approached her bed.

"There was somebody in here."

Gracie looked around. "Nobody in here but you." She put her hand on Erika's head. "You're not too warm. I think you just had a bad dream."

"It was right there." Erika pointed at the end of the bed.

The nurse took her outstretched wrist and looked at her watch. "Your heart's beating like a little rabbit. Just a dream. You want me to leave the light on for a while?"

"Sure." Erika climbed out of bed after the nurse left and hobbled to the bathroom. When she was finished she washed her hands and turned out the light. She regarded the outline of the cat in the chair for a moment, then picked it up and crawled into bed, lying on her side with it against her breast.

At 10:00 a.m. the last dose of antibiotic was finished. Sam and Teresa arrived, Sam carrying an old brown attaché in one hand that Erika recognized, and a Dillard's sack in the other. He set the attaché on the bedside table and opened it.

"Your mother picked these out," he said, pulling a pair of CK jeans into the air and letting them unfold, then a knit camel blouse. "I'm merely the courier." He flipped a package of underwear onto the bed like a playing card. "But I picked this out," as he handed her the sack. "We didn't have time to find another pea coat."

She sat looking at the sack, so he took it back and emptied it next to her. A royal blue quilted jacket slid onto the bed. "Duck down." He bobbed his head as he said this. "Supposed to be duck down."

She took a handful of it and squeezed. "Melinda had a coat like this, didn't she?"

"I don't know." Sam looked at Teresa. "Did she?"

Teresa smiled. "I believe you're right dear. It was her ski jacket."

Erika dressed while her parents stood in the hall. Doctor Farag arrived and talked with them for a little while. "Hypoxic encephalopathy," he explained. Events closest to her injury might be erased forever.

"Will she eventually remember more?" Teresa touched Farag's arm.

"The body eventually expels things, like a sharp sliver of wood under the skin. It may be uncomfortable for a long time, but relief will come."

Sam shook his hand.

The door to the room was still closed. "Please tell her I said good-bye," Dr. Farag said. "I am awkward at such ceremonies, and must be at another hospital in a few minutes." And he gave his card to Teresa and told her to call him if there were any questions. Then he was gone. A rosy-cheeked, white-haired aide arrived with a wheelchair as Erika opened the door.

"I can walk fine. I walked all over yesterday."

"It's just our policy," the woman said.

Erika sat in the chair with the cat in her lap, and all of them headed for the elevator.

At the airport Erika looked up at the parking garage where the taxi had dropped them off and tried to imagine Majij there, but couldn't. He wouldn't have left. He would have stayed nearby, angry or critical, but near her. Erika watched the faces in the current of passengers that coursed around them in the concourse and back over her shoulder, aching for his familiar presence. Perhaps he had left on some purpose, or with his brother. Yes! He had a brother. She tried to imagine what he looked like, but could only picture Majij. Angry Majij.

They sat on aluminum and Naugahyde benches at the gate. Erika watched small tractors pull trains of suitcase-laden carts to and from planes on the glistening tarmac. A few small patches of snow persisted in the shade nearest the window where the sun had not shone. I am boarding a flight for Iran with my husband, she thought, but could not picture it, it had become like a story someone had told her about someone else, dizzying in its absurdity.

"I talked to Mister Cordova," Sam said. Theresa looked at him with a question on her face. "He's the high school principal."

"Yes?" Erika sat up straighter.

"He says you can test straight into tenth grade if you want. He looked at your grades. You wouldn't have to go back to Wilson."

Erika took a seat by the window and twisted the air nozzle overhead until it was off. The concourse moved away from them slowly and they thumped and rumbled along the tarmac past tails of other planes with different colors and emblems, while a flight attendant mimed a peculiar ballet with a belt in the aisle two seats ahead.

"Have I ever flown before?"

"Your father and I took you to England. You weren't quite two. My mother wanted to see you before she died."

"I don't remember that." The air roared louder, numbers and lights raced past, then they were aloft and Erika watched the shadow of the plane pass in shivers over the snow, the streets, hundreds of irregular little rooftops where vapor rose in the sun and the shingles were shiny as slate, tiny cars moving below along the highway like a labor of ants.

They had not mentioned Steve, she realized, in the two days they had been there, and she wanted to ask, but felt it would reveal a longing to return to some juvenile club in which she no longer desired, or could even claim, membership. Steven and his devout mother might just as well belong to another species now. For nine months, she had been in a different world, she thought, and now was off to a third, some sort of graduation or revelation, but not shame. Her memory of Steven had served her well, but the thought of seeing him again struck no chord. The whine of the engines began to subside.

She leaned forward after the climb, after they reached level flight. "What do you think the Romanians are going to do now, Dad?"

Sam closed his magazine and shoved it into the seatback by his knees. "Oh, I suppose there will be chaos for a spell. There always is. But eventually, they'll have to confront their past, if they're going to move forward."

A rectangular cart rattled a few feet behind them and the flight attendant locked the wheels. Erika noticed she was the same woman who had demonstrated the seat belt.

"What can I get you?" she asked.

"Coffee." Erika spoke before her parents could answer, before it occurred to her that the woman might be asking them.

"Cream in that? Sugar?"

"Black." Erika took the diminutive cup and sucked the bitter brew over her teeth. It tasted *clean*, she thought.

"You're drinking coffee now, are you?" Teresa asked, with the hopeless tone a mother might address the loss of virginity.

"Thought I'd give it a try."

The attendant was bobbing about, snapping napkins off the top of the cart as she spoke to Sam and Teresa. "My niece is already back in school for a week. What's the special event for you three?"

"Family reunion." Sam offered her a flash of teeth at once diplomatic and territorial.

The attendant eased back. "I see." And gingerly handed Teresa her tea. "Well, it must be a joy to travel with your granddaughter." She unlocked the cart and moved up the aisle.

Erika turned to the window and looked out over the confluent white sea that extended to the curvature of the earth beyond them, and wondered if every conversation to come would be an exercise in subterfuge. A small nausea came—the motion of the plane or the coffee, she thought. It didn't seem to matter yet, for now, so high above the world.

20

The backpack flopped onto the desktop in a crumple, skidding as it landed, Aaron landing in the chair in front of her with equal chaos, like a piece of debris falling from the sky after the passing of a tornado. It was an arrival he had polished to a trademark, for most of her life he had startled her with it, and for most of her life, she had practiced looking unperturbed. A bubble of unoccupied chairs had surrounded her, and Aaron had entered that bubble. He turned the plastic chair and sat on it backward, facing her. "Hi."

"Hi to you." She smiled.

"I'm glad you're here. I was afraid they'd make you do ninth grade all over again."

"Do you remember anything you learned last year?"

"Not much."

"I rest my case." She took a deep breath. "There're only a couple of classes that are actually prerequisites for high school. I'm going to do those this summer." She cast a glance over Aaron's shoulder. "Cordova said I might even graduate early, if I do both summers."

Three boys across the room were staring at her. Aaron glanced at them and they turned away. "American Lit?"

"Challenged it. How do you think I got in here?"

Mr. Galbraith walked in and cleared his throat, and the murmur in the room subsided. Aaron turned and sat in his chair sideways. They spoke in whispers. "What are you reading?" He turned the book before her to look at the cover. *Edgar Lee Masters*. "Have we read this?"

"We're going to, you'll like it. It's poetry."

"You always know everything. Can I sit here all semester?"

She shrugged. "Your risk. Some mornings I can't even remember my own name."

"So what happened to your ear?"

"Which one?" They kept each other's secrets like photographs exchanged. She rubbed the Masters book thoughtfully. "A bear bit it off."

In the second week after her appearance in the hallways, a rumor circulated among students who had known her only superficially at Wilson, that she had been duped and taken away by a man who had been a physician impersonator. She had been taken, right there on the exam table, and had been too ashamed to return home or go to the police. In the third week, the man was Middle Eastern and had taken her for the slave trade as a sex worker. She'd been apprehended in a shipping container in Galveston. Or was it a brothel in Barbados? She had been injured by police gunfire in her rescue. Another rumor cast her abductor as a cocaine dealer, and she had been riddled by machine gun fire from a rival in a territorial dispute in Omaha. It was agreed by the fourth week of March that she had gone willingly with a sociopathic loner. With an arsenal in the back seat, they had murdered their way through a series of convenient stores and gas stations and had robbed a bank in Denver (a large bank had indeed been robbed that summer in Denver, by someone else), and she had fallen in a hail of shots from the Kansas Highway Patrol. The details, of course, could never be known by the public, since these things were kept secret when minors were involved in felonies. Everyone knew that. No one ever asked her directly, and Erika remained mute. Melinda would report each story verbatim between puffs, while they stood across the street from the campus, Melinda with an upturned cigarette in her sleeve. She had started smoking only that fall. Erika would lean against the building, cane in hand, to take the weight off of her back.

"I like the one about the robberies. Try to keep that one going," Erika said. "Tell them the police put a transmitter under my skin, so they can tell where I am, day or night."

"What was it like, really?"

Erika screwed up her face. "Everything sort of runs together. We drove a lot, stayed in a lot of motels." She was quiet for a while, scattered fragments, torn pages from a magazine carried on the wind that whipped past, an air-conditioner that never worked, a souvenir shop where she loitered, an arid vista from a rest area where they had fought, late in the afternoon; a lot of emptiness, it seemed to her, linked together by hours of perspiring in a bucket seat in the grip of some tension, some sadness. "Maj seemed pissed off a lot, at me. My psychiatrist…" She closed her eyes and shook her hair. "God, it feels weird, saying that," she laughed, "My psychiatrist says, anger and fear are two sides of the same coin." A car passed, decelerating as it came abreast of the two girls. It was no one they recognized. Among the forms within the tinted glass, a hand pointed at her. "I've become a legend in my own time."

"Aaron and me, we've decided we should, we're going to…"Melinda halted.

"Have sex." Erika finished her sentence without looking at her. The car sped away.

"Yeah." Melinda exhaled, relieved at Erika's interjection, and tried to blow a smoke ring. "He's been buying rubbers at the Eagle's lodge, in the bathroom. He goes and picks up his dad if he drinks too much."

"So you're going to do this more than once. That's good."

"I'm serious. You're the only one I can talk to about this."

"I'm sorry. I think it's great." She pushed her hair back.

"Did you ever, with Steve?"

Erika shook her head. "I was afraid. Maybe of getting pregnant." She took the cigarette from Melinda, pulled a long drag, then dropped it on the ground and snubbed it out with her toe. "Shit. We never even talked about it. He was Catholic, you know." She looked away, down the street. "Now I can't." It was then that Erika remembered one of Majij's dismal pronouncements and realized the irony at having spent so long in the naked embrace of a man who thought everyone in North America should be killed for their lascivious sins.

"Can't what?"

"Get pregnant. What did you think?"

Erika listened as Melinda went on, and smiled with her and held her hand, all the time wondering whimsically if Melinda should be stoned to death. It seemed a bit harsh. "Just make sure there's not four witnesses," she told her. "Light another cigarette. We've got time."

Melinda would sit with her in the cafeteria until Aaron had finished eating, and then they would leave her alone for a while, and she would be lost, briefly, completely unsure where she was. She knew that this was a place where people ate, and some of the faces were familiar but all of them detached, and though she knew some of the names of the faces, she didn't know *them*.

High on the wall over the serving line in the cafeteria hung a banner in black and red that said, "The Roosevelt Bulldogs," and between the two words was the face of a dog wearing a football helmet, the dog having a grizzly underbite. Erika supposed it was intended to look like a bulldog, but it was uncomfortably familiar to her as the dog she'd seen one morning under Mrs. Curtiss's chair. "Fuckface" or "Fuckhead," what had she called it?

A psychiatrist in Portland said she had PTSD, as well as Stockholm syndrome. "No, I was in love with him," she said. A neurologist in Yakima thought she had partial complex seizures and gave her a medication to take four times a day. A sleep specialist at OHSU called them 'hypnogogic hallucinations.' "Anxiety. You're going to bed each night with unanswered questions. Find the answers, and they'll go away." He prescribed a bitter white antidepressant to be taken each night before bed. The new pills made food much more appealing and reawakened other hungers as well. Each night she drew her pillow against her chest and placed another between her knees and thought of men, clean and smooth and always silent in their attention. Sometimes she thought of Majij—his arms and lips, the muscles of his back, the enormity of him inside of her. She watched boys in the hallway at school, pimply-faced, infantile, sweating, and unkempt, exaggerated swaggers or awkward, pubescent mincing past clusters of girls, who were giggling or coy or foolishly confident. Sex was a dare for them, something you lunged for, stole, and hid behind the curtain of its prohibition later, lying about how long or how loud or how easy it had been. Dr. Aziz remained in her world atlas, she ran across him quite by accident, the stiffness of his photograph flipping the pages for her, appearing like a jack-in-the box. She opened the book several more times in the month that followed, each time lingering less on the page, feeling less familiarity, until she started to read some deceit in his face which she didn't want to explore.

In Junior English, she watched Mr. Galbraith more closely, the clatter of his chalk on the board, the power of his hands, the patches on the sleeves of his corduroy jacket, the hair visible at his open white shirt. Every student's insight had value, and he found "exceptional passages," he would say, in every student's essay to read to the rest of the class. One afternoon he spent almost the entire period discussing her essay, 'Utopia Doomed.' After school, she walked with him to his Volvo, crossing her arms beneath her chin on the passenger roof, resting her back while trying to look like Audrey Hepburn as he unlocked his door.

"That was a nice piece of work," he said. "You've read some Orwell?"

"Just '1984.' Last year."

"Who else?"

"Hannah Arendt."

He glanced skyward. "Heavy stuff for a kid your age, but good work." He tossed his briefcase into the car, then looked across the roof at her again. "So you really think that the Iranian Revolution will touch Americans, right here in this country someday?"

"They're utopians, religious utopians. If we don't fit, they'll try to exterminate us."

"Interesting idea. You really think they're doomed?"

"I hope so."

"You wouldn't have an ax to grind, would you, Miss Etulain?"

Erika shrugged.

"Maybe you should keep reading about those things. Might be a career there." He disappeared into his car and drove off.

*

The phone rang on an afternoon in late April. Erika had arrived home while the house was still empty. "They don't tease you at school anymore, do they?" There was no salutation, it was Aunt Helen, and she spoke as if they had just talked for an hour. "How are you getting along?" she asked.

"I do fine if I don't move real fast." She tossed the cane on the sofa.

"Your father asked me to look at your records. Everyone thought you were dead, young lady."

"It's not all it's cracked up to be."

"You came back. People sense that. Life will be special for you."

"I'm not holding my breath."

"Your parents are fine people. You know that?"

"I know that."

"They never stopped looking for you."

Erika sat quietly and turned a globe that had been moved from her bedroom to the living room table.

Helen went on. "Will you be coming back to the hospital?"

"I don't think so."

"It's probably time to move on. The girls there this year seem so young, silly. If you think, later, if you find yourself considering nursing, I have a friend at OHSU I could recommend you to."

"I'll think about it." She could hear her aunt pause and wondered if she had seemed too arrogant, equivocal.

"When you think about last year, aside from being almost killed, do you think you learned anything?"

The question stunned her and for a moment, sounded condescending. Erika sat up in the chair defensively. "I don't know. Probably learned more than I would have at Wilson."

"I only asked because, when I was nine, and I've never told your parents this, a gardener took me from my parents' house in Shanghai. I didn't realize it was a kidnapping but it was. They took me up the river on a junk, about ten miles. I remember that trip as if it were yesterday. I was gone about a week, before the soldiers from the embassy came and retrieved me."

"Wow. Did they do anything, hurt you or rape you or anything like that?"

"Oh heavens, no. I was worth money! I do remember an old China-woman who didn't like me." Helen took another deep breath and went on. "I just wanted to tell you that, on that trip, I think I learned more about the Chinese than in three years at the missionary school."

Erika turned the globe again, stopping it at China. "And you think maybe I learned some things last year?"

"Probably more than you realize."

"Besides immortality?"

"Don't be too full of yourself. You think about the nursing program."

"I will. I really have to go now."

"I understand. Stay in touch."

Erika placed the receiver back on the phone, held the globe in her lap, and pressed her head against it. People wanted things, a show, evidence that everything inside was really all right, that they could rest easy that no real damage had been done, so they couldn't be guilty by association. She couldn't give them that.

*

Her father put his head in her room one late morning and asked her if she would like to come to the Safeway with him.

She rolled over from the book she was reading on the bed. "I'm fine here." Her parents' distrust had lingered for several weeks after her return, then evaporated. "You just want to keep an eye on me?"

"No, really. I'd like your company."

"Let me get some shoes on."

He started to turn away.

"Can we stop at Clayton's?"

"If it's a book you need, I might already have it."

"They've got posters there too." She rolled her eyes around the empty walls of the room. "Art."

"I'll wait outside in the car."

When she arrived outside a few minutes later, he was seated on the passenger side. She started to take the door handle and he rolled down the window. "You didn't happen to learn how to drive during your year of living dangerously, did you?"

She gazed down the street at the highway for a moment, then glanced down at him. "Kind of," she said.

"Then get in."

She limped around to the driver's door and got into the seat, staring at the panel quizzically, then at the pedals.

"It's an automatic," he said.

"He had a clutch."

"Just put your foot on the brake and move the shifter to reverse."

She did as she was told, taking her foot off the brake in halting increments while the car moved backward in a staccato rhythm until it settled, half-turned into the street.

"They're power brakes. Just press slowly and you'll be fine." She moved the selector to Drive and they crept toward the highway.

In the Thriftway parking lot Sam took out his wallet and handed a slip of paper to Erika. "Here's a list your mother made." He unfolded a crisp fifty and held it toward her.

She stared at the bill. "You feeling okay, Dad?"

"I'm fine. I just thought you might enjoy…"

"Going by myself?"

"If you like. Just watch the prices. Conserve your money."

"Sure."

He rolled down the window as she walked away. "Pick out a dessert. Anything you think we'd all like."

Her father was asleep when she returned to the car, where she studied him through the passenger side window for a few minutes. Exhausted, like an old king after a lifetime of battles. He awoke when she closed the driver door.

At Clayton's Books, Sam looked at the new nonfiction rack while Erika stood in the back, turning stiff, hinged frames of glossy posters of black-and-white landscapes, metal bands, mischievous kittens, bowls of fruit, optical illusions, and stark horizons. She pulled a cardboard tube from the rack and rejoined her father at the front of the store.

Sam had a paperback under his arm. "Let me get that," he said, and took the tube from her.

"What if it's one you don't like?"

"I'm sure I will. I owe you a couple, I believe." He spoke without apology or an invitation to discuss the past.

"Thanks."

She unrolled the poster that evening and anchored it above her desk, a forest scene that might contain a unicorn on the road that disappeared into the dark canopy, where words were printed in a Germanic script: "If you do not have good dreams, you will have nightmares."

But the murky form returned, almost every night, fifteen or twenty minutes into sleep, ethereal and ominous, she would shake her head and cry out, and her father would appear and hold her hands and tousle her hair and say, "That's my girl" and "It's fine. Everything's fine." And she would take one of the huge, bitter pain pills and go back to sleep, solid and dreamless.

"She's made her own punishment," Sam whispered to Teresa in the dark. Teresa did not respond, but Sam knew that she was awake, and both of them understood. It was a delicate equilibrium and further conversation was avoided. They both believed that anything could unsettle the balance and unearth a complexity that Sam and Teresa, in their own lives, lacked the experience to address.

Erika took the car alone on weekend afternoons, driving as far as Hood River, high into the hills above the Columbia. Tiny fragments of recall tumbled into her life each day like snowflakes. A view from a window haunted her. She leaned in the bathroom door while her father shaved one morning.

"Dad, is there a Masonic Lodge in town?"

"Think so," he said, without looking away from the mirror. "It's just for men, though. You want to think about Eastern Star?"

"Kipling was a Mason, somebody said at school. I just wondered what it would look like."

He rinsed the razor and tapped it on the sink. "Other end of town, Third or Fourth, I think."

The apartment building stood pale green with burgundy trim, and she drove past it once, certain that it had been white, then pulled into the parking lot behind it. Most of the windows were dark and at the far left on the top level, a fluorescent orange sign said, 'For Rent.' She ascended the stairs, each step familiar, with a trepidation she remembered from a night in March, fifteen months and another world prior. She leaned far out over the rail and saw the tower of the Masonic lodge a block away. She pressed her hand above her eyes on the glass and looked in at the plaid sleeper-sofa she he had unfolded so many times. "Where are you?" she whispered.

*

She took twelfth grade composition in the autumn of eleventh grade and loitered in Mr. Galbraith's classroom in the mornings as he graded his papers. She came by again at noon when he sat at his desk eating his lunch from a brown paper sack, and offered to go to the vending machine to buy him a Pepsi. A few weeks later, her father sat on the edge of her bed one night while Erika sat at her desk. "Jenny and Bob Galbraith have been friends of your mother and I for a long time. Jenny just had a little girl, last year while you were gone." He wove his fingers together and looked at the floor and wondered how direct he could be, without seeming crude. Perhaps it was just admiration, and he was overreading the situation. "It takes a fine balance for a man to find that kind of happiness," he said finally. "It would really break my heart if anything upset it." He got up to leave but turned and waited in her doorway.

"I understand," she said without looking up.

"You'll be at college in less than a year. You've got a lot to look forward to."

She graduated from high school the following spring, two months before her eighteenth birthday, crossing the stage in the auditorium at her point in the alphabet, without the cane. A few weeks earlier a letter had arrived from Mr. Slupsky, the school counselor, who offered to arrange for her diploma to be sent to her in the mail. Sam had opened it without looking at the first name, thinking that it was school business, and tore it up as soon as he read it.

*

In September Sam and Teresa drove her to Portland and helped her carry three suitcases, two boxes of books, and several bags of linens into a room of Clara Sommers Hall. Sam pressed three hundred and thirty dollars into her palm and an AT&T calling card. "Bus money," he said and winked. "Call us. We're still your best friends."

She arranged her books by height, bought an incense burner for her desk, and an Andrew Wyeth poster of a dog sleeping on a bed. "Don't wake up the dog," she told anyone that stopped by to visit Heather, the girl on the opposite side of the room, who was studying computer science. She took her showers late at night when no one else was in the bathroom and dressed behind the opened door of her closet. She went to campus dances with a crowd of girls, sitting in restaurants in the early hours with the boys she met, who bought her breakfast and talked about all of their plans, nice boys who went to class and dreamed of having families with a beautiful college girl like herself, how they would teach or be graphic artists or great authors or scientists. She would go home with this glimmer of iridescence of the future in her chest, undress, and look at the scars, and the awareness of some terrible knowledge, just around the corner, out of sight, would tarnish it away, corrode the dream until it collapsed. In the morning, not even a pile of ash remained. She went to a movie alone one night, *Dances with Wolves,* and it was not so bad, she thought, walking home, I could do that. Her need for solitude and her frequent night terrors drove away three roommates in the year that followed.

Erika began her sophomore year with Karen Rutgers. Reliable, sensible Karen with her sensible boyfriend, Brad, who never swore and always left by ten, in an apartment over a Lebanese restaurant at the opposite end of campus, adorned with crosses in every room and a poster in the living room with a story about walking on the beach with Jesus. "That's when I carried you," Jesus said in the story. Erika accepted a paperback New Testament from Karen because her own King James Version was full of inaccuracies, Karen told her, and she went to church with Karen on Wednesdays, Saturday nights, and Sunday mornings, absorbing every word with blind but shallow faith, finding no context in her life, already a clockwork of measured movement and silent tension.

For three months she played the electric Wurlitzer during the Sunday service, but the melodies were bland, dull, contemporary hymns written by people with bland names, and the lyrics, she thought, sounded like religious greeting cards. Brad sang in the choir, sexless as a Moonie. He never looked at Karen like he really wanted to drag her into bed. Whatever purpose they served each other was invisible to Erika.

"My throat's getting really sore," she told Karen one Wednesday evening. As soon as Karen had backed her old Pontiac out of the driveway, Erika took out her calling card and picked up the phone. *Seven-eight-five, five-five-five, one-two one-two.*

"What city please?"

"Topeka."

"What listing?"

"Stormont-Vail Hospital."

Erika scribbled the number on the back of a Kleenex box, hung up, then dialed, worried she would not know what to say first, her tangled thoughts dense as a ball of yarn in her throat.

"Stormont-Vail Hospital, how may I direct your call?"

"Doctor Farag, please." The line beeped, and Erika wondered if she was being recorded.

"I'm sorry. I don't have anyone on staff by that name."

"You must. He took care of me. Right there."

"When were you a patient here, Miss?"

"Christmas. Eighty-nine."

"Maybe he was with the university, Miss. Those doctors come and go all the time. Let me connect you." And the woman's voice was replaced with several long chords of violins and a voice-over about cancer care, then a recorded voice said that the campus switchboard was closed for the night. Erika dashed the number on the inner flap of her French text and closed it.

The next day she stood in the warmth of the morning sun in a phone booth by the student union and waited for the line to pick up.

"Doctor Farag?" The woman said and then added in a motherly tone, "Oh, Souly, why yes, of course. Let me see now." She made small smacking noises with her mouth, and Erika pictured the woman flipping through a Rolodex. "He's at the Veteran's Hospital in Amarillo, Texas." And then added, with a tone of pride, "I hear he's the director down there now."

Erika wrote that number next to the first. "Thank you." She sat in the cafeteria and stared at the number through lunch and into her next class, feeling small and foolish, as if she had neglected a great talent or forgotten a language she would now be required to speak. She jotted down a small list for herself, dissonant questions and fragments, then closed the book without finishing her thoughts.

She stayed in the library until the lights flickered off at eleven each night, choosing a study cubicle in the northwest corner of the building, on the fourth floor near several bookcases on Native American History. She had gathered up a copy of the *Seattle Times* one evening and had just started an article on a blast in the parking garage of the World Trade Center, when a willowy boy walked past her chair, a boy with a cherubic face, brown eyes, a "Free Tibet" sticker on his backpack. She put the paper down. He walked by more frequently in the weeks that followed, and on the one night she chose to test him, stare him down, put him in his happy, stupid place wherever he came from, he said "Hello," and walked on past. A small tide of frustration and panic washed over her. She stopped going to the library for a month following and did not see him until spring semester, when he sat down on a bench in the courtyard outside of the student union and took out a sandwich. He waved to her. She surprised herself and smiled at him.

By January of 1994, she lived alone in a one-bedroom apartment, two stories above a tavern at Thirteenth and Washington. She bought two used electric keyboards and gave lessons to children, in the afternoons between four and six, while their mothers shopped just a few blocks away. "Twelve and younger," she'd printed on the flyers she taped to lampposts around the downtown district. For the first forty minutes she would stand over them or behind them or squeeze onto the bench alongside, and guide their fingers and recite each note, and from time to time think of the hours with Miss Turner at her side, and pray her own students wouldn't regard her with the same disdain. The last twenty-minutes were fun time, she would play them records, Bob James and Lyle Mays and Errol Garner, then rhythm and chords, rhythm and chords. With the volume up, they would rock from side to side, and she would do this until she could break into their young souls, forgetting in those moments everything that had passed, playing through her hands alone, student and instructor free of the notion of time. They would pass the hour mark sometimes, another student's mother thumping on the door over their laughter. When the last student left it was quiet but for traffic below in the street, and she sat at her kitchen table eating ramen and laid the money, usually eighty or a hundred dollars, in front of her.

In the evenings garage band music filtered through the floor beginning at nine, the rhythm of the bass, the drums, the window panes buzzing like Morse code. Sometimes she would go down and listen, floating through the web of stares, longing gazes from one rotating stool to the next, smoke falling off the armor of her indifference. Sitting at the bar at the end of the evening, Axel, the bartender, would feed her—egg rolls, curly fries, Jo-Jos, mini pizzas, anything that had been ordered, fried, and not picked up in the previous hours.

Back in her apartment in the diminishing echoes of the street after two, she would stand insensate before the mirror at the sink in the darkness, the flicker and glow of the night in her eyes, first gray, then black, then neon.

*

The pain in her back went away, and in its place rigid scars that forced her to turn her trunk unnaturally to look behind her. The sensation was mechanical, gradually overtaken by another unfeeling but indestructible being. She assumed an otherworldly sense of immortality, free of the monthly bleeding that stained lesser beings.

Lovers were tried and unceremoniously released in the months that followed. One of them, Jeffrey, his olive arms tracked with small bruises and pustules, was later found dead in his car. A week later Erika searched the backpack he'd left in her apartment, giving the clothing and a few paperbacks to Goodwill. She kept a pair of 2-B drumsticks and a large black automatic pistol she found tucked in the inner pocket. All of her lovers were in some way dangerous; in choosing men who were out of their element in her company, she was out of her element in theirs. Above her refrigerator, in a black eight-by-ten frame, she'd mounted two blood-stained, perforated hundred-dollar bills.

*

The pistol sat on the kitchen table for a week, covered by a towel. She picked it up one morning while she ate her Grape Nuts and examined the tiny lettering along the side, 'Beretta and Sons 19x9mm.' Another snowflake of memory. She flipped the lever up on the side and a red dot was exposed. She grasped the slide and pulled with all of her effort, and it slid back a half inch, revealing a fat little brass cartridge. Leaning forward in her chair so the sunlight would pass down the barrel, she stared into the muzzle and could see the silver nose of the bullet, five inches into darkness. Bad things happened in slow motion, she'd learned. Would you actually see the bullet come up the barrel, and would it be so bad if that was the last thing you ever had to look at? She pulled a dozen books out of her bookcase and propped the gun behind them and had started to replace the books when she picked up her French text. She opened the cover and stared at the number. A moment later she took out her calling card and sat down next to the bookcase on the floor with her phone.

"Veteran's Administration Medical Center. Can I help you?" It was a man's voice, gravelly and brusque. It seemed fitting, Erika thought.

"Doctor Farag, please," and prepared herself for a long explanation of her identity. But the phone was already ringing.

"This is Doctor Farag."

"Hello?"

"Yes?"

"This is Erika."

"Erica. Erica Thomas in records?"

"No. Erika Etulain. You took care of me, in Topeka."

"Erika, why yes. Erika Etulain!"

"You remember…"

"Of course. My student of the Middle East. How are you?"

"I'm okay, I guess."

"You must be eighteen now."

"Twenty."

"And you are in college?"

"University of Oregon, in Portland."

"Ah, this is wonderful. I knew you would be indomitable. You are doing well?" He sensed her hesitancy. "Not so well?"

"I'm, well," but her voice settled into a small wail. "Oh God, I don't know what to believe anymore."

"You are passing your classes?"

She wiped her eyes. "Yeah."

"Your health, it is good?"

"Yeah. I'm fine, that way. I pass everything with A's. I just don't have any idea what I am learning." She glanced at the list. "I wondered if it could be my brain, you know. How I was."

"Are you seeing anyone?"

"There have been some guys, but God, they're all fucking crazy."

"No, I mean, have you spoken to a therapist?"

"There were a bunch in high school. Nobody now. It's so expensive. My folks spent…" But she could not think of a figure, only that their plans to buy a newer house had somehow become a remodeling project of the back porch.

He thought out loud to himself. "You never had seizures, no. And we looked at your brain." He hummed briefly. "And there was an MRI, I recall…"

"You told me once, 'Go back and become a good Episcopalian.'"

"I did?"

"Yes. You did. But I feel like nothing matters. Nothing. Not my classes, not my life, nothing. And religion, it's like the Emperor's new clothes." A stone loosened, one tumbled after another, until a thousand tons of malice poured down; she would let it bury them both. "I say I believe and all my friends say praise God and I know it's all lies. They pray when they don't have anything to pray about, they don't know, they don't have any fucking idea what could happen to them in a second, except to just get on with buying stuff and bitching and making a big mess they call a life and I don't think they believe any of that shit either." And she ran out of breath. Someone on the street below yelled and she stood and looked out the window, but they were running up the street, lost in the river of people that flowed there. "I feel invisible," she said, "not indomitable at all."

"I see."

People say that when they think you're crazy. "I'm sorry. You've got better things, I mean, I shouldn't have…"

"No. No, this is fine. Maybe you are just making things harder."

He stopped, and she could hear him think that he had just blamed her and feeling bad that he had done so. She wanted to forgive him.

He spoke again. "Are you thinking of hurting yourself?"

"No." She lifted the gun off the shelf again, hefted it at the refrigerator, then set it down. "Do you think you're a good Muslim?" The line fell silent again, and for a moment she believed he had hung up, she had so offended him, or her service had been disconnected, or their conversation had all been imagined. "You still there?" The second hand made three-quarters of a sweep around the face of her watch.

"I will tell you what has worked for me. I don't concern myself with matters of faith anymore. I look at conduct." He sighed, and with an impersonal exasperation, "I think most people, they do whatever gratifies them at the moment, and try to make it fit their religion later. So," he said with some finality, "forget about religion. Conduct yourself well, look for other people who do the same."

"That simple?"

"It works for me. You trusted me in the hospital?"

"Yeah."

"Then trust me again. Faith is just something people argue about, which they cannot prove."

"You should be on TV."

"No thank you."

She paused. "You still smoke Camels?"

"Whatever in the world made you think of that?"

"You had them in your pocket in the hospital. When I woke up."

"It was an empty box. I quit them that week. Nothing the matter with your brain."

"Thanks." She leaned back into the bookcase of her home in a beautiful world.

"You have chosen a major area of study?"

"Not yet. Just breadth requirements. Biology, French, Calculus."

"Well, all of that matters. Foundations for other courses."

"I know." An awkward pause followed, each listening to the other's hesitation.

"It was a blessing to hear from you again. You understand? It would be very distressing for me if something bad happened to you, after all of my hard work."

"I understand. Thanks again."

"But please, start seeing someone there, regularly. It is free in some cities. I will be glad to be in touch with a counselor when you find one. We were lucky to talk today, but often I am not in my office."

"I understand." She felt the briefest sting of rejection.

"Good-bye, until then."

She said good-bye and hung the receiver back on the hook, slowly absorbing the concrete. Her life was indeed two points on a curve, so it did exist outside of the moment, and it might be headed somewhere else.

*

Her journey to her apartment from campus became a patchwork of bus transfers, and as her stride improved, she chose to walk more. When a white Corolla pulled over one afternoon near Harrison, it was the boy from the library. She considered the street for a moment and her menu of options, then got in.

"I'm Eugene," he said. "I don't see you at the library anymore."

She took his hand. "Erika. I moved off-campus. It's too big a hassle to go back up there at night." She looked over his shoulder. The back seat was heaped with papers, textbooks, a folded white jacket, and a stethoscope.

"Fuck," she said softly. "Don't tell me you're a doctor."

"You don't like doctors?" He glanced over the seatback. "Oh." He raised his voice over the sound as he shifted. "I teach karate at a grade school in Bedford. I picked up the stethoscope for my mom. She checks her blood pressure about six times a day and writes it in a little book." He smiled. "And you?"

"I think I'm something different every day."

A few weeks later, he lay with his head across her abdomen, in the light of the television, kissing her, his arm beneath her bare thigh. They had finished a bottle of chardonnay. "What happened here?" He moved the tip of his finger over the stellate dimple beneath her right breast.

"Karate injury."

"Really. I've told you everything about me." He followed her sternum with the palm of his hand, at every unnatural ridge. When the television grew brighter for a moment he leaned back. "God, did you have a heart transplant?"

She spoke into the pillow, alcohol in her voice. "I was the donor."

"Erika, trust me." He kissed the scar. "Talk to me."

"Right." She sat up on her elbows. "My dad used to do this William Tell thing when I was a kid. One day he missed."

"Sometimes I feel like you don't want me to know who you really are."

"You are sooooo right." She pulled him up to her face and kissed him.

Eugene wanted her to take vitamins, to eat more protein, to go running with him in the mornings down along the river. He wanted her to go to bed each night by eleven. When she pointed out that she couldn't do this because of the music from below, he wanted her to move into his apartment. He wanted her to meet his parents. He wanted to know what she thought about children. He wanted too much.

When at last the weight of him on the mattress next to her became too familiar, his caress predictable, his conversations concerned with classes and groceries and job applications, he was discarded like the rest. She watched the phone until it stopped ringing; twenty-seven times she counted, once, and sensing his approach with that same familiarity, stood across the street in the Vintage Clothing Exchange. He appeared on foot, going up the staircase and down again, loitering, eventually walking off slowly, turning in one direction, then another. He slowed by the shop window, and she knew that he sensed that she watched, with a telepathy she had never known before, and she wept with this loss as she watched him walk away.

A dentist came next, out of the black in the stroboscopic flashes of The Comet, where she danced until four a.m. some nights, studying his face in single frames, it was too deafening to talk, every communication of the body alone. Lewis F. Klipper, with a ruddy nose and silver hair and perfect teeth. He said he was fifty-two, but she discovered he was sixty-one when she looked in his wallet the next morning while he was in the bathroom. A gold wedding band was on his key ring, and a key with a leaping cat. He did push-ups on her floor and wanted her to stop drinking coffee. "It stains your enamel." He only wanted her to move to a quieter apartment with a view of East Portland, which she would not do. He bought her lacy nightgowns that were stiffly uncomfortable, and left expensive bottles of cognac in her cabinets. After he bought her a black, used Yamaha baby grand, she agreed to sleep with him on Monday nights and Thursday nights. He didn't talk when he lay on top of her, and she liked this, because she could close her eyes and picture anyone she liked. She imagined he did the same.

It was a late afternoon in February when she walked in the rain, a circuitous route downtown, rudderless in the aftermath of an exam, all the while considering dissolving herself in the river, if that were possible. Far preferable to the icy shock of asphyxiation, just melt one's molecules away, off into the Pacific. She had procrastinated studying, she knew, not for diversion or pleasure, but for fear of knowing she might give her best and still be beaten. Now she procrastinated going home. The sky had darkened early with the weather and she walked with the flow of employees in the city on their way home, wishing she were one of them, finished with school, wishing she could go somewhere and simply stop. At a crosswalk on Fifth and Broadway she stood alone in the crowd of coughs and sneezes, beneath the umbrellas. Her own form felt like a waste of order; it might be so much better to be part of a tree, or eaten by fishes. The rain became snow and she looked up, enchanted by its sheer opacity, so sudden, something that had been invisible only moments before. She moved forward with the crowd when the light changed, looking skyward through the flakes into the empty night between the buildings, like so many tiny stars falling to earth.

She slowed, and those behind her walked around until she stood alone a few yards from the curb. The light changed, engines roared and headlights moved forward, and she looked across the intersection. Through the falling flakes, she saw the silhouette of a man standing in the glare of the cars behind him, pointing at her. There was a blast of horns. Tires skidded on wet asphalt.

A grasp, not by the arms, not by the neck, nor hand, nor waist, but by all of them, by the coat perhaps, pulled her, lifting, dragging her over the curb to the safety of the walk. To the face of a man stubbled, furrowed, gray and acid, a breath of cigarettes and the stale fruit of wine, inches from her own.

"Wake up, girlie!" He growled, his throat full of phlegm.

She turned her head away, her face to the street, to the passing cars and the draft that followed, the cold fresh oxygen. When she looked back, there was no one beside her. No one so unseemly walked away in either direction on the sidewalks. Two older women sharing an umbrella occupied the remaining crosswalk. She struggled with this incongruity, standing bewildered at the curbside for another minute until her pulse slowed to the pace of the footsteps that passed, to the rhythm of the traffic, until in the silence of the huge flakes that fell, she was uncertain it had happened at all.

*

Three place mats remained on the dining room table. Sam liked seeing them there, believing that if the slightest void could be opened in their lives for just a few minutes, Erika might drop in. "She's only two hours away," he would say and hug Teresa if she stood near his chair, drawing her hip to his shoulder. He dreamed of Erika arriving home some day with a young man, someone he could talk with, some young fellow who read, understood history, with a keen eye and a strong arm, who would keep his daughter from harm's way after he was gone.

Spring break had arrived for his community college, but the high school would not be out until the following week. Teresa had gone back to full time, and taught a literature course as well. It had put color in her face, he thought, as lovely as that morning at Cambridge. Thirty-eight years had not blemished her one whiff.

The University of Oregon would be out next week as well, and Erika would be home then, at least part of the week, but he would be back on campus, and it would be Teresa who sat with her for long hours in the morning over tea. Coffee, the girl drank coffee now, he had to keep reminding himself. Some things a parent just couldn't control.

He unfolded the *Oregonian* on the table. Well, there they were, they had caught the buggers. All of them Egyptian. No, a couple of Iraqis and a Jordanian, their faces next to a familiar photograph of smoke billowing from the parking garage beneath the World Trade Center. The article went on about an FBI failure and some knowledge beforehand. Only in American history was there such a passion for conjecture, how one or another agency had fumbled or let a vital warning pass without notice. One of the suspects caused some confusion, Hakim Hassan Malouf. The same man was supposed to be in custody in Leavenworth, Kansas, for killing two federal employees in 1989. Grains of silver in an emulsion. He stared at the photograph until his tea grew cold, then slid his chair back and went into the living room and pulled a photo album from the top shelf where he had wedged it beyond anyone's reach but his own. The plastic pockets inside held newspaper clippings. He turned a few pages and carefully pulled out the yellowed picture he'd snipped from a newspaper four years before, taking it back to the table and laying it next to the photograph of Malouf. In that moment, he understood something he knew no one else on the planet comprehended, this irregular little slab of history before him turned once and then again until it fell perfectly into place. On the window sill a foot away stood a gilded, framed photograph of Erika, cap and gown, her high school diploma in hand.

He pulled Haynes's card from another pocket of the album and sat down with the telephone.

"Captain Haynes retired in January," the duty officer said. "You want to speak with Captain Rodriguez?"

"No. Thank you."

"Do you need to file a complaint?"

"No. It was personal. We're old friends." Sam set the phone in the cradle. He thumbed the Portland Government pages until he found the number for the FBI, then hesitated and closed the book. There was a time for each point in history. Perhaps that time had already come and passed.

21

"Look, you'd be the same distance from the campus, and you'd have a view of the river." Lewis leaned over her and flattened the city map with the palm of his hand on the kitchen table where she sat. "The first floor is a bank. Quiet after five."

Erika stared at the map quizzically.

"There's a restaurant too, but it closes at three. The rest of the building is all condos."

"But I like it here, I like the noise. It would be creepy."

"There's other condos, people to talk to. You'd have a balcony to look over the river. People have hibachis outside."

"But it's all concrete."

"Just on the outside."

"And it would be lonely. How many units did you say? Two hundred and twenty-five, and only twenty-six of them filled? Boy, we could have quite a block party."

Lewis went to the other side of the table and faced her, leaning against the refrigerator, and cast a flinching glance at the cryptic, bloody bills in the frame. *Enigmatic girl.* "I just want you to be safe, that's all. I could unlock the door you have now with one of my dental probes." He glanced down at the street beneath the window.

"It's still there."

"What?"

"Your Jag. They don't steal the really big stuff around here until after dark."

"You could put the grand by the window and look out over the river."

She shook her head slowly and looked at him with a pained expression. "I don't know, it just doesn't feel like me."

"Erika, I care about you. Let me do these things."

"If you care about me, be here. I want somebody I can be spontaneous with."

"You know I can't."

"Mondays and Thursdays. I get tired of reading on weekends."

"Two more years, till my daughter is out of school. We could travel. Africa, Italy, Sweden. In any other city of the world, we could walk down the street together."

A week after their first night, she had watched him at the crosswalk below her apartment, wearing a bow tie, a vest, and looking at his watch. His nose was red, and those teeth—billboard white and as large. As a child, she'd thought the Mad Hatter was Lewis Carroll because of the picture on the cover. Now here he was, two nights out of every week. Lewis. He preferred to be called "Lou," he said, "Like Lou Reed." Loo. It was what her mother called the toilet.

"What are you smiling about?" he asked.

"Oh, you just make me smile inside sometimes, and it overflows."

"And that bartender, Axel," he went on. "Who would name a son that? I don't have a good feeling about him. I hope you haven't slept with him."

She flashed him a half smile intended to inspire doubt. "He listens to me." She turned the map over and there were colored paths for the bus routes printed on the other side.

"I don't see how. He's got to be deaf from all that racket."

"Besides, this condo is..." She bent over the map and squinted. "At least eight blocks from a campus bus."

"You and the damn bus. That's another thing."

"You want me to walk?"

"You could drive. Let me get you a car."

"Where would I park? No. I don't need..."

"You could park over there." He pointed through the window to the parking arcade across the intersection. "I'd rent you a spot."

"Then I'd have to park it at school."

"I'll put a dental school permit on it. Faculty. That lot's never full."

"Somebody would notice."

"You could meet me for lunch at Tigard." He took her hands between his. "At the Pamplona Club."

"Oh, Lewis."

"Lou."

"Loo. Let me think about it."

"I've thought about it for you." He pulled a business card from his pocket and pressed it on the table. "Ask for this guy. He expects you."

She looked at the card. 'Craig Anderson, sales associate. Mercedes Benz and Audi.'

"Am I getting a Benz?" She wagged an imaginary tail.

"No." He looked at her reproachfully. "I'd have a hard time hiding that kind of money. He does have some lease-return Audi coupes, and a convertible."

It was a long time before she fell asleep that night, the singer's voice in the band below reflecting off the building across the street and penetrating her window. An angry voice, angry with her. You can't make good things happen. They happen or they don't. Fucking random, it is. A car would be useful, if he would pay the insurance. Or it could just be his, that would be fine, ameliorate any sense of indebtedness. He'd find someone else eventually. Maybe he already had, on Tuesdays and Wednesdays. She pictured herself at the Yamaha by a plate glass window, sunrise over the Columbia, a pencil in her teeth, composing. The voice in the street screamed again.

On the bus the following morning, a disheveled unshaven man sat across from her, clutching several plastic bags of carefully stacked used soft drink cups from various restaurants, as if they were irreplaceable. The collar of his wrinkled white shirt was brown with sweat and the knee was worn through one leg of his trousers. When the bus stopped and the air stopped blowing through the windows, she could smell him, a rancid, oily smell with the sweet aroma of old urine.

At four fifteen after her last class, she took the trolley down Sixth, got off at Pioneer Square, and walked another six blocks. The breeze had grown stronger and came up the river from the south, pulling her hair across her face. When she turned onto Naito Parkway, she walked face into it, squinting, one block after another uphill, until she found herself passing a long row of plate glass showroom windows, where she stood for a moment and looked at her reflection. Thinking her purse over her back looked too girlish, she put it over her right shoulder. Yellow-and-black plastic pennants fluttered and snapped. She walked up to the plate glass door at the end of the building, swung it open, and the wind quieted behind her.

Some men in suits sat at a chrome table, talking, where one of them was smoking a cigarette. She stopped at a dove gray sedan, bent forward and looked at the sterile, empty seats, the idle wheel, the dark instruments within it's closed windows, as if in a vacuum. She backed away from the car and turned to a row of desks where lamps were on and papers scattered and computer screens lit, but at least temporarily, no one sat. At one desk, a small nameplate read, 'Craig Anderson, Associate.' The screen was off and the desktop was clear. She felt relieved, though until that moment, she hadn't realized that she was uncomfortable, the absurdity of the contract to which she was about to commit, so many strings she had ignored, surrounding her now like a room full of snakes. It was time to go. She looked up but it wasn't immediately apparent which of the great glass panels was the door she had come in. The air felt thick as oil.

"Somebody, see what she needs," someone murmured.

Beyond the end of the desk on the showroom floor sat a red convertible, and she ran her fingers along the doorsill. It occurred to her that she could easily swing her leg over the door without opening it, and it seemed very vulnerable. She turned to a sea mist sedan with a three-pointed star on the hood, much larger than the convertible, vaguely threatening, like a machine built for the military.

"Miss, can I help you?"

She was aware of the voice and did not want help, except to get back to the door, to get away from taking something she didn't deserve, which would require far more than she gave now, until it was rusted or wrecked or burned. And it was as close to evil, as the spirit that always hovered behind her, that stood at the end of the bed, that now, in a terrifying revelation, had become clear; it had become human and had sent her here, and its name was Lewis Frederick Klipper.

"Miss?" A hand touched her shoulder.

She spun around and backed into something cold and solid.

"Can I show you something, perhaps, within your budget?"

Dressed in fine navy gabardine, he was only a few years older than herself, she thought, and she smiled at him but moved sideways, spotting at last the door at the far end of the showroom. "I was just looking." And she tried to remember the name of the salesman she was told to speak to, but it had vanished like a mirage. Her hands found the car door handle behind her, and she grasped it and turned away from him.

"On the other hand, this one's very affordable," his voice droned on behind her. "Not much more than a new Honda. Just forty-one thousand miles and all the maintenance in our own shop."

"It's nice," she said and stroked her hand over the obsidian sheen of the roof.

"Nineteen seventy-nine, five-sixty SL. Car like this today lists out at seventy-two grand." He leaned over the hood, trying to recapture her gaze. "Of course, it's not the best gas mileage, but it's safe and solid."

The floor moved beneath her and he was ignoring this. He kept talking. The door handle was still in her hand and she pulled it open and swung herself into the front passenger seat and closed it behind her. He was still talking, she could see his lips moving on the other side of the glass, he had bent over like a bird might chase a spider. The car was warm, too warm inside, and someone breathed and coughed, and she turned. Behind the wheel sat Majij, the windows behind him obliterated by night. She drew her legs up on the seat and backed against the passenger window. Snow fell in the beam of the headlights. The heater fan roared. She grasped the door lever, frigid and immovable. The fan roared more loudly. He pushed her and she struck the upholstered bolster, the chrome of the seat belt buckle pressed into her cheek. She cried out, furiously tugging at the door lever, beating the glass. The snowfall and the night absorbed it all.

"What's going on?"

"I don't know. I was talking to her one minute, and then she jumped inside and hit the power locks."

"She's panicked. Tommy, go get the goddamn key. She's going to pull the goddamn latch off."

A moment later the door unlocked and she bolted out, bouncing off of it and falling back against the car before righting herself.

"Are you all right?" one of the men asked. Three men stood around her in a semicircle. "You just scared yourself," another one said.

Erika focused on the three curious faces before her, none of them Majij's. She took a step back and her breathing slowed. She stooped with a quick glance into the open door of the Mercedes, then stood and flattened the lapels of her jacket and adjusted the straps of her purse. "I'm fine, really. I'm just fine." She gave them a nervous smile. "I don't think I need this car." And she began to move around them, stepping sideways, and backed away while they kept watching her. She stopped. "I don't think I need a car at all."

She pivoted and crossed the showroom and went out into the wind of the late afternoon and marched another four blocks in gusts that shifted her on the sidewalk from side to side before she realized she was walking away from her home. At the corner of Jefferson she stopped at the crosswalk. Cherry blossom petals were blowing across the street from a row of trees planted in the median of the boulevard, like so many huge flakes of snow. My God, how beautiful, she thought. She went west uphill until she crossed Broadway. It was six fifteen. She looked back down the hill she had just climbed, toward the river. I could go back and look at it again, she thought. I should touch it, get this through my head. It's just an old car, a big metal box, probably owned by some old couple with money to waste on cars they never drove. An image came to her then, of Majij and his brother. Hakim! It had been his brother's car in Salinas. No, after Salinas. Topeka. In the garage, polished. Odd, when their own car had been so filthy. Hakim. Where was Hakim when they argued, driving out of Topeka on the snowy night? If he had been in the back seat she would have seen him just now. She was absolutely certain of this, the image had been so cinematically vivid. She sat down on a granite retaining wall in the shaded street and drew her hands back through her hair and stopped on her right ear.

She remembered now that there had been a loud pop, a sudden hurt, like a horrendous paper cut. He had been right there, no farther away than the width of the street. The wall sank beneath her and she thought she might be sick. Another pop had followed and she saw now the blue flash, remembered the impact, the torch in her abdomen that rose through her chest, the nausea that came, her bladder emptying that night. She crossed her arms over her belly and leaned over, cold moisture formed over her face and neck, and a dark curtain covered everything momentarily. She threw her head back and tried to breathe in the evening cool, and above her a magenta cloud hovered in the remaining sunlight. Her ears roared and she was unsure whether it was her own voice that alarmed a flock of pigeons into the sky from the lawn behind her. "Why?" she repeated, and the wind dried away the wetness of her hair. She sat still for many minutes, playing and replaying the scene in her mind, and each time another detail materialized, crisp and bloody as a thorn.

She stood and began walking north on Broadway, and as she walked shops closed and restaurants grew noisy. She walked as nighttime fell, and headlights went on, and the song of the traffic changed. She was walking downhill now, the wind at her back. As she approached Morrison Avenue, a black hatchback Saab parked at the curb came into view. She had seen dozens of them in four years, and each time the sight had plucked a solitary note, a memory of a frustrated man, who in the end had done some cruel things in anger. Perhaps he was shot too, Farag had said, and she had seized on the notion. It was a memory she had assembled to satisfy the casual inquiry, the psychotherapist, anyone she wanted to dismiss simply from a debate, including herself. His car had burned at an airport; both of them had been in more danger than they had realized, and he had died so that she could live, that noble, brave man she had been wise to choose. Her choice. An Erika choice that could not be questioned. A *fable*, she realized now, that she had nurtured and defended, smoothed between the leaves of a book.

"I lied to myself," she said out loud and understood then that he might still be alive, anywhere, and the car ahead precipitated a sense of dread. When she stood by it, finally, at the crosswalk, she ventured a glance. It was, directly beneath the streetlight, navy blue. The interior buckskin, a child's seat buckled into the front passenger side. She pictured a single mother talking to a toddler, a chubby little girl, groceries in the back. The crosswalk light changed, and she started walking again. I'd need a car if I had children, she thought. A little girl just wouldn't be able to keep up. *What I don't have now, I don't need*, she subvocalized, then said it aloud and repeated it the length of several blocks, determined, with a growing anger, a syllable with each footfall.

Just before the corner of Alder she stopped. If Majij was still alive, so was Hakim. She had no grounds to believe otherwise, and this new understanding chilled her. One was like the other, changeable as a chameleon, as Majij had started to look like the man at a motel. She turned and looked south, up Broadway. A block away, a male figure hobbled in her direction, small-framed, stooped. Hakim had limped, maybe in that same way. The figure turned into a liquor store, and in the light, she could see that he was not Hakim, but knew Hakim or Majij could be any of the dozens of figures walking behind her, silhouetted by the headlights. He could look like an old man, or he could look like a woman. He could have been watching her apartment for a week, waiting. At midblock she slowed, and the floor plan of the house in Topeka lay before her like a hologram. She took two measured steps forward and hopscotched to her left. "That was the living room," she said, as a couple scurried widely around her. Qtab's portrait hung on the wall. She turned about face toward the street. "And the bedroom." Between her and the approaching intersection lay the hallway, the kitchen, and the back porch. A bathroom passed on her right. At the curb, she stepped through the back door and was free, and she realized only then she had been holding her breath. Something wasn't right about his house. She could almost identify it now, that she had been in the presence of some terrible conception, silent and mercurial, a vulgar process that thrived on contempt, that had consumed all of the light and had almost consumed her. Her terror confirmed, her apartment now felt more like a blind corner than a citadel against the supernatural. She would require more if she were to stand a chance. Allies. Family.

A dumpster sat near the sidewalk at the end of the alley two blocks from her apartment, a large pile of boxes marked 'Chiquita.' She slowed. I'm going to need some boxes, she thought, and lifted the top one. Its bottom was wet and smelled of rotting bananas. Some clean, dry boxes. I'll ask Axel.

After she locked her apartment door and pulled the curtains, she took the pistol from the bookcase and randomly worked the levers and buttons on the sides until she pressed the magazine release and the clip fell on the table. She racked the slide, and a cartridge bounced onto the floor. She studied it longer, intuitively, then reinserted the clip and racked the slide, like she'd seen in movies, and carefully lowered the hammer. Satisfied, she put the pistol in her backpack and set it by her bed.

*

The first morning she awoke in her old bedroom in her parents' house it was early June, but felt like a childhood Christmas, the day a blank page with unlimited potential. She got up, dressed in some gray sweats, then lifted the corner of her mattress. The pistol was too large for her pockets. She covered it again and went to the front door. Her father stood in the living room sorting laundry he had spread out on the sofa.

"Good morning," he said. "Take this, will you?" He handed her two corners of a warm sheet, and she mirrored his movements until they had folded it neatly.

"Where's Mom?"

"Down at the church. Setting up for a bake sale tomorrow morning." He handed her the two corners of the fitted sheet. "I hate these," he said. "If you weren't here I'd just wad it up, try to make it look square."

She glanced at one chair, where stacked, folded, feminine squares of color sat, and at the other, a tangle of large white briefs. "You fold all Mom's underwear?"

"That's how she likes it."

"But not your own?"

"That's how I like it."

"I think I might just go for a walk around the neighborhood." She sat down and pulled her laces tight.

"The people who bought the Grants' house have a Corgi. Mean little tyke."

"I'll go the other way."

At the curb a new concrete gutter was being installed, and she stepped wide over the forms and began to trot along the hard-packed gravel. Halfway to the highway, asphalt had been laid, smooth as a pool table. She jogged more quickly, and at the highway turned left past the mailboxes and looked out over the river and breathed in the summer heat. She ran another sixty yards, where she turned left again onto Trish's street, which now bore a brilliant green-and-white sign on a galvanized pole, 'Asherwood Lane.' The entire length of the street was freshly paved in asphalt as well. Five new houses stood at the end of the street, with dirt yards and great piles of scrap near the curbs. Men with nail guns scurried around the plywood roof of a sixth, to an irregular rhythm of pneumatic thumps while a compressor grumbled somewhere. She slowed and turned around and began to wonder if she had taken the wrong street. She walked back, looking between the houses, until she saw a wire fence, a hole near the corner, and a few strands of dead vine. She took a step closer. The picket fence was gone. And the porch. A new front room had been added, and the door now entered the side near the driveway. The house was whiter and straighter than she remembered. A metal sign in the yard read, 'Offered by Dave Lavender Realty.'

*

Her parents let her sleep as late as she liked. In the early afternoon she would go visit Melinda, and on Tuesdays and Wednesdays, when Melinda went to the community college, babysat her nine-month-old son, Anthony.

"You don't awaken at night like you used to," Sam said to her one morning. He sat at the table with a checkbook. "Is that all better?"

"I guess it is." She had pulled on a pair of blue jeans and a tank top, but her feet were still bare. Teresa stood at the edge of the yard wearing a straw hat, snapping at the hedge with a pair of pruning shears.

"No more nightmares, headaches?"

"No." She slumped into one of the overstuffed rockers. "Qtab's gone." She swiveled to face the living room window, curling her toes on the sill. "Should I go help Mom?"

"It's going to get up to ninety-four today. We should all go to a movie."

Natasha lay on the front lawn beneath the crab apple, legs straight and her neck arched, tail straight in the grass. Any passerby might think she was dead. "Natasha doesn't play anymore," Erika said. "She doesn't stalk birds or fight with my toes. Just sleeps all the time."

"She's getting old, Erika. She's…" Sam calculated for a moment. "Ninety-one in animal years."

"I feel old," she said.

"You're not even twenty-one yet." In the radiance of the late summer morning light, she looked like his mother, in the strength of her youth, every gesture and motion.

"I feel like I'm forty." She turned the chair to face him. "Ever since Kansas." She stood and paced the living room several times and then stopped and twirled the globe so violently that it rocked on its base and started to fall. She caught it and steadied it on the table top. "I missed being a goddamn teenager, and there's got to be more than this."

Sam closed his book and looked at her, circumspect, and saw her eyes brim.

"I know who shot me." She flopped back into the chair and crossed her arms over her drawn-up knees and sobbed. "People are supposed to love you back, and then the world is easier. Together." She rubbed her eyes and wiped her nose on her arm. "It's like somebody took everything apart. I've got all the pieces back. I don't piss myself anymore, but I can't…" And tears flooded her face and her nose, a cough choking away her voice.

Sam stood, went to her, and put a hand on her shoulder, patting her head as she lay against him. Her gasps gradually subsided.

"But why, Daddy?" She looked up at him, her face wet. "I just wanted to love him. He said he wanted to go home to his country." She snorted and rubbed her face on her sleeve. "Jesus. Look at me." She tried to dry her sleeve against her jeans. "I bought all that bullshit. I was good to him, I loved him. I felt sorry for the sonofabitch. And he just got worse and worse and worse. And then he shoots me. Tries to kill me? It makes no goddamn sense." She pulled herself away from him and stood and spun the globe again. It skittered off the table and bounced across the floor. They both watched it until it stopped rolling.

"You were only fifteen," Sam picked up the globe with a little grunt and inspected it. "I suppose it is fair to say that he didn't value you as much as he valued himself." He set the globe on the end table farthest from her. "But you might ask him."

"We'd have to find him first." Erika dried her eyes with her fingers. "You want to go to Iran? I don't."

"I know where he is." Sam looked out the window, where Teresa was putting hedge clippings by the curb. "I don't think he ever left Kansas."

*

Erika loitered near the Avis counter and heard her father ask for a midsize. She watched other passengers in every direction with duffels slung over their shoulders or pulling wheeled bags. A few chauffeurs stood at the bottom of the escalator, silently holding cardboard signs with names. She imagined 'Etulain' written on one of them. She walked over to the glass where the traffic moved outside, in the sunshine on dry pavement, and looked left and right, trying to determine where they had entered the building on their departure four years earlier, on a day that had been so insular in its numbness that she decided after several minutes that she could not remember anything about their trip to the airport at all. She recalled only the acceleration down the runway and their levitation skyward, and a sense of enormous liberation.

Sam touched her on the arm.

"You have the keys?"

"In a moment."

They boarded a shuttle to the rental lot and sat across from each other, the only passengers on the little bus. Erika watched the driver in the rearview mirror, black skin with three parallel scars on each cheek. Nigerian maybe, she thought. How odd it must seem for him here. The driver noticed her stare and gazed back in the rearview mirror, and she looked down at her feet. When she looked up again, her father was watching her.

"Small world we have, with jet airplanes." He glanced toward the driver. "You can be on the other side of the planet in the time it would take us to walk from The Dalles to Hood River. If someone had told me when I was twelve, that I would visit Topeka, Kansas, in the United States twice in my lifetime, I'd have thought them loony."

Erika smiled at her father and pressed the bottom of her shoe against his. "You've walked a lot of places. I don't think I realized that until last year or so."

He looked forward through the front of the bus. "The trick is ending up where you actually intend to go."

The shuttle stopped at a guard booth, then clattered over the steel teeth in the pavement. A few minutes later, they drove out of the lot in a Taurus. Sam unfolded a small map and handed it to her. "You navigate. I can't read and drive at the same time." He took off his glasses and folded them into his shirt pocket and turned up the airconditioner. "Highway Seventy-three, northbound."

Broad rolling hills spread out before them, benignly green, with silos and barns at intervals, small figures in tall combines and glass compartments moving snaillike through the fields, all of the colors bleached in the glare of midday. The armrest of the car was almost too hot for her elbow in spite of the airconditioning. It was nothing like she remembered; a cold, gray, nightmarish time in another world, and she startled at the possibility that it had all been a bizarre dream and her accusations unjust. They would go to the federal penitentiary and ask for a man whom she would not recognize, perhaps he would not be there at all. "Are you sure?" she asked her father twice. The first time he smiled and nodded. The second he simply reached over and took her hand.

A sign on the shoulder warned them not to pick up hitchhikers for the next twenty-five miles. They were getting close. Five years, since she first met him,—that would make him thirty-seven now, if she knew when his birthday was, and it now seemed profoundly significant that she didn't, because he had never told her. She had stolen a peek at his driver's license once while he showered, and counting to herself, had been stunned that he was thirty-two, and failed to make note of the month or day before slipping the wallet back into his trousers. She ruminated for several minutes, trying to remember the town or the state they had been in at the time, when her father spoke.

"Looks like this may be it."

A chain link fence at least ten feet high bordered the right shoulder of the highway, topped with razor wire. They slowed and took the next exit, and a few minutes later rolled up a four-lane driveway, stopping at a gate where a guard gestured for Sam to roll down the window.

"State the nature of your business," he said.

"Visiting."

"Proceed ahead, turn left into the visitor's parking. No weapons of any kind are permitted in the facility. No key ring tools. No cameras either."

They drove on into the lot. When they stopped Sam rummaged through his pant pockets, laid a Swiss army knife on the console, and started to open the door.

"Dad, I can do this." She took his hand and held it to the seat.

"They could be difficult. I'd better…"

"No, really. You've brought me this far. But I need to see him alone." She opened her own door and then stopped. "Do I just ask for Doctor Aziz?"

"Malouf. He's listed as Hakim Malouf."

"What?" She pulled the door partially closed.

"Just trust me. This time. They think his name is Malouf." He tore a small sheet from a pocket notebook and handed it to her. "Hakim Malouf."

Sam watched her cross the parking lot past the corner of the fence and trot up the concrete steps as if she worked there. At the top, a steel door opened, and then she was gone. He rolled down the windows, halfway expecting to hear the song of men on a work crew somewhere, but only the summer heat blew in.

At the end of a long hallway she came to a thick glass window where a cadaverous looking man who spoke through a disc in the glass told her to fill out a form on a clipboard. *Name, address, social security number, driver's license, current employment, relationship to the prisoner, purpose of visit.* She would need to leave her identification with the form until she left. She thought for a moment and then penciled 'wife' and 'reclamation' into the last two boxes. She approached the window when she was finished and placed the clipboard in a steel drawer pulled under the glass.

The cadaverous man took the board mechanically and placed it under a computer monitor and began to type. He looked up at her a moment later with a sardonic grin. "Married. Who woulda' thought? You gonna make his day. You're the only one who's visited him since he come here." His grin vanished as quickly as it had appeared. "Go to the door to your right. When the lock buzzes, turn the knob. Wait in that room."

The door locked behind her. Four plastic armchairs sat in a row in a windowless concrete cube about twelve feet square. Almost twenty minutes passed. Jesus, she thought, are they just going to put me in here with him? A second door buzzed, and a porcine little man swaggered in with a black baton.

"Hold your arms away from your sides," he said, and he stroked the tip of the baton the length of her torso beneath her arms and to her fingers and then traced each leg, pressing a little more firmly. He drew the baton up the backs of her legs, over her buttocks and then her abdomen, and stopped with the tip between her breasts. The light on the wand glowed, and beeped weakly. "What do you have there?"

She pulled a thin gold chain with a small medal from beneath her sweater. "Cross of Saint George." Next to it, a small gold crescent.

He looked at her indifferently. "Whatever." He pressed a code into the lock on the door on the far side of the room. "You have thirty minutes. The prisoner may choose to visit with you only part of that time or not at all."

"I understand." She studied the back of the person who opened the door for her and decided that it might actually be a woman.

"Take the second booth from the end, number thirty-one." The door slammed behind her. She sat in a plastic chair between two partitions, padded and perforated like a phone booth. A beige handset hung in a cradle on the right. The chair on the other side of the glass was empty. Minutes passed, and she briefly entertained the thought of leaving, telling her father it had been the wrong man, or that he hadn't come at all.

An iron gate slammed somewhere, and then a shuffle of steps. In a blue jumpsuit, he was there. A guard pressed him down into the chair and unlocked his hands from behind him, then walked away.

His moustache was gone, his thick wavy hair shaved to a bristle, dry and stiff on his scalp, with little feathers of gray. He glanced at her, then leaned back in his chair, looked right and left, and started to push the chair back. A muffled voice shouted something at him and he stopped where he was, and considered her again, head half turned, eyes wide, like a horse regards a snake.

"It's me, Maj," she said, her voice soaked up by the partition. The figure remained mute, the profile vaguely familiar but every other detail she had carefully committed to memory in four years dulled or absent, and she wondered if it was the wrong man after all. She noticed the handset and lifted it and spoke again. "Maj. It's me. It's just me. Erika. Remember?" Majij shook his head and rubbed his eyes and stared at her more intently. "I guess you weren't expecting me today. Or ever, huh?" Expecting a response, she was without words, and she studied his expression, the tension in his jaw, and the fasciculation of his eyes. "Jesus, you look terrified. I can't hurt you from over here."

Majij buried his face in his hands and his nails into his scalp. Erika could see the marks they made in the skin. He had no scar on his temple, and his ears were symmetric. It was indeed Majij.

"God, don't you have anything to say to me?" She shifted in her chair. "They put me back together. Is that what you're wondering?" She stood but had to stoop because the handset was short. "You want to see what it looks like? They took some stuff out." Her voice raised, she started to lift her sweater.

A female turnkey she hadn't noticed was behind her almost instantly. "That's enough of that, miss."

Erika ignored her but sat down again. "Try to remember the trip, into Topeka." Majij sat on the other side of the glass, his palms pressed against the side of his head, eyes still closed. "Open your eyes, Doctor Aziz."

He squinted at her.

"That's a start."

He seemed to settle to her voice.

"Now take your hands away from your ears."

He laid his hands on the counter in front of him.

"I'm not a ghost. Somebody just got me to a hospital, that's all." She felt her own resolve falter, her voice cracked. "I came a long way today, all the way from The Dalles, just to ask you something. Just one thing. That's all I want. Then I'll go away." He was looking down at his hands. "Pay attention," she said. He looked at her again. "I just want to know. The night we drove. In the snow. Why did you shoot me?"

He blinked several times, as if he had only then begun to recognize her.

"Why, Maj? I was sixteen-fucking years old. What did I do?"

He only shook his head slowly from side to side.

"Why? Did I see something, something Hakim had?" But he had gone somewhere else, as if a whole new puzzle had flashed before him. "You could say you're sorry. Just say that." The cubicle he sat in mimicked her own, the same chair, the same Formica, the same glass reflecting her own profile overlapping his, both of them prisoners, it seemed, his inertia to blame for her impotence. "Goddamnit, why don't you answer?" And the full measure of her disdain rose up. She lifted the small chain from her blouse, teased away the medallion, and held forth the gold crescent. "Remember that?"

The crescent captured his focus, but elicited only clueless wonder.

"Ma' shuge." She spoke coldly. She looked at the handset as if it might be faulty, then smashed it against the glass. Majij flinched. A ring of beige plastic fell away from the mouthpiece, and the microphone tumbled out. She set the handset on the desktop and slumped, defeated, in the chair. Her eyes filled, but she did not tear.

He reached forward, slowly, his face strained as if he pressed against an invisible web, and put the palm of his hand against the glass. His fingers seemed stubby and malformed, and tiny patterns of dirt filled every convolution on his fingertips. They were not the hands she had held, the hands that had undressed her, scrolled the signature she had worshiped. He had become, in his journey to this isolated, barren place, something else. She reached forward and placed the tip of her index finger opposite his, but not her whole hand. It was cold, thick glass, flat and smooth, the sort that keeps people from reaching into the world of dangerous reptiles at the zoo. "Good-bye, Majij Aziz."

"Well, you managed to break the handset." The turnkey stood behind her.

"I'm sorry." Erika started to stand.

The turnkey took her by the arm. "We replace about half a dozen a week," and led Erika back to the door.

Erika turned at the last moment, and he had risen from his seat and pressed both of his hands and his cheek against the glass. Only then did he seem to recognize her, his lips moving in something of a prayer.

The turnkey let go of her arm when they reached the little cubicle. "You have a nice trip home," she said. The door buzzed, and Erika stormed down the hallway. "Miss Etulain," someone called, but she was anxious to get into the light and back into her own world.

"You were right. It was him," she said and slammed the car door shut. She snapped the seat belt across her waist. "Let's get out of here."

Thirty minutes of silence ticked by as they cruised down the highway. It was four thirty in the afternoon. Sam watched her from the corner of his eye, her posture full of resolve. She pushed the sun visor down, then dug in her purse and pulled out a small ring-bound pad and a ballpoint and wrote, intermittently pausing to stroke her lips. She would speak when she was ready.

"I didn't know what to say." She shoved the pen through the wire binding and set it in her lap. "It was like it wasn't really him, so weird. Like I'd never known him." She shook her hair and tried to shake off the frustration. "He wouldn't talk. Maybe he can't."

"It's been a long time. Four years." His answer felt shallow, like it had all raced past in a blur, too fast for an aging man to seize and set right. "A fifth of your life, Princess."

"Is there a federal building in Topeka?"

"One in Topeka. One in St. Louis."

"I'd like to go there tomorrow."

"I thought you might want to see the arch anyway," Sam said. "It's only five hours away. Our ticket isn't until nine forty, day after tomorrow."

"Topeka will be fine," she said. "How long have you known?"

"I didn't for sure." He shook his head with his own disbelief. "Until I realized how important it was to you, I didn't think it was worth the risk."

The sun was lower in the sky, and all of the color had returned to the landscape when she spoke again. "*Ghashang.*"

"Hmm?"

"Ghas-hang. It's Farsi for 'beautiful.'" She gestured at the sunset. "I remember thinking one time he was the smartest man in the world. And he was kind, sometimes, he really was. He could have done so many things, so many good things, but he ended up in that place." She looked out of the back of the car and then touched her father's arm. "Did I do that to him? Did I lead him somewhere I shouldn't have?"

"You feeling guilty?" Sam looked over and realized that she had been saying something to him all of his life, but he was only hearing her now. "Did you get up every day and wonder how you could be better for him? Make him happy?"

"I think so. It's become a blur since then. Do you think people do whatever they want at the time they want it, then try to make it seem right, later?"

He paused, perplexed. "It's certainly an interesting way to look at things, at history."

"I don't know. I came here thinking that it would help if I forgave him. I was going to say that. Just that. 'I forgive you.'" She flipped the pad open and looked briefly at it and then shoved it in her purse. "We never got that far. And now I feel like I should ask him to forgive me."

"I think you did the best you could. I imagine at some point, he seemed like the most exciting person in the world. But maybe being with a good person is better than being with the most exciting."

"It was an awful, awful mistake. I don't know what I thought."

"You'll make a few more. We all do."

They drove further and the sun began to set. Erika turned on the radio, scanned the dial, then turned it off. "Did you and Mom really meet in school, like in a class?"

"No, actually. She was clerking in a bookstore, Keatings, I think it was called. I went in to get a summary of Herodotus, sort of like Cliff Notes. I didn't read English all that well then." And he realized that he had never told anyone this, that it had been an important secret. "She marched me all over that bloody store, even made me climb a library ladder. Then she handed it to me from a rack by the register."

Sam began to laugh, and then Erika, until her cheeks ran wet, and she wiped them and blew her nose. "But why?"

"She said…" And he cocked his head sternly, saying in his best King's English, "'If you're going to cheat, you still ought to work hard at it.'"

"That was pretty forward."

"I thought later it was fine. You see, she'd seen something in me, something that needed to be addressed, a little empty place she could fill."

"You were pretty handsome, those days. Didn't you have any other girlfriends?"

"No one of consequence. I was a pretty somber fellow. Since my father was killed." His thought stumbled for a moment. "You might say I missed being a teen too. T'was your mum that taught me to laugh again." The exit for Topeka loomed in the distance and Sam began to let the car slow. "Don't you think I'm handsome now?"

Erika smiled gently. "Do you ever think, wonder what life would have been like, with someone else?"

"Not for a second."

*

"You're sure you want to talk to these people?" Sam asked, as they sat in the front seat of the car.

"I think I need to tell my story to somebody. Just for the record, just once."

They got out into the morning sun that had flooded down between the buildings. Sam put a handful of quarters in the parking meter and they walked between the traffic across the street, into the cool shadow. In the lobby an armed guard sat at the information desk.

"Federal prosecutor's office?" Sam asked.

"That would be Mr. Jewell, nineteenth floor."

A receptionist with dyed red hair and a gray business suit interviewed them, harsh formal interrogatories, and asked if Mr. Jewell was expecting them. Erika said no, and took a deep breath and was about to explain when the door to the inner office opened and a barrel-chested, silver-haired man, somber, indecipherable and firm, came out and laid something on the desk next to the woman. He looked at his two visitors, and his composure softened.

"I'm Lawrence Jewell," he said, "and you must be Erika."

Sam and Erika looked at one another.

"Please come in. We've got some questions for you." He closed the door behind them, and they sat down. A martial looking gentleman sat in the corner. "This is Mister Quigley, with the Federal Bureau of Investigation." The man nodded but did not get up. "And you left this at Leavenworth yesterday." He handed over her driver's license.

"So are you *the* federal prosecutor?"

"It's the title of the office, not me." He sat down behind his desk and smiled. "I'm just a lawyer who works for the government, young lady. There are lots of federal prosecutors."

Sam and Erika sat on a black leather love seat. He repositioned his arm behind her in a protective gesture.

"You called Mister Malouf 'Majij Aziz' yesterday. Can you explain that?"

"You listened?"

"Ordinarily, prisoners must tell us in advance who'll be visiting them, and we decide if we approve." Jewell closed a folder on his desk and tossed it to one side. "Malouf's been an enigma. He's never spoken a word. Tried to hang himself twice when he arrived. We moved him to Springfield for a while."

"Springfield?"

"Missouri. There's a psychiatric ward down there." He leaned back in his chair with his hands clasped. "We've waited over four years for someone to show up. When you came, they gave us a call, and I approved it."

"I called him 'Aziz' because that's his name." She took out the ring-bound notebook and told her story.

Mister Jewell scratched periodically on a yellow legal pad, listening to her without interruption, hesitating from time to time as if a question lurked just ahead. Quigley listened quietly for most of the interview, then stood and turned his back to them and looked out over Topeka.

When she had finished, Quigley turned for a moment, and the men exchanged glances. Then Quigley spoke. "Were you aware that there was an alleged embezzler in eighty-nine, a physician from The Dalles, named Aziz?"

The question blindsided her. "No. I don't think I was."

"You don't *think* so?" He looked at her unsympathetically. "Did Aziz seem to have a lot of cash on that trip, the time you were with him?"

"I know we ate a lot of junk food, stayed in a lot of dives. Am I gonna have to worry about this now?"

"The word 'accessory' comes to mind." Quigley turned away, his hands behind his back. "The man he embezzled later defaulted on some enormous loans and moved to Iraq. So, in short, no."

"But you better hope he doesn't come back to the United States," Jewell added, and then flipped a page of his notepad. "There are some fundamental questions that remain unanswered," he said, "if your story is true. First of all, why did he shoot you?"

"That's what I came here to ask him."

"And where is the gun? Fingerprints? Even a confession would be helpful."

"I don't know. I'd never seen him with a gun before."

"If you had even stepped forward earlier..."

Erika looked at her father, and he shook his head. "It took a long time for all of it to come back to me," she said and looked down at her pad. Her father looked away, Jewell stared into the web of his fingers, and Quigley stood vanguard at the window, each lost in his own silent review of the tale they had just heard.

After several minutes Mr. Jewell stood up with the pad in his hand and stepped to the front of his desk and sat on it. "Young lady, I think everything you've told me is the absolute truth. Nobody could make up such a thing about a prisoner the rest of the world doesn't know exists." He gestured to his companion. "But opening a case that is predicated on changing that prisoner's identity will automatically raise doubts about the man who killed two of Mister Quigley's best investigators. Those men had families, and those families have seen justice and closure in knowing that Mister Malouf is going to serve two thirty-five year sentences consecutively, without parole. I can't take that away from them without reasonable cause."

Mister Quigley stepped over to the desk and looked at a sheet of paper there. Erika could see that it was a photocopy of her driver's license. He spoke, his voice concise. "We'll look into this. Don't think we won't. But it may be a long time before you hear something. We'll be in touch." And he opened the door to the outer office and bid them leave.

Sam turned to thank Quigley, a thank-you of decorum, when the door closed. Erika and her father stood facing each other, jaws slightly agape. The receptionist hunched over her desk like a gargoyle, a headset on, typing away as if the room was empty. Sam cocked his head slightly toward the closed door but could hear nothing. He looked at Erika, opened the door to the hallway, and they went out. Erika moved ahead of him. "They're not going to do a bloody thing," he said.

"I know." Erika pushed the down button. "I knew it before we came here. But it feels good, to be right about something."

"What was the word he used?" Sam asked. "Accessory? You were a minor. He can go piss up a rope."

They had dropped a few floors in silence when Sam looked at his daughter. "You did well in there. I'm proud of you." He mused for a moment. "If I ever have to deal with the FBI, I'll let you do the talking." The doors opened and they were in the lobby.

Erika stopped halfway across the marble expanse. "I want to call Mom," she said and walked back to a row of phone booths and stepped into one, leaving the door open. Sam stood nearby.

When her mother answered, Erika hesitated for just a moment and thought of the call she had made once from Majij's apartment. "Hi," she said. "We're just about done here," and she told her of the day before, and the promise the FBI man had made.

"Oh Erika, do you know a young man named Eugene?" her mother asked. "He called from his car. He has one of those cordless phones."

"It's called a cell phone, Mother. What did he want?"

"He was driving down to Pendleton to see his parents. Said he just wanted to stop and say hello. He was very polite."

"Oh."

"Are you two going over to see the Arch today?"

"I don't know. Dad, are we going up in the Arch today?"

Sam nodded his head. "We've got another day to kill."

"We might," Erika said. "I don't know. I've got the rest of my life to go up in arches."

"What do I do if this Eugene fellow calls again?"

"I guess, tell him 'hello' from me." She watched her father stroll away from the booth nonchalantly, his hands in his pockets. "If he wants to stop by, tell him it's fine."

"Should I ask him? I could invite him to dinner."

"No. Just tell him I'd like to see him. I want him to stop by." She watched her father, who had stopped in front of a portrait across the lobby and was reading the plaque below it. "Tell him this. I'd like to see him. I'll meet him at Cousin's at fourish on Friday."

"Four-ish. Friday. What if he's not…"

"Anytime is fine. But I bet he will."

Erika called to her father, who came back to the booth and took the receiver. He spoke in a tender voice, and then he hung up.

"Did I hear you say you're not too interested in the Arch?" he asked her.

"Not really. I think the train yards in Kansas City might be better. More jazz history down there, too."

"Good. I've never really liked heights that much," Sam said, clasping his hands behind him as he walked by her side.

"I never knew that," she said, and held the door for him as they stepped back out into the humidity and the summer glare of the Midwest sun. They crossed the street, stopping on the lines as traffic passed, Erika reaching the far side of the Taurus first.

A young man approached along the sidewalk, his black hair wavy, his moustache trim, his skin a warm latte, the smooth folds of his linen suit and the crease of his trousers falling over him with a grace that bespoke litheness, a readiness for life to begin. As he passed Erika, the silver of his cufflinks flickered, and she turned to watch him, as if to face into a light breeze. She willed him to turn around but he did not, and at the corner, he did not wait at the crosswalk but turned instead and was gone from her view. She stood watching where he had been until her father spoke her name, twice, and still she looked back as she took her seat in the car and closed the door.

Acknowledgements

What has been presented in this work of fiction in no way reflects the opinions of these authors but the following works were reviewed and were indispensible in the preparation of this text.

Tedisco, James, Paludi, Michele. *Missing Children*, Albany, State University of New York Press. 1996

Simmons, Rachel. *Odd Girl Out*, Orlando, Harcourt. 2002

Patai, Raphael. *The Arab Mind*, New York, Macmillan 1983

Dehghani, Yavar. F*arsi (Persian) Phrasebook*, Victoria, Australia, Lonely Planet 2001

Ramazani, R. K (editor). Iran's Revolution, Bloomington and Indianapolis, Indiana University Press.

Mackey, Sandra. *The Iranians*, New York, Plume 1998

Sciolino, Elaine. *Persian Mirrors: The Elusive Face of Iran,* New York, Simon and Shuster, 2000

Brooks, Geraldine. *Nine Parts of Desire*, New York, Anchor Books, 1990

Shakir, M.H. (editor). *The Qur'an,* Elmhurst NY, Tahrike Tarsile Qur'an Inc. Publishers, 1999

Shaikh, Khalid Mahmood. A Study of Hadith, Skokie, IL. IQRA International Education Foundation, 1996.

Arendt, Hannah. *The Origins of Totalitarianism*, Boston, MA. Houghton Mifflin, Harcourt. 2001

The following works of music are quoted under the doctrine of Fair Use:

Bart Howard, *Fly Me to the Moon,* 1954

Benny Andersson, Bjorn Ulvaeus, Tim Rice, *One Night in Bangkok*, 1984

Irving Berlin, *White Christmas*, 1942

Havens Gillespie and J Fred Coots, *Santa Clause is Coming to Town*, 1934

Rod Stewart, *Maggie May*, 1971

Mel Torme and Bob Wells, *The Christmas Song*, 1944

Kim Gannon, Walter Kent, Buck Ram, *I'll be Home for Christmas*, 1943

Howard Jones, *No One is to Blame*, 1985

Clark Datchler, *Shattered Dreams*, 1987

And finally, I would like to extend a heartfelt thank you to those myriad souls, faculty and fellow writers, who have patiently workshopped this piece since that first summer in Iowa, so long ago. I am indebted to you all.

10835451R00218

Made in the USA
San Bernardino, CA
28 April 2014